SLAVES OF THE AMETHYST BOOK 10

THE ASSASSIN AND THE ARRIVING ANGELS

Michaela Francis

SLAVES OF THE AMETHYST BOOK 10

THE ASSASSIN AND THE ARRIVING ANGELS

SILVER MOON
ADULT FICTION

A SILVER MOON PAPERBACK

ISBN: 978-1-78695-149-6

Silver Moon is an imprint of
Fiction4All

Published 2018
Fiction4All

Narrators Foreword

In that pivotal summer of the history of the House of Mathom, so many factors came to be of significance that it is sometimes difficult for the researcher to separate the threads and identify the specific events which were instrumental in the founding of the new age. There was, of course, the beginning of the Wars of the Goddess which impacted directly on the Imperial House in many ways, not least of which were the refugees of war that drifted like flotsam onto the very steps of Mathom Hall itself with consequences that were barely understood at the time. It is occasionally said that the new dynasty was forged in the crucible of war and there is much truth in the statement. The young slaves, who arrived in Mathomdale that summer to rejuvenate the Line, came through many routes but, undoubtedly, a high proportion arrived through their displacement as a result of conflict.

It is important to recognise the effect and ultimate contribution of these new arrivals. Whereas many historians have focussed primarily on the more central characters in the rich drama unfolding in Mathomdale, these newcomers were also of critical importance in the foundation of the dynasty that would emerge from those chaotic and troubled times. It seems indeed, in hindsight, that while the House of Mathom's attention was distracted by the necessities of war, the immediate threats within Mathomdale itself and the frightening unfolding of Prophecy One, it almost overlooked the steady stream of quiet arrivals that would have such profound consequences to its future.

We do a disservice to the story to overlook these arrivals in our turn. The simple fact remains, that, virtually unseen, an extraordinary collection of young people, from all corners of the globe, were gathering in Mathomdale; the future Slaves of the Amethyst who would invest the dynasty with such dazzling promise and glittering hope.

Chapter One

Danny and Darren were up a tree. It was a venerable old tree, many of its branches sagging with senility towards the clear waters of the still pond. The pond was called the Golden Pool and it was easy to see why with the fringes of yellow water lilies about its banks and the odd almost, gilded tint to the water as the sun lanced down into it. It was a fairly shallow pool, heavily grown with weeds and lilies, and beautiful in its concealed location, sheltered among the trees. Dragonflies hawked along its margins and bright blue, metallic damselflies perched on the weed stems above the water surface. The surface of the water was unruffled by any breeze and the flat tranquillity was disturbed only by the meanderings of the odd moorhen and the humping dark shapes nosing about in the weeds. "Bloody 'ell!" breathed Daniel in excitement "Look at t' size o' that bastard! It's forty pound if it's an ounce."

"Where? Where?" asked Darren caught up in Daniel's excitement.

"There! Just by that sunken branch. Yer must see it!"

"I got too much glare off the water there."

"'Ere. 'Ave a look through me glasses." Daniel handed Darren the polarising sunglasses he wore.

With the glare reduced by the glasses Darren saw the big carp immediately. "Holy shit! That's a real lunker." Even as Darren watched another even larger shape joined the first nuzzling around the branches of the partially submerged tree. "Jesus Christ! There's another one Danny. Damn me if it ain't even bigger!"

"Give us the friggin' glasses back quick!" Daniel snatched the sunglasses and whistled in astonishment. "Sod me! I don't even like ter think 'ow big that sod is."

"How big do you reckon?"

"Robin said as 'ow t' carp in 'ere went up inter t' upper thirties but that bastard's closer ter fifty! Bugger me! Just 'ow big do the bloody things grow in 'ere?"

"Does Robin fish this water then?"

"Not much Ah don't think. 'E's more ov a salmon an' trout fellah. I tell yer summat though, there'd be bloody carp anglers wot'd flog their own mothers fer a crack on this place. It don't look as if anybody 'ardly fishes it either. Far as I know it's only t' odd folk wot works on t' grounds wot even know about this pond."

"Maybe we should have brought a couple of rods with us."

"Nay not yet Darren. We know where the buggers are. They're not going nowhere. We'll come back an' bait a patch off that bush there fer a few days, gerrem used ter findin' food an' then we'll lay a trap fer 'em."

"You're the expert here Danny. I ain't fished much for carp."

"Don't yer get 'em where you come from then?"

"Sure. We got carp all over the place in the States but most folks don't bother with them much. Kinda figure like they're trash fish. Most folks fish for game fish or pan fish, like trout, bass, bluegills, catfish and the like."

"Bloody heathens!"

"Well in the last few years there's been more interest in fishing for them. Some folks go fly fishing for them now."

"Yer wouldn't shift those buggers out from under yon tree wi a bloody fly rod."

"Nope. Got to agree with you there. You'd need a pole could stop a moose to hold those lunkers."

"This place is bloody fantastic! Look at that group ovver on that gravel bar. That tail end fish is well ovver twenny and 'e's just t' babby in t' gang. There's got ter be at least two thirties among 'em. We've got ter give this place a go Darren. Do yer fancy it?"

"Hell yes! Count me in. You got the rigs to deal with this place?"

"Oh aye. Still got all me carp rods an' what 'ave yer. We 'ad ter flog off a fair bit o' stuff ter mek ends meet me an' Alice when we got wed but I weren't givin' up me fishin' tackle fer nobody."

"You got gear I could borrow?"

"Oh aye. No need ter worry about that. We'll mek a proper English carp angler out o' you yet Darren."

"Suits me! I got me a hankering to see what forty pounds of carp feels like on the end of my line." Darren paused "Hey somebody's coming."

Daniel looked away from the water to see a familiar figure walking through the bushes along the bank side. "Ey up!" he whispered conspiratorially. "It's our Becky. Shurrup an' we'll give 'er a surprise." Rebecca was wending her way slowly along the bank. When she was beneath their tree Daniel called "Now then Becky!" Rebecca jumped in alarm and her eyes flew wide in surprise to spy the two young men above her as she staggered against a tree trunk.

"You bastards! What the devil do you mean by giving me a shock like that? I thought for a second it was a pair of goblins sat up there or something."

Daniel and Darren laughed delighted by the surprise they'd pulled on her. "Yer ought ter be more careful Becky love." Daniel told her. "Yer never know what might be lurkin' in t' trees above yer."

"And just why are we up a tree boys might I be so bold as to ask? In retrogression toward our primeval instincts are we? Shall I slip back to the hall and fetch you a bunch of bananas for your lunch?"

"We're just watchin' t' fish like." Daniel told her.

"Oh really? What are men like? Remove the smallest veneer of domestication from them and they can shed thousands of years of civilising influence and evolutionary progress in a twinkling. You can take the man out of the jungle but you can't take the jungle out of the man it appears."

Daniel laughed "At least we're not after draggin' you off to us cave Becky. Wot are yer doin' out this way anyway?"

"I'm out looking for Jenny actually. She still hasn't come back to the Hall yet and I'm starting to get worried about her. Have you two seen her when your attention could be spared from your precious fish?"

"No ma-am." Darren told her "Surely she'll be safe enough here on the Hall's grounds though won't she?"

"Well...." Rebecca began but she paused and with her hand on her hip. "Look will two do me the honour of coming down out of that bloody tree. I refuse to hold a conversation with a pair of barely domesticated lower primates." Grinning the two men scrambled to the ground.

"So where's she's got to then?" asked Daniel.

"I'm damned if I know. I've been looking for her everywhere. Nobody among the ground staff or the security forces seems to have seen her either. I thought she might be up on the sports fields but there's no sign of her. I'm checking out around some of the lakes and ponds now because Jenny's got a thing about water. It would be just like her to be sat somewhere staring wistfully into some pond while she feels sorry for herself."

"I'm sorry ma-am." Darren interrupted, "I guess this is mostly my fault."

"No of course not Darren. It's just the way Jenny is. With all the best will in the world you can't be expected to take responsibility for her conduct."

"Excuse me ma-am but isn't Miss Jennifer a grown woman? Isn't she allowed to go off somewhere on her own if she feels the need for a little solitude?"

"Well it's not quite as simple as that Darren. For one thing she has duties that she is neglecting and for which she could be punished if I don't get her to attend to them. But that's not the main reason that I want to run her to earth."

"That is ma-am?"

"I'm concerned for Jennifer herself Darren. Jennifer's on an emotional roller coaster for the moment and she needs somebody to keep an eye on her. We're under strict instructions to make sure that she's well protected and given plenty of love and attention Darren. Jenny's the youngest among us and she can be dangerously unstable."

"But hell.... what harm can come to her?"

"With all due respect Darren you don't know Jenny as well as I do. This summer she's had her world turned upside down, lost her family and been asked to grow up too quickly. She's got other troubles bothering her as well and her mood swings can be wildly unpredictable. I just want to make sure that no harm comes to her."

"You mean she could do something crazy, hurt herself or something?"

"Goddess! Don't even say that Darren. Jenny can swing from euphoria to black depression in an instance at the moment and there's no telling what sort of idiocy she might get it into her mind to do."

Darren looked at Rebecca closely seeing the evident anxiety there "I'm sorry ma-am. I thought you were just being overly invasive of Miss Jennifer's privacy but I see that you're genuinely concerned."

"Tell yer what," Daniel suggested. "Why don't me and Darren 'elp yer look Becky? You can go off in one direction an' we can try in another."

"The grounds are huge Danny and you don't know them well yourselves. You could end up getting lost."

"Give ovver Becky. We can allus find us way back ter t' 'All! It's not like it in' t big enough for 'eaven's sake. Yer can see it from miles away."

“Are you sure your fish won’t pine for you whilst you’re neglecting them?”

“Fish ’ll still be ‘ere when we come back ter reacquaint our sens wi ‘em.”

“In that case thank you for your offer. I’ll look over towards the Oriental Gardens in case she’s wandered that way if you two cover the area to the east. If you don’t find her, we’ll meet back at the Hall in two hours for lunch. If she doesn’t turn up or we don’t find her by lunchtime I’m sending out security to look for her. If necessary I’ll have her dragged back to the Hall in chains and confined to the cellars until the Lady’s return.”

“Jesus!” said Darren, “Let’s not get too dramatic. She’s probably just lost track of time or something.”

“I hope you’re right Darren.”

“Listen Miss Rebecca. I’m sorry but I do have some responsibility in this. Miss Jennifer was kinda upset with me last night so I’ve got to take some blame if she’s gone off in a huff.”

“Oh Darren. Don’t concern yourself with that. Let’s just find her and see if she’s all right. Maybe I am being a bit of a drama queen but I can’t help it. I’m worried sick about her. I love her you see.”

“Aye well we’re not doin’ owt about it standin’ ‘ere talkin’.” Daniel pointed out sensibly. “Let’s get lookin’.”

Chapter Two

Jennifer was walking down the slopes towards the distant Hall when the assassin decided to make his move. She was isolated now... the young one, far from help. It would only take seconds and then he would melt back into the trees where he had been hiding these last days, waiting for his chance. The others were dangerous but this young one was terribly vulnerable. He'd stalked her for days now, on her morning runs in the grounds, but the heavy security about the Hall's grounds had denied him his chance. But he was patient in his craft, this lone killer. He was a solitary wild card infiltrated into the inner domain of the Hall, there to kill and disappear, as wraith like as he had entered. It had been easy to identify a target. The young auburn-haired girl was the weak link in this perilous inner sanctum where a single mistake could mean death. He'd been virtually invisible during his patient wait in the vast grounds. From the camouflaged den he'd created in the woods in the grounds he moved silently about garnering information from afar about his victim. She was apt to wander away from the Hall and its heavy military presence on her daily runs and she had favourite routes she liked to take. It was almost too easy.

He'd hoped originally to catch her on one of her sorties away from the Hall's grounds but the witch that ruled this land had trumped that possibility and no longer was her little favourite allowed away from the grounds without an escort. Very well then, he had infiltrated into the grounds themselves; creeping in under cover of darkness to lie concealed until his moment to strike. It was a fantastically dangerous move. There were eyes everywhere in these grounds and, behind those eyes, people who would kill without hesitation but his target was making his life easier; drifting away from her umbrella of security, flouncing about with her head in the clouds and unaware that death stalked her in the peaceful surroundings of the parklands. She seemed sad today the assassin thought. Well she would not have much longer to mope about her worries. He was within fifty yards of her now; moving silently through the bushes, his tread quieter than that of a stalking cat. He had already earmarked the killing spot a little further down the path. He let the thin metal cord slip through his fingers. It took five seconds for an expert garrotter to kill his victim once he had whipped that cord about their neck. It was fast, quiet and deadly and the assassin was very expert indeed.

He moved closer to the interception point watching her. She was walking very slowly now, her head bowed, her mind concerned with her own petty worries. He was fixated on the slim neck above the running vest. It would be a few quick steps and then his garrotte would be about her throat. There would be a few moments of silent struggle with his knee in the small of her back and then the slender body would fall limp. She would die without even seeing her murderer. There would be a few seconds of incomprehension as she felt the garrotte about her neck and the life ebbing from her before oblivion. Quickly and efficiently, that was how the assassin liked his victims to go. It was quiet up here on this hillside. By the time they found the body he would be long away. Maybe he'd have time to violate her dead body before fleeing. She was pretty this young victim he noticed. Well they were all ugly in death. Sometimes they soiled themselves in their death throes. He liked that. He felt the familiar sexual thrill at the thought of her last struggles with his garrotte about her throat. He enjoyed killing.

He moved into position; the killing very close now. His loins were aching with the desire of it. Taking life was food and drink to him, a sensual pleasure that he took greedily. He yearned for her death agony like a sexual release. Sometimes he would whisper in the ear of his victims in their last moment of consciousness so that they would die hearing his voice as the last thing they would ever experience. He would do that with this one he decided. Slowly he moved into position to pounce. Then he froze into rigid immobility, his heart pounding in his chest. Somebody was coming. A man with a double-barrelled shotgun under his arm stepped out into the path to intercept the girl. He sucked his breath silently between his teeth and slunk back into the undergrowth in great stealth, foiled at the very moment of the kill. But he could wait. There would be other opportunities. His craft had taught him great patience and the assassin was a very patient man.

Jennifer jumped with surprise as the figure emerged before her on the pathway. "Good afternoon Miss Jennifer Walstow-Mathom." the figure said grinning at her in delight.

"Why Mr Baxter! You startled me."

"Aye well a bit ov a shock's allus good for the soul they allus say. Yer've wandered a bit far from t' All terday aven't yer Jenny love?"

"I.... I was just out running Mr Baxter."

Baxter looked at Jennifer in her tiny shorts and skimpy running top in unholy glee. "Well yer should be more careful Jenny lass. Runnin' about wi' next ter no clothes on. Yer don't know oo might be about up this end o' the park. Didn't yer know there's a bit of a scare on?"

"I.... I thank you for your concern Mr Baxter but I was just on my way back to the Hall. If you would excuse me please?"

"Now then Jenny. Just being considerate is all. I'll escort yer back if'n you want. Can't be 'avin' yer traipsin' all ovver t' place on yer jack when there's an alert on can we? Any road I've bin meanin' to 'ave a little chat wi yer when I could get t' chance."

"I'm sorry Mr Baxter but it's not very convenient. I do have to get back to the Hall."

"There's no rush Jenny. I just thought yer might like ter discuss some o' t' difficulties your young Miss 'Awthorne 'as got her sen inter."

"Julie? I'm sorry Mr Baxter but I fail to understand you."

"Do yer?" Baxter chuckled meaningfully "Well yer've a bit o' time surely ter pass t' time o' t' day Jenny." Baxter reached into his pocket "'Ere would yer like a cigarette Jenny?" Baxter proffered a packet of cigarettes.

"I… I don't smoke Mr Baxter."

"Nay? Well that's funny cos neither does young Julie either. Funny why she should want so many cigs isn't it?"

"I'm at a loss Mr Baxter. Perhaps you would care to explain yourself more clearly."

"Cigarettes Jennifer love. Lots of them! Your little girlfriend's bin a bit of a naughty girl 'asn't she?"

Jennifer looked bewildered "What on earth are you talking about Mr Baxter?"

"'Ave a look at that packet Jenny love." Baxter tossed the packet to Jennifer who caught it by surprise. "All the way from sunny Spain them are. Contraband Jennifer. Black market. Cigarettes wot never saw a customs stamp on 'em Jennifer. Nay don't 'and 'em back. There's plenny more where them come from. Couple o' thousand cartons by my reckoning. I 'appened ter slip inter t' 'Awthorne's depot one afternoon Jenny. There they was. Fifty odd thousand-pound wuth of illegal fags 'idden under a tarpaulin. Not just a couple o' cartons from t' duty free shop. Oh no! Your Julie's bin up ter no good Jenny. There was tens o' thousands ov fags in there wot t' custom and excises would be right interested in knowin' about."

Jennifer was staring at the cigarette packet in horror. "Surely you can't think that Julie has anything to do with contraband. It can't be true."

"Nay? I've been seein' your little madam about recently Jenny. Come up a bit in t' world 'asn't she? Expensive new clothes, jewellery, posh cars pullin' up outside t' village shop; doin' right well for 'er sen isn't she? Nice little racket she's runnin' down in t' village be looks o' things."

"That's a monstrous suggestion." Jennifer was white with shock.

"Aye well we'll be seein' as to whether or not t' authorities think so Jenny. It's time some conscientious citizen were 'avin' a quiet word wi t' police about Julie 'Awthorne's illicit activities."

"But it doesn't follow that Julie's involved Mr Baxter."

"Now come on Jenny love. Yer not that daft. It's common knowledge in t' village that young Julie runs t' Awthorne business. If there's any funny business goin' on your Julie 'll be up to 'er neck in it. I've allus said that class will tell. A leopard can't change its spots. She might be 'angin' about wi t' likes of you an' t' other fine misses from t' All but common she were born and common as muck she'll stay. Well I don't suppose yer'll be seein' much ov 'er in days ter come. I'd say a nice long 'oliday at 'Er Majesty's pleasure in a juvenile correction facility is Miss 'Awthorne's most likely future prospect an' even when she gets out I can't see 'Er Ladyship allowin' yer ter mix wi the criminal classes now."

"You…… you can't be telling the police about it Mr Baxter. Please no!"

"Oh but I can. I've me duty as a law abidin' citizen ter be thinkin' about." Jennifer reeled in shock. So much now seemed to make sense; Julie's secrecy of late, her mysterious absences, new clothes, sapphires and pearls.

It all added up. No wonder Julie hadn't wanted to tell her what was bothering her. She was involved in criminal activities. "Of course." Baxter continued "I might be persuaded ter be reasonable about it. Like as not Julie's just fallen in with the wrong people. I might be open ter givin' 'er a second chance. She's only young after all an' maybe it's not too late for 'er ter see t' error ov 'er ways an' go straight. Of course I'll 'ave me price like."

"Wh.... what do you want Mr Baxter?" whispered Jennifer hardly daring to breathe.

In two quick steps Baxter covered the ground between them and took Jennifer by the elbows. His voice grew deep and husky as he gripped her arms in sudden lust. "Yer know what it is that I want Jenny. I want you! I want you down at my cabin, stripped down for me pleasure. That's what I want Jenny. That's what I've allus wanted."

"No Mr Baxter! Please!"

"Aye! I want yer naked Jenny." Baxter's ferocity was relentless "I want yer naked an' dancin' ter t' tune o' my whip Jenny love. Yer know a bit more what to expect now, I'm thinking. Yer got idin's enough while you was in t' cellars didn't yer? Oh aye! I know all about it. I were watchin' that day when old Sebastian gave yer a good leatherin' in t' prison garden Jenny. A right bonny picture yer were tied to that stake whimperin' after 'e'd tekken 'is lash to yer. Well it's my turn now little Jenny. That's 'ow I want yer. This very afternoon. Young Julie 'Awthorne 'll 'ave nowt to worry about just as long as you present yersen nicely fer my pleasure this afternoon. Your body fer my whip. That's the price o' my silence Jennifer."

"No! No please!" Jennifer was trembling in fear.

"Oh but yes Jenny. Of course yer could be tellin' yer Mistress about me an' I'd be losin' me job but then your girlfriend 'd be facin' a nice salutary sentence wouldn't she? So I think we'll keep this just between ourselves Jenny. 'Alf past two this afternoon Jenny. Down at my cabin in t' Low Woods. I'll be waitin' for yer. Say nowt to nobody about it an' your Julie keeps er sen out ov jail."

"I.... I can't leave the grounds Mr Baxter. We're under restrictions."

"That's easy enough Jenny. Just take the little path wot goes past the old mill on Barling Beck down the east end. After a while yer'll. come to a little secret gate wot leads inter t' woods an out o' t' grounds. Nobody 'll see yer that way if yer take care. Go down the path through t' woods an' after a mile or so yer'll come to a lane. Cross that an' there's a gate on t' far side that leads down inter t' low woods. Foller the track inter t' woods and another mile or so an' yer'll see a big old tree by the side wi a path leadin' off ter the left. I'll leave a sign on t' tree so yer know yer way. My cabin's a couple o' undred yards down that path. It'll tek yer about three quarters of an hour all told if yer don't 'ang about. I'll be waitin' for yer. Mek yersen pretty afore ye come along Jenny. I'll want yer lookin' yer best when yer strip down fer me whip."

"I.... I can't do it!"

Fiercely Baxter grasped the front of Jennifer's shorts and hauled her to the tip of her toes by them, the material cutting into her sex. "Yes yer can Jenny. I've waited too long fer this now. That's my price fer keepin' me mouth shut. Just you an' me tergether down t' Low Woods nice an' quiet where there'll be nobody t' 'ear yer squeals when I tek me whip to yer."

"No please!"

In a sudden dart Baxter thrust his hand into Jennifer's shorts and grasped her sex. "Oh yes Jenny! Yer want ter come don't yer? Don't lie ter me now." Jennifer moaned despairingly, the violation of her sex compounded by the betrayal of the moisture seeping from it. "Say yer'll come Jenny. Say yer'll come an' nobody ‘ll ever ear a thing about wot Julie’s got ‘idden in her depot. Yer’ve ‘ad whippin’s before. One more won’t ‘arm yer.” He released her sex and stared at her a dangerous glint in his eye.

“I… I’d have the promise of your silence if I do as you say?”

“Aye! I’m telling yer. Julie ‘ll ‘ave nowt to fear from me Jenny. It’ll just be between the pair of us. ‘Alf past two Jenny. Don’t be late now.”

Jennifer surrendered completely knowing that once more Mathomdale demanded a sacrifice of her. “V… very well Mr Baxter. If you swear to hold by your promise. I…. I’ll be there.”

Baxter exulted. “Good girl Jenny. I’ll be true ter me word yer can bank on that. Now be running on along an’ be getting’ yersen pretty fer me. I’ll be expectin’ yer at ‘alf two sharp.”

“Very well.” she whispered in quiet, ultimate despair. Then she was reeling away down the path her face white and her eyes staring beyond tears.

Baxter watched her go in triumphant satisfaction. Even in the moment of his exultation however, a worm of uncertainty insinuated itself into his consciousness. Perhaps it was just the tiniest rustle from the undergrowth, the merest whisper of unexplained movement or perhaps it was an unfamiliar scent on the air. Whatever it was Baxter whipped around to glare at the dense bushes intensely. For all his insanity Baxter was an Alpha Sensual and possessed the keen acuity of the senses that his inheritance had bequeathed him. For a second he was sure that he was not alone on the quiet path.

He snapped the breach of his shotgun back into place and thumbed back the hammers, his eyes scourging the undergrowth fiercely “Oo’s there?” he called “Come on! Show thee sen!” He strode forward to the bushes his weapon held before him and paused to listen in intensity. But there was silence from the bushes now and just the cawing of the crows from the poplars along the path to disturb the morning air. A blackbird flew out from the bushes. Perhaps it had been just that. Perhaps all he had detected was the thrush scrabbling in the detritus beneath the bushes for worms. But he was troubled, his instincts screaming caution at him. Slowly he backed away from the thick bushes but he kept his weapon cocked, his eyes alert. He moved off down the path but his attention never wavered from the bushes until he had turned the bend in the trail and they were lost to view.

The assassin made it back to his hidden culvert with his heart pounding knowing just how close he'd come to death. The man with the gun had known he was there. He had trained for years in the art of stealth and silent movement yet the man had detected him. Had he persisted in his scrutiny of the undergrowth he would have found him. The killer was a veteran of many assassinations but none had carried the peril of this infiltration into the nest of vipers these seemingly innocuous parklands represented. He wondered, not for the first time, if the money was worth it. These people were dangerous. He didn't know who they were or what they stood for but their innate peril was clear and evident. He was living on borrowed time here on these grounds. His employers had sent him into a poisoned garden, alone and expendable, some discardable pawn in the game they were playing.

He looked for the thousandth time at the small collection of photos he had concealed in his culvert. They were the pictures of five young women, his targets, and he wondered why his employers wanted one of them dead. He fingered the newest photograph almost lovingly. It showed the auburn-haired girl that had been just seconds away from death before the intervention of the man with the gun. She could thank him for her life now he thought. But only for a short while. He'd overheard the conversation between them. He pulled out his plans of the grounds. They were inadequate these plans he knew. Nobody seemed to have a firm grasp on the topography of these parklands and he'd been pencilling in details almost constantly. Nevertheless he thought he could find the track over the Barling Beck by the mill and somewhere, down in the woods beyond, he'd whisper in the young girl's ear.

Chapter Three

Jennifer staggered back toward the Hall in turmoil knowing she was trapped. Baxter had struck her in her most vulnerable quarter. Why, oh why had Julie been so foolish? She didn't doubt Baxter's story. It all made horrible sense. A nightmare scenario unfolded before her, Julie in handcuffs at the police station, Julie in a cell far removed from the loving prisons of Sebastian's underworld. She saw Julie in her best dress at her first court appearance, the presentation of the devastating evidence, Julie's tears at her sentencing and the van that would take her away to a young offenders institution. She wondered what they made them wear in such places. Would they give her some chance at rehabilitation she wondered, perhaps address her neglected education, or were they just sink holes for the unwanted flotsam of failed society? For society had failed Julie hadn't it? It had even created her crime through its avaricious tax system and claimed it needed the revenue from her wretched cigarettes to defray the costs of caging her. It would have cost them far less to ensure that she'd had a proper education and a chance to make her life worthwhile without the resort to crime. And now Jennifer was all that stood between Julie and the ruination of her young life. Jennifer would make the sacrifice on her behalf because that was the imperative of love and that imperative was the one that ultimately ruled the heart and mind of Jennifer Walstow-Mathom.

She paused on the path, a new thought occurring to her. On the hilltop it had been apparent to her that she was powerful. That was still true wasn't it? Baxter thought he had trapped her. The truth was rather different wasn't it? A clear shaft of sunlight leaked from behind a cloud and it seemed to clear Jennifer's head with its illumination. Baxter himself was the one in the trap. He had walked into a snare of his own making. She could rule him now couldn't she and he had provided the very mechanism by which she could do it. The Lady had told her that she could destroy Baxter whenever she wanted and Baxter himself had given her the means to do so. A single sacrifice and he was her creature forever. By the time he realised the power she had over him it would be too late. She could eliminate his threat forever. He would rue the day he'd dared to play his games with Katherine's daughter.

She was still lost in this reverie when a voice hailed her "Miss Jennifer! There you are! Where the blue blazes have you been?"

She looked up her eyes dangerously calm now. "Why Mr Morgan. What a surprise to see you so far from the Hall."

Darren scrambled down a low bank to join her. "You ok ma-am? We've been looking for you all over the place. I was kinda getting worried."

"I really don't understand why my whereabouts should concern you Mr Morgan." Darren looked at her keenly. Her face was white and her eyes red from tears.

"Jenny are you ok?"

"I'm perfectly all right thank you Mr Morgan."

"Dammit! Stop calling me Mr Morgan."

"As you wish sir."

Darren paused in agony, not knowing how to deal with her but understanding that it was critical to handle her well. "Jenny we've been worried about you. Danny and me have been scouring the whole goddamn place looking for you. Danny's gone off way over east and Rebecca's looking for you westwards."

"Really! How absurd. I've only been out taking some exercise in the grounds. Hardly due reason for sending out a search party for me."

"Ain't a search party ma-am, just folks as are worried about you. Folks that think a lot about you.

Nobody's seen you all day. We just wanted to make sure you were all right. We thought you were avoiding us."

"A little runaway huh? I'm surprised you didn't set the dogs on my trail. Isn't that what the cotton planters did when their slaves ran away?"

"Sure is ma-am. Then they'd drag 'em back in chains and have 'em whupped in front of the whole plantation. You want I should do that with you?"

"I would hardly have thought I had much say in the matter."

"Well sure you do Miss Jennifer cos I ain't your master and you ain't my slave. What I might do is kindly ask you to honour me and allow me to accompany you back to the Hall. Of course if you don't want to then that's just dandy too. I'll just mosey along and leave you in peace. I just wanted to put my mind at rest and make sure you were all right. I'm just one of those folks that thinks a bit about you see."

Jennifer awarded him a watery smile. It was hard to be annoyed for long with his disingenuous charm "Thank you for your concern Darren. I'm having a bit of a bad day is all. Forgive me for neglecting you."

"Jenny I want to apologise for what happened last night. In my defence, feeble though it is, I can only say that I didn't understand some of the things about this place. Well I still don't but I realise now I should have kept my fool mouth shut until I figured out the ins and outs of things round here. Danny and Rebecca have been putting me straight on a couple o' things and maybe I see it a bit more clearly today. I'd kinda like a second chance ma-am if you could see your way to forgiving my foolish words."

Jennifer was not insensible to the pleasurable charm of a man admitting that he was wrong and, in any case, she had to concede that her own conduct had left a good deal to be desired. Her Mistress had warned her to treat this young man gently, be diplomatic and not to shock him too much and she'd done a pretty wretched job at it. He was looking at her concernedly now with a trace of anxiety in his features and she knew very clearly what her forgiveness would mean to him. He was a kind man she realised, kind and gentle and she could grow very fond of him. Right now however she needed him. Her mind was still reeling from her conversation with Baxter and formulating its plans. She needed this young man in those plans.

"But there is nothing to forgive Darren. It is I who should be ashamed of myself. My behaviour yesterday was inexcusable. As soon as my Mistress returns I shall confess my failings to her and you will have the satisfaction of knowing that I have been suitably punished."

"Hellfire and damnation Jenny! I don't want to see you punished. I just want to see you smile at me and tell me that we're still friends."

"Of course we're still friends Darren. Forgive my foolishness. I've had a trying day Darren and I'm afraid I'm rather upset."

"You're upset with me?"

"No Darren it's nothing to do with you. It's something personal. Something private. Please excuse me."

"Would you like to share that with me Jenny?"

"I'm sorry but I can't Darren."

"You sure Jenny? My old Uncle Bob used to say, "Son if you don't open your hand folks can't put anything in it.""

Jennifer laughed and although the laugh was weak it was like an unexpected glint of sunshine through the clouds on a rainy day. "No really Darren. This is very private. But we are still friends Darren. Heaven knows I need a friend today!"

"At your service ma-am."

"Would you do something for me Darren?"

“Your wish is my command ma-am.”

“Would you kiss me?”

“Gee! Hell! I don’t know. Kind of an onerous task that ma-am. I’d have to think about that one.”

“Well if you don’t want.....”

“For about half a second.” continued Darren, grasping her firmly in his arms. Jennifer started to say something but her words were stifled under Darren’s lips on hers. Darren gloried in the feel of her against his body, the thin top and shorts of her running clothes slightly slick against her flesh. Within seconds the scale of mounting arousal ratcheted up between them and the embrace became heated in mutual yearning. Darren found his hand cupping her buttock through the light shorts and she shuddered in the passion of her need pressing hard against him in overt invitation. Almost of its own will, his hand quested beneath the material of her shorts to grasp the rounded orb and she was murmuring wantonly as he pulled her hard against his crotch. In wonder he felt her rub herself against the bulge of his erection and her hands tugging at his shirt to free it from his trousers and find the flesh of his back.

For long minutes they were lost in their desire, insensible to the possibility of prying eyes. Her top was free of her shorts now and he was caressing the silky texture of her back beneath it, feeling the heat rising from her in tangible waves. He held her slightly away from him so that he could run his hand up her front seeking out her breasts beneath her bra and she took the opportunity to slide her hand between them fumbling with the zip on the front of his trousers. He trembled as she gained egress and her hand urgently found his penis beneath his boxer shorts. He was lost now. He wanted her right now, here, this instance, on the grass by the side of the path. She moaned falteringly as he thrust his hand into her shorts and his fingers slipped into the moistness of her sex. “Take me Darren! Take me now! Please!”

“I.... I love you Jenny.”

“Now Darren! Quickly!”

“Darren? Darren? Where the ‘ell are yer?” The voice was Daniel’s from some distance away.

“Jesus it’s Danny Jenny!”

“Tell him to go away.”

“Steady Jenny. Behave yourself now.”

“I don’t want to behave.” Jennifer pouted.

“Hush honey. He’ll be here any moment. Make yourself decent.”

“I bloody well will not... Ow!” The last remark was elicited by a sharp slap on the rear.

“Nice young ladies don’t swear Jenny. Now behave yourself and adjust your clothes.”

“But I want you Darren.”

“I want you too Jenny but not now. Later maybe. This afternoon perhaps.”

“Darren do you really love me?”

“Cross my heart and hope to die.”

“Darren quickly. This afternoon... I need your help.”

“What for? Other than what we just had in mind of course.”

“I..... I have to do something. Something private. I don’t want the others to know Darren. I.... I need you to cover for me. Say that I’m going to be spending the afternoon alone with you.”

“Jesus Jenny! What the hell’s all this?”

“Please Darren. It’s important. Very important. Please help me.”

“What is it?”

“I..... I have to help my best friend Darren but to do that I have to do something very secret. Something wicked. Please don’t ask me to tell you. Please.”

“Damn it Jenny! I don’t like the sound of this.”

"It'll only be for a couple of hours Darren. Nobody will know. But I have to have your help because the girls won't let me out of their sight unless I'm with you. Please believe me this is very important. Afterwards we'll find a quiet spot and carry on from where we left off. Please Darren tell me you'll do it. For the love of me tell me you'll do it."

"Jenny I….."

She clutched his penis tightly and pleaded urgently. "Darren if you love me then do this for me. Then I'm yours. Yours to do as you wish with. "

"Is this thing you have to do dangerous?"

"No Darren. I won't come to any harm. I promise you. I just need you to cover me for a few hours that's all. Now swear to secrecy and tell me you'll do it."

"Ok! Ok! I'll do it. Just for heaven's sake make yourself decent. I can hear Danny coming." Hastily Jennifer adjusted her clothes whilst Darren attended to his own state of undress. They were just in time for Danny came around the corner seconds after Darren had fastened up his trousers.

"Oh there you are. Aye up Jenny. We've bin lookin' for yer."

"Oh thank you Daniel. Darren found me. I've been out running and lost track of the time. I do hope you haven't been worried about me."

"Nay. Nay. Well a bit I suppose. Anyways as long as yer all right. Did yer just find 'er Darren?"

"A few minutes ago Danny. We've been passing the time of day before going back to the Hall." Daniel looked at the two of them still flushed and flustered and made a fairly accurate guess as to how they been whiling away the time.

"Right then. Well er it's getting' on. Are you two comin' back fer dinner….. I mean lunch."

"Yes of course Daniel." Jennifer told him. "I'm hungry after all that exercise. The three of them walked back to the Hall together.

Chapter Four

As Jennifer and Darren were wending their way in the direction of the Hall, a tense looking Julie was sat in mounting trepidation in Dr Chandra's waiting room in Brawton. Astrid was with her and it had taken her a good morning's work to wheedle and cajole Julie into the clinic. Julie had been white faced and on the verge of tears as they'd driven into town and it hadn't helped that Astrid had found it incumbent on her to warn Julie about the good doctor's notoriously less than sympathetic surgery manner which Jennifer, Alice and Daniel had recently had the misfortune of being subjected to. After they'd waited for several tension filled minutes the secretary announced, "Dr Chandra will see you now ladies." And Julie and Astrid had been ushered into the Asian woman's surgery. Dr Chandra took one look at Julie and asked,

"Is this it?"

"Yes Doctor." Astrid told her "This is Julie. The girl we hope to be buying."

Dr Chandra shook her head sadly "Well let's have her in the examination room down the corridor and see if anything can be done with her."

"Oh doctor there is something we have to tell you. "Astrid announced and quickly explained about Julie's intermittent fits and blackouts. Dr Chandra looked thoughtful before asking how long she'd been having these episodes. "Tell the doctor Julie." urged Astrid gently.

"Yes come along girl. Have you no tongue in your head?"

Hesitantly Julie recounted the history of her illness encouraged by Astrid and not at all encouraged by Dr Chandra's barked questions and non-committal grunts as she scribbled notes on her pad. Eventually Astrid asked, "Well doctor what do you think."

"Can't tell you until I've made a few tests Astrid. Hopefully it won't knock too much off the girl's value, such as it is, but I'll be able to tell you more when I get some test results."

"P…Please ma-am is it epilepsy?" Julie dared to ask.

"Epilepsy? Whoever's been putting that fool notion in your head girl?"

"I… I read something about it ma-am."

"Hmmph! I swear I'd put a ban on unqualified people reading medical articles. They're the country's leading cause of hypochondria. I have one patient comes in regularly and I can tell you exactly what she thinks is wrong with her as soon as she walks through the door just by knowing what the medicine column in the Guardian was about that week. Leave the medical diagnoses to me girl. Have you seen a doctor about these episodes?"

"D.. Dr Atkinson in Mathom's 'ad a look at me ma-am." Dr Chandra made a less than respectful snort at the information that her country colleague had examined Julie.

"Well don't concern yourself with things you know nothing about girl." Dr Chandra turned to Astrid, "Let's have her in the examination room then." Once in that room Dr Chandra turned to Julie "Come along girl. Get your clothes off. We're not here to examine the couture in your finery you know." and Julie shyly disrobed. The presence of the gentle Astrid seemed to have some ameliorating effect on Dr Chandra because she was considerably less acerbic during her examination than her usual style but it was still bad enough as she ran test after test on Julie for the next two hours which was an hour longer than the examination had originally been scheduled for. By the end of it, Julie had been subjected to the full gamut of medical humiliation in Dr Chandra's considerable armoury. She'd been prodded, poked, sampled, x-rayed, ultra-scanned, weighed, measured, put through a barrage of bewildering tests, had her eyes tested, her teeth looked at, blood, skin, hair and urine samples taken, obstetrically examined, had her pulse monitored on an electro-cardiogram, had her blood pressure taken, her joints flexed, her skin examined, her cervix swabbed and virtually every other thing the doctor could think of. She had never been the object of such a comprehensively thorough examination in her life and her entire remaining ambition was to get out of this foul clinic, preferably after setting fire to it, and never to return again. At last Dr Chandra had exhausted her repertoire of intrusive medical humiliation and laid down her note pad with a weary shake of the head. "You can put your clothes on now girl." In enormous relief Julie began to dress.

"What do you think Akuti?" asked Astrid eagerly.

"How much are you and Rosalyn paying for this girl?"

"Oh upwards of half a million Akuti."

"Great Goddess!" Dr Chandra looked thoughtful "Well I'd like to run over the test results at leisure Astrid. I'll be able to give you an opinion at the end of the week if that's all right with you."

"Of course doctor." Astrid looked disappointed.

"I don't think these blackouts are anything to be worrying about but I'll be able to tell you more clearly then. I'll be able to give you a better opinion on the girl's value by then as well. I might need to see her again to run some more tests."

"Yes doctor."

"In the meantime I'd advise you to keep her under lock and key and make sure she gets whipped regularly."

"Oh she hasn't joined out household yet Akuti. She's still residing with her parents."

"Really? Oh well can't be helped. You going to the Mathomdale festival this year?"

“Yes and so is Rosalyn with her two girls.”

“Hmm how are those two? Long time since I had them in my surgery.”

“Fine I believe Akuti.”

“Prime stock those two. Especially the Asian girl. The Italian girl’s top of the Line as well but Rosalyn’s far too soft with her. Thoroughbreds like that need a strong hand.”

“I’ll pass your suggestion on Akuti.”

“I’ll probably be at the festival this year as well. I’ll try and have the results for you by then in case we run into each other.”

“Thank you Akuti. We might be able to finalise the offer for her at the festival in that case.”

“Well we’re on the lookout for a suitable girl or two as well if anything comes up at auction. Does the wench have any sisters by any chance?”

“Yes but much older Akuti and I don’t think they’re available.”

“Oh well we’ll just have a look around in any case. There’s usually a few youngsters coming on the market at the Mathomdale festival but the competition for them is horrendous. Quality slaves are worth their weight in gold these days.”

“There might be more on the market this year Akuti. There’s a rumour going about that there’s a lot of displaced youngsters from the troubles in the Third World that need new homes. They’re evacuating lots of them to this country and offering good terms for them. I’m keeping an eye open myself because I need at least one or two sisters for Julie.”

“Well if you hear of any that might interest us Astrid I’d appreciate it if you’d drop me a quiet word. We can’t afford to lay out the kind of money that you and Rosalyn are throwing about but if any good bargains come up we’d be mighty interested.”

“I’ll keep an eye open Akuti.”

“Anyway I’d best get on. I’m behind schedule what with looking at your girl.”

“Thank you Akuti. I do appreciate you taking the extra time to look her over.”

“My pleasure Astrid. If you’re paying a cool half a million for the wretched wench it’s the very least I can do to give her a thorough going over. I’ll see you at the festival then.”

“Yes until then Akuti and thank you again.” Astrid turned to the subdued Julie and said, “Come along Julie and we’ll go and get some lunch.”

They took lunch at a small pleasant bistro with a sunny terrace overlooking a small square. Astrid was highly pleased with the morning’s work and chattered interminably although Julie was rather quiet following her strange examination by Dr Chandra. It hadn’t been at all what she had expected and, quite apart from the residual resentment that was the normal aftermath of an encounter with the doctor’s inimitable style, she was somewhat bewildered. She wasn’t at all sure what the examination had been about. She’d assumed that she was being examined to ascertain the causes of her fits but that couldn’t be true could it? She was at a loss to explain what a detailed examination of her teeth, hearing and eyesight could possibly tell the doctor about her condition for example and why had she been obliged to submit to that intrusive gynaecological examination as well? Then there’d been other tests that she’d simply had no idea as to the purpose of. Julie was baffled. On the one hand she was somewhat reassured by the doctor’s curt dismissal of her fears of epilepsy but that worry had been replaced by another anxiety. What had the doctor been looking for? Eventually she summoned up the courage to raise the issue with the animated Astrid.

“Why it’s perfectly normal Julie.” Astrid explained, “All prospective young indentured people have to undergo a medical examination. That way any possible problems that they may have can be isolated and their new owner made aware of them. Also it's a protection for the buyer so that they know how healthy the person they are thinking of buying is. After all, whether or not the young person is healthy can affect their value. It's a necessary condition of any sale Julie. I know it sounds awful but it's a bit like buying a car really. You want to know if there are any problems with it before you lay down your money. It's not quite as mercenary as that however. It's also for the benefit of the young person. A clean bill of health and a high AS score on their medical enhances their value."

"AS score ma-am?"

"Alpha Sensual score Julie. The examining doctor does all sorts of tests to ensure the purity of your Alpha Sensual characteristics. They determine the purity of your bloodline and the extent of your enhanced facilities. They are obliged to produce a certificate detailing your Alpha Sensual profile. It's a bit like your documentation of pedigree if you like. High scores on that certificate bestow high value and status on the person involved. It's not unknown for the parents of a young person with a high AS score to demand a higher price for their son or daughter and they'd probably get it as well because such young people make very valuable slaves Julie."

Julie was more fogged than ever. "An' if these AS scores is low ma-am?"

"Well there might be some renegotiation on that basis Julie. You've got to remember, however, that it's not only that that determines the value of a slave. It's important yes but there are all sorts of other factors to take into consideration."

"T' doctor seemed a bit surprised when yer said yer was payin' 'alf a million fer us ma-am."

"Well it's a good deal of money Julie. It shows how much we think of you. I think you're easily worth it though."

Julie wasn't at all sure however and she had more than a nasty feeling that neither would Astrid and Rosalyn be by the time that Dr Chandra delivered her report on her "characteristics". She groaned inwardly at the thought. She had begun to enjoy her new-found status and presumed value. By the end of the week Dr Chandra was liable to be sticking a rather large pin in her balloon. She was staring undeniable exposure as a fraud in the face.

Chapter Five

The safe house was a little farmhouse on the outskirts of a small hamlet on the windswept flat coastal country to the East of the port of Kingston. Eugene looked at the three young girls critically as she organised bedding and other requirements for them. It had been simplicity itself smuggling them ashore on the dockside at Kingston. She'd kept a close eye on Ana as they'd bustled them ashore but she'd been reasonably co-operative and less trouble than Eugene had feared. The waiting team had spirited them away in a car and Ana had hugged the frightened Vesna on the back seat as they wound their way through the city streets. They'd had a nervous moment when a police car had pulled up behind them on a traffic light but it had passed without incident and they'd soon found anonymity along the dark country roads beyond the city limits. At the house they'd fed the girls, bathed them and organised some clothing for them but they'd had very little sleep that night, so Eugene had dug up a couple of cot beds and a mattress and tried to get them to get some rest. They were all exhausted but they were jittery in their unfamiliar circumstances and Eugene was having a hard time reassuring them.

"Please lady why are we locked up?" a wide-eyed Mali asked her.

"It's just for your own safety Mali." Eugene told her truthfully if somewhat economically. She was worried about Ana taking it into her head to make a run for it. "It's only for a short while until we find somewhere safe and permanent for you."

"Please we not go to a puff?"

Eugene sighed. "Mali darling. I promise you. You are not going to a puff. I haven't dragged you girls out of one whore house just to send you to another. You are all going somewhere nice and safe where you can be looked after properly and have a nice life. I promise you. Until we arrange that though I want you all to promise to be good and keep very quiet. It'll only be for a few days at the most. You're safe and you'll come to no harm here. I want you two older girls to look after Vesna and make sure that she's not too frightened or anything and hopefully by the end of the week we'll have found a home for all of you. Have you got that Ana?"

"Ja gad dama! Ja ne lonimau!"

"Don't bullshit me Ana! You understand perfectly well what I'm saying. I know very well that you speak English as well as Mali here so don't try to pull the wool over my eyes. You're in England now Ana so the quicker you start to use your English the better."

"Nobody ask me if I want to be in England." replied Ana in sulky subordination.

"No Ana they didn't. Neither did anybody ask me to pull you out of that goddamned brothel in St Pauli either. Maybe you'd like to go back there.! How about it Ana? Do you fancy a nice future career as a whore? Just say the word and we can arrange it if you want."

"You say we not go to puff no more!" Ana's fear showed through her defiance.

"Nor will you unless you want to, Get this straight Ana. In Hamburg they were going to sell your virginity to the highest bidder. Some old guy was going to pay money just to do what he wanted with you. Then you'd have been put to work serving the customers of some filthy puff. You might have had to let twenty men a day use you Ana, maybe more. Does that sound nice? They'd probably have kept you chained up in a disgusting room whilst the customers queued at the door for their turn. That would have happened Ana if I hadn't have got you out of there. If it wasn't for me you'd still be handcuffed in that puff now Ana. But I did get you out of there. Because of me you, all of you, have got a chance to make something decent and worthwhile out of your lives. Now I don't expect you to fall on my neck in gratitude but you could at least try saying thank you."

"Thank you." said Ana sarcastically.

"Please lady we are thankful." interjected Mali nervously "Ana she thankful too. She just don't want to go to a puff. We scared."

Eugene glared at Ana "Just what is your problem Ana? There're people that are putting their necks on the block to help you and you're barely even civil to them."

"Maybe I see too many people what they are like. Why you should help us?"

"So Ana going to do it all on your own huh? Run out of here and take on the world on your own little lonesome huh? Let me point something out Ana. You're an illegal immigrant, underage and with no family, connections or help here. You have nothing. No money, no home, no chance of a job, not even any clothes to stand up in except what I give you. Do you want to walk out of that door right now Ana? Going to sleep on the streets are you? How long do you think you'd last out there Ana? You'd better shape up Ana because right now I'm the only hope you've got and I'm getting pissed off with your attitude. I start getting a little co-operation out of you or I throw you out of the door myself. Do you understand?"

"Yes lady." Ana looked subdued.

"Please Lady. Don't throw Ana out." Mali pleaded, "Ana will be good. Won't you Ana? Tell her Ana."

"I'm sorry lady." Ana murmured, with tears threatening in her eyes.

"Come here Ana!" Eugene ordered. The Russian girl approached Eugene warily as Eugene sank onto a sofa. When she was close enough Eugene snatched her hands and pulled her down to kneel at her knee. Ana stared at Eugene fearfully.

"Please you not hurt me!"

"I'm not going to hurt you. Don't be frightened of me you foolish girl."

"Are you killer lady?"

"Yes Ana I am. I've killed people Ana. I'm not proud about it but I've had a hard job to do and I've had a hard life. But I only kill the enemies of our people Ana. Your enemies. You have nothing to fear from me. I promise you." Eugene reached out to stroke the blond hair, her voice softening. "Listen Ana you've had a bad time, been mistreated by a lot of bad people, seen some terrible things. But that's all past now. I'm sorry I was angry with you. I know it must be hard for you to trust anybody any more. But I'm telling you the truth Ana. There is nothing more to fear. I've brought you here to England to give you another chance. A chance to have a nice life Ana, a nice home Ana, nice clothes, your own room in a nice house, plenty to eat and money in your purse. I'm giving you the chance to go to school and learn so that one day you'll be able to make your own way in life. When was the last time you went to school?"

"Before my mother died lady."

"Where did you learn to speak English?"

"One of the servants he speak English. He teach me. He have lot of American films in English with the Russian underneath and he let me watch them. I wanted to learn so I could run away to America."

"You're quite something aren't you Ana?"

"Sorry lady?"

"Never mind. Can you read English?"

Ana shook her head "No lady. Only little bit. The letters are different."

"But you can read and write Russian?"

"Da lady."

"Well you'll have to go to school to learn your Latin alphabet and to learn to read and write in English Ana. It won't be hard for you if you already speak it. In fact I don't think many things will be hard for you Ana.

You've got quite a little brain under that sulky exterior haven't you?"

"Please lady where is this home you say we go to?"

"Not far away Ana." Eugene turned to beckon to the other two girls. "Mali, Vesna, come here." When they had joined Ana at Eugene's knee she looked at them softly. "You'll have to explain this to Vesna afterwards Ana." Vesna spoke a related Slavic language to Ana's and she could understand some Russian "Listen girls once upon a time I was like Ana here. I ran away from what should have been my home. I ran away from my Mistress who was the kindest and most generous woman in the world. She forgave me because she loved me but I never went home. Until now. Now I want to go home. I'm having a baby girls."

"You lady?" Mali was wide eyed in astonishment.

"Yes Mali. I'm having a baby and I'm scared as hell. I never had a baby before. Now I want to go home. I want to bring my baby home. I want to beg my Mistress for her forgiveness and find a home for my baby. I have another home in Austria but I've betrayed that home and my baby doesn't belong there. My first home, the one I've never lived in, is here in England a couple of hours drive from here. It's in a beautiful valley in the hills to the north of here. At the weekend there is a big festival in that valley. At that festival people may petition my Mistress for her favour and there I hope to find a home for myself, my baby and for you three as well. I want to find homes for all of us. I will throw myself at the mercy of my Mistress and beg that she find a place for all of us. But you must trust me girls. We will go to my Lady's valley, the four, no the five, of us and present ourselves to her. There we'll find sanctuary girls for my Mistress is the wisest and kindest woman in the world."

"Who… who is your Mistress lady?" asked Mali.

"She has many names Mali. She calls herself the Lady Jennifer of Mathom now but she's known as the Purple Lady, Queen of the Line, Empress of the Purple Empire, first among our people, the people of the Line."

"But... but I have heard of her!" Ana cried "My mother told me about her. She is the Tsarina of the Goddess is she not?"

"Yes ... yes!" Mali answered in excitement "I'm knowing of her too! We say in my country she is the Queen Maya reborn, Mother of Siddartha Gautama, the Buddha."

Eugene smiled "They say a lot of things about her Mali and there's an awful lot of things we don't know about her. That's a very big book to read."

"You.... you take us to the Tsarina lady?" asked Ana in wonder.

"Yes Ana." Eugene grinned and pinched Ana's cheek playfully "And you'd better bloody behave yourself when I do. She's a very powerful lady Ana and not liable to be patient with young ladies that don't know how to behave themselves. Now tell Vesna what I've just said." Mali and Ana's excitement was transmitting itself to Vesna and the younger girl was babbling helplessly in her own tongue. Haltingly Ana tried to explain the gist of what Eugene had said. The young girl looked puzzled to begin with but as comprehension dawned her eyes grew wide with wonder.

"Purpuran Carica?" she breathed at last.

"Da Vesna!" Ana told her, "Carica! Boginja!" Vesna bit her knuckle staring at Eugene in astonishment.

"So you see girls," Eugene continued. "I haven't just brought you to England to sell you to a puff! There's a great future ahead of you but you must trust me a little bit longer. Will you do that?"

Ana looked at Eugene solemnly "Da lady. I sorry I was bad, lady. I will behave. Please don't be angry. I want to see the Tsarina."

Eugene smiled at her "It's all forgotten Ana. You'll get to see her all right." Eugene laughed gently. "I think she might quite like meeting you too Ana. You're quite a young lady." Eugene pulled the other two girls closer to her and kissed them all fondly. "In fact I've got a feeling she's going to like meeting all of you. I think I found three precious little gems in that Goddess forsaken whorehouse."

Chapter Six

Jennifer's walk to her rendezvous with Baxter that afternoon was the doom-laden trea condemned. Darren accompanied her but she wa and pale and he was liking their agreement less and less by the minute. He had tried to coax what it was she intended to do out of her but she had told him that she was unable to tell him and he found himself pledged to secrecy under terrible oaths of love and thoroughly unhappy about it. The others had largely accepted that Jennifer wanted some quality time alone with Darren that afternoon, although Rebecca had been less than convinced and there'd been a minor row between them, with Rebecca refusing to accept that Jennifer had merely gone for a long run through the grounds that morning and lost track of time. Jennifer for her part had expressed her discontent that Rebecca should be so concerned about her as to come looking for her and had invoked her right to some degree of privacy. It was a lover's tiff between two girls that adored each other but, by the nature of these sort of things, it had been painful to both concerned and they'd barely been on speaking terms at lunch. Rebecca knew that Jennifer was hiding something from her and Jennifer's private, guilty acknowledgement of the justification of that fuelled her already smouldering resentment; the resentment that burned in shame in her breast from her shock in the gallery the previous night. A coolness had fallen between the two girls and Jennifer's icy determination upon her drastic course of action that afternoon exacerbated it.

At the gate beyond the Barling Beck Jennifer took her leave of Darren with admonishments to wait for her there until her return. By now Darren was convinced that Jennifer had some dreadful deed in mind for her afternoon's clandestine activity and he was not prepared to leave it at that. He let her get some distance ahead and

.en he made to follow her discreetly at a distance. Dodging between the trees and undergrowth he managed to keep her in sight as she left the grounds on her way to the Low Woods. At one point however he let her get too far ahead and struggled to catch up. Rounding a bend in the lane he saw a figure before him. It was not Jennifer but the furtive figure of a man emerging stealthily from the undergrowth in front with his attention focussed on the path ahead. In a terrible moment he realised the figure was stalking Jennifer and he called aloud "HEY!" There was a dart of surprise in the figure and a pair of eyes flashed briefly in his direction then the figure was gone melting back into the woods with remarkable speed. Darren dashed forward to where the figure had disappeared and pursued it into the wood at the side of the path but it seemed to have vanished completely. He hunted around with the hair tingling on the nape of his neck, certain that the elusive creature had been on Jennifer's trail and for no good reason. In panic he darted back to the path to catch Jennifer but she was far ahead by now. He ran along the path with his heart beating wildly only to find that it ended in a country lane. Here he made a mistake. He barely noticed the gate on the far side of the lane and assumed that Jennifer must have walked off along the road. To the left the road was visible for some distance but, to the right, it vanished around a bend and it was in that direction that he pursued her, losing her completely as she walked ever on into the Low Woods. By the time that Darren had realised his mistake Jennifer was beyond his reach.

The assassin was furious with himself. He'd spent the time since his aborted effort of the morning surveying this trail through the peripheries of the grounds and, finding a concealed spot for the ambush, he'd been waiting patiently since. He'd been delighted to see her walkin down the trail right on schedule, walking with admirable punctuality to her death. It hadn't occurred to the assassin that she might have a shadow however. He had nearly jumped out of his skin when the man had yelped at him from behind whilst his attention had been fixed upon the slim figure walking ahead. He must be some personal bodyguard or something the assassin reasoned and he'd seen him. He must have been in full view for over a second before losing himself in the woods once more. He'd never get near the damn girl now. They'd clamp a security blanket over her you wouldn't be able to penetrate with a small army. He'd jeopardised his entire mission with a momentary lack of caution.

It was just typical of this job he reflected sourly. The whole damn thing had gone awry from the word go. When he'd first taken this contract it had seemed simplicity itself. A rural quiet and isolated country estate, how difficult could that be? Just locate and isolate some girl belonging to the foul witch that owned these lands, take her out nice and quickly and get the hell out. He'd expected to be in and out within twenty-four hours, forty-eight at the most. His employers hadn't told him that the whole fucking valley was an armed camp bristling with highly trained counter insurgency troops armed to the fucking teeth. And now it was likely that he would be the hunted one. Once that guy reported his presence there'd be an all-out sweep of the grounds and surroundings for him. The assassin was under no illusions about what would happen if they found him. At the start, when he'd first taken on this job he thought he might have had a chance of bluffing his way out if he'd been detected. Not anymore. He'd seen enough to convince himself that these people would shoot first and ask questions later.

He toyed with the idea of just getting out now and telling his employer to go screw himself. He didn't much appreciate being sent as an expendable pawn straight into a death trap. He might have known that the money he was being offered was too good to be true. But he'd been so close not once but twice. He'd been that close to cashing in that money. The damn girl lived a charmed life it seemed. He allowed himself to calm down and think rationally. The first priority was to get out of the grounds of this hell house as quickly as possible before he got caught up in the sweep. Lie low until the hue and cry had died down. There was some big fair on in the valley at the weekend he knew. There'd be all sorts of people, strangers and so on, at that. There might be a chance then. It would be easy to blend in with the crowds and keep an eye open, waiting for his opportunity. He didn't think that guy had seen him well enough to furnish a description. He could become invisible in the crowds. There had to be some moment when his target was left exposed.

He could earn that money yet. Retire some place where the weather was better maybe; Spain perhaps or South America. Somewhere where the witch that owned this valley would never find him. New identity, new passport, a little place on the beach, open his own little bar and invite the girls in their bikinis in. Just one slip up from that little auburn-haired beauty and her goddamned overseers and it was all possible. But he would have to be careful. Damn careful and patient too. But there'd be a chance. There always was.

Jennifer had steeled herself into fatalistic acceptance of her coming ordeal as she approached Baxter's inner sanctum within the Low Woods. In a way she sensed the inevitability of her upcoming showdown with Quentin Baxter as if it had been something pre-ordained ever since the day that he had caught Julie and herself trespassing in the woods. The arrows of fortune had all seemed to lead toward this day when she would sacrifice herself to her nemesis in the woods of his domain on behalf of her love for Julie. She seemed to have done this all summer. She seemed to have spent her entire time marching to the cadence of destinies beyond her control and walking with her eyes open into ever enclosing entrapment. This valley was a honey trap and she the fragile insect lured into it. She wondered if she possessed any free will left at all other than the will to simply walk into her own slavery.

She found the place, where the path lead aside by the bole of an ancient, gnarled oak tree, easily enough. There was a large arrow carved into the bark of the tree and she followed its command resignedly, although she was very frightened. It was only a few hundred yards into the thickest part of the woods to the beautiful and quiet open glade where her tormentor had his den and there Quentin Baxter was waiting for her. He watched her approach his heart soaring in glee. She was as beautiful as he had ever seen her. She was dressed simply in white with a long cheesecloth skirt and a halter neck top that tied in a bow behind her neck leaving her arms, shoulders and back bare although she covered herself with a woollen shawl. She looked almost preciously virginal, a fitting picture of innocence walking to her sacrifice. Baxter felt a great lump in his heart and he hardly dared to breathe as she approached in silence her head lowered in submission and the sun radiating in her thick auburn tresses. He wanted to capture her in this moment forever in his mind's eye, freeze the vision of her in his memory knowing that however long he lived he would never lose the magic of this moment. Hoarsely he willed himself to speak to her.

"Yer look a right picture Jenny love."

Jennifer raised her head to look at him. She was astonished. Baxter had dressed up in his best for this encounter in smart gypsy style breeches and a flamboyantly ruffed white shirt under an old-fashioned Renaissance style jerkin. The powerful muscular man was almost handsome in his dashing old world finery, like some romantic bandit or highwayman of long ago.

She felt she had stepped out of the twenty first century and into some earlier time zone like a tavern's serving wench meeting her clandestine outlaw lover in the woods beyond the sheriffs' questioning eyes. It was perfect for they were both outlaws now joining in their wicked tryst and damning the consequences of their devil's agreement. "Thank you Mr Baxter. I have come as we agreed."

"Just stand there and let me look at yer Jenny. Yer a picture fer sore eyes an' no error." Baxter drank his fill of the sight of her as she stood there her lovely hazel eyes looking sorrowful yet calm, windows of her resignation. He loved her he realised. Whilst yet his cruelty demanded her agony, he loved her still and he was torn between the urgency of his cruelty and the overwhelming sense of tenderness toward her. Had fate and life not determined otherwise, had he not grown to manhood crippled by the evil of his insanity and had he been yet young and uncorrupted by that wickedness, he would have folded this young girl in his arms and declared his love for her and begged her to be his. There'd once been a young Quentin Baxter who'd dreamed of love and romance, a young man still innocent in youthful idealism and untainted with bitterness and cynicism. Given the chance, that young man might have emerged triumphant in the battle for the soul of Quentin Baxter, but he lay deeply now, buried beneath the hard cruelty of his dark brother. Yet the sweetness of Jennifer could talk to that young man still and awaken him in the dark recesses of Baxter's mind.

"Let… let me take yer wrap Jenny love." He requested hoarsely. Jennifer slipped her shawl from her shoulders and he took it from her almost gallantly to hang it carefully on the branch of a small sapling. "Come love." he ordered gently and took her by the hand to stand beneath the enormous oak tree that dominated the sunny glade in magnificent isolation. Jennifer glanced up and saw, with a thrill of horror, the rope he had looped over a stout branch well above her head. He steered her quietly into position beneath the rope and took her wrists in his hands. She watched, almost hypnotised, as he pulled the rope down and fashioned two loops firmly about her wrists. With her hands bound together, he surprised her for he raised them softly to his lips and kissed them gently. The glade seemed to be on the verge of explosion, in the silence of the afternoon. She waited trembling as he stepped to one side to take up the other end of the rope and then she whimpered in pain as he hauled on the rope to drag her hands high above her. The rope bit into her wrists as he pulled her taut and onto the tips of her toes, stretched tightly from the branch above. She grasped the ropes with her hands to relieve the pressure on her wrists as he fastened a firm hitch around a root.

Baxter stood back to admire her. She was breathing heavily now her face in a grimace of pain as she tried to gain purchase on the ground with the extremities of her toes. He took her legs and lifted her feet clear of the ground and she gasped as her arms took the full weight of her body but all he did was support her legs with one arm as he slipped her sandals from her feet. He placed them carefully by the little sapling he hand hung her shawl from, as she watched him, wild-eyed and biting her lip to still her moans of desperation. He was walking around her now, as if to see her helplessness from every possible angle and savour it at his leisure. Then he was behind her and she felt his breath hot on her neck as he cradled her waist with his hands. She could hear the mounting excitement in his deepening breath and feel the heat of his body now so close to her. She closed her eyes and swallowed the bile in her throat knowing that she had only one card to play and she must play it well.

"This is 'ow I've wanted yer Jenny." he was whispering "This is 'ow I've allus wanted yer."

“You… you said that if I came….. if…. if I submitted to your will you would leave Julie alone. Do you mean it?”

“Aye…. Bugger Julie ‘Awthorne! It’s you I want! My sweet Jenny…. that’s all I want. Your Miss ‘Awthorne can flog ‘er black markets fags all ovver the county for all I care.”

“Then swear it! Swear it to me now!”

“Ye ‘ave me promise Jenny.”

“Do you love me Quentin?”

“Eh? What’s all this about?” Baxter stiffened with surprise.

“I asked if you love me. I want to know! I want to know before….. before you …. do what you will. I want to know!”

“Yer blatherin’ lass!”

“Tell me! Tell me now!”

Baxter gripped her waist tightly “Of course I love yer lass!” he growled “I’ve loved yer an’ wanted yer ever since that day I come upon yer wi Julie ‘Awthorne in t’ woods. I’ve thought o’ nowt else all this summer. Yer my little sweet Jenny an’ allus will be.”

“Then swear to me! Swear that you’ll stand by your word. Swear that you’ll remain true to me. Swear it! By the Goddess swear it!”

Baxter was in turmoil knowing he was being bewitched. He had this girl at his mercy yet she dared make conditions of her helplessness and he was bound to acquiesce in them. For an awful moment he felt that it was he that hung by the ropes from the old oak tree. His heart was hammering wanting her so very badly but knowing that he must sell his soul to her. “I swear then! By the Bloody Goddess I swear! May she strike me down dead if I prove false. Now are you ‘appy?”

“Yes.” she breathed and let her head fall to her chest. “Yes Quentin! Thank you. I am.”

“Oh bloody ‘ell!” he suddenly rested his head on her shoulder breathing deeply. Jennifer could feel the roughness of his chin against neck.

“Are.... are you going to beat me Mr Baxter?” she whispered in a tiny voice.

“Aye Jenny! I am! I’m afraid I ‘ave to.”

“P... please don’t mark me permanently sir. You wouldn’t want me scarred would you?”

“Fer ‘eaven’s sake lass still yer blatherin’!” Baxter stood up straight and glared at her fiercely, almost panting in his turmoil.

“P.... please Mr Baxter!” she whimpered softly tearing his heart in two. She mewled piteously as she felt his fingers at the nape of her neck and then he was lifting her heavy tresses aside and laying them over her shoulders. She could sense the unsteadiness of his hands as they sought out the bow on her halter neck and teased the knot apart, holding the two ends apart for long seconds before allowing them to fall and for her top to slip away from her torso to her waist, exposing her nakedness. Bare to the waist she stared ahead at the great oak tree as the breeze played on her breasts whilst he stood back to admire his handiwork. Then his hands were slipping about her flanks from behind and cupping her breasts. She winced as he pinched her nipples hard and felt his body against her back, the bulge of his erection through his breeches against her buttocks. She felt tears in her eyes as his hands fumbled at the fastener at the back of her skirt.

When her skirt was loose, he stood back to watch it slip slowly under gravity, along with her top, over her loins to crumple in a heap about her ankles. Astonishingly, he lifted her feet one by one to remove the garments and then to brush the twigs from them carefully before hanging them up on the little tree, as if he cared deeply about her clothes. Only her knickers stood between her and nakedness now and he knelt to pull them down her legs and these he did not hang up but pushed them into the pocket of his breeches before sliding a hand around her to caress her sex. She moaned involuntarily as the fingers of his right hand pushed themselves into the moisture between her legs whilst his other hand grasped her left breast. He was panting heavily against the nape of her neck.

"Now then Jenny! Yer stripped naked fer me whip! Are yer ready fer this Jenny? Nobody 'ere fer miles around. Yer can scream yer pretty little 'ead off. I want to 'ear yer. Are yer goin' ter sing me a nice little song Jenny love? Are yer goin' to give me a nice little dance?"

"Oh please!" she whispered, "Please don't!" She was very frightened now.

"Too late now Jenny. Yer come o' yer own free will. This is the price o' my promise Jenny. I'm goin' ter whip yer till me arm aches Jenny. I'm fore sworn to yer bewitchment lassie but I'll 'ave me devil's due an 'ear you scream an' beg fer mercy."

"Oh Goddess!"

"Aye Jenny. You just 'ang there nice an' pretty while I be fetchin' t' tools fer t' job." Baxter strode away to the little hut beyond the tree and vanished inside. When he emerged Jennifer groaned in despair for he carried a long switch in one hand and a coiled long whip in the other.

"Oh Goddess help me now!" she pleaded to herself. "Give me strength please." Baxter was taking his jerkin off and hanging it up beside her clothes before rolling his sleeves up and turning to her. He laid the long whip aside on a tree stump for the moment and flexed the riding switch evilly in his hands. Walking across to her he stroked the front of her body with the switch, tickling her breasts.

"D' yer remember this Jenny? It's t' crop I used on yer t' first time when I caught yer trespassin' wi your young Julie. I've bin keepin' it for yer ever since. Yer only 'ad a dozen then Jenny but yer know what it feels like. Well yer goin' ter be renewin' yer acquaintance with it now Jenny. It'll be more than any dozen yer'll be getting' now though."

His eyes dancing in glee, Baxter walked around the back of her, savouring the sight of her long slim naked torso hanging before him. She sensed him raise the switch and she clamped her eyes shut her buttocks clenching in dread anticipation. She shrieked in shock and pain as he brought the dreadful implement down across her body for he'd landed the blow across her shoulder blades and not, as she'd expected across her buttocks. She took a firmer grip on the ropes and gulped a deep breath, the stinging pain agonising across her back. The breath exploded out of her as he lashed her again, this time directing the force across her bottom. She swayed forward dangerously, losing grip on the ground with her toes. He grasped hold of her and straightened her up again before raising his arm to whip her again. A flock of birds flew in alarm from the trees above as she pierced the stillness of the glade with her scream. Baxter gloried in that scream and brought the whip down harder his excitement mounting furiously with every contortion of her tortured body and every shrill howl wrenched from her throat. He had a rhythm now as she twisted and squirmed under the cruel onslaught of the switch, the deep red weals scarring her back, buttocks and the back of her thighs and her screams growing ever more desperate in the accumulation of her agony.

Jennifer was nearly demented with the pain as Baxter's strong arm flailed at her. Some particularly vicious strokes made her lift her feet from the ground and hang by her wrists writhing desperately at the scorching impact on her flesh. Her voice was hoarse with screams and her vision blurred with the tears from her eyes. At the moment she believed herself beyond any further endurance, he stopped. Baxter gazed at her, his excitement huge, as she hung limply sobbing with the back of her body laced with innumerable red weals. He walked around the front of her and lifted her chin with his fingers for he wanted to see the pain in her eyes. Her cheeks were wet with tears; her eyes red and her mouth hung open gasping breath. Almost tenderly he lifted her hair back across her shoulders, smoothing it away from her front. Then he stepped back, took a long look at her heaving breasts and raised the switch once more. Through the blur of her tears Jennifer saw him raise the switch above her breasts and she gasped in horror.

"No! Please No!" The switch exploded on her breasts in agony. She jerked backwards with a terrible howl. Her keening continued as he lashed the front of her body matching the back with a latticework of angry red stripes from her hips to the top of her breasts. He seemed dissatisfied with the perfection of the pattern he was laying upon her and he stepped close to lift her breasts by the nipples in turn to deliver a series of short sharp strokes to the soft flesh on the underside of her breasts in quick succession bringing a new purgatory to the tormented girl. At last he seemed satisfied and he laid aside his switch to fortify himself with a quick pull from his hip flask. He sat down on a tree stump to watch her taking his pipe from his pocket and enjoying the soothing smoke as he observed the fruits of his handiwork. She was the most satisfyingly beautiful thing he had ever seen hanging there in her pain. This he wanted to remember forever. He let the aromatic smoke linger in his mouth as he watched her fight back from the brink of her agony. He felt a deeply contented man. But he was not finished yet. In great satisfaction he knocked out his pipe and picked up the long-coiled whip.

"No Quentin! Please! No! I can't take anymore!" she pleaded.

"I don't think yer've much option Jenny lass." he leered at her. He was getting warm with his exertions so he pulled his shirt off and hung it up. The taut muscles of his chest were slick with perspiration as he uncoiled the long whip and stood before her. Like a striking snake the whip curled around her body and she screamed once more at the searing flame across her skin. He took his time over this last infliction of pain walking slowly about her and directing the whip from every different angle, delighting in her agonised dance beneath its caresses. To Jennifer it was horrible. She never knew where the lash would strike next and slowly she began to descend into a red fog of agony. At some point where each individual whiplash was indistinguishable from the others, when her whole body seemed ablaze with fire she found that curious elevated detachment that she'd experienced in the Oriental Gardens, almost as if she were leaving her body to escape from the torment of it and staring down at the tableau in the glade as if from a height above.

Then the whipping stopped. She didn't know how she knew that it was finally at an end only that it was and that Baxter's excitement had finally overcome him and now he was fumbling with the fasteners on the front of his breeches, panting in rising lust as he surveyed her tortured body. He struggled clear of his pants and now he was descending on her, his erection thrust firmly before him. Jennifer was beyond pleading now. She watched him approach her almost objectively, as if his rape of her was a fitting climax to the violation of her sacrifice. Her senses were very intense now and her throbbing flesh felt like the burning heat of some powerful engine kindled within her. The red mist cleared from her eyes and now she saw him with terrible clarity. She gritted her teeth as he lifted underneath the legs, supporting her burning buttocks to push himself between her limbs and lower her onto his erection. A groan escaped her lips as he forced his way inside her but it was her last protest for now the Goddess was ascendant within her and she felt triumphant in the moment of her rape.

His face was very close to her now as he thrust frantically at her and she stared closely at it. In that moment she thought of Julie but where the thought came from she had no idea. Her awareness was massive now and there were no secrets under her searing hazel gaze. His eyes! She had never looked closely into Baxter's eyes before. Now they were inches from her. They were clear blue, full of lust, alien and yet strangely familiar. Where had she seen those eyes before? Her brain sought clarification rooting back in its data files but it would not come. Then her body was betraying her as she'd known it would for it could not help it and the waves of treacherous arousal were already overwhelming her. The heat of her agony and the ascendancy of her ecstasy became blurred into a single passion and she screamed a last time as her body became convulsed in the climax of that passion even as she felt the urgent quickening of Baxter within her. In a terrible bonding of insanity they rode the madness of that climax together.

It was quiet in the aftermath of that dreadful moment, the stillness of the glade broken only by Baxter's stertorous breathing, her own gasping breath and the sound of a woodpecker tapping on the trunk of the great oak tree above. Her body was slick with sweat and his musky odour filled her nostrils. He had released her legs and she found some purchase on the ground to relieve the strain on her arms. But he held on to her still burying his face against her neck and his penis still buried within her. She was calm now and though her body shrieked with pain with every movement she felt an exultant triumph.

For she owned him now. It might take some time for him to realise it but she possessed him completely.

He was her slave, her animal; she could destroy at her whim now. Soon he would realise the power she had over him. He had blackmailed, misused and raped a Slave of the Amethyst. His life was forfeit to that reality. Her Mistress would eradicate him without hesitation. A mere word from her and her Mistress would destroy him utterly. Jennifer had baited her trap with her own sacrifice. Julie was safe. So was she. Baxter would soon come to realise that he lived only by her sufferance. Should she finish him off straight away, she wondered. Go straight to her Mistress and confess all? She would be punished but she knew she could endure that. He would be doomed. The terrible icy calculations of his fate frightened her. She knew she was the Goddess at this moment and she could extinguish his life so very easily. And he loved her. He was powerless before her. He could hurt her but ultimately it was she that carried the whip. She felt almost pity for the man whose soul she had just stolen.

"Look at me Quentin." she commanded quietly. In triumph she saw him obey and she searched those disturbing eyes keenly. In her heightened awareness she saw the truth in their enigma and knew at that moment that there were betrayals within betrayals within the enchanted land of Mathomdale. It was the Valley of Love and it carried the betrayals of love like a curse within its bewitched gardens. In the name of love she decided to let Quentin Baxter live. "Release me Quentin!" she ordered and the voice seemed to come from another being within her, a powerful being that brooked no argument or dissent. It was a voice that carried the ultimate authority of command.

"Aye Jenny. Just a minute now." He broke away from her. She could feel his semen trickling down the inside of her thigh as he withdrew from her and he was fumbling hastily and clumsily with the knot he had tied around the tree root. Then the strain was relaxed and

Jennifer collapsed to her knees thankfully. Her wrists burned where the rope had scored them but it seemed a small matter in the overall fire that consumed her body. He was knelt by her now tugging at the knots about her wrists and she waited patiently whilst he teased them loose. When they were free he rubbed her wrists concernedly and she let him do it watching him dispassionately. "Are ye all right Jenny love?" he was asking anxiously and she saw no contradiction in his sudden frantic concern for her well-being. "Tell me yer all right love. Speak ter me!" he begged her. "Talk ter me Jenny. Tell me yer all right." How easy it was, she thought to herself, to capture a person and chain them to you forever. She raised her face to look at him directly and Baxter was shocked at the icy tranquillity in her face.

"Do you truly love me Quentin?"

"Aye! Aye I do!" and in that second she believed him.

"Then remember you are sworn to me. I've accepted your love through the pain you have given me. Don't betray me Quentin."

"Never!" he cried and he snatched her in his arms hugging her tightly. "This day 'll allus be precious ter me Jenny love. Yer a brave lass. I'm not a good man Jenny but I'll do all right by you I swear. Give me t' chance an' I'll show yer I can be a good man Jenny." Baxter believed it himself. For a few heady minutes he allowed some distorted fantasy to possess him, a fantasy in which he would have a place in the heart of Jennifer Walstow. He honestly saw a future in which he could prove himself worthy of that place, become a better person, make himself a bedrock of reliability to her, a champion of her. He would protect her, defend her against all her enemies. One day she would be queen over these woods and he would be her faithful knight, defender of her realm and carry his lady's colours on his shield. Perhaps she would reward his loyalty with her favours and perhaps she would come willingly to his arms. His cruelty was sated for the moment and he allowed himself the luxury of impossible dreams.

"I.... I must go." she said at last. "Would you hand me my clothes please?"

Aye of course Jenny." He brought her skirt, top, shoes and shawl from the sapling as she struggled painfully to her feet. She never asked for her knickers still in his breeches pocket. Carefully, for her flesh was still tender, she dressed herself, wrapping her shawl about her tightly to conceal the weals of the whip. Her tangled hair she could do little about however besides pushing the wayward locks into some order. She turned to him expectantly and he snatched her and kissed her, the first time he had done that. Then she was turning to go but she turned her head one last time and reminded him,

"You're mine now Quentin. Don't ever let me down." and then she was gone. Baxter pulled his clothes on and collapsed against the bole of the tree fumbling in his pocket for his pipe and his flask. He stared up at the rope still looped over the bough above and saw her once again hanging there in her sweet agony. He knew he would see that in his mind every day for the rest of his life. He would never take down that rope he swore. It would stay there always as a memento of her pain within these woods. He'd call this tree the Jennifer Tree and he would turn this glade into a shrine for her. He would come here every time the troubles in his mind became unbearable and find some semblance of harmony and peace as he thought of her whipped body hanging from the Jennifer Tree. Maybe in that memory he could find some of the happiness that had always eluded him.

Chapter Seven

Darren had finally found the correct trail but he was frantic with worry now. He'd spent hours hunting for Jennifer up and down the lane and he was on the point of betraying his promise and going back to the Hall to declare her missing when he finally saw her walking slowly back through the woods toward the country road. "Jenny!" he gasped in profound relief and then he was flying toward her to grasp her in his arms. Jennifer winced as he held her tight inflaming the soreness in her swollen tender skin beneath her clothes. "Jesus H Christ! Where the hell have you been Jenny? I looked everywhere for you."

"You were supposed to wait for me at the gate Darren." she admonished him.

"I.... I couldn't help it Jenny. I was scared sick. There was someone following you honey. I just had to see that you were all right."

"Who? Who was following me?"

"I dunno Jenny. Some guy. I didn't get a good look at him but he was trailing you as sure as damn and he vanished mighty quick when I yelled."

"Probably just one of the groundsman being nosy Darren."

"I dunno Jenny. He didn't look like no groundsman to me. He was up to no good. I'd put my shirt on it."

"Come then let's get back into the grounds. I... I need to sit down for a while."

"We can take a seat right here."

"No Darren. Let's get back. I'm not supposed to leave the grounds of the Hall."

Darren held her at arm's length to look at her. She was pale faced and her eyes were red. She was shivering slightly, hugging her shawl tightly around her and her hair was a mess. "Jesus Jenny what happened to you?"

"I.... I can't tell you Darren. Forgive me but I can't. Please don't ask me to."

"Ok let's get the hell out of here then!" Darren helped her along for she seemed suddenly frail. He would not allow himself to relax however until they had regained the grounds and within sight of people working within them. There was a little rustic bench by the side of the trail and Jennifer sank thankfully on to it. He joined her and held her hand dreadfully worried about her. "Jesus Jenny what the hell have you done?"

"Oh Darren don't. Don't ask me. Please. I beg you!"

"Hell Jenny! I ought to tell your friends. Really I ought."

"No Darren! Please. You promised! Nobody must know besides you and I."

"Jenny I don't know what it is, but you've been doing something crazy; something dangerous. I'm worried sick about you."

"Oh Darren I'm sorry. It was something I had to do. One day I'll tell you but please don't ask me right now. I beg you. And please don't tell anybody."

"Ok Jenny. I don't like it but ok. There's something rotten in all this but if you want me to keep my mouth closed about it you're going to have to make me a promise now."

"Anything Darren. Anything you want."

"You're going to promise me that you don't go wandering off on your own on some fool adventure again. You'll promise me that you don't go out of sight of the Hall again without somebody with you. You'll promise me that Jenny or all deals are off. Either I have your promise on that or I go straight to your sisters and tell them about your days' work. I don't care if that gets your ass into trouble and gets you locked up for a month. Leastways I'll know you're safe. Now promise me!"

"Yes Darren. I promise. I won't go off on my own. I promise." Jennifer was near to tears.

"Oh Jesus Jenny! Come here." He held her for a long time whilst she wept on his shoulder. When her catharsis seemed spent at last he kissed her gently. "Come on honey let's see if we can sneak you back into the house without anybody seeing you. You're a goddamn mess."

"Thank you for everything Darren. Truly I mean it. I'm very grateful."

"Jesus Jenny! A guy needs nerves of steel round you"

"I'm sorry I'm so much trouble Darren."

"Well my Old Uncle Bob used to say, "Son troubles come to those as go looking for them." I guess I kinda looked for trouble with you ma-am. Come on let's go."

In the event they were only seen at some distance by Helen as they crept furtively back into the Hall. Helen reported their return to the others who were gathered on the back veranda for tea. "Well Jenny and Darren just got back." she announced. "Saw them sneaking into the Hall."

"Where the devil have they been?" asked Rebecca in some irritation.

"Dunno. Somewhere quiet and private at a guess."

"Why didn't they come over here?" Abigail wanted to know. "Darren knew we were having tea on the back terrace. Even if they're late they could have come up to let us know they were back."

"I guess Jenny needed to do some emergency repair work Abi." Helen noted. "She looked like she'd been dragged through a hedge backwards from where I was. What's she like? Goes off for an afternoon of hanky panky in the bushes with Darren Morgan and hasn't even the sense to take a hairbrush with her."

"I don't like this." Rebecca commented "Jenny's up to something."

“Well we know that sister.” Heather commented, “They didn’t go off for an afternoon’s bird spotting.”

“Might have done Heath.” remarked Helen “Different avifauna in America sis. Maybe Darren’s never seen a Great Tit before.”

“Stop it you two.” laughed Rebecca “Seriously I’m worried about her. She’s got some other agenda going on.”

“Come on Becky!” Helen said “Just because you two had a bit of a row at lunchtime. No need to start getting paranoid. She’ll be all sweetness and light again by dinner, especially if Darren’s mellowed her out a bit in the rose bushes somewhere. You watch. She’ll be as sweet as cherry pie by the time we sit down for dinner.”

“I agree with Becky.” Abigail commented, “Jenny’s spending too much time going off on her own. She’s definitely brooding about something.”

“She wasn’t on ‘er own this aft.” Daniel pointed out “She were with Darren. Can’t see ‘er comin’ ter much ‘arm with ‘im. Seems like a sound bloke ter me.”

“Well ok.” conceded Abigail “But there’re a few undercurrents I don’t like. I think we need a solidarity get together sisters and brother. It’s driving everybody loopy being cooped up at the Hall with the Lady away and when all the excitement for the festival preparations are down in the village. Anyway this afternoon I sent a message to Shiro-san asking permission for us to have a dinner party in the Oriental Gardens tomorrow evening. If you’re all agreeable I think it would be cool. We can get to show Alice, Danny and Darren the gardens too.”

“Hell yes I’m up for it!” Helen said gleefully.

“Me too!” yipped Heather.

“Eee I’d like that.” said Alice, “I’ve never seen these gardens wot yer all allus on about.”

“That’s a great idea Abi.” Rebecca interjected “Jenny loves the Oriental Gardens. That’ll be one way to get her out of her mood.”

“’Ere ‘ang about though.” warned Daniel “I’m workin’ down in t’ village puttin’ up them flippin’ stands tomorrow. Don’t know when I’ll get away.”

“Surely you can be back up by sixish.” Said Abigail.

“Well I’ll try but it’s an ‘ell of a job be sounds o’ things.”

“Well leave the rest up to the minions Danny and get away around tea time.” Rebecca told him “Come on you’ve got to see the Oriental Gardens. They’re one of the wonders of Mathom Hall.”

“I’ll see wot I can do Becky. I’d like ter see these gardens mesen. Jenny were tellin’ us that they make all t’ rest o’ t gardens look like a cabbage patch an’ that’ll tek some doin’.”

“Ok folks.” Said Abigail holding up a hand “We should get confirmation this evening if it’s convenient for Shiro-san. I don’t see that there should be a problem though. It’ll be great. We haven’t had a party in the Gardens since spring and never with all of us together.”

“Will there be a problem with Darren?” Helen wanted to know. “I mean he’s not part of the household is he?”

“Not yet he isn’t.” remarked Abigail “Reading between the lines though I’d say that was a pretty temporary condition. Darren may or may not be aware of it but I’d say it was overwhelmingly likely that he’s due for a permanent change of address!”

“Suits me.” remarked Heather “We need a few more fellahs on board. Poor old Danny here is starting to look gaunt and wasted.”

“That’s not wot yer said last night.” Daniel pointed out.

“’Ere!” objected Alice in mock outrage “Wot ‘ave you bin up ter me lad?”

“Nowt wuss than wot you was doin’ love.” Daniel told her.

“Can it guys.” laughed Abigail “OK then are we all on?”

“Sure Abi.” said Rebecca “Hey what about dress code?”

“Hmm I dunno. What do you think?”

“Why spoil the ship for a ha’porth o’ tar? Let’s make it full formal traditional Japanese dress! We’ve got all afternoon to get into our kimonos! We can use the kimonos from the Japanese collection. There’re plenty of men’s kimonos too.”

“’Ere I’m not wearing a bleedin’ frock!” Daniel yipped in alarm.

“They’re not frocks Danny dearest.” Rebecca told him. “They’re correct Japanese traditional men’s wear. You’ll look like a samurai warrior.”

“Perfect.” Abigail stated in satisfaction. “We’ll get Mrs Yakamura to help us get dressed.”

“Why do we need ‘elp?” asked Alice.

“Honey have you ever tried getting into a full formal kimono?” asked Rebecca, “It’s a good hours job at least and you need an expert on it. It takes somebody that knows the bloody things just to tie your obi for you. You’d never do it on your own.”

“Then there’s all the hairdo and cosmetics Alice.” said Helen “We’re looking at a full afternoon’s work here.”

“Bloody ‘ell! I’d no idea.”

“Come on Alice it’ll be fun.” Heather told her. “Hey, we haven’t got really dressed up like this in ages. We’ll be a perfect little bunch of geisha girls. Parasols and everything.”

I can’t wait to pick out a kimono.” Helen said excitedly. “You ought to see the collection we’ve got here Alice. They’ll blow your mind.”

“All right I’m up fer it then. This sounds like a laugh.”

“Sorted then.” said Abigail “It’ll show respect to Shiro-san to dress up Japanese style formally as well.”

“We gonna sleep in the gardens?” Helen wanted to know.

“Let’s just see what the magic of the night brings us!” said Abigail with a smile.

Chapter Eight

A palpable air of excitement seemed to have gripped the village of Mathom that week. With the summer festival now only days away, the whole village was galvanised into frenetic activity. The place was being scrubbed and decorated. New flower boxes and licks of paint were in evidence everywhere, as the inhabitants prepared the village to look it's best for its visitors. Stands, marquees, flagpoles, stalls and amusement rides were starting to sprout like weeds around the green, the square, the sports fields and school yards and the stray by the river was a bustle of activity with fencing going up and the erection of tents and viewing stands. Bunting was already beginning to festoon the houses and strong men everywhere were muscling heavy equipment into place to provide the logistics for the festival. Up and down the valley schoolchildren were being put through their last-minute rehearsals for their dance and choral routines or busily decorating their floats whilst their parents and teachers fussed endlessly over their costumes. Every village was alive with the sound of music as the brass bands and choirs practised interminably and the marching bands were being drilled into perfection up and down the streets until their feet ached. Farmers were grooming their prize beasts assiduously and the market gardeners were agonising over their choices with the same fanaticism that the valley's women folk were worrying themselves into a decline over their choice of dress.

Housewives were perfecting their pickles and preserves or baking formidable cakes and pies. It was a bad time to be a fatted beast or fowl in Mathomdale for there was a great slaughter and dressing of those destined to be the roasted pigs, lambs, bullocks, geese, chickens and turkeys to feed the festival. The hangers in the butcher's shops groaned under the weight of strings of glistening sausages, whole hams and sides of bacon. The dairies were producing prodigious mountains of local cheese. The bakeries seemed to be working around the clock. All leave was cancelled at the Mathomdale brewery as its labourers sweated to churn out the enormous quantities of festival beer to quench the festival's thirst. In every corner of the valley there was the aroma of baking and cooking on the air.

In the back room of every pub or the recesses of the village hall, earnest committees were meeting to finalise plans for their contributions to the festival. People argued and swore, fell out with each other or declared their solidarity, caught up in the overall excitement of the coming festivities. There was very little work being done that was not directly involved with the festival. Those with no immediate involvement were apt to be found lounging around the village, content to be at the centre of the mounting anticipation and frantic activity. Parents despaired of keeping their children in the house as the youngsters dashed excitedly from one scene of action to another, getting under the feet of the sweating labourers, begging tit bits from those preparing the feasts or being chased away from the firework display being prepared down on the stray. It was a wonderful time to be a Mathomdaler.

Not all was well however in this burgeoning ascendancy toward the climactic event on the valley's calendar on Tuesday morning. Conspicuous by their absence were the large grandstands for the ceremonies on the main square and the sports fields. These large structures presently resided on a series of flatbed trucks in the yard of Joseph Cartwright, senior builder responsible for their erection, on the outskirts of the village, being regarded with mounting trepidation by Joseph and his two assistants. "'Ow?" asked Thomas Granton in desperation, "are we supposed ter get this bloody lot put up before Friday Joe?"

Joseph pulled of his cap and wiped a wrist across his forehead. “Buggered if I know Tom. Not on us jacks that is fer certain. I ‘ardly know where ter flippin’ start.”

“It’s no good Joe.” commented Richard Cartwright, Joseph’s nephew, “We ‘ave ter ‘ave some ‘elp. Yer just goin’ ter ‘ave ter go ter t’ committee an’ tell ‘em it’s too much work fer three men. We’ve only two ‘ands apiece after all.”

“Ah’ve bin ter t’ flippin’ committee. Every bugger’s tied up. T’ only ‘elp they could offer us was some fellah wot’s supposed ter be comin’ down from t’ All ter give us an ‘and.”

“Oh bloody great! A bloke from t’ ‘All. Worris ‘e? A bloody footman or summat?”

“Nay, nay. They said as ‘ow ‘e were one o’ t’ buildin’ consultants up there an’ ‘igh in ‘Er Ladyship’s favour an’ all. Supposed ter be right ‘andy.”

“Even if ‘e is it’s still only four of us.” Thomas pointed out.

“Well it’s better than nowt. We’ll just ‘ave ter see if’n we can rustle up some extra ‘ands from somewhere.”

“We’d better or folk ‘ll be sitting on t’ cobblestones or on t’ grass come Friday.” Thomas remarked sourly.

The masses of scaffolding and planking lay like a portent of doom on the trucks. It would take most of a day just to unload them Joseph thought, let alone begin the laborious task of heaving them into position and bolting them together. It was a nightmare. Joseph’s stomach turned over every time he thought about the job. “Well we’ll just ‘ave ter get on with it.” he told them “We’ll just ‘ave ter do t’ best we can an’ ‘ope somebody comes up wi some solution fer us.”

“Right then!” Thomas stated, rolling up his sleeves, “We’d better mek a start.”

“Aye up! Are we in t’ right place ‘ere?” Joseph and his workers spun around to see Daniel and Darren walking into the yard from the street beyond.

“Excuse us gents but oo might you be?” asked Joseph.

“Sorry but they said as ‘ow this were t’ place fer these ‘ere stands wot ‘ave ter be put up.” Daniel announced. “Are you Mr Cartwright?”

“Aye that’s right.”

“Well I’m Danny Foreman an’ this is me mate Darren Morgan. Pleased ter meet yer like.” Daniel held his hand out politely.

“Er.... pleased ter meet you an’ ‘all.” Joseph told him, taking Daniel’s hand “Are you down from t’ All like?”

“Aye that’s right. Darren ‘ere’s come down to ‘elp an all. That’s if it’s all right wi you like.”

“Sure Mr Cartwright sir.” Darren smiled “Don’t know too much about this kinda thing but I’m a pair o’ willing hands should you need me sir.” Joseph took Darren’s hand liking the look of these two young men.

“Aye well. We can use all t’ ‘elp we can get an’ no mistake lads.” Joseph waved a hand in the direction of the materials loaded on the wagons. “Look at this bloody lot. We’ve got us work put out shifting all this. ‘Eaven knows ‘ow we’re goin’ ter get it sorted out in time.”

Daniel stepped forward and regarded the mass of scaffolding and accoutrements critically. “Shouldn’t be much problem Mr Cartwright. Couple o’ days an’ t’ job’s a good ‘un I’d a thought.”

“Yer blatherin’ lad! It’ll tek us best part o’ today just ter get t’ stuff off o’ t’ wagons.”

Daniel laughed and placed a hand around Mr Cartwright’s shoulder. “Nay don’t worry about it Mr Cartwright. It’ll be sorted. ‘Ang about a minute.” Daniel walked back to the yard gates and issued a piercing whistle. “Right lads! This is t’ place. Let's be ‘avin’ yer.” From the two big lorries parked outside the gates a solid looking gang of young men dressed in fatigue dungarees emerged and walked into the yard. “These lads look a bit ‘andy don’t yer think Mr Cartwright?” Daniel asked, “Soldiers like. They’re with an engineering company so they should know t’ ropes. I’ve brought fifty ov ‘em with us but if we need any more I can call up their gaffer an’ ‘e can send us as many as we need. I reckon we should be able to ‘andle owt wi this little lot.”

Mr Cartwright staggered against the tailboard of one of the trucks. “Well I’ll be buggered!”

“Right then!” said Daniel decisively “Let’s get this stuff down t’ square then. Are you t’ sergeant?” he asked one particularly authoritatively looking man.

The man snapped an immaculate salute. “Yes sir! Sergeant Oldfield.... First Battalion Amethyst Guard sir!”

“Right well. I need three drivers ter get these trucks ter t’ square and then we need ter offload. I want that fust stand up be this afternoon so let’s not ‘ang about.”

“Yes sir!” Sergeant Oldfield turned to his command and barked, “Come on then you miserable set of pansies! Shift your arses! You Thompson, Bartlett, Smith, get on those trucks. Rest o’ yer down the square now. Don’t prat me about Wilkins! Goddess ‘elp you if that stand isn’t up by teatime! Move it! Go, go, go! Let’s see some bloody movement around ‘ere!” Sergeant Oldfield’s command burst into admirable activity. Daniel turned to the shocked Joseph with a grin of satisfaction.

“Well Mr Cartwright! I think yer worries is over!.

Which was more than Jillian Peters and Margaret Wilkinson could say as they wrestled with the accommodation lists for the festival over a cup of coffee in a back room of the Mathom Arms. Mathomdale it has been noted was fairly thin in the way of a tourist infrastructure but there were some small hotels and guest houses and most of the valley’s pubs had a few rooms to let. Then there were private households with rented accommodation and a number of cottages and lodges open for letting. Jillian and Margaret needed all the space they could get because festival time was the one time of the year that the valley was inundated with visitors.

These visitors were not the usual low level of summer tourists however. They were mostly Alpha Sensual people of the Line with familial connections or bonded ties and kinship with the valley. Many were the scattered slaves of Mathomdale returning to the valley where they had served their youthful indentures and bringing their families with them. Others had been born in the valley or were close friends of the valley's high families and these could often find accommodation with the families in question but there was always a large surplus that had to be housed or boarded for the duration of the festivities. To co-ordinate this influx and prioritise the visitors according to their importance a committee was formed to act as a central agency to provide accommodation. It was an important job because these visitors were an important and integral part of the festival. In a sense it was the time of year when the sons and daughters of the valley came home and renewed their ties with their heritage. It was a gathering of the clans, a family reunion of the valley of the Goddess, and these people were very welcome indeed but finding places for them all was a nightmare.

Three large fields on the outskirts of the village had been designated as camping and caravan sites and these alone were a headache because all of them had to be provided with lavatories, water supplies and power, and somehow had to be organised into a semblance of order. Every place in the valley with a few rooms to let had to be marshalled to handle the influx, every empty cottage, disused hunting lodge or spare caravan husbanded. The hostels at Marveaux and other places were already booked solid, as was the hotel at Cropton, which, with its sixty rooms, was the only large hotel anywhere in the valley. The Mermaid's twenty odd rooms were already spoken for as were most of the other inns in the valley yet still there were requests for accommodation landing on the committee's table and places had to be found.

Margaret was deeply involved in all manner of activities to do with the summer festival but, she reflected, this was one headache she could have done without. Compounding the problem this year was the fact that accommodation up at Mathom Hall was limited in the extreme. The barracks up at the Hall were already taken up with soldiers and security problems had precluded the use of most of the Hall's other buildings for accommodation. Jillian picked up a piece of paper and sighed. "Here's another one Margaret. Just got this last night. A high born lady with three young slaves looking for a place. She'd like at least two rooms but she says they'll share if we're pinched."

"Do we have a name?"

"Yes. Collette, Eugene Collette."

Margaret's eyes snapped up from her perusal of the list of cottages in surprise. "Eugene Collette? Are you sure you got that name right Jill?"

"Definitely. I spoke to the lady myself."

"Well I'll be blowed! Eugene Collette!"

"Do you know of her then?"

"Oh yes! I know of Eugene. She's a Slave of the Amethyst Jill."

"Well why the hell is she phoning me up looking for a place then? Why isn't she staying at the Hall?"

"I don't rightly know Jill but there's a story behind that somewhere. I think she's under some sort of penance, a proscription if you like. I don't think she's allowed at the Hall."

"You mean she's out of the Lady's favour?"

"Not entirely. She wouldn't be bearing the Amethyst if that were the case. No it's more like a penal separation or something. I don't know the ins and outs of it Jill. Damn it! It must be twenty years or more since Eugene Collette so much as set foot in the valley."

"Well do we accommodate her or what?"

"Absolutely Jill. She's a VIP! Right up there on the Line. She's some sort of big-wig in the Line's intelligence agencies as far as I know."

"Could she be here because of the security issues then?"

"Possibly but it doesn't seem likely she'd be here as a private visitor and with three slaves in tow. Unless they work for her of course. Did she say how old they were?"

"She said three young girls, fourteen to sixteen."

"Well they're not intelligence operatives then. They're not even fully accredited slaves. I wonder what the hell she's doing here."

"I'm blowed if I know where I'm going to put them."

"Goddess I'm going to have to find some room for them here. We can't just be sticking Eugene Collette in any old place. She's one powerful lady Jill. I wish to hell the Lady was here. I could do with her advice on this one. Why the devil did she have to take off a week before the summer festival?"

"She's got her own worries Maggie."

"Yes I guess she does but this is a hot potato. I wonder if she knows that Madame Collette is flouncing back into the valley as bold as brass."

"Do you have room for her?"

"I've still got the honeymoon suite free and I suppose we can clear out a room for her girls. A couple of my lasses might have to double up for a few days. Shouldn't be an imposition on them. They'll probably not be sleeping in their own beds during the festival in any case. Trouble is I've got to house Jenny and her ladies in waiting during the festival as well. Trust bloody Jenny to pick half a dozen of them. We'll probably have a bunch of security goons camped out around the place as well just to make things more complicated."

The Mathom Arms was the traditional neutral residence of the festival queen and her entourage during the festival. Their costumes and assorted regalia were housed at the big pub and a whole ground floor wing was devoted as their accommodation and dressing rooms for the duration of the festivities. They would not necessarily all sleep there during the festival but the rooms had to be allocated in any case. Jennifer, in all probability, would have to remain in residence at the pub since tradition precluded her from residing at the Hall because of the exclusion of young Slaves of the Amethyst from the office of Festival Queen. It had required some finicky diplomatic juggling to maintain the pretence that Jennifer was qualified for that office whilst in residence at the Hall. It was agreed that her formal indenture would not be announced until the Grand Ball but she would have to reside away from the Hall until then to keep up the appearance that she was as yet unfettered. In the original plan, she was supposed to have maintained an official residence at the Appletons for the week up until the festival but the ongoing security alert had ruled that out. As it was there was liable to be a heavy security cordon thrown around the pub whilst she was there. It was one more problem to add to Margaret's woes. She could really have done without the illustrious presence of Eugene Collette and her retinue.

"Damn it!" Margaret remarked again. "I wish the Lady was here."

Chapter Nine

Lady Mathom was not in Mathomdale. Instead she was walking out onto the tarmac of a private airfield in the south of England at that moment. She was beautiful indeed this day, having shed the power suits she had worn, the past few days, for a much softer look in flowing lilac chiffon and wearing the diamond and amethyst jewellery of an Empress around her neck, on her ears and wrists and in the simple tiara set in her raven hair. Her ensemble was carefully chosen this day. She looked like the beautiful mother figure of her people; a gentle matriarch, soft and kind yet bearing the symbols of her power and influence, protective and reassuring, a champion of the vulnerable, a mother to the lost and frightened. There was a good reason for this appearance for, being marshalled on the airfield tarmac, was a bewildered collection of young people flown from terrible danger into heart rending alien exile.

It tore at Lady Mathom's heart to see the miserable youngsters gathered together clutching their few pathetic belongings. There was a whole library of tragedy in their stories of upheaval, the deaths of their families and the destruction of their familiar surroundings. She knew all too well the terrible feelings of a lost and lonely young person for her own youth had been scarred by such loss and, while it had been long, long ago, she could still feel the bitterness and few things could arouse her compassion more than the sight of a forlorn child. And they were children to her. Many were little boys and girls sucking their fingers and staring in hopeless confusion about them. Some were little toddlers, barely away from their mother's breasts and crying piteously. Some were in their teens, even very early twenties but they were all Her children. It was a warm day in England but many of them were shivering after the summer heat of their homeland. The aeroplane that had brought them from the tortured land of Afghanistan was idle on the apron in front of the hangars and harassed stewards and stewardesses were trying to form their precious charges into order before they mounted the buses to take them to the designated camps where they would be looked after until permanent homes could be found for them all.

Such scenarios were being played out all over the First World at the moment where the Line took in its displaced refugees and gave them sanctuary for the Line looked after its own and the sacrifice of these children's parents, giving their lives that their children could yet come to safety, would never be betrayed. The concerns of immigration officials had been blown aside. These were children of the Line. The corporations of the Purple Empire would look after them. Not one penny of state money would ever be asked to nurture them and foster accusations that these young people were parasites on the taxpayer. The Line looked after its own.

Lady Mathom had wanted, above all, to see this process with her own eyes and she had insisted that she be here today. She could not greet every young refugee that landed in desperation on the strange soil of England but it was important that at least she saw some and granted her blessing over all of them, in symbolic welcome, so that every petrified young exile would know that the legendary Lady of their peoples had cared about them and extended her formidable protection over them. Her aides were bleating about trivialities as she strode across the tarmac and her security detail was feebly protesting at her exposure but she heard them not. Her entire attention was fixed on the little wretched survivors.

She saw to the second when the objects of her interest became aware of her. The stewards and stewardesses looked up to see her approach with startled eyes and began to communicate her presence to the young people, urging the older ones at least to stand and genuflect politely to her as she approached them. A ripple of excitement ran through the youngsters like a shock wave. All of them had heard stories of the Purple Lady in their mother's arms. She was a legend to them, the Queen of their people. They had known her by distant repute all the conscious days of their lives. They had been encouraged in their darkest dreams with the tales of her magnanimity, reassured in their confusions by the stories of her wisdom and comforted in their loneliness by the legend of her unlimited love.

Most of them recognised her for there was neither house nor hovel within their villages and enclaves that did not possess at least some old faded photo or portrait of her adorning its walls even though it was only some old picture torn from the pages of a magazine. In most, that old picture was tantamount to a shrine and a candle would burn throughout the night beneath it and their mothers would have taught them to say a prayer for the Purple Lady and ask her blessing before they were tucked into their beds. Now this quasi-religious figurehead was striding into their midst in all her electrifying presence of flesh and the young people were awestruck in the moment. They were jumping to their feet, their eyes wide with wonder, and finding some clumsy parody of curtsy or bow to acknowledge their profound respect for her.

The chief stewardess rushed forward to curtsy low before her. "Serenity! This is a great honour. I thank you for gracing us all this day."

"It is my pleasure young lady. Are the kids all right?"

"Oh yes Serenity. A little confused and scared but they are all very ok Serenity."

"Thank you. Can they all speak a little Farsi?"

"Oh yes Serenity. Or Dari anyway. Some of them speak a little English too!"

"I'll try Farsi thank you. I'm a little rusty and it may not be their dialect but we'll see how we get on." Lady Mathom was gratified. It had been long since she had conversed in that tongue but she considered it to be one of the most beautiful and poetic languages on Earth.

"You wish to speak to them Serenity?" The young lady was astonished.

"But of course!" Lady Mathom walked closer to the milling young people, now ecstatically excited by her presence. They were milling forward to come closer to her but their minders were holding them back out of respect for their august visitor. One stewardess apologised breathlessly to her.

"Oh sorry Serenity! They are not knowing to be polite. They too excited to see you Serenity. Please forgive their bad manners."

Lady Mathom laughed, "Let them come! Let them all come." and then she was among them, letting them touch her, the youngest ones clinging to her skirt, the elder ones trying to kiss her hand and all of them babbling in glee. She walked into their midst glorying in their naïve wonder, stroking their heads, bending to kiss them and speaking little endearments in their own language to them. She sat on the edge of airfield trailer and sat the very youngest ones on her knee to smile at them and ruffle their hair. Many of them were dirty, travelled stained from their long voyage, and a desecration upon her fine clothes but she cared not. There was not a miserable little urchin among them for whom she had no time. There were over three hundred of them but not one would she pass without a word, a smile or a swift caress. She possessed the genius to let everyone of them feel that they were special to her this day and in years to come all of them would remember this day in tearful fondness. It meant so much to these tragic orphans of war that the Great Lady herself had come to welcome them and bless them. She kneeled down among them and let the little ones play with her jewellery. She'd hug them with soft laughter and if she could not erase the horror of the days past she was nevertheless a healing balm upon those dreadful wounds. It was a fine hour, a proud moment for the First Lady of the Line. It was the Purple Lady at her finest. In that simple outpouring of love she stated irrevocably and in the most fundamental of fashions exactly what she meant to the people of the Line. She was the Goddess in all Her mercy and unlimited love at that moment and the stewards and stewardesses watched on with eyes that shone with tears that came from breaking hearts at the joy she spread among their forlorn wards.

Jamila was hanging back in the crowd, clutching Laila's hand. Laila was biting her thumb and could not take her eyes away from the beautiful black-haired lady. "It … it is She Jamila!" she whispered in wonder. "The Great Lady!"

"Yes little princess. Didn't I promise you that we would fly to see the Great Lady? That is She! Come to greet us in person Laila. Isn't she beautiful?"

"Yes, yes Jamila. She is more beautiful than her picture we had above the fireplace." Laila clung fiercely to Jamila shyly. "See Jamila. She talks our tongue."

"Yes Laila but she is English in this life. If we must talk to her then we must speak to her in her own language out of respect. Do you remember the words that mama taught us in that language?"

"Only a little Jamila. She won't talk to us will she?" Laila buried her head in Jamila's tunic terrified at the thought.

"I don't know little one but if she does then you must remember to be very polite and to bend your knee as we used to do before her portrait every night before bed. Can you do that?"

"I… I'm frightened Jamila. What if I forget how to conduct myself as mama taught us?"

Jamila kissed her little sister "Have no fear little jewel. The Lady will forgive us. Come let's get a little closer so we can see her better." With Jamila urging Laila on the two girls weaved their way through the crowd until astonishingly they were a few feet away from Lady Mathom as she enjoyed herself among the adulation of the young refugees. Jamila's heart nearly stopped the moment that the Lady caught sight of them and smiled, beckoning them forward. Even among the litany of tragedy and heartbreak there was something about Laila's wistful vulnerability, her mix of dread and excitement and the touching protectiveness of her older sister that tugged at Lady Mathom's heartstrings. Laila was nearly holding her breath as she eased little Jamila in front of Lady Mathom, her hands in firm protection on the young girl's shoulders.

"What is your name little princess?" asked Lady Mathom in a soft purr.

"English! Tell the Lady in English!" Jamila whispered urgently in Laila's ear.

"Please Majesty I am Laila." the young girl lisped in broken English nearly fainting with fear at her boldness.

Lady Mathom laughed, touched deeply at the small girl's courage in spite of her dread. "So you speak English." she said as she reached out to caress Laila's face. "You're a little pearl indeed."

"Sorry not understand Majesty."

"Never mind Laila." Lady Mathom looked at Laila. "Is she your sister young lady?"

"Yes Serenity." Jamila bowed politely, "I am Jamila, daughter of Amin and Nura of the Hindukush, born of the Line of the Lady of the Prophet, sworn to you Serenity, Purple Lady, beloved of Allah." Jamila repeated the formal testimony taught her by her parents. She gripped Laila's shoulder. "Laila my little sister." Lady Mathom looked at her in wonderment. The children of the Goddess were always extraordinary but, even so, there were those that transcended even that level of remarkability.

"Where is the rest of your family Jamila?" Lady Mathom asked gently in English

"They are dead Serenity. They die so we can come over the mountains. The evil ones kill them. We are all that left."

"Goddess!" sighed Lady Mathom in grief. Little Laila unable to hold her silence any longer babbled a machine gun rattle of words in her own dialect. Lady Mathom didn't understand her. "What did she say Jamila?"

"Oh Serenity! Sorry. She want to know where your garden is. When we flee over the mountains I tell her we go to your garden Great Lady. She frightened. I tell her we go to the garden of the Lady so she not be frightened. It was bad time Lady. Mother and father dead so I tell her this so she not be sad. I not want to be no respect Serenity."

"You are not disrespectful Laila. I think you are a very special young lady." Lady Mathom held Laila's face in her hands and spoke to her in Farsi. "Would you like to see my garden little one?" Laila could only nod her head in dumb wonder. Lady Mathom called over an aide. The man scurried to her side. "Jonathon I want all these young people housed and fed immediately. I want all of the homeless ones to have residences found for them as soon as possible. There are enough families with space to take them all in. We've been rich and comfortable for long enough. Now it's time for us to put our ease and comfort at the disposal of our less fortunate. I want these kids to have homes within the week. Do you have a problem with that?"

"No My Lady. We'll find places for them. I guarantee it."

“Excellent! I shall set an example and start the ball rolling. Make sure that these two youngsters,” Lady Mathom indicated Laila and Jamila, “are on my transport for Mathomdale as soon as they are rested and fed. I will take personal responsibility for them. We’ll find a home for them in Mathomdale. Please be aware that they are under the full protection of the Imperial household. Do you understand?”

“Absolutely My Lady!”

Jamila was looking confused trying to understand the flurry of words. “Please Serenity what are you meaning?”

“I mean Jamila that you and your sister are going to come to my garden.”

Chapter Ten

Back in Mathomdale Julie had to get away from the house for a while. It was lunacy in the Hawthorne household at that moment as the family prepared their stands for the shop's festival display. Even Julie's slothful sisters were caught up in the excitement and displaying admirable levels of energy in making sure that the Hawthorne business would not be disgraced during the forthcoming festivities. Mr Hawthorne, with his son, was busy with his tools on the street outside the house erecting the stalls that were the Hawthorne contribution to the festival whilst Mrs Hawthorne bustled about in the kitchen surrounded by pies, tarts, preserves and other foodstuffs in the process of creation. Julie's heart wasn't in it. Astrid had brought her home the previous day as confused as ever and, despite her central appearance in the festivities as Jennifer's chief lady in waiting, she could not for the moment rustle up any enthusiasm.

She needed, most of all, some time to be by herself, to think through the extraordinary events of the past days. She had decisions to make and she was by no means sure that her decisions would, in the long event, mean anything. Her stomach turned over every time she thought about the likely conclusions of Dr Chandra's report at the end of the week. Then there were the figures from the household business. Julie had gone over them again the previous evening and the unmitigated tale of disaster they had portrayed had simply refused to ameliorate itself however rose tinted a pair of spectacles you looked at them from. It was of increasing urgency for Julie to sell herself to protect her family from impoverishment and, given the imminent likelihood of exposure of her worth, of diminishing probability of her being able to do so.

Adding to her worries was another crisis that had burst upon the Hawthorne household that very morning and it had precipitated a considerable row between Julie and her mother. The crisis had its origins in Jennifer's demeanour up at Mathom Hall the night before. Darren had joined the other young people for dinner with the startling announcement that Jennifer was feeling ill disposed, had retired early to her bed and had begged leave to be excused from joining them for dinner. It was a sensational announcement and Rebecca had had to be restrained from immediately marching along to Jennifer's rooms to demand what the devil was the matter with her fiancée. Darren had been quietly insistent that Jennifer needed some rest and recuperation although he had been unable to shed any light on the reasons for her malaise. Rebecca had reluctantly granted Jennifer the privilege of privacy but with a determination to determine what ailed her at the earliest possible opportunity. As they'd all relaxed after dinner Rebecca had discussed the matter with Abigail in private.

"I don't like it Abi." she'd stated flatly "Something's going on with Jenny and I damn well don't like it."

"Come on Becky. Relax. Maybe she's just having PMT wobblies."

"I know Jenny's periods better than she does Abi. It's not that. She's got a bloody bee in her bonnet about something."

"You worry about her too much Becky. I know you adore her. Well we all do but maybe we're too over-protective of her. She needs a bit of space like we all do. Darren says she's promised not to go off on her own any more so at least we know where she is. Ok maybe she's got a monk on about something. Big deal! We all have our moods from time to time."

"Jenny's moods tend to be spectacular Abi. We're talking one pretty intensive girl here. She isn't just sulking because somebody borrowed one of her tops the other day without asking. She's got something on her mind and you can bet your last chemise it'll be something serious."

"Ok. Let's look at it rationally then. It can't be a fall out with Darren because it seems to be hunky dory on that front. She hasn't spent the whole afternoon telling him he's a beast. Heath and Hell said they were all cuddly when they came back and Darren goes all misty eyed when he talks about her. Maybe they've had the odd bit of rough shoals but they seem to have come into calmer waters at least."

"Hmm. Maybe."

"Listen sis. I don't want to insult you or anything. You and me we've been through plenty together and you know I love you but is it possible that you're jealous of her? Are you jealous of her going off with Darren?"

"No Ab. Seriously. I like Darren and I think he's fine with Jenny. If she wants to drag him on board I've got no problems with that. Really. No there's something else."

"Julie then?"

"You could be right there sister. We still haven't figured out what to do with Julie. It's possible that Jenny's pining for Julie! In a way she's Jenny's first love and Jenny's miserable without her." Rebecca sighed, "There's something I never told you Abi. One of Jenny's reasons for becoming a slave to the Amethyst was that she would not have to be separated from Julie. It hasn't exactly worked out that way has it? Now they're more separated than ever! Because of this blasted security alert they can't even see each other. Jenny can't go down to the village and Julie for some reason won't come up here. Before Jenny came to the Hall they spent all day and every day together. Now they're hardly seeing each other at all. Julie's got some other bloody programme going on as well and Goddess knows what that is."

"Yeah you're right there Becky. I don't know what Julie's doing but she isn't telling the truth by a long margin."

"Jenny's devoted to Julie Abi. If there's something wrong there she'll be going loopy."

"And you sister?"

"Oh Goddess! I don't know Abi. It all seemed so simple at one point. I took Jenny, Julie and Robin on. We were going to forge a family. Now look at it: Robin's away; I have to go away; Julie and Jenny are falling apart and I'm damned if I know what happened to our dreams."

Abigail had taken Rebecca's hand compassionately "Becky was it really a realistic dream? I mean could Julie have really been part of that?"

"I don't know Abi." Rebecca had sounded terribly sad. "I'm not as good as you at analysing these sort of things Abi. I just fall in love and devil take the hindmost."

Abigail had taken a breath and a moment to consider. "All right then we can't do anything until we've sorted out Jenny and Julie's problems. So our first priority is to get them together."

"How for heavens' sake?"

"Easy. We'll just invite Julie up here for our dinner party in the Oriental Gardens tomorrow."

"Goddess! Do you think she'll come?"

"She won't have any option Becks. While the Lady's away I have de facto her authority as senior slave. I'll send a formal invitation to the shop requesting Miss Hawthorne's presence at the Hall tomorrow evening for formal dinner in the Oriental Gardens. I won't even address it to Julie. I'll send it to her parents. A full formal, official, type written letter on the Hall's letterhead, with my signature underneath, acting on behalf of Her Ladyship. Julie's family won't dare to refuse. Can you think of any problem that we can't sort out with the pair of them in the Oriental Gardens?"

"Goddess that's brilliant Abi!"

"Yep we'll sit the pair of them down together and give them the old third degree. We'll soon settle their hash for them."

"Are we going to sleep in the gardens? Or Whatever?"

"We'll play that one by ear. If we get to the bottom of it all I think a little bit of sisterly bonding might be on the cards. You can do an awful lot of reconciliation under the lanterns on the maple bushes."

"We might have to finesse Darren Morgan in that case. He might have ideas of his own about the programme under the bushes."

"Tell him to stand in line Becky. Jenny and Julie are your girls first. We'll find some way of deflecting him away from Jenny. If necessary we'll unleash Heath and Hell on him. Even the most noble of devotions is going to come unstuck at the prospect of fun and games with a twin sister act."

"Hey, we're under proscription to behave ourselves with Darren."

"Heath and Hell won't mind a little caning for the chance to get their claws into Darren Morgan in a good cause. They can join Jenny on punishment parade when it comes to her turn to explain her conduct in the Lady's chambers."

"Damn I never thought about that! Jenny's not exactly stuck by the letter of the law either has she? She's due for one serious arse tendering isn't she?"

"Well it'll serve her right for giving us all so much grief with her moodiness. A nice cosy session with the Lady's cane will soon sort out our little drama queen. She won't be giving us her "I want to be alone!" routine when the Lady's finished with her."

“Poor Jenny!” Rebecca had laughed, “She’s the sweetest and best behaved of all of us generally and it doesn’t do her a bit of good by way of keeping her out of trouble.”

“Do we tell Jenny that we’re inviting Julie?”

“Let’s wait and see how she is in the morning. If she’s gung-ho on this dinner party we’ll keep it a secret and drop it on her as a surprise. If she kicks we’ll just have to dangle Julie as a carrot in front of her.”

“Ok then let’s grab a terminal somewhere and draft out this invitation. We’ll send it around to be hand delivered by a courier in the morning.”

Abigail’s formal bombshell had landed on the Hawthorne breakfast table like a napalm strike that morning. Her mother had sat her down alone to batter the matter out. At first Julie had adamantly refused to have anything to do with the invitation. “I’m not going!” she’d insisted.

“Now don’t be daft Julie!” Mrs Hawthorne had told her crossly “You ‘ave to! That’s an official summons. That’s tantamount to an order.”

“They can’t order me about like that. I’m bloody well not goin’!”

“Listen Julie ‘Awthorne! You know as well as I do that if the ‘All whistles round ‘ere we all go runnin’. If the ‘All tells yer it requires yer presence fer a party up there then inter yer party frock yer climb and yer get yer backside up there sharpish. No ifs, buts or maybes about it!”

“It’s not Lady Mathom wot’s sent this invitation. Just one ov ‘Er lasses.”

“Oo makes it plain that she ‘as full authority in ‘Er Ladyship’s absence Julie. It’s no good wailin’ and tearin’ yer ‘air out Julie. Yer’ll do as yer told. At ‘alf past six this evenin’ yer’ll show yer face up there, all spruced up an’ on yer best be’aviour or woe betide you young lady.”

“I can’t do it mam. Don’t ask me to.”

“It’s not me wot’s doin’ t’ askin’ Julie. It’s t’ ‘All wot’s orderin’ yer to.” Mrs Hawthorne had sighed, “Come on Julie love. I can’t understand wot’s t’ matter with yer. I’d ‘ave thought yer’d be all too willin’ ter get ter see your Jenny. You ‘aven’t seen a lot ov ‘er since she’s been up at t’ All. I’d ‘ave thought you was missin’ ‘er.”

“It’s not Jenny wot’s invited me.” Julie had been close to tears.

“Well that’s cos it’s all done official like and ‘as ter go through ‘Er Ladyship’s senior young lady Julie. But Jenny ‘ll be there. Letter meks it plain that yer ter dine wi ‘Er Ladyship’s personal maids. That means Jenny an’ all. That means that Rebecca Walpole ‘ll be there too. I thought you liked ‘er.”

“I do mam. I just can’t go up ter t’ flippin’ ‘All. I don’t like it mam. It scares me. Wot’s likes o’ me wantin’ ter be doin’ there? I can’t just walk up ter Mathom ‘All and walk in there. I just can’t.”

“Now don’t be daft an’ don’t be givin’ me any guff about not bein’ good enough ter walk inter Mathom ‘All. Yer good enough for Mrs Waterstone’s establishment, yer good enough fer Mrs’ Ramone’s and this ‘ere letter says yer good enough fer Mathom ‘All. So yer can walk in there wi yer ‘ead ‘eld ‘igh an’ I’ll not ‘ear any more of yer nonsense about it bein’ too grand for yer.”

“Mam it frightens me.”

“Fer ‘eavens sake Julie. It’s only an ‘ouse. Grand as it is, it’s only an ‘ouse when all’s said and done. Anyway, if yer that worried about it, yer don’t ‘ave ter go into t’ ‘All.”

“Eh?”

“T’ letter says this party’s in the Oriental Gardens. They’re right out in t’ grounds. Miles away from t’ ‘All.”

“I’d still ‘ave ter go through t’ ‘All ter get ter them.”

"Not at all. If yer like I'll drive yer round ovver t' fell an' drop you off at the top gate an' you can walk down from there. Yer wouldn't ave ter go anywhere near t' 'All."

"What top gate?"

"Why there's a little secret gate that lets down into the Oriental Gardens right up the fell side. Yer go through and pass through a little gorge and it opens out inter t' gardens. It's a bit of a walk mind cos them gardens is huge but yer won't 'ave ter go through the main gates and up through the parklands."

"Ow do yer know this?"

Mrs Hawthorne's face had grown soft. "Oh I often used ter sneak inter t' Oriental Gardens when I was younger Julie. It were me favourite place. I used ter take a pack up an' have meself a little picnic there. Yer've never seen them gardens 'ave yer love? Well yer've never seen owt so bonny in yer life love. They're a little bit o' paradise is them gardens."

"Didn't you ever get caught?"

Mrs Hawthorne had chuckled "Nay Julie lass. T' lady wot runs them gardens allus knew when I were sneaking in. She didn't mind. I met 'er a couple o' times. She's Japanese and right nice. I got ter know one or two ov er lasses an' all." Mrs Hawthorne had paused and Julie had been shocked to see her mother blush. "I got right fond of one o' them. She were called Delilah and I used ter 'ave picnics with 'er. She left a couple o' years later an' I never found out wot became ov 'er."

"Yer've never told me any o' this mam."

"Aye well it were long before you was born. Before I married yer dad even. You know I once thought o' goin' ter live and work in them gardens Julie. I used ter 'elp out in there at times. I've allus loved gardens. There's a little rock garden by one o' t' streams what I made all on me own an' it's got me name attached to it. I used ter dream o' bein' one o' the gardeners in t'

Oriental Gardens Julie. That isn't just bein' any old gardener either let me tell yer. Yer 'ave ter be the best ter be allowed to turn yer 'and to them gardens. It were one o' t' proudest moments in me life when I was permitted ter mek that little rock garden."

"Bloody 'ell mam! I never knew all this."

"Well don't think yer t' only one wot's 'ad 'er dreams an' got up ter some adventures in this 'ouse Julie."

"Wot 'appened mam?"

Mrs Hawthorne had looked wistful "Well Delilah left an' then I met yer dad an' nowt came of it in t' end. Still I wonder sometimes 'ow it would 'ave turned out otherwise. I often think o' them gardens Julie. It's bin many a long year now since I saw them last. I'd love ter know if me little rock garden's still there."

"Oh mam!"

"Aye well that's as never mind Julie. You can see 'em yersen this evening. Yer'll love 'em Julie. There's nowhere else as bonny as them gardens. I right envy yer."

"I'll do it then mam. Just fer you. I'll see if I can find yer little garden an' I'll tell yer all about it."

"Yer a good lass Julie. I lost me gardens Julie but I grew me a lovely daughter ter be proud of in their place."

"Oh Mam." Julie had hugged her mother overcome with love for the gentle woman that had borne her.

"Come on now love. Let's not get soft. I've plenty on today an' later we'll 'ave a look an' see if yer've got a nice frock ter wear for yer party tonight." Peace had reigned once more in the Hawthorne household.

Chapter Eleven

In spite of her promise to her mother Julie's resolution was still wavering as she stepped out into the square shortly after lunch. The square was a bustle of activity as all the businesses and private households around it worked on their decorations or the erection of their displays but the most fevered centre of activity was on the far side where a brisk looking gang of men were throwing up a grandstand with remarkable alacrity. Julie walked past the men and her humour was restored to receive a chorus of appreciative wolf whistles. Then however a voice hailed her.

"Aye up Julie!" Julie turned to see Daniel scrambling down from the partially built construction. Julie had only met Daniel the once but she liked him and she liked Alice as well. Although they were apparently now high members of the Mathom Hall household they seemed much closer to Julie in station somehow. Certainly there were no airs and graces about them. They just seemed solid down to earth people. Julie curtsied politely to Daniel.

"Good afternoon sir."

"Bloody 'ell Julie! Don't be callin' us sir. I get enough o' that from all t' bloody servants up at t' 'All. Ow are yer anyway?"

"All right ta."

"'Ere you 'aven't met Darren yet 'ave yer?" Daniel beckoned over the attractive young American. "'Ere Darren this is Julie. One o' Jenny's best mates."

Darren removed his baseball cap liking the look of this girl immediately, "Very pleased to meet you ma-am. Miss Jennifer has mentioned you to me."

"Oh 'as she? Well send 'er my love won't yer sir."

"Indeed I will ma-am."

"Darren's coming up to stay at the 'All Julie. 'Ere are yer comin' up to this shindig in t' gardens this evenin'?"

"'Er I got t' invitation like." Julie stated non-committally.

"Well I 'ope yer can make it Julie. Our Jenny's bin missin' yer something rotten." Julie's heart skipped a beat. "So's Becky." Daniel continued, "In fact we're all lookin' forward ter yer company this evenin'. T' girls are right excited about it." Daniel had been carefully primed by Rebecca as to his approach on the likelihood of bumping into Julie whilst working on the square.

"I…. I don't know sir. I've never bin to a formal do up at t' 'All."

"Well that makes two of us Miss." Darren interjected "Thank the Lord I won't be the only rookie at this affair. I ain't much of a guy for these formal English garden parties. I'd kindly appreciate your moral support Miss."

Julie laughed, liking the charming young American. "Aye well I'll probably be there sir. I'm not comin' be way o' t' 'All though. I'll be coming straight to these gardens wherever they are. Will that be all right Danny?"

Daniel scratched his head "Don't see why not. Can yer find 'em on yer own though?"

"Oh aye. Me mam knows 'ow ter get to 'em."

"Well I'll tell t' lasses then. Anyway Darren we'd better get back ter work an' be showin' t' lads a good example."

"You aven't 'alf got this lot up fast." Julie commented.

"Oh aye. These lads are brilliant. Work like bloody donkeys. I 'ave ter beg 'em ter slow down."

Julie laughed "Well don't work too 'ard. I'll see yer tonight then." Julie took her leave of the two men feeling far more reassured about the evening to come by the presence of Daniel and his charmingly ingenuous American friend.

In a feat of engineering that Joseph Cartwright would have regarded as nearly impossible the big stand was to all intents and purposes fully erect by four o'clock. Joseph took Daniel to one side. "'Ere Danny I don't know 'ow ter thank yer. I'd a never 'ave got that bloody thing up without you an' your lads' 'elp."

"Well we've come on right well. I think we'll be able ter get t' other stands up on t' sport field tomorrow and then a bit o' tidyin' up an' wot 'ave yer an' t' jobs done."

"D' yer reckon we should call it a day for today then?"

"Oh aye. No point knocking our sens out. I could do with a pint anyway."

"Aye me an' all. Right then we'll knock off fer today. We'll go down t' Lady Anne. They've got t' festival ale on already. Worrabout your lads though?"

"Well I think they've earned them sens a pint an' all. They've worked like bloody Trojans today."

"Ee Danny I'd be all too willin' ter get t' beer in but I don't think me budget 'll stretch ter fifty odd pints o' draught."

"Hey, don't worry about that Joe. I've got a Mathom 'All credit line. We'll just charge it up to t' 'All."

"Bloody 'ell! Power's a wonderful thing."

Daniel laughed then emitted a shrill whistle. "Right lads tidy everything up an' get t' tools away an' we'll knock off fer today. We're off down t' pub. Beers are on us." A roar of approval greeted this last and within minutes the site was tidy and surrounded by fences bearing ominous warnings that everybody knew were going to be of no use whatsoever in deterring the village youngsters from climbing all over the newly erected construction. A short while after, leaving the troop of soldiers on the benches in front of the pub, Daniel, Darren, Joseph and his two co-workers marched into the quiet interior of the Lady Anne. It was a beautiful old pub on the main street leading up to the square but it was by no means as busy an establishment as the Mathom Arms on the square. In fact the pub's interior was currently occupied by about half a dozen locals and two bored looking barmaids. The locals weren't involved much in conversation either. There seemed a cathedral like silence within the dim interior that Daniel was at a loss to understand. The locals seemed put out by this sudden disturbance of their reverent meditation. Joseph strode up to the bar determined to extract the full amount of pleasure from what promised to be a shining moment.

"Now then gentlemen." the barmaid greeted them "What can I get yer?"

Joseph swelled up his chest. This was his big moment. "Fifty five pints o' best bitter if yer please love."

"Eh What!"

"I said fifty five pints o' yer best bitter. T' festival beer if yer please. In fact mek it an' 'undred and ten. Yer might as well be pullin' t' second round whilst t' lads are suppin' their first ones."

"Oo's payin' fer all these?"

Daniel intervened "Mathom 'All love. Just stick 'em down on t' 'All's account."

"An oo might you be?"

"Daniel Foreman-Mathom pet. Personal assistant an' buildin' engineer to 'Er Ladyship."

"Oh bloody 'ell!" The flustered girl dropped a quick curtsy. "Sorry sir! Didn't mean ter be disrespectful or owt."

"No problem love but I'd get pullin' them pints if I were you. It's warm out an' our lads is thirsty!" The two bar girls were galvanised into action and for the next few minutes there was a flurry of activity as a shuttle of foaming pints of ale were transported out on trays to the thirsty soldiers without. The five men retired to a corner table, delighted with the effect they'd just made in the pub.

"Bloody 'ell Joe!" said Thomas laughingly "I thought that lass were gonna wet 'ersen when you ordered a 'undred an' ten pints."

"Aye it were a grand moment. I'll carry that look on 'er face in me memory till me dyin' day."

Daniel laughed "Right then. 'Ere's to us. Cheers lads!" Daniel picked up his pint tankard but as he did he became aware of an expectant silence in the pub. Joseph and his two workers were looking at him keenly and so were the local inhabitants. Puzzled, Daniel took a draught of his beer. He was thirsty enough to have quaffed half the contents of his pint in a single swallow but after a mere mouthful he lowered his glass and stared at it in growing wonder. The looks among the locals and Joseph's contingency had developed into knowing looks of deep satisfaction and smug self-congratulation. Simply put, the beer that Daniel had just sampled was, beyond all measure of doubt or question of argument, by far and away, the best pint of beer that he had ever tasted in his life. It was smooth to the palate, yet rich in its earthiness. Not too bitter with its hoppy flavour but just right in its tang and creamy with its malty after-taste. There were hints of honey and the suggestion of glowing summer sunlight on fields of growing barley. It was golden in the mouth, a nectar that left a warming pleasure on the tongue and an impossible to describe filling, satisfaction to a man's thirst. It was very nearly perfection. It was the pint of beer that you had spent a lifetime looking for.

Daniel considered himself a connoisseur of fine ale. He was a devoted follower of some of the best small breweries in Northern England but, in a moment of revelation, he realised that he had just been taken to see the elephant. Everything else that he had considered to be beer was mere folly and vanity compared with this ethereal brew. Had Daniel been an eloquent man he would have waxed long and feelingly about its nutty texture, its richly gratifying rustic aroma and its hints of sharp bitterness sneaking out from its warming malty fullness. As it was he just gasped and said "Bloody 'ell! This is t' best pint o' beer I've ever 'ad."

"Aye!" said Joseph, deeply satisfied, "Yer'll go along way ter find owt wot 'll match t' local festival beer Danny." The locals chuckled in contentment. Daniel realised now the meaning of the reverent silence within the pub. This wasn't a pub at all. It was a shrine. The locals here were in fact worshippers before the holy grail of the brewer's art. Conversation and like-wise triviality was but earthly distraction in the presence of such a divine combination of fermented grains.

Joseph leant across the table and whispered as if divulging some deep and inner mystery. "T' Mathomdale brewery brews this ale specially for t' festival Danny. T' recipe's a closely 'idden secret. Supposed to 'ave bin in t' family fer 'undreds o' years. We call it t' festival beer but it's sometimes known as t' Lady's Milk. Yer'll not find a finer brew anywhere ter my way o' thinkin'."

"Yer not far wrong Joe. By 'ell if'n CAMRA knew about this stuff there'd be coach loads o' bearded fellahs in anoraks and corduroys parked half way out ter Cropton an' back. I thought t' beer were good in Mathomdale already but this teks the biscuit."

"Aye well t' brewery 'as a few specials wot they bring out for various events on t' calendar. T' Christmas ale's right good but most folks reckon t' festival beer's t' best o' t' lot. It's allus a day ter look forward ter in t' year when t' first barrels appear in t' pubs."

"What do you think of it Darren?" asked Daniel.

“It’s good Danny. Kinda rich for me though. I usually drink Bud.”

“Bloody Americans! ‘Eathens the lot o’ yer!”

The men drank their beer in profound contentment until the pint pots were sadly empty vessels with the foamy remnants of the head clinging to the sides. “Same again lads?” asked Joe unnecessarily.

“I won’t say no Joe.” said Daniel “We can’t be stoppin’ too long though. T’ lasses are throwin’ a garden party this evenin’ an’ if we’re late fer that our lives won’t be worth livin’.”

“What sort o’ party Danny?” asked Thomas eagerly fishing for details. The rumours of the sort of parties the young ladies of Mathom Hall were apt to throw enjoyed a certain notoriety locally.

“Oh just a formal do in t’ Oriental Gardens wi t’ chief gardener so I’m told.”

“Oh!” Thomas sounded disappointed “Bit borin’ then?”

“Give ovver Tom!” chuckled Richard “Them lasses could start an orgy at a Sunday School picnic be all accounts. In ’t that right Darren?”

“’Ey steady on Dick.” warned Joseph in the midst of the laughter “Bit o’ respect like.”

Darren grinned, “I’m only recently acquainted with the ladies in question Dick but I’d guess your comment is a fair one.”

“That’ll do now lads.” Joseph pontificated “Don’t forget that Danny ‘ere’s married to one o’ them.”

“Aye well.” remarked Daniel ruefully “She’s not much better than t’ rest ov ‘em truth be told.” The men roared with laughter.

“By ‘ell! I’d give me ‘ind leg ter get an invitation ter that party.” observed Richard.

“I’m getting t’ beers in before this gets out ov ‘and.” said Joseph firmly.

"I'll help you carry them Joe." Said Darren standing up. "I need to use the bathroom anyway."

"Why do Americans call it a bathroom when there's no bath in it?" Tom wanted to know.

"Why do you guys call it a lavatory when you're not going to wash in it? And as for calling it a water closet….."

At the bar Darren noticed a framed oil painting on the wall.

"Hey Joe, is that a picture of Lady Mathom?"

"Er…. er no Darren. Well not the current Lady Mathom at any rate. Not our Lady Jennifer. That's supposed to be the Lady Anne what t' pubs named after. One ov 'Er Ladyship's ancestors."

"You're kidding!" Darren stepped forward to examine the portrait closely. "Jesus she's the goddamned double of Lady Jennifer."

"Er aye! Aye there is supposed ter be a great familial resemblance." Joseph shuffled uncomfortably not at all certain of this young man's status yet. There were deep secrets in Mathomdale that it didn't do to talk about in public. Darren stood hypnotised in front of the picture of the black-haired lady with the startling purple eyes in a flowing 16th century gown, suddenly sure that Joseph was lying to him.

Chapter Twelve

At the Hall, Lady Jennifer's younger namesake was wincing in pain as Mrs Yakamura wrestled her into her kimono. Jennifer had been mildly excited by the prospects of a garden party in the Oriental Gardens when it had been announced that morning and the idea had gone a long way to restoring her morale after the events of yesterday. She had been even more thrilled when she'd been told that Julie was invited to the party as well. With the Oriental Gardens weaving their magic she felt sure of addressing the growing separation between them. Of course she'd detected Rebecca's manipulations behind the invitation and had sighed. There was unfinished business between Rebecca and herself now too. Life was complicated all of a sudden but surely it would simplify in the glades of the Oriental Gardens.

She would have been less enthusiastic about the whole business had she had any inclination of just how complicated and time consuming the preparations for the party would be. The last time she had worn Japanese dress she had simply worn an informal yukata. The kimono she was being bullied into now was quite a different matter. It was a formal homongi or visiting kimono with enormously deep sleeves and a full pattern in rich shades of greens and golds. It was an awesome sheath of heavy silk, hand woven, sewn and dyed, richly patterned and ridiculously valuable. It had come folded in its own special case and Jennifer had gasped when Mrs Yakamura had presented it to her. It was worth several thousand pounds. Jennifer would have been horrified to discover that her entire ensemble that evening would have left little change out of ten thousand pounds.

Before she could even get near to putting the kimono on however there had been elaborate preparations to be made. Her hair had been tugged, wrenched, waxed and beaten into a highly formalised Japanese style bunched up on her head and decorated with kanzashi hair ornaments. The make-up hadn't quite been the white porcelain doll like look of a geisha but it had been far more elaborate than Jennifer's usual cosmetic appliance. Then there'd been all the undergarments! There'd been the hadajuban like an under vest and a slip called a susoyoke that you wore next to your skin. Then on top of those there was an under kimono that Jennifer had learned was called a nagajuban and the funny socks with divided toes called tabi. Only when she was dressed in these garments, could the full kimono be placed upon her.

In her ignorance Jennifer had assumed that a kimono, like a dress, came according to the size of the wearer. She was astonished therefore to discover that kimonos came in a single standard size; T-shaped great bolts of silk, that had to be folded, tucked and arranged according to the body shape of the wearer. The whole affair was then bolted into place by the huge wide obi that was wrapped around you from the hips to the breasts and tucked and tied into place as firmly as a corset. It had taken the combined efforts of Mrs Yakamura and her two assistants to muscle the garment into place, squeezing the breath out of Jennifer as they did so. To top off the whole outfit was a haori that was a sort of formal kimono coat worn over the kimono. Once into this and perched on the wooden geta sandals, Jennifer began to understand the delicate little careful movements that Japanese women displayed when dressed in their finery. It was nearly impossible to move any other way. These were not costumes for dashing about flamboyantly in. Just trying to kneel down, as they would have to at a formal Japanese dinner, was a taxing activity. Even walking. You had to sort of tip toe along with little tiny steps with the trail of your kimono waggling behind looking almost silly.

Thank the Goddess she wasn't a slave of some high Japanese family thought Jennifer. She could never have gone through all this rigmarole every day. It had taken Mrs Yakamura the better part of the afternoon dressing the girls up. She'd dashed from one of their rooms to another with her assistants because none of the girls had wanted the others to see them until they were fully attired in their finery. Jennifer wondered if the other girls were as thoroughly fed up with the whole business as she was.

At last Mrs Yakamura seemed satisfied. She stood back to admire her handiwork critically and clapped her hands. "Ah very pretty lady. You perfect little Japanese girl now."

"I feel like a blooming stuffed doll." grumbled Jennifer ill humouredly.

Mrs Yakamura laughed. "Ah no lady. You just perfect."

"I can't believe that Japanese ladies have to go to all this fuss just to get dressed up for a dinner party. I can hardly breathe."

"Ah lady what's a little pain? We want to look beautiful so we endure our pain. Pain is price we pay for being women. Come please. Look in mirror." Mrs Yakamura had not allowed Jennifer to look at herself in the mirror until she was satisfied with her dress. Now she led Jennifer to the big floor length mirror in Jennifer's chambers and let her drink in the extraordinary vision. Jennifer stared at herself in astonishment. Her familiar reflection had disappeared to be replaced by the exotic looking lady in the glass. She seemed to glow in the greens and golds of the elaborate kimono, the golden obi, matching haori and the kanzashi in flashes of colour in her hair. She looked like a precious doll, an Emperor's concubine from some bygone age; fragile and beautiful.

"My goodness!" she breathed. "It's.... it's amazing!"

Mrs Yakamura chuckled in delight. "You very pretty lady. Your sisters too. Come now they all waiting for you."

The other girls greeted Jennifer with a resounding cheer as she shimmied carefully into the common room. They were an amazing sight. Abigail's kimono was an incredible affair in blues and silver whilst the twins had opted for fantastically patterned kimonos with floral designs in a bewildering combination of colours. Alice was looking comically self-conscious in a stunning creation of warm pinks and white. Rebecca looked like an oriental sorceress in flaming scarlet and black designs. "Wow Jenny!" Helen expostulated "You look fantastic!"

"You too. You all do." Jennifer replied.

"I should bloody well hope so." Heather muttered "The effort it took to get me into this thing. There were times I could slapped Becky for her daft idea of us all getting dressed up in Japanese formal clothes."

"You look great sis." Rebecca told her.

"What are we wearin' on us feet lasses?" Alice asked. "We can't be goin' out in t' gardens in us socks."

"Our geta are at the slave's entrance Alice." Abigail told her. "Japanese ladies don't wear shoes in the house. Anyway there's a pair of Japanese slippers for you by the hearth. If you need to go to the loo there's another pair outside the door of the common bathroom."

"Eh? What the 'ell for?"

"Oh Alice. In Japan you never wear the same slippers in the bathroom as you do in the rest of the house. You have to change them at the door before you enter and back again when you come out."

"Bloody hell! Don't even mention going to the loo." groaned Heather. "The thought of hitching this little lot up just to sit on the thunder-jug doesn't bear thinking about."

"The Japanese manage it Heath." grinned Abigail. "Come on we've plenty of time girls. Let's have a drink to set the proceedings in motion. I've got some saké warming in the kitchen. We might as well do the job properly." Abigail waddled tentatively in the direction of the kitchen.

"Your kimono train looks like a duck's arse waggling behind you." Helen told her.

"Stop it Hell! Don't make me laugh for pity's sake. I swear everything will come adrift if I do."

"Mine bloody well won't." Heather commented, "I think Mrs Yakamura used a tyre iron to get mine on. It feels like it's set in concrete."

The saké was hot and aromatic and the six girls became more animated as they admired each other's costumes. "Damn it! Have we got a camera?" asked Rebecca.

"I've got mine tucked inside my obi somewhere if I can ever find it again." Abigail told her. "I thought we could take some pics when we get in the Gardens."

"Brill! We've just got to have some photos of us all dressed up like this."

"I was going to bring mine as well." said Helen, "but I didn't know how to carry it. Are we allowed handbags?"

"Sure." said Rebecca, "There should be matching little bags with your parasols ladies. You can stuff a lot of things down your obi but even Japanese ladies need something to carry all their bits and bats in."

"Well let's get some photos before we set off anyway." Helen decided, "While our costumes are still in one piece."

"Are we supposed to 'ave t' collars on us under kimonos showin'?" asked Alice.

“Oh yes Alice.” Said Abigail. “You’re supposed to show about an inch of the collar on your hadajuban. It’s called the haneri actually. Also you’re supposed to expose part of your neck, which is considered to be the most erotic zone. That’s why Mrs Yakamura painted our necks with those white V shapes. It’s supposed to be alluring.”

“Sod me! Must be complicated bein’ a Japanese lass.”

“Japanese women only go to these lengths on formal occasions Alice. Most of the time they just wear western dress now.”

“That’s not necessarily true Abi.” Rebecca noted. “In many Japanese Alpha Sensual households the slaves are required to wear traditional dress at all times when on duty. I met some Japanese girls off the Line at uni and they were telling me about it. They had to get up two hours before the rest of the household just to get dressed because they were obliged to wait upon their masters and mistresses in full kimono. It’s supposed to instil self-discipline, self-awareness and respect for tradition.”

“Goddess!” breathed Abigail “And we think we’ve got it rough sometimes. I think I’d lose the will to live if I had to hitch my kimono up for the cane every time my okumi wasn’t laid just right or something.”

Rebecca laughed. “They didn’t seem to mind. They seemed quite proud of their ability to wear kimono. They were sure as hell a lot better at it than we are. I mean it’s an acquired skill isn’t it?”

“That’s true enough.” Abigail agreed. “It must take shed loads of practise to look elegant in these costumes. Don’t geishas have to go through years of intensive training to get it right?”

“Well for the love of the Goddess don’t mention it to the Lady.” quipped Heather. “I’d hate her to get it into her head that we’d all benefit from a regime of geisha training.”

“What are we doing about the boys?” Jennifer asked.

“They’re joining us a bit later Jenny.” Abigail responded. “Danny and Darren have to get back from their work in the village so we’re going on to the Gardens ahead of them. Mrs Yakamura will be intercepting them when they get back so they’ve no hope of getting out of proper formal wear.”

“That’s a point.” said Helen “It’s getting on. We’d better be shifting. I don’t know about you ladies but it’ll take me flipping ages to walk over to the Oriental Gardens in this gear. It’s bloody miles and I’m worried enough just about getting downstairs. This kind of kit isn’t exactly designed for athletic enterprise. If they ever had a fire at a formal Japanese banquet there’d be bloody carnage.”

“Never fear sister.” Abigail reassured her smugly “Transport is arranged. I sorted it all out at lunch time.”

“What sort of transport?” asked Heather suspiciously.

“Never you mind. Something special. It’s a surprise.”

At that moment the telephone rang in the common room. Abigail stood closest to it picked it up casually. “Hello?” As the others watched her face turned pale with shock. “Yes! Yes of course. Thank you.” she put the phone down and leaned heavily against the wall. “Oh shit!”

“What’s the matter Abi?” asked Rebecca in alarm.

“That was downstairs. The Lady just breezed in about ten minutes ago.”

“You’re pulling our legs Abi.” Helen protested, “She’s not due back till Thursday at the earliest!”

“I wish I was Hell. She’s just flown in from the south by helicopter. She wants to see us all in her chambers in twenty minutes flat.”

“Wot dressed like this?” cried Alice “We can’t.”

"We don't have any bloody option Alice. There's no way we can do a turnaround in twenty minutes."

Panic and consternation overtook the slave's wing. Rebecca held up her hands. "Ok ladies we're just going to have to talk our way out of it. We'll just have to explain that we're invited to dinner in the Gardens and we've dressed up like this out of respect for Shiro-san. With a bit of luck she'll be too tired from her journey to thrash us all on the spot."

"Oh Goddess! I hope not." said Helen. "I'd hate to have to wait until she's fully recovered from her travels and able to do the job properly."

"Let's not panic ladies." Abigail told them "If she's in a good humour we might just worm our way out of this one. We'll all go down, give her a pretty Japanese bow and explain the circumstances."

"What about our inviting Julie?" squeaked Jennifer in concern.

"Oh hell yes! I'd forgotten about that." said Abigail.

"Wait a sec." Alice interjected "Danny phoned us up from t' village. 'E met Julie on t' square. She said she's not comin' ter t' Gardens be way o' t' 'All but goin' straight there or summat. Is that possible like?"

"Well yes if she knows the way in by the top gate from the fell." Rebecca commented.

"Then she wouldn't come near the Hall." Abigail said.

"Won't it be guarded?" asked Alice.

"I don't think it is Alice." Rebecca told her. "Not many people know that gate. I'm surprised Julie does."

"Julie knows every nook and cranny of this valley Becky." Jennifer piped in. "If there's a secret way anywhere she's likely to have found it."

"Well ok then." Abigail decided, "If the Lady lets us get away with it we'll diplomatically omit to mention Julie's presence. If she puts the mockers on it we'll just have to call Julie on her mobile and warn her off."

“She’s bound to find out sooner or later.” Helen pointed out.

“We’ll cross that bridge when we come to it. Come on girls we’d better go down and face the music.”

Chapter Thirteen

If the girls at the Hall were facing the immediate future with some trepidation then the same could not be said of Mrs Hawthorne. In fact, thought Julie, she had never seen her mother so excited as she drove Julie over the high road to the back entrance to the Oriental Gardens. She seemed to have shed years from her age in her almost girlish like anticipation. She was like a young woman again, bubbling with chatter and her eyes shining with beautiful memories. For the last hour or so, as they'd picked out a dress for Julie and dressed her up for her dinner date, Mrs Hawthorne had chattered on endlessly about the Gardens, describing them in detail and telling Julie anecdotes about them. Ostensibly she had been trying to give Julie directions to get from the upper end of the gardens down to their heartland but her own directions seemed to get lost in a labyrinth of memories and she turned aside from the trail often to lead Julie into little favourite corners where the past held some glowing jewel in the recollections of her life.

Julie was delighted with this facet of her mother that she had never seen before. Julie's mother had years of hard toil behind her, raising four children and struggling with the family business that her husband had so often led into stormy waters. She had worked hard and unselfishly at her task and it grieved Julie that her sisters and brother so took her devotion for granted. None of them appreciated the work and sacrifices she had made on their behalf except Julie. There'd been little time for herself in Mrs Hawthorne's long struggle. Only in her little garden at the back of the shop had there been some small place of tranquillity and peace. Julie now realised that that little garden was all that was left of her mother's dreams and she had tended it with the loving care for a last trace of her youthful aspirations like a drawer full of old fading photographs of past happiness.

They'd even called it "mam's garden" and they'd never realised, when they played in it as children, that it was the place where their mother had kept her dreams.

It was strange thought Julie how you could live with a person all your life and still not know them and her mother's reviving excitement showed her just how little she really knew about the woman whose body had given her life. She'd fussed over Julie like a broody hen as she'd dressed as if she were sending her favourite daughter home to the place where she lived in her dreams. In an insight Julie realised that the events of the past week were terribly important for her mother. It was as if through Julie that Mrs Hawthorne could realise her own lost dreams, that Julie could aspire to the heights that had eluded her in her own youth, close the circle and heal a quarter of a century of bitter regrets. Julie understood now the deep pride her mother had kept barely concealed when Mrs Waterstone, Astrid and Rosalyn had vied for her daughter's position. There was another dream then that Julie could ruin and in some ways the most terrible of all. She could yet shatter the last hope of her mother's life. It would be nearly a fatal blow. Julie could see some dreadful time when the little garden lay neglected, perhaps turned into some utilitarian back yard, with the final denouement of her mother's dreams.

"Nearly there love." Mrs Hawthorne told her as she steered the little car over the moor tops.

"Wot? 'Ere?"

"Aye that's right love. Just over that next rise."

"Blimey mam! We're miles away from t' All."

"Well I told yer these gardens was big Julie. That's why I were keen on getting' you 'ere early. It's a fair old walk down into 'em love. 'An' they're like a maze an' all. Yer might get lost."

"Mam! I never get lost. Yer know that." Julie was mildly proud of her unerring navigational facilities.

“I know love. Anywhere else and I’ve ‘ad no fears on that score but, no matter ‘ow clever you are at findin’ yer way yer can still get lost in them Gardens.” Julie’s mother shook her head in reminiscence, “Everybody gets lost in there Julie. That’s what they’re made for.” Julie looked at her, bemused by the strange comment so apparently untypical of her mother. “’Ere we are then.” Mrs Hawthorne pulled the car over to the side of the road. “Just down this trail ‘ere.” She pointed to the little rough track leading away over the rise.

“Blimey mam! That track’s a bit rocky. I could ‘ave done to put some other shoes on. ‘Ow am I supposed ter walk down that in these ‘eels?” Julie’s mother had insisted upon Julie wearing an elegant pair of high-heeled shoes with the lovely pink party dress that Eleanor had bought for her in Brawton.

“Well tek ‘em off love an’ carry ‘em. We don’t want yer ruinin’ yer best shoes on t’ stones.”

“Me feet ‘ll get mucky.”

“Yer can allus wash ‘em in t’ beck love. T’ paths are a bit smoother once yer get down into t’ Gardens.”

“Oh ‘ell!”

“Tell yer what love I’ll come part way with yer. Just ter t’ top meadow past t’ gorge ter see yer on yer way an mek sure yer don’t go wrong.” It was a transparent excuse. Mrs Hawthorne just wanted to see her beloved gardens once again.

“Come on then mam.” said Julie grinning, “Let’s go in tergether.” They were almost like a pair of schoolgirls on an adventure as they set off up the track with Julie stepping gingerly over the stones with her shoes in her hands and Mrs Hawthorne’s face flushed with excitement. At length they came to the gate where the track passed into the Gardens. Mrs Hawthorne struck the gong three times.

“Mek a wish Julie. You allus ‘ave ter mek a wish at t’ gate.”

“Go on then.” Julie closed her eyes and made the most fervent wish she had ever made. “Your turn then mam.”

Mrs Hawthorne put her arm around Julie “’Ee love mine’s already come true.” and, with that, she led the pair of them down to the gorge where the two great sphinxes, carved in the cliff face stood sentinel over the entrance to the gorge. Julie was staggered by the enormous figures. She had never even heard of the two guardians of the gardens before. There were few places in the valley that Julie had not explored on her adventures but the realm of Mathom Hall and its great parklands was an enclosed mystery to her. She had lived within walking distance of the boundaries of the grounds of the Great Hall all the days of her life, heard fantastic tales about them but had never once set foot inside them. The vast swathe of that enormous sprawling territory was terra incognito to her, a blank space on the map known to her only through rumour and clandestine report. She felt a thrill of fear as she stood before the two gigantic figures and the watchful tension of their silent vigilance. Her mother stepped forward and, to Julie’s astonishment, curtsied low before the two great statues. “These ‘ere two ladies beg leave to enter an’ ask t’ blessin’ o’ the Goddess in ‘Er Gardens.” She straightened up and turned to Julie, “Right then that’s t’ formalities seen to! Let’s be getting’ on.”

“Wot were all that about mam?”

“Oh it’s just t’ palaver yer ‘ave ter go through before yer pass t’ Sentinels. It’s just tradition like. It’s supposed ter be bad luck not ter ask permission ov ‘em.”

“Bloody ‘ell! They give me the creeps.”

“Hush Julie! Don’t be talkin’ like that in front ov ‘em. Yer’ll bring us bad luck.” Julie shook her head in bewilderment. Superstition was not one of her mother’s more notable traits but then her mother seemed a very different woman in this place. That difference was notable as they wound their way down the long gorge beyond the Sentinels. Mrs Hawthorne chattered excitedly pointing out the features within it. There was a little hanging bridge where they crossed the stream that caused her some comment. "By they've shored this up nicely. This bridge were a bit rickety in my day. I was allus scared of falling off inter t' beck." Julie looked down at the rushing cascade below and shivered.

"Seems daft they'd leave it so unsafe mam."

"Well I don't suppose they think ovver much about 'ealth an' safety regulations in 'ere Julie. It's not like it's a public park after all. Folks come in 'ere at their own peril. Anyway we're nearly out o' t' gorge an' where t' gardens start proper like." They emerged onto the little tranquil hanging meadow where Jennifer had stood before them gazing down in awe upon the vista of the gardens. Julie caught her breath at the glowing perfection shimmering in the late afternoon sunshine below her. Julie was no artist like her beloved Jennifer nor did she possess much in the way of a poetical nature but she did have the deep aesthetic appreciation of natural beauty that only a girl that had lived all her life among the splendour of Mathomdale could fully acquire. She might not have had the words or other means to express her joy in the world in which she lived her life but her heart was firmly rooted in the glory of the soft meadows and sparkling brooks beneath the imposing fells of her little homeland. Nature spoke to her in a deep and fundamental fashion and she felt inextricably linked with the woodlands, pastures, hamlets, hills and flowing waters of her beloved valley.

In the artful contrivance of the wondrous gardens below her Julie felt an instant rapport. She had expected to find a highly stylised formal layout of flowerbeds and shrubbery, as regimented as the rows of crops on an arable farm. She found instead a mind that adored the natural world as much as she, had nurtured it, cherished its uniqueness, crafted it lovingly and aided it toward some perfection impossible to describe in her own faltering vocabulary. Here had humanity found some final truce in its battle with nature, had melded it into its own vision and then subjugated itself into harmony with it. Her mother had been right. This was a little piece of paradise. This was where her mother lived in her dreams. This was where everybody should live.

“Bloody ‘ell mam!” she choked at last, the words catching in her throat, “I’ve never seen owt as lovely as this.”

“I told you it was bonny love.” There was an odd soft timbre to Mrs Hawthorne’s voice and Julie tore her eyes away from the scene laid out before her to look at her mother. She was gazing down across the landscape with a soft sad smile and with the hint of a tear in her eyes. She was the woman that Julie had seen nearly every day of her life but, in that moment, Julie scarcely recognised her. She had undergone some strange metamorphosis. In place of the care worn harassed house wife of the Hawthorne household stood a woman that seemed half her age, wistful and yet glowing with some inner place of tranquillity, lost in sweet memories and quite beautiful. Julie had never thought of her mother as beautiful before but there, discernible once the magic of the gardens had stripped the care of years away, lay somewhere still the warm loveliness that had carried Julie’s father’s heart.

“Aye Julie.” she said softly. “Everybody ‘as a place wot’s special to them an’ this were mine. I can’t tell yer all t’ days wot I spent in ‘ere, walkin’ about, tendin’ ter t’ plants or t’ lawns, ‘elpin’ maintain t’ pavilions an’ summer ‘ouses or just sittin’ about doin’ nowt an’ lettin t’ world go by. Me an’ Delilah used ter go off on us own fer a picnic somewhere an’ just spend all day messin’ about an’ paddlin’ in t’ stream or swimmin’ in one o’ t’ lakes. There were a little picnic ground by one o’ t’ lower meadows wot we loved. There were a little 'erd o' deer wot allus used ter come ter graze there of an evenin'. They were dead tame an' sometimes they'd come right up ter yer an' tek food out o' yer 'and. We gave 'em all names an' they was us special friends. Sometimes we'd stay out all night in one o' t' groves an' light a little brazier an' 'ang lanterns in t' trees." Mrs Hawthorne shook her head sadly. "Ee they were grand days Julie."

"Oh mam!"

"Aye well I'd best be off now love. Now do yer think yer can find t' way? Just try an' keep that big pagoda in view as yer foller t' paths down an' work yer way toward it. That should bring yer somewhere near t' centre. I don't know where your lasses are 'avin' their do but if yer get inter t' middle yer should run inter one o' t' gardeners an' they'll probably be able ter put yer right."

"Oh mam come wi' me!"

"Nay love. Another time maybe. I 'ave ter get back an' get yer dad an' sisters' tea on."

"Bugger them mam! Let 'em get their own tea fer a change. They're old enough. Come with me."

"Nay Julie love. I must go. Another day perhaps. Now 'ave yer got yer phone in yer bag?"

"Yes mam."

"Well if yer need pickin' up later on just give us a call. Doesn't matter what time it is. Now get on wi' yer. Yer've a fair walk."

"Oh mam!" Julie rushed to her mother and grasped her in a great hug. "Oh mam! I love yer!"

Mrs Hawthorne patted her favourite daughter in heart rending fondness "I love you too pet. Now get on wi' yer or yer'll be late for yer party." With a last embrace Julie set off down the path into the gardens. Before she was out of sight Julie turned to see the small figure of her mother stood alone by the stream in the little meadow watching her go. Then she pressed on.

Within a few minutes, in spite of her uncanny sense of direction, Julie Hawthorne was quite lost.

Chapter Fourteen

Lady Mathom's unscheduled early return to the Hall had precipitated a small domestic crisis in that establishment. The girls in the slaves' wing weren't the only ones caught on the hop by her sudden arrival. There was no evening meal planned for her for example and the kitchen staff had had to be run to earth to provide for her. She sighed and informed her hastily summoned butler that a light repast in her chambers would suffice for that evening. Did she want her young ladies to attend upon her this evening he wanted to know? No she'd told him but she did want to see them. She was in a strangely listless and sad mood, worn out by the whirlwind of meetings and functions and saddened by the horrors she had heard about the war. She wanted to take a light meal, take a long bath, relax with a brandy, a cigarette and her own thoughts and then retire to her bed. Most of all she wanted to see her slaves. She'd missed them.

She'd changed out of her clothes whilst a chambermaid ran a bath for her and she was reclining in a negligee when the knock came at the door of her chambers. After being bade to enter, the six girls shuffled in nervously. Lady Mathom stared at them in total astonishment as they all bowed to her in oriental fashion. "What the blue blazes is this all about?" she demanded at length her eyes flaring.

Abigail took a deep breath and stepped forward "Please My Lady, your wretched slaves humbly beg your forgiveness. They were so missing the presence of their beloved and benevolent Mistress that they had decided to ameliorate their misery at Her absence by dining formally with Her guest Mr Morgan in the Oriental Gardens this evening, unaware of their Mistress's early and joyful return. In deference to Your Ladyship's many admonitions to embrace and pay due respect to the culture of other people, they decided to dress in full formal Japanese style in homage to their hostess, the Lady Shiro in her Gardens. They did not intend to displease you Serenity and if they have done so then they humbly request that you beat them all for their foolishness. So overjoyed are they by your return that there is no whipping so hard that will detract from their pleasure and gratitude over your safe return to your home."

The corners of Lady Mathom's mouth were twitching in a furious effort of control. It was hopeless however. She laid her glass to one side, threw back her head and roared with laughter. "Oh my!" she gasped at last brushing the tears from her eyes. "You girls are just utterly precious. I might have known you'd be getting up to something as soon as my back was turned. Come here and let me see you all properly." The six girls skittered across the room encouraged by their Mistress's evidently restored humour. She stood to examine them all still chuckling. "Goddess! You girls have been snuffling into the Japanese collection like a bunch of truffle pigs on a hot scent haven't you?"

"We're sorry if we've been presumptuous My Lady." said Rebecca nervously. "It was my idea, I'm afraid, so I should take the punishment if we've displeased you."

"You haven't displeased me Rebecca. On the contrary. I've had a bloody awful few days with one or two exceptions and you girls are just the tonic I needed. I think you all look absolutely wonderful. You could have taken one of those feathers out of your hair and knocked me over with it when you all walked through that door however. Goddess you must have taken hours to get dressed up like this. You're sensational."

The girls were flushing in pleasure at their Mistress's delight. "We're so happy that you're pleased My Lady." Abigail told her. "Do you wish us to change before we wait upon you this evening?"

“I wouldn’t dream of it Abigail. If you’ve gone to all this trouble to dress up for a party then I’m not going to put a damper on it. You girls can run along and enjoy yourselves. Where is Darren Morgan? And Daniel as well for that matter?”

“Not back from the village yet Ma-am.” Alice told her. “They’re puttin’ up stands for t’ festival.”

“Oh yes of course. Are they both joining you all in Japanese dress for this party as well?”

“Yes Ma-am.”

“Goddess! That’ll be funny to see. All right girls have a nice evening and for heaven’s sake be careful with your food and drinks. That’s a small fortune in antique kimonos you’re flouncing around in. Before you go however I have one or two things to tell you and somebody I want you to meet.”

“Meet My Lady?” asked Abigail puzzled.

“Yes Abigail. Two people in fact. There may be some more to come in the next few days as well. Let me show you.” Lady Mathom rang a bell and within a few moments Mr Carmichael, the butler, appeared.

“Yes My Lady?”

“Ah Joseph! Have they eaten yet?”

“I believe so My Lady. My wife attended to the matter.”

“Good. Would you care to bring them here for a short while?”

“Of course My Lady.” Once he had departed Lady Mathom turned back to her six young ladies.

“Girls before I left I started to tell you all something about the conflicts that are currently waging around the world involving our people. I’m afraid as a result of those conflicts we will all have to make some adjustments. The security issues, onerous as they are, are among those adjustments but there will be others. It will be a trying time for all of us but I expect you all to conduct yourselves as high ladies of this House. We here must set an example to the Line and display courage, fortitude and compassion in these difficult days. There will be many demands upon my attention girls and in the case of my absence you are my representatives of this House. I want you to bear that responsibility with the dignity and humanity of the First House of the Line."

"We won't let you down Ma-am." Abigail told her.

Lady Mathom smiled. "Of that I feel quite certain Abigail. You, all of you, are among the most impressive young slaves it has been my privilege to possess. I am very proud of all of you."

"Oh Ma-am!" cried Heather in uninhibited delight and they would have rushed her in a body of pleasure except, at that moment, there came a knock on the door.

"Bring them in Joseph." Mr Carmichael ushered two girls into the room. The six slaves looked at them in astonishment. One was an older girl who looked to be in her late teens with olive skin, dark hair and wide brown eyes. She looked to be of Middle Eastern extraction and she was undeniably pretty, dressed in a white and black floral dress of simple design in which she appeared to have the discomfort of unfamiliarity with. Huddled fearfully at her side was a young girl of perhaps eight or nine years old dressed similarly. She was quite obviously the older girl's sister for there was a resemblance between them but, if anything, her eyes were even larger and they grew to an enormous pair of orbs at the sight of the six girls dressed in Japanese finery. The older girl curtsied hastily and whispered urgently in the younger girl's ear after which her young sister managed an unpractised and clumsy curtsy. Lady Mathom beckoned them forward. The young one clutched at her sister's dress afraid to approach these incredibly dressed women but her sister propelled her closer gently, even while her own eyes darted with nervousness.

"This is Jamila and her younger sister Laila girls." Lady Mathom told them. "Jamila, Laila, these ladies are my young slaves Abigail, Rebecca, Heather, Helen, Alice and Jennifer."

Jamila curtsied once more "I honoured ladies. May the blessing of the Lady be upon you." The girls bowed in Japanese style puzzled by the presence of these girls.

"Jamila and Laila are refugees girls." Lady Mathom informed them "They come from the northern regions of Afghanistan, born of the Line in the foothills of the Hindukush Mountains. A little over a week ago the enemy struck at their village and destroyed it killing everybody they could catch. A few survivors fled over the mountain passes to safety. A very few. Jamila brought her sister over the mountains with great courage and determination obeying the wishes of her parents." Lady Mathom lowered her voice that Laila might not hear and understand "Their parents died holding the enemy at bay on the approaches to the passes girls so that their children could escape. Jamila and Laila are all that remain of their family."

The girls listened to the tale in mounting horror "Oh no!" cried Alice "That's terrible!"

"Their story is not a unique one Alice." Lady Mathom continued. "All over the world there are young people in the same circumstances. Young people that have lost all their families and loved ones, utterly destitute and with everything they have ever known torn from them as they are cast into exile. Today I met over three hundred of them, on an airfield, girls, and it broke my heart, but that was just a tithe of the misery our enemies have brought upon our people. A great evil has been perpetrated girls. It is up to us to heal that evil. I have sworn on my honour as the Lady of this House that not while it lies within our capacity shall a single one of those unfortunate young people be without sanctuary and care. I brought Jamila and Laila back with me after ensuring that all their fellow unfortunates were cared for. There will undoubtedly be more of them to come. We must find space for all of them. In some way they must become a part of our family and have the umbrella of safety that this House can provide extended over them. Do you understand?"

"Absolutely My Lady!" declared Rebecca. "We'll not let anybody harm them."

"Very well. For tonight Mrs Carmichael will take care of the girls. Tomorrow I want you to find a place for them in your wing. It is only a stopgap until we decide on a permanent placement for them but I shall sleep easier in my bed if I know that my trusted slaves are caring for them. It is possible that you may have to take in some more girls over the next days as well, at least temporarily. I want you all to help them and look after them. They may come from very different backgrounds and cultures and you'll have to make allowances for that."

"What will become of them in the long run My Lady?" Rebecca wanted to know "Will they become our sisters?"

"Some of them possibly Rebecca. Other's we may absorb into the household in different departments and others we will find homes for among our daughter households or allies. In the meantime you should regard them all as your sisters and brothers. If the events of the past days can teach us anything it is that we of the Line are but one family and it is time to remember that." Lady Mathom turned to Jamila "Do you understand all this Jamila?"

"A little My Lady."

"Well please explain to Laila what you can. Jamila speaks some English girls." Lady Mathom told them "Laila has a few words as well. You can speak a bit of Farsi can't you Heather, Helen?"

"We studied a bit My Lady." Helen told her, "because it was such a beautiful language. I don't know how much good it will be though. They speak a different dialect in Afghanistan."

"Well I managed to communicate with the children off that plane in Farsi and Goddess knows it's years since I spoke any at all. I think with your bit of Farsi and their English you should be able to talk to each other. I think they'll pick up English quite quickly in any case. They are a remarkable young pair of girls. You should honour them and make them most welcome girls. They've demonstrated high courage in fleeing from that hellhole. Jamila's protection of her little sister is nothing less than heroic. You should be proud to consider her your sister."

"Oh we are!" declared Helen. She turned to Jamila and spoke in Farsi telling her "You are very welcome in our house Jamila. We hope you find great happiness here."

"Thank you honoured lady. You do us great honour."

"By its 'andy 'avin' someone as can talk different languages." Alice remarked breaking the tension with laughter.

"We'll teach you Farsi if you want Alice" Helen told her. "It's a lovely language. You'd enjoy it."

"Ee I don't know. I was rubbish at languages at school. I could never get me 'ead around French. Mind you I'm not that good at English."

Lady Mathom laughed "Very well then Alice. You've just talked your way into language courses in Farsi. That means you'll have to learn Arabic script as well so that should keep you occupied."

"Oh 'ell! Oh sorry My Lady."

"Farsi has a rich vocabulary in swear words Alice. So you should be able to add to your repertoire of oaths. You're a musician too and Farsi is a very musical and poetical language so it should appeal to you. You can be studying it in between your German lessons."

“Sorry Ma-am? My German lessons?”

“Half of your favourite composers were German speakers Alice, so you can learn their language as well as your Farsi and French.”

“French an’ all?” asked Alice pale with shock.

“Oh yes Alice. You’re a Slave of the Amethyst. Don’t ever let me hear you say that you’re rubbish at anything again.”

Alice looked so comically deflated that the others laughed in glee. “Cheer up sister.” Abigail told her. “It happens to us all. I was once stupid enough to tell Her Ladyship that I couldn’t swim. Oh boy did she prove me wrong!” The older girls laughed. Two years before Abigail had been the Northern England freestyle champion. Encouraged by the merriment little Laila’s irrepressible inquisitiveness exerted itself and she babbled out a query in her own tongue.

“What did she say Jamila?” asked Rebecca.

“Sorry lady. She want to know if we live here should we dress as you ladies.” The girls looked at each other’s elaborate Japanese costumes and burst into laughter.

“No Jamila. This is just for a special occasion. We are dressing up for a party. Something special. Do you understand?”

“Yes lady. Sorry we not know.” Jamila looked down at her own unfamiliar costume. She had not worn western dress before. “We are not knowing how slaves of the Great Lady dress.” Quickly she explained to Laila. Laila looked disappointed and rattled off another incomprehensible barrage of words.

“What’s the matter with her Jamila?” asked Rebecca.

“Oh she is sad lady. She say you are all very beautiful. She want to dress like you every day and go to party.”

The girls grinned at Laila and were rewarded with a shy smile in return. "Believe me Jamila if she knew the grief it takes to get into this clobber she wouldn't think that." Helen said laughing.

"Sorry lady I am not understanding."

"Sorry." quickly Helen translated as best she could into Farsi.

Jamila smiled. She had been in awe of these exotic looking young ladies to begin with but their friendliness and humour had eased her nervousness. They were high born young ladies she could see but they were so warmly pleasant they had quite disarmed her. She particularly liked the look of the youngest one in her green and gold fabulous costume. She was of an age with Jamila and although she'd said little she'd smiled warmly and encouragingly. Here was one that Jamila knew could be a special friend. She felt a little flutter in her heart every time the lovely hazel eyes turned upon her.

It had been another bewildering day for Jamila and her sister. To their astonishment the Lady had singled them out and they'd been shepherded away to a private aeroplane. They'd been stripped out on the tarmac much to their shame but the Lady had explained, carefully, that it was only a security measure. A brisk looking young woman had appeared with some clothes for them and they'd had to dress in the unfamiliar garb before boarding the aeroplane. The Lady had boarded with them.

They'd been getting used to flying by now but this aeroplane had seemed very small although very luxurious inside. The Lady had held their hands as the aeroplane had taken off and talked with them softly explaining that she was taking them to her own home. There'd been more adventures waiting for them when they had landed for they'd been whisked away into a helicopter and had been back in the air again almost immediately. They'd gazed out of the window in wonder as the helicopter had circled over a great parkland. This, the Lady had told them, was her home. They'd seen the huge edifice of Mathom Hall on the slope above the lake and the enormous stretch of the Lady's gardens stretching back to the hills.

They'd landed on what Jamila recognised was a sport field and The Lady had taken them firmly by the hands and led them along a path to the Great Hall. Here she had handed them over to a kind lady who had given them food and drink. Laila had been very hungry and had forgotten her manners, snatching at her food until Jamila had slapped her hand and told her that she was in the house of the Great Lady and must behave like a good girl. It was hard to be annoyed with her for long though for, ever since they had met the Lady, Laila had been in a fever of excitement tinged with fear. To be sitting in her very home was almost unbelievable. And now this. Jamila had thought she must be dreaming when she'd seen the six exotically dressed young women. It was another astonishment on a day when their senses had been overwhelmed by new experiences but slowly Jamila was coming to understand that after all the horror and fear of the past days she and her sister had found sanctuary.

"Come along then girls." Lady Mathom told them "You and Laila have had a very long day Jamila so I think you'd better get some sleep." She rang the bell and Joseph duly arrived. "Mr Carmichael will take you to the lady looking after you tonight and she'll show you to your room. Do you understand Jamila?"

"Yes My Lady and thank you. Thank you very much."

"Entirely my pleasure young lady. Go with Mr Carmichael now. I want to speak with my young ladies for a minute or two. I shall see you tomorrow." The two Afghan girls curtsied respectfully before Thomas led them away. Lady Mathom turned back to her finely dressed young slaves. “They are a very courageous and resourceful pair of youngsters girls. I want you to look after them well whilst they are with us. I’ll decide what to do with their future as soon as I can clear my present headaches out of the way. In the meantime I hold you all responsible for them. You can sort them out with some clothes tomorrow. They don’t seem to have much experience of western dress so you’ll probably have to help them there. Oh yes, and while they are lodging in your wing, I want you all on your best behaviour. Little Laila is very young and Jamila too is from a somewhat conservative and sheltered background and not accustomed to your girly antics. So please keep things a little respectable in their company.”

“Yes My Lady. Abigail told her “We won’t let you down.”

“Good girls. Now Rebecca?”

“Yes My Lady?”

“How is your work on your research papers coming along? The special research that is.”

“Slowly My Lady. It was so long since I last went over them. and they were in somewhat of a chaotic state. I have managed to get them into some semblance of order though.”

“Good. Well I want you to spend tomorrow morning gathering up all the material you have and let me have it after lunch. I’m expecting important visitors tomorrow who wish to see your research. They may well want to interview you about it as well so please be available throughout the afternoon and evening.”

“Yes My Lady.” Rebecca looked very subdued suddenly.

“Oh and Jennifer?”

“Yes My Lady?”

“Did you pick that kimono out yourself?”

“Er Mrs Yakamura brought three or four for me to look at Ma-am. I…. I liked the look of this one so I picked it.”

“Extraordinary Jennifer. Did you know that that kimono belongs to your mother?”

Jennifer blushed in sudden confusion “No…. no My Lady. I had no idea.”

“Well it’s true Jennifer. Your mother loves Japanese dress and there are several of her kimonos in the collection. That one was always special to her however. Shiro san and her ladies made it with their own hands in her honour.”

“Oh My Lady! I’m sorry. I didn’t know. Perhaps it is inappropriate for me to wear it then.”

“Not at all Jennifer. I think it is entirely appropriate. You will do Shiro san great honour by wearing it to The Oriental Gardens tonight.”

Jennifer was flustered and felt tears pricking dangerously at the back of her eyelids. “Thank you My Lady.” She whispered. “I will wear it in that case.”

Lady Mathom looked at her keenly. “Is there something wrong Jennifer? You seem distracted this evening.”

“N… no My Lady. You caught me by surprise. That’s all.”

Lady Mathom considered ordering Jennifer to attend upon her in her chambers tomorrow to receive the cane for lying and so that she could get to the bottom of what was bothering her youngest slave. She let it go however. She had so much to do and Jennifer’s adolescent problems and prevarications would have to wait. “Very well then have a good time girls and I’ll see you in the morning. No don’t all kiss me. You’ll ruin all your careful make up.” The girls laughed and bowed in Japanese fashion and scuttled away. Lady Mathom watched them go with enormous fondness. There was part of her that wanted to dress up and join them.

Goddess knew she needed the stimulation tonight. But at least they had relieved her earlier weariness.

Chapter Fifteen

After the girls had left her, Lady Mathom luxuriated in a warm bath for a while, caressing herself with the suds, just glad to be back home. After her bath she donned one of the filmy, soft sensual negligees she so loved, its gauzy wisps little more than a misty film over her nakedness, and sat before the mirror admiring herself as she dried out her hair. She felt refreshed and invigorated. The girls in their Japanese costumes had entirely restored her humour. One day she thought she'd have them dress like that for her own pleasure. Perhaps she'd take them visiting and show them off proudly to her friends. Maybe though she'd just have them for herself for one evening. Perhaps she'd have them all report for punishment dressed like that. Have them all strip one by one out of their kimonos to be whipped. Her body grew warm at the imaginative erotic dalliance and almost automatically her hands started to caress her body beneath the thin material of her negligee.

Her intercom interrupted her revelry. It was Joseph. "Excuse me for disturbing you My Lady but may I ask if you are receiving this evening?"

"I am undressed Joseph. I'm just out of my bath and wearing next to nothing. I wasn't planning on getting dressed again. Who is it anyway?"

"My daughter My Lady."

"Margaret? Oh well that's different Joseph. Show her in."

"She's not actually here My Lady. She is calling from the pub and asking for an immediate audience with you if it is convenient. She said that if you were disposed to see her then she could be here in a few minutes."

"Of course Joseph. I would enjoy Margaret's company this evening. Tell her to come up."

"Very well My Lady." After Joseph had rung off the intercom, Lady Mathom enjoyed a delicious tingle.

Margaret was just what she needed to alleviate her loneliness this evening. She applied make up quickly and expertly but she left her hair loose knowing how Margaret loved it so. She wondered what to wear. Then she looked at herself in the mirror and saw her perfect body shimmering in promise below her negligee. She decided that she was dressed just fine. Laughing to herself, indulgently she walked over to her computer desk to open her personal email files. There were plenty of new entries but one in particular caught her eye. She opened it. It read,

"My Dear beloved Mistress,

Your miserable slave begs leave to inform your Serenity that he has obeyed your commands. He and his new fiancée are now having a wonderful time in Venice and would like to thank your Serenity for your benevolent gift of each other's pleasure. Your humble slaves trust that their wise Mistress is well and as undiminished in glory as ever.

We remain your devoted vassals

Alex and Evelyn

P.S. Say hi to Darren for me."

Lady Mathom clapped her hands in joy. "Oh well done Alex!" She felt thrilled by the communication. She wondered if they'd like to have their marriage here at the Hall. It had been long since they'd celebrated a marriage. It would be marvellous to throw a big wedding once again. Evelyn had no slaves of her own so she could lend the bride her retinue for her bridesmaids. Then again why shouldn't Evelyn have her own slaves. That was a new thought. There would be plenty of youngsters up for auction now. She'd pick out three or four suitable ones and give them to the couple as a wedding present. Perfect. She'd have them fettered in gold chains and have them presented before their new Master and

Mistress on their wedding day. Alex was certainly wealthy enough to maintain a stable of slaves. Evelyn could have her own slaves to fuss over and to wait upon her and three or four young people would find a loving home. She leaned back in her chair happily. Now then should she put one or two boys in with the coffle? Evelyn liked admiring young lads. She'd need a couple of girls though. Evelyn had a thing about dark Mediterranean looks. Perhaps some of the kids from Latin America might prove suitable. Alex had a weakness for blonds though so perhaps she'd better sneak some peachy little rosy cheeked girl with golden tresses into it. She was still mulling ideas in her head happily when there came a knock on the door.

"Come in Joseph." Joseph entered and noted with gratification that Her Ladyship seemed eminently restored in humour. In fact she was glowing with pleasure and as lovely as she'd ever been. That she was nearly naked, her nudity barely concealed beneath the transparency of her negligee, bothered him not at all. He had seen her naked many times. In fact once, years ago, in one of her wild moods, she had requested that he whip her. He had been greatly honoured to take a whip to that exquisite body. Few were ever granted the privilege of chastising her these days. Secretly he thought that a bad thing. Her temperament would benefit for more regular beatings he believed. But then it was long since she'd had anybody in this house that could master her occasionally. Not since her husband had died and her wife had left her in fact. It was lamentable. The Goddess still needed to be tamed.

"My daughter My Lady." He announced. Margaret walked in and curtsied low.

"Thank you for receiving me at such short notice My Lady. I am sorry to have disturbed your privacy with my trifling worries."

"Oh stop being so stuffy Maggie. Take your jacket off, kick off your shoes and come and join me on the sofa. Joseph would you pour us a couple of brandies?"

"Where on earth are your girls Ma-am?" asked Margaret puzzled.

"Gone flouncing off for a party in the Oriental Gardens Margaret."

"Really My Lady! You're far too lax with them. Your first night back at home and they're off on a party instead of waiting upon you. You ought to thrash the lot of them."

"No Maggie I turned up back home unannounced and they'd already got dressed up to go off. In full Japanese kimono no less. I didn't have the heart to put all their efforts to waste."

"Hmmph! You're too soft with them." said Margaret as she settled down on the sofa next to Lady Mathom.

"Oh Margaret let them have their fun. They've been cooped up in the house long enough with all this blasted security. I scared the poor little dears half to death when I arrived home unexpectedly demanding their presence in twenty minutes flat. They must have spent all afternoon getting dressed up as well. You've never seen the like. They were like a little bunch of geishas out for a hard Saturday night in Kyoto." Margaret laughed. "Anyway Margaret dearest," Lady Mathom continued stroking a fingernail down the side of Margaret's face. "Your own little spy network must be working overtime. How the blazes did you know I was home so quickly?"

Margaret chuckled deeply "Oh no big secret there My Lady. Your helicopter flew clean over the centre of the village on its way in. I was out in the garden at the time."

"They're using that helicopter for all sorts of liaison purposes Margaret. It could have been anybody in that aircraft."

“Not when its got two fully armed attack choppers riding shotgun on either flank and two more full of commandos bringing up the rear it couldn’t. Only one person around here that can make an entrance on that sort of scale.”

Lady Mathom sighed, “This bloody military security is starting to get on my pip. I can barely go to the loo nowadays without half a dozen sharpshooters hiding in the cistern.”

Margaret laughed, “Well Ma-am we don’t want the nasties taking out the best we’ve got do we? I wish I’d got here a bit earlier though. I’d have loved to have seen your little bunch of lovelies dressed up in full kimono.”

“Oh they were just precious Margaret/ I couldn’t believe it when they all shuffled in tarted up like that. I thought I was hallucinating or something! I swear I can’t take my eyes off them for a second and they’re up to something. How are your girls anyway?”

Margaret grinned, “In big trouble actually. Well Sally and Patricia are anyway.”

“Oh yes? Do tell.”

“Well I made an unexpected return home myself last night. I was supposed to be staying over in Brawton but in the end I just decided to come home. I turn up at nearly two in the morning and find that Sally and Pat have decided that while the cat’s away it’s time to do a bit of snuffling around for some cheese.”

“Oh my what have they got up to?”

“They’d got their claws into those two young slave lads from Hartley’s mill. Persuaded them to stay back after closing time for a game of doubles snooker.”

“Well that sounds relatively harmless.”

“Not when they were playing for an item of clothes per frame it wasn’t.”

Lady Mathom laughed richly “Oh dear! How far had they got?”

"Well the girls get to practise their snooker a fair bit living in the pub so they were a bit better than the boys unfortunately. They had the two lads in their birthday suits by the time I walked in on them and they hadn't even divested themselves of their underwear yet."

"Oh Goddess what did you do?"

"I threw the two lads out. Told them they could come back and collect their clothes in the morning."

"You threw them out in the middle of the night without a stitch on? Goddess it's nearly three miles up to Hartley's Mill."

Margaret grinned evilly "That's right! It's worse than you think as well. They didn't even have the keys to get into the mill. Mrs Hartley phoned me up today and told me that she caught the pair of them trying to climb in through a back window at three in the morning. Scared the life out of her. She thought it was burglars or something. She took a good stout stick to their backsides on the spot. It was a very penitent pair of young gentlemen that came shuffling around humbly asking for their clothes back just before lunch today."

"Oh my! What about your two?"

"Oh I bent the little darlings over the snooker table and thrashed their pretty little bottoms red raw for them. Probably ruined the baize. The snooker club will play war with me. Never mind we're supposed to be getting the tables re-clothed next month anyway."

Lady Mathom laughed in pleasure "Oh Margaret aren't they wonderful? What would we do without our treasured slaves? They keep us all young."

"They do indeed Ma-am."

Joseph laid the decanter of cognac on the coffee table "Do you require me any further My Lady?"

"No Joseph that will be all thank you." When he had left Lady Mathom said, "All right Margaret what's eating you? You didn't come rushing up here just to relate all your domestic disciplinary problems."

“No My Lady. Actually I want your advice.”

“On what?”

“Well you know that I’m on the accommodation committee for the festival?”

“No surprise there Margaret dearest. There aren’t many committees you’re not on.”

“Well yes and a pain in the butt it is too, sometimes. Anyway today we got a request for housing for the duration of the festival. An unusual one, high-born, very VIP, no less a personage than Eugene Collette in fact.”

“Ah Eugene! So this is what this is about.”

“You don’t seem very surprised.”

“No Margaret. I’ve been expecting Eugene to turn up sooner or later. She sent me an email in formal language requesting an audience with me some time ago. She’s got a bee in her bonnet about something or other. Goddess knows what.”

“Well what the devil am I supposed to do with her My Lady? Am I right in presuming that she is under some sort of penal prohibition from entering the Hall?”

“She is under no prohibition from my part Margaret. Eugene is a favoured Slave of the Amethyst. She is a courageous and honourable scourge of our enemies and she has proved her worth to the Line a thousand times over. The Hall is her home whenever she wants it.”

“Then why for heaven’s sake is she asking for accommodation? Can’t she just come to the Hall?”

“No Margaret. It’s not that simple. Eugene is a lady that finds it very difficult to live up to her own principles Margaret. Many years ago she used to visit occasionally although she has never taken up residence in the Hall even though she was always welcome to do so. Nearly twenty years ago however she placed a penance on herself. She swore that she would never again defile the floors of my house until she could repay me for the terrible loss she had incurred upon me. Eugene is very good at punishing herself."

"Goddess whatever did she do?"

"It's a long story Margaret but the gist of it is that Eugene blames herself for Donald's death."

"Donald? Your husband?"

"Correct Margaret. Eugene holds herself responsible for that. I'll not go into details but Eugene made an error of judgement and it probably cost Donald his life. She has atoned for that error a hundred times since and I forgave her long ago. Eugene finds it very difficult to forgive herself however. She's had a hard life living up to her principles Margaret. She's placed herself in danger time and time again on behalf of the Line, sacrificed her own happiness a thousand times over and still cannot assuage the demands of her guilt. Few people are more welcome in my home than Eugene Collette and nobody believes themselves more unworthy to be there than herself." Lady Mathom looked sad. "Poor Eugene. Some people have tragedy forced upon themselves others just carry it about within them."

"Why do you think she's here?"

"Possibly, hopefully she wants to come home. That's my best guess. Perhaps my little wayward bird is coming home to roost at last. It will have taken all her considerable courage to do so Margaret. Maybe, just maybe she finally got tired of running away."

"Well where should I put her? Should she be ordered up to the Hall?"

"No. Give her her space Margaret. Let her have time. I think she'll probably ask for a formal audience with me and make a request to meet on neutral ground. If so I'll grant her that. Then I'll judge what's biting her. Where were you thinking of putting her?"

"I was a bit flummoxed My Lady. There's a complication. She's dragging three young slaves in tow.

I was going to put them up at the pub but we're going to be damned crowded."

"Three slaves? It's the first I've heard about any new young slaves. Oh she's got her boys and girls in Hamburg and I believe her family in Austria have a couple of slaves but it hardly seems likely that she'd be bringing them along. Did she say how old they were?"

"Between about fourteen and sixteen My Lady. Three young girls apparently."

"That's odd. I'm sure I'd have known about it if Eugene had registered any new slaves. Why is she bringing them with her?"

"Perhaps she's looking to sell them at the festival."

"Eugene's got plenty of markets to vend her slaves at Margaret. She's not coming all the way to Mathomdale just to speculate on the slave trade."

"A gift then? A peace offering to yourself."

"A possibility. Goddess we're going to be crowded at this rate. Apart from Jennifer I've taken two new slaves on this summer and Alex has just sent me a young man he wants me to put my brand on."

"The American boy?"

"That's right. I've only seen him once but he's in the house now. I'll have a good look at him tomorrow when I get a minute. Then again, I just brought back two new girls fresh off an aeroplane from Afghanistan this afternoon. I've got homes to find for them as well. They're refugees, lost their family out there. They're impressive youngsters. They'll fetch a high price I would think."

"There're a lot of young slaves coming on the market. There'll be a lot of wheeling and dealing at the festival I would imagine."

"Well a lot of them are displaced youngsters from the troubles. I'm having quite a few coffles sent to me. We'll have to start putting them up in the barns at this rate. It's going to be quite a market. Have an ask around and see if anybody's interested. I'll get Akuti up here to vet them so the buyers will know they're getting good quality."

"If you see any girls that might be suitable for my place I'd be grateful if you singled them out for me Ma-am. With Sally going off to college full time come the end of September I'm going to be a bit short. I'm looking for a nice presentable girl, over eighteen whose religion doesn't preclude her from serving alcohol."

"Looks?"

"Doesn't have to be drop dead gorgeous but a nice full-bodied bosom would help. I know it's a cliché but the punters like a nice pair of boobs to be looking at whilst they're getting their pints pulled."

"Well I'll keep an eye open for you Margaret. Anybody else you know might be interested?"

"Oh stacks! We've had a shortage of decent quality slaves for a long time now. I'm forever having people come up to me and ask me if I know of any decent youngsters on the market. Send me a few dozen and we'll hold a private market in the back function room one night. Selected invitations only. Get quality families with a bit of brass behind them. They'll go like hot cakes. I could flog as many as you send me."

"That's a good idea Margaret. Goddess knows there's going to be plenty of these kids up for sale. We've got to find places for them somewhere."

"We advertise it right and there's no end of people that would jump at the chance. Get some of the shipping families up from Kingston and the sky's the limit. There're heaps of ships running under-crewed. Some of the ships are even having to hire Beta non-slave crewmembers just to fill the shortage and nobody's happy about that. Then there're all the families in the valley and in Brawton. I bet I could flog a gross of them without too much sweat. If I charge a commission I'll make a mint."

"Hmm. I like this. I'll get the refugee authorities to send us up a sampling. We won't sell all of them in open auction however. We'll pick out the ones with something really special about them and offer them up for private viewing to a very select clientele. Only the very best families. We'll give them a Mathomdale stamp of approval and charge the earth for them/ We'll use part of the proceeds to set up a trust fund for each kid and the rest we'll funnel back into assistance for the refugee effort. I don't mind you taking a commission but no more than eight percent all right."

"It's a deal My Lady. I'll use the money to buy one or two for myself."

"Now then whom in the valley should we be thinking about?"

"Well My Lady, I know of several. One of them, however, is very curious indeed."

"Oh really?"

"Yes. I don't want to bother you with trivial local gossip however."

"Bother away Margaret. After the last few days I've had I can do with all the trivial gossip I can get."

"Well remarkably Eleanor Waterstone is in the market for a new slave, so rumour has it."

"Nothing remarkable there Margaret dear. I should imagine she's looking for a sister for that Debra girl of hers. She's a very valuable young slave is Debra. I own part of her contract myself."

"It's not the fact that she's looking for a slave that's remarkable Ma-am. It's her choice that is a bit startling."

"Why? Who's she after?"

"Well my contacts in Marveaux tell me that it's common knowledge there that Eleanor is in serious negotiation to buy Julie Hawthorne no less."

"What?"

"That's right Ma-am. Julie Hawthorne! The very same. Of the Hawthorne business consortium on

Mathom Village Square; your darling Jennifer's little girlfriend. I couldn't believe it either when I heard it myself."

"Impossible! Why would Eleanor be after buying a Beta girl as a sister for a thoroughbred Alpha?"

"It's not unprecedented for an Alpha family to buy a Beta Ma-am."

"True but I can't see Eleanor doing it."

"Perhaps she doesn't know that Julie isn't of the Line My Lady."

"I can't believe that. The Hawthornes go back generations in this valley. I've known them myself since time out of mind. There's never been a hint of Alpha Sensual blood in that family."

"Well something must have persuaded Eleanor that Julie has some value. The rumour has it that she's offering a great deal of money for her."

"I'm astonished. It seems incredible."

"Oh but that's not all. The tale gets curiouser and curiouser. My friends in Brawton tell me that Eleanor was parading Julie and Debra around in the Royal Hotel one afternoon. So what happens next gets very peculiar."

"Go on."

"Well apparently no less a personage than our dear Rosalyn Carter-Bannister was among the company present. Nothing unusual there, Rosalyn likes to get down to the Royal on a Friday afternoon to swap gossip. Well Eleanor introduces her new slave Debra and her prospective buy Julie and Rosalyn comes over all thoughtful."

"Just a moment Margaret. You're not telling me that Rosalyn Carter-Bannister is weighing in with a bid for Julie Hawthorne as well?"

"Absolutely My Lady! Within days of that afternoon Rosalyn was up here in the valley with her old girlfriend Astrid Ramone and I know for a fact that their car was sat out on the square all afternoon and I've more than enough reason to believe that they spent that afternoon cloistered with the Hawthorne family. I think they made an offer for Julie."

"Goddess! What on earth is going on?"

"I might be wrong of course."

"I doubt it Margaret. Your informer network is pretty reliable. If Rosalyn so much as powdered her nose in Mathomdale you'd probably know about it. But why for heaven's sake? Why the devil are two high houses suddenly haggling over a simple village girl?"

"It's pretty serious haggling too My Lady. Rumour has it that there's some very serious money being wafted about for Julie's contract."

"Something odd is going on here. What do you think?"

"Well there's the obvious possibility My Lady."

"Jennifer?"

"Yes My Lady. It's pretty much common knowledge that Jennifer is deeply attached to Julie. Eleanor surely knows about their relationship and it wouldn't have taken Rosalyn five minutes to sniff out that fact. Kind of puts a bit of a different value on Julie if she's intimately connected with a high slave of Mathom Hall doesn't it? Rosalyn's got a nose for money like a hound on a hot scent and Eleanor's not above a little creative speculation if it comes to the prospect of holding a contract, that might be worth millions, in the future marriage negotiations of the most expensive slave in England either."

"Yes you're right Margaret. It makes sense too. Recently I found out that Rosalyn was sniffing around the Hall's current contract applications with a view to seeing whom we were acquiring. I didn't know what the devil she was playing at."

"Well there you are Ma-am. She was digging around to make sure you hadn't put in a formal bid or taken out an option on Julie yourself."

"There's something odd here though Margaret. Why have the Hawthorne's suddenly decided to sell their youngest daughter? I mean they've got three other children haven't they? They've never attempted to sell one before."

"Hmph! No mystery there My Lady. The Hawthorne's are in deep financial trouble. The business is going tits up on them."

"I've heard nothing about this. That shop is one of the busiest and most successful retail outlets in the whole valley so I'm told."

"Nothing wrong with the shop My Lady. It's the haulage business that's the stone around their necks. They're up to their necks in debt over that. They could go under. Well if somebody suddenly comes along with a substantial chunk of cash for their daughter then they'd be bound to take it seriously. They might even have a done a bit peddling on their own behalf when they realised they had a possible asset in Julie. Goddess knows they wouldn't get much for her two sisters. Julie's the best they've got and, with her profile as your Jennifer's favourite, well they could do worse."

"Damn it! I've been neglecting my domestic duties Margaret. I've been putting off this relationship that Jennifer has with Julie for too long. I've never been happy about it and I'm less so now. I should have forbidden it long ago. Now look what's happened. She's placed her girlfriend in the position whereby greedy investors are crawling out of the woodwork trying to get their claws on her contract. There's too much of this sort of financial speculation in the slave trade these days Margaret. It's high time that somebody reminded some of our families that the institution of slavery exists firstly and fore mostly for the benefit of the slave in question."

"Well I agree My Lady. However, it wouldn't be entirely out of Julie's interest to be enslaved to a wealthy family now would it? I mean they'd still have to make provision for her under the terms of the contract legally whether or not their motives are purely speculative wouldn't they. That's the legality of it. Julie could do very nicely out of it. Goddess knows she doesn't have too many prospects as it is. She has hardly any school qualifications and her family's facing bankruptcy."

"She'd still be a Beta girl being brought up in an Alpha environment Margaret. It's a minefield. The legal ramifications alone don't bear thinking about. She could contest that contract in the future and open up a whole can of worms."

"Why would she if it was favourable enough for her?"

"She might want to get married Margaret and suddenly find that her owners have effective veto powers over the union. If she was an Alpha then she'd simply wed into an Alpha marriage and everyone would have a fine old time negotiating terms and coming to arrangements. But she's not. She's an overpriced Beta girl who might just want to marry off with any old boy she meets. The more money her owners have invested in her the less likely they are view with sympathy the fact that she wants to run off with the butcher's boy down the street."

"Well if you forbade any further relationship between Jennifer and Julie publicly you'd soon scare the investors away Ma-am."

"Yes and then have Jennifer going loopy on me. She's a tad highly strung is Jennifer at the moment Margaret and I don't want to destabilise her further by telling her that she can't see her girlfriend anymore."

"Perhaps you could have a quiet word with the persons involved and warn them off My Lady. Let them know privately that there is no future prospect of Julie marrying into the House of Mathom."

"Yes that's certainly an option. Perhaps I'll have a chat with them at the festival. Rosalyn will certainly be in the valley for that. That still leaves the Hawthorne family in deep water however. I can't have one of the local businesses going to the cleaners right under my nose. It looks as if I might have to do a bail out there."

"And Julie?"

"Maybe I can find a place in the domestic service for her here at the Hall. I could take out an open option on her contract myself to frighten the vultures off and find her a place with one of the departments. I don't know what the girl's capable of though. I've been meaning to take a look at her ever since I knew she was entangled with Jennifer but I've never found the time. Trouble is that I've only met the girl once or twice and that when she was only little. I know she was very poor at school and she used to get into trouble a lot so Goddess knows how reliable she is."

"She's settled down a lot in the last year or two My Lady. She runs the shop virtually single-handed or did until she became ill. She's not very well educated but she's by no means stupid. I'm sure she's hard working and conscientious if a bit flighty on occasion. I certainly think she's got some potential. She's definitely superior to her sisters and brother."

"Well I'll have to think about it. In the meantime keep your ears to the ground and let me know if there are any other hyenas snuffling around her. We'll get the festival out of the way and then I'll see what action to take." Lady Mathom sat back and sipped her cognac thoughtfully. "There's just one thing that puzzles me."

"That is My Lady?"

"Astrid Ramone. Rosalyn Carter-Bannister getting involved in something shady I can understand and Eleanor isn't averse to this sort of thing but Astrid doesn't add up. I know her well and while she's wealthy she's the last person I would have imagined getting into this sort of deal."

"She's Rosalyn's long-standing friend My Lady. She shared the same chains with her as young slaves. She's probably just along for the ride on Rosalyn's schemes."

"Not Astrid. No she's a fine lady Margaret and goes her own way. No she'll have her own agenda Rosalyn or no Rosalyn!"

"Maybe she's just a spectator My Lady."

"Perhaps but I doubt it. If she thought that Rosalyn was up to something unethical then she would be no mere spectator I think. No there's something else going on here."

"Well I'll put my spies to work Ma-am and see what they can come up with."

"Thank you Margaret. I will leave the intelligence gathering in your capable hands. See what you can find out. Anyway.... about Eugene Here's a suggestion Margaret. What about putting her and her slaves in Rose Cottage up at Marveaux? It's Hall property theoretically but it's far enough away from the Hall to be considered neutral. It's empty at the moment and it's a beautiful place. We can invent some fiction about it being on the official accommodation lists so we don't spook her by making her think that it's part of the Hall."

"Brilliant! If you can give me the keys I'll get a couple of cleaners up there to get the place into shape."

"I'll let you have them before you leave. Now then... to other matters. What are you doing this evening?"

"Oh much the usual at the moment. I'm supposed to be at a meeting later to allocate space for the market garden stalls at the festival. Apparently there's some tiff or other about the damn matter, or so Tom Wilson seems to believe. Nothing I can't worm out of if there's something you require me to do Ma-am."

"The pub?"

"I've left Sally in charge. She's reliable and she won't be risking any more misadventures with her bottom still sore after yesterday's little seeing to. I can usually rely on three or four days of good behaviour from my girls after a decent thrashing."

"It's more than I can boast. My little darlings seem to think that I've nothing better to do with my time than beat their backsides for them. I swear they think that I relax my vigilance immediately after punishing them because they usually are straight into some other mischief."

Margaret laughed, "Well your little pack are true thoroughbreds Ma-am. I wouldn't expect anything else. Anyway was there something you required me for My Lady?"

"Oh nothing important Margaret. I just wanted you to attend a little meeting that's all. I'm sure the fruit and veg stalls for the festival take precedence however. I mean we wouldn't want the season's parsnips to be poorly displayed after all."

"What sort of meeting My Lady?"

"Oh just an interrogative sort of thing in reality. A small commission of inquiry you might say."

"Inquiry into what My Lady?"

"Well into a few things actually. Such as what you are wearing under that dress and how quickly I can divest you of them, drag you into the bedroom and abuse you. Minor stuff really. Nothing to keep you from your marrows and turnips."

"Bugger the marrows and turnips My Lady!"

"Are you sure Margaret? I mean I hate to keep you from your wildly exciting social life by asking you to perform a tedious chore such as stripping your clothes off and spending the night allowing your tyrannical Mistress to use your body for her pleasure."

"Tom Wilson can take his market stalls and shove them up his arse" Margaret grinned in delight. "Duty calls! My Mistress has demanded that I attend upon her and I'll have no one saying that I'm not a dutiful slave. I am entirely at your disposal My Lady."

Chapter Sixteen

Atlantic Lady was tied up alongside the quayside at the big cruise liner facilities in Bridgetown. She'd been there ever since six o'clock that morning when her arrival had caused somewhat of a diplomatic stir in the island democracy of Barbados. Three other big cruise ships shared the port facilities for the moment for this was a popular cruise destination and Atlantic Lady was well known to the port authorities. But, unlike the other ships, Atlantic Lady was not carrying a cargo of well to do tourists about to come ashore and leave their money to the benefit of the local economy. Much to the authorities horror, she was stuffed to the gunnels with penniless refugees, many of them without passports or any sort of documentation at all. Immigration had thrown a minor fit at her expected arrival and at first had refused to allow the liner into harbour, insisting that she take up a quarantining anchorage at Carlisle Bay. This was, by now, largely resolved.

There had been a furious round of diplomatic wrangling that had started days ago while the crisis in Colombia had been unfolding. The bewildered refugees on board had little idea of the powerful forces being unleashed on their behalf in this diplomatic struggle. Amethyst International and its hydra like, multi corporate spin offs were heavy investors in the island economies of the Caribbean. Their voice carried the substantial weight and authority of the billions of pounds of investment the archipelago so relied upon. The forces of the Line were quietly asking for nothing more than transit for its displaced persons.

There were five big, chartered jets waiting on the tarmac at Grantley Adams International Airport, just twenty-one kilometres east of Bridgetown. Three were flying to a safe destination in South America, another to Central Europe and the last to England. With admirable efficiency the Line had organised a small fleet of buses to speed the refugees to the airport. All they required was the authorisation to do so. The government officials of the island had huffed and puffed, waffled about immigration restrictions and quarantine requirements and would have dragged out the discussions interminably had not the main office of Amethyst International on the island, an institution that was to all intents and purposes an embassy for the most powerful non-national organisation on the planet, unmasked its batteries and quietly tapped its finger on the rows of figures indicating that the island economy needed them far more than they needed it. "Let our people go!" they said and in the face of the massive amounts of capital woven into the structure of the local economy the authorities had capitulated. The kids were only in transit after all. Let them board their planes and then they're somebody else's problem.

Some of the young people would not leave the ship. Atlantic Lady, in common with other ships of the Line, had her own eyes open for suitable young people to serve her. Captain Delamonte had urged his senior crewmembers to scour the masses of youngsters and single out the best of them as potential crew. The ship was not losing money on its humanitarian mission for it was being well compensated for being requisitioned for the duty but the captain was not above taking a little cream off the top of the milk and picking out the best of the crop for his own crew. Atlantic Lady was not as big as some of the other liners tied up around her but she was a fast modern vessel and very luxurious. She needed a good crew to man her and, in common with all ships of the Line, she needed the sons and daughters of the Goddess enslaved to her and to sail her beneath the flags of the Mermaid and the Purple Lady. Such slaves were hard to come by as the fleet expanded and this influx was a golden opportunity for the captain to bring his crew up to full capacity. He had the pick of some two thousand potential young slaves to choose among and he needed fifty or sixty good hands. His departmental officers had been rummaging among the refugees, ever since they'd left Santa Marta, with admirable enthusiasm and now he had a satisfactory list of potential new hands growing on his purser's desk. In fact, he had rather more than he needed. As a result of this Gitana would make it off the ship after all.

She very nearly didn't. She was already a favourite with the crewmembers that had come to know her and Nathan Roberts; the steward that her originally assigned her her cabin was a vocal supporter of her being indentured into the crew. It was not entirely sympathy that had endeared Gitana to the crew, although her personal tragedy was particularly poignant, but also a consideration that she represented a terrific asset to the ship. Certainly with her intelligence and abilities, her good English and her admirable character she would have made an excellent crewmember and could have forged out a successful career among the ships of the Line. She was really a prize asset but there were a lot of very impressive young people aboard Atlantic Lady and possibly her young age told against her. She had barely turned sixteen after all and, unless they were born into the sea-going families, Captain Delamonte preferred to buy his slave crews at a little more mature an age. He had hesitated over her in any case because of the glowing reports he had of her but in the end had reluctantly let her go. Nathan, who had befriended her and taken a special interest in her, was devastated but he was determined to see her safely away anyway.

That duty had fallen on him now as he raced up the companionway to the first class cabins where Gitana was bunked. Gitana was sitting fearfully in her cabin with her little suitcase of donated clothes already packed beside her. She had found the voyage to Barbados soothing after the horrors of her family's murder and her abduction and Nathan had told her he would try to get her a berth aboard ship. For a little while she had dreamt of a life afloat, plying the seas safe from the terrors of the land and only the capriciousness of the ocean to worry about. It had seemed a very attractive and romantic life but it was not to be and now she, along with her fellow refugees, was under stand-by for immediate debarkation and diaspora to whatever uncertainty the future held. She was frightened.

Nathan rushed into her cabin. "Gitana honey. Have you got your kit together? The buses for the airport are due here in one hour."

"Si Senor Roberts. I have been packed for hours. I don't have very much. Please Senor, where am I going?"

"To England Gitana. I wrangled it so you could get on the plane for England. The bloody Purser was after putting you on a flight for Buenos Aires and I told her to stuff it. You'll be better off in England."

"If you say so Senor."

"Look Gitana I've got some family in England and I've put some addresses in this envelope." He handed Gitana a slim white envelope. "When you get settled down, drop them a line and if you have any problems they'll help you out. Just mention my name. There's also a contact address for me in there. Write me a letter and let me know how you're getting on. We're going to miss you."

"I will miss you too Senor. You have been very kind. I promise I will write."

"You have any problems just drop a line ok?"

"Si Senor."

"Here look. Me and the other stewards had a whip round for you Gitana." Nathan handed her another envelope. "It's not much but it'll be a bit of pocket money for you when you get to England."

“Oh Senor! No! You are too kind. I cannot take your money.”

“Stop arguing honey and tuck it away safely somewhere. We don’t get to go ashore much these days in any case so it’s not as if we’re spending much.”

“But it is too much. How can I thank you for all your kindness Senor?”

“By being a good girl and sticking that money away somewhere. Don’t let the other girls in the cabin see it. Where are they anyway?”

“Out on deck Senor. They were told to muster there.”

“They won’t get away for hours yet. They’re embarking the passengers for your flight first. Listen have you used the heads recently?”

“Sorry Senor?”

“The heads; the toilets. If you haven’t, I’d go now if I was you. Goddess knows how long you’re going to be on that bus or hanging about at the airport.”

“I am fine Senor.”

“Good girl. Come on then let’s grab your bag and get down for debarkation. I’ll see you off the ship.”

“Senor I want to thank you for your kindness. You and all your friends”

Nathan smiled at her and took her gently by the shoulders. “Honey it was our pleasure. You’re a little joy Gitana. We’re all going to miss you.” Impulsively Nathan pulled her to him and hugged her, tears pricking at his eyes. “You take good care of yourself in England sweetheart and write to us soon. We’ll all be waiting to hear how you’re getting along.”

“I’m frightened of England Senor Roberts.”

“Don’t be honey. You’ll be just fine. Oh its got its problems just like anywhere else but it’s still a good place to live. You’ll be happy there I promise you.” he said huskily.

“Then I will go Senor. I will write to you and the others. I will miss you.”

“Come on honey. Don’t cry now. There’s a big future ahead of you and you’ve got a plane to catch.” Nathan led her to the debarkation station and kissed her fondly before sending her off into the haze of the future.

Chapter Seventeen

Outside the slave's entrance to Mathom Hall the six girls looked on in wonder at the magnificent sight before them. "Abigail you are a bleeding genius!" Rebecca told her.

"Cool huh?" said Abigail smugly, delighted in the effect her surprise had had on the other girls as they contemplated the transport she had arranged to take them to the Oriental Gardens.

"It's bloody awesome!" Helen gasped, "How the hell did you wangle this from the stables?"

"Oh one has ones ways. I haven't been rolling around in the hayloft with Billy Harrison entirely for recreational purposes you know."

"You must have put up one hell of a performance to organise this." Heather commented. "It's gorgeous." And it was. Waiting outside the slave's entrance was a beautiful, polished, antique open landau being pulled by two colossal, black, matching Shire stallions, dressed in full livery, with their coats gleaming, their white mains brushed and decorated and with gleaming white spats, feathering over feet the size of manhole covers. They were just beautiful as they stood there placidly under control of the liveried driver responsible for them.

"Goddess!" breathed Alice, "Those osses must be eighteen 'ands if they're an inch. Goddess knows what they weigh."

"Over four thousand pounds between them." Abigail told her. "Let me introduce you. This is Toby and this is Tommy. Look great don't they?"

"They're so big!" breathed Jennifer a little fearfully. "Would they let us stroke them?"

"Go right ahead. Don't be frightened of them. They're the most sweet tempered creatures you could imagine." The girls skittered forward to fuss over the two enormous beasts that endured their petting with the stolid placidity of their breed.

"We've just got to get a photo of this." said Helen excitedly snatching her camera from her bag. "Billy? Would you do the honours?" This last was directed to the young man holding the reins of the two big shires, a good-looking young man in old-fashioned coachman's livery.

"Yes ma-am!" he grinned climbing down. William Harrison was one of the many young Alpha slaves that worked the vast estates of Mathom Hall. He worked primarily in the stables and helped in the maintenance of the pastures in the grounds. It was a dream position for him for he loved working in the outdoors and he adored working with horses. He was in his element exercising the large stable of horses and ponies on the estate and he was good at it too. He was one of only two people, other than Lady Mathom, that was allowed to ride Shaitan, her favourite stallion. William loved all the horses but the girls' effusive delight over the two big shire horses warmed him particularly.

Of all the horses on the estate Tommy and Toby were his favourites. They were his particular responsibility and he had long since lost track of the hours and hours he had spent meticulously grooming them, dressing their manes or brushing their coats till they shone. He was immensely proud of his two charges and there was no quicker way to his heart than a person's admiration of them. Occasionally he was used to partake in ceremonial processions with the two magnificent beasts pulling one of the Hall's considerable collections of carriages and they were the proudest moments of all for him. Only this last week he had been hired out to the Mathom Brewery to distribute the first of the summer festival ale and he'd driven the big dray around all the pubs in the village gleaming with pleasure as the village folk had dashed out into the street to admire his two handsome dray horses. It had been this that had given Abigail the idea of having him transport them all to the Oriental Gardens.

William had a crush on the beautiful Abigail. There were few things that could drag William away from his precious horses but Abigail was one of them. She was a bit above his station however. She was after all a high slave of the big house and he was just a stable lad with his austere room above the stables in the grounds. The stable master would have been horrified to know that his young apprentice was spending clandestine quality leisure time carousing with one of Her Ladyship's personal attendants. Generally speaking there was even a certain division between those slaves that worked in the grounds and the household domestic slaves. It was bad enough for one of the stable hands to be found having an affair with one of the housekeeping staff, although of course it happened. It was nearly unthinkable for one to be dallying with the small elite of high slaves. But of course that happened too and most of the girls that became high slaves in the Hall soon accumulated their own private harem of lower slaves in and around the Hall. This naturally led to some wondrous entanglements and the occasional crackdown or imposition of penal sentence. This latter rarely had much effect. Abigail for her part had only to bat her eyelashes at William and no amount of whippings up in the hayloft would have kept him from rushing to pander to her wishes.

After a protracted round of photo taking, with the girls all posing in front of the two magnificent horses, they mounted the landau and, with William driving, they set off across the estates for the Oriental gardens. There was ample room in the landau and they sat three abreast facing each other chattering animatedly whilst trying to avoid poking each other in the eye with their parasols. It was a remarkable little procession that wound its way across the park lands and a very gay one with the girls' faces flushed with excitement as they condescended to bow their heads demurely to the astonished gardeners that paused in their work to remove their caps politely in deference and watch them go by, shaking their heads in bemused wonderment at the latest caper of the Hall's notorious but well-loved High slaves. At one point they passed a group of soldiers from the military garrison loafing around by a small copse. The troop leapt to its feet and granted them a formal military salute. The girls' majestic acknowledgement of the salute was somewhat spoiled by their having to hide their giggles behind their fans.

Shiro-san with her full retinue of slaves met the girls at the Bridge of Despair bowing politely at them from across the stream as they dismounted on the far side where they returned the bow and begged leave to enter into the gardens. Shiro-san granted them leave with all the high graciousness that was characteristic of her and they stepped over the arched wooden bridge and into the domain beyond where their hostess and her escort and, leaving two behind to await the arrival of Daniel and Darren, led them through the gardens towards her palace on the island in the lake. Alice, who had never seen the Oriental Gardens, was struck dumb by them from the moment they set foot within them. She had thought that she was by now getting used to all the wonders that Mathom Hall could produce but the glory of that incredible manicured landscape left her speechless. Finally she gasped "Bloody Nora! I've never seen owt like this place."

Jennifer laughed and put her arm around Alice's waist. "It's quite something isn't it? Becky brought me here the first time and I couldn't believe it either."

"It's….. well it's….." Alice paused unable to articulate her wonder at the enchanted landscape. She shook her head. "I saw this programme on telly once. All about some of the most famous gardens o' stately 'omes in Britain. I can't believe they overlooked this one. This would of med t' others look like bramble patches."

"Oh there's a story there Alice." Rebecca laughed. "Doris!" she called.

The beautiful smiling blond girl of Shiro-san's escort turned back towards them, her blue eyes dancing with amusement, their colour the same as her kimono. "Yes?"

"Tell Alice how you came to the Garden Doris."

"Oh it's a simple story really. I was a reporter for a gardening and country life magazine, my lady Alice; a big glossy weekly, probably the best publication of its kind in England. Well we did this series on the big formal gardens of Britain. It was fun. I was only twenty one and I travelled all over England with a photographer and visited some beautiful gardens; Kew, Blenheim Palace, Windsor, Burton Constable, Castle Howard, you name it. We went everywhere. Then one day we were visiting a gorgeous garden in the south of England and I interviewed the head gardener. She was a lady called Arabella and I got friendly with her. I took her out for a meal in a little country pub and we got on really well. It was funny though. I didn't know then that I was Alpha Sensual but Arabella saw it straight away. I was going through the sort of sensory turn on that can make you think you're losing your marbles and had no idea what was happening to me. I guess Arabella saw that the sooner I was chained up the better.

So, after she'd sounded me out, she asked what I thought of her garden. Well I waxed lyrical about it for a few minutes. Well I mean it was lovely. She stopped me in full flow however and told me that it was nothing. "You haven't seen the best by a long margin." she told me. "Have you ever been to Mathom Hall?" Well the answer to that was no. I'd never even heard of Mathom Hall. Well she told me that she served her apprenticeship as it were at Mathom Hall. She told me that the Hall had the most extraordinary collection of gardens anywhere in England; miles and miles of them. I thought she was pulling my leg. I mean I thought I was pretty well cued up on just about every stately home and its gardens in England and I'd never even heard of the place. But she was insistent and she told me that she'd learned her craft in a garden called the Oriental Garden at Mathom Hall. Well that interested me because I've always loved formal Japanese and Chinese style gardens so I asked her to describe this garden to me."

Doris paused and laughed, "It took her three hours until we got thrown out of the pub at closing time! She just couldn't shut up about the place. We went back to her cottage on the estate and she showed me her photographs of the gardens and, even on the photos, it was obvious that it was somewhere very special indeed. She had hundreds of them. We sat up all night with a bottle of port whilst she showed me through her photographs. She described every last detail of the photos. There was all kinds of stuff: historical details, the names of the people responsible for certain features, the names of particular aspects, the stories behind every piece of the garden. I was enthralled. I decided, then and there, that I had to see these gardens.

Arabella told me that she'd give me a letter of introduction to the owner of the gardens and the head gardener. I didn't think much about that at the time. I just thought it was a common courtesy. Goddess I was naïve. When I got back to London I looked up Mathom Hall to see if I could garner more information. I came up with nearly zilch. It was incredible. Hardly anybody seemed to have written anything about the place. There were a few references to it in the history books, the odd casual mention here and there and a few very brief descriptions but otherwise nothing. It started to feel unreal. I mean here according to Arabella was one of the greatest stately homes in Britain and you couldn't even find a brochure on the place. That was quite new in my experience. I mean most stately homes are all too eager to publicise themselves and get the paying public in but not this one. I tried some inquiries to find out what were the public opening hours and found out that there weren't any.

I didn't have much better luck when I tried to look up the owner of the place. When you think about it you'd think that a fabulously rich and influential, beautiful widow would be in and out of the socialite press nearly continuously. You'd think she'd have paparazzi camped out permanently on the front lawn. But no. I was damned hard pushed to find anything at all about her. It was days before I even found a photograph of her. When I did see a photo of her I was more puzzled than ever. I mean even on film she was just stunning. You'd have thought that every tabloid photographer worth their salt would have been making tracks towards Mathomdale. This after all was a woman it was nearly impossible to take a bad photo of. I asked around a few journalist friends but very few seemed to know much about her and those that did tended to go all quiet and thoughtful on you. It didn't seem credible. This was one of the most eligible women in Britain after all. I mean talk about your Aussie dream girl; rich, beautiful and owns more public houses than most breweries do.

Well I took the question to my editor and when I told her that I had a letter of introduction to Lady Mathom she nearly peed herself. It turned out that she'd been trying to get inside Mathom Hall for the better part of a decade without success and I just come flouncing in with a personal letter of introduction. I found out that the magazine had run one story on the Hall and its grounds but that had been over ten years ago. We dug the story out. It didn't amount to much; a couple of pages, a few photographs of the Hall and grounds and no mention whatsoever of the Oriental Gardens. There was one stunning photo however of Lady Mathom herself reclining against the big fountain in front of the Hall with the front façade as a backdrop. I couldn't tear my eyes from it. The reporter that had run the story had retired in the meantime and was living down in Somerset so I drove down there to see him. He was nearly in raptures when he described the Hall and its grounds. He was almost bitter that space had precluded more than a brief article. In his opinion the place deserved a whole book on it. I wanted to know if he'd heard of the Oriental Gardens. Oh he'd heard of them all right. He'd even been in them but he hadn't been allowed to take photographs. He was spitting blood over that. I told him about Arabella and how she thought them to be the finest landscape gardens in England. Well, to be honest, I think he felt that she was doing them less than justice. I had to beg him to shut up about them.

Well I sat down and wrote a grovelling, fawning letter to Lady Mathom begging permission to visit her lovely gardens. My editor thought I had no chance actually. Personal invitations to visit Mathom Hall were as rare as rocking horse shit she told me. She couldn't believe it when about a week later I received this hand written letter, on Mathom Hall letterhead in the most exquisitely crafted copper plate handwriting you ever saw, formally inviting me to Mathom Hall to visit her gardens. Of course, what I didn't know was that Arabella had already been in private correspondence with Her Ladyship. I don't know the exact details of that correspondence but it doesn't take much working out. Something along the lines of "My Dear Lady Mathom, about that vacancy for a slave in the Oriental Gardens, well I've just met this girl that……" The upshot of it was that I walked straight into a classic Mathom Hall trap.

I came up here with a photographer believing in my naivety that I was just coming up to visit some gardens without the foggiest notion that the real purpose of the exercise was for Lady Mathom and Shiro-san to have a look at me. I didn't have an earthly. The Lady took one look at me and to all intents and purposes that was me; sealed, signed and delivered. She brought me over to the Oriental Gardens to meet Shiro-san and she might as well have had her chain me up on the spot. I stayed for the next six weeks in the garden whilst my editor had screaming blue fits back in London wondering what the hell was happening to me. Those six weeks changed my life entirely. After them there was no other place in the world where I wanted to live. I'd found my way back to the garden. I left for a while to resign my position and set my affairs in order and then I returned here and I've never left since." Doris giggled, "That article never did get written."

"And you're not allowed to leave Doris?" asked Jennifer.

"That's right lady. We seven are forbidden to step beyond the boundaries of the garden except in very exceptional circumstances."

"Doesn't that cut you off from the world a bit?" Jennifer wanted to know.

"Oh I suppose so though not as much as you might think. I mean we do have lots of contact with people outside. People visit us all the time and so on. We get the newspapers delivered every day. We even watch television. We're all fanatic Manchester United fans and we never miss a game on the television."

"Yer kiddin' me!" laughed Alice. The vision of these cloistered elegant ladies and gentlemen gathered around a television set in their kimonos rooting for a football team was just too incongruous to imagine.

"Not at all. If United have a slump in form we all go into collective grief around here. We reckon they've got a chance in the league this year as well. Bloody Chelsea can't win it every sodding year."

"Give over!" Alice giggled. "Yer'll be tellin' me you 'ave a picture of Wayne Rooney on yer flippin' bedroom wall next."

"Oh I wouldn't go that far. He's a great player but I wouldn't like to have to wake up and see his face every morning." Alice shook her head in disbelief. Things at Mathom Hall were never quite what they seemed to be. This was further evidenced by a sudden commotion in front of the party. A party of four young boys in shorts came tearing around a bend in front of them in a body shouting gleefully. Shiro-san smiled at them but Doris clicked her tongue in exasperation. "Boys." she commanded. "We have visitors." The four youngsters skidded to a halt guiltily and bowed hastily before the guests in polite deference.

The eldest one who appeared to be about eleven years old acted as spokesman. "Thank you for gracing our garden miladies." The girls smiled at the youngster and bowed in return.

Doris addressed the eldest boy. "Terry what on earth have you done to your knee?"

The young boy looked down at his scuffed and bleeding kneecap shamefacedly "I fell off the swing mam."

Doris clucked in irritation and squatted down to examine the boy's knee. "I can't take my eyes off you for one minute. Look at the state of you! Go and wash it and put some ointment and a plaster on it this instance."

"Yes mam."

Doris turned to the amused girls and introduced the young boys. "I don't think you've met my sons Jennifer, or you Alice, have you. This is Terry and this is Richard and these are two of their friends Paul and Martin."

"We're pleased to meet you boys." Said Jennifer with a smile.

The boys bowed once more. "Pleased to meet you too ladies." Terry told them "Thank you for t' gift of yer presence." Alice shook her head in bemusement. They were just boys like any boys, apt to get into scrapes and mischief but they were well brought up and you couldn't fault their manners.

"Now run along and see to that knee and play a bit more quietly boys. We're entertaining the High Ladies of the Hall this evening and they don't want you disturbing them."

"Please mam?" Terry ventured nervously.

"Yes Terry?"

Terry bowed formally to his mother. "These two boys would ask their mother a favour mam."

"Go on."

"We would 'umbly ask that Paul and Martin be allowed to stay over tonight mam."

"Have you asked your mum and dad Paul?" Doris wanted to know.

"Yes lady. They say we can if'n it's all right wi you."

"Well if Dave and Janet say it's all right of course Paul and Martin can stay. But don't be playing around near the palace whilst we're entertaining visitors, all right Terry."

"No mam. Thanks mam." Terry's eyes were shining with joy.

"Go along then and get that knee seen to and for the love of the Goddess play a bit more carefully!"

"Yes mam. Come on guys... let's go up the dragon pagoda." The boys rushed away in glee.

Doris sighed "Dammit! You need nerves of steel to be a parent."

"Yer raise yer kids in the garden 'ere ma-am?" asked Alice in wonderment.

Doris laughed and swept a hand around to indicate the glory of the enchanting landscape in an encompassing gesture. "Can you think of a better place to raise kids?" Alice looked around and saw the thousands of corners and crannies, every bewitching pavilion a secret den, every copse of trees a hiding place, every lake a boating pool, every stream an obstacle, every tree a challenge, every pool a hunting ground and around every corner a new adventure. It would be a truly golden childhood spent among the glory of these gardens she realised. It was the ultimate adventure playground; a child's paradise.

"Are there more children in here?" Jennifer wanted to know.

"Oh heavens yes!" Doris told her "We've got eleven of them between us. Ming alone has got four of them."

"You 'ave four kids Ming?" Alice asked the beautiful Chinese girl.

"Ah yes lady. One I brought to the garden when I came here. One I have had while in the garden and two we have adopted."

Shiro-san smiled "What would a garden be without the laughter of children lady?"

"Yes there's always kids around." said Doris. They're always having their friends over during the school holidays as well. Kids love it in here. I'll be glad when the school term starts and we can get a bit of peace and quiet during the day again."

"They go to school?" asked Alice.

"Of course they go to school."

"There're lots of kids living on and around the estates Alice." Abigail told her. "During term time the school bus picks them all up at the Hall each day."

"Blimey I 'ad no idea. Does Terry and Richard's dad live 'ere as well Doris."

"They have different fathers Alice. I have two husbands. They don't live permanently here in the same way that I do but they visit often and I keep a house for them. They dote on the two boys and spoil them wretched when they're here."

“It must be a very safe place for children in the Garden Doris.” Jennifer observed.

“Yes but is the garden safe from them?” asked Doris with a laugh. “Earlier this summer my two little villains started a fire in one of the pavilions. Shiro was just amused but I went bloody ballistic. The two little horrors won’t forget that leathering in a hurry.”

The girls laughed. Jennifer was touched by the image of the Garden’s families. It was strange that she hadn’t thought of it before. Now she realised that it was entirely appropriate, inevitable really that there would be children in the Garden. Shiro-san’s domain grew all manner of things. In a sense the whole garden was a celebration of fertility. It was only right and fitting that the carers of the garden blessed its perfection with their own seed. Shiro-san led them on into the heart of her realm.

Chapter Eighteen

Following the girls but at some distance behind, still in the outer gardens and parklands in fact, Daniel and Darren were making their way on foot to the Oriental Gardens and grumbling mightily about it too. "I," declared Daniel firmly, "feel like a complete prat dressed like this."

Darren was apt to agree with him. "Why the hell do we have to wear these swords?" he wanted to know. Mrs Yakamura had equipped the two young men with two pairs of matching samurai swords, a long katana each matched with a short wakizashi, tucked into the obis of their kimonos.

"Dunno, Cos it looks good and makes us look like a pair of samurai I suppose. As opposed to a pair of idiots."

"It's a hell of goddamn fashion accessory."

"Tell me about it. I'm scared ter death o' doin' mesen a mischief on 'em."

"How much further are these damn gardens anyway? These damn clogs are murdering my feet."

"I 'aven't a clue. I think we have to get over that rise and they're down in the next valley. So that Japanese woman told us anyway."

"Jesus! It's goddamn miles! This place is huge."

"I thought you'd be used ter big properties Darren. Didn't yer say yer lived on a ranch back 'ome?"

"Sure and it's a day's ride to cross it but that's wild open country. This is a goddamn garden for Chrissakes!"

"Yeah an' Becky said that t' bloody Oriental Gardens themselves is ovver four mile long. God knows 'ow we're gonna find t' lasses!"

"Jesus!

"It's all Becky's fault. This were 'er idea to get all dressed up in these poncey clothes. She don't 'alf come up wi some daft ideas that lass."

“Hey what was that message that guy brought you just before we set off?”

“Oh aye. I’d forgotten about that. The Lady’s back. She wants ter see t’ pair of us in ‘er chambers fust thing tomorrow. Straight after breakfast before we go off ter work.”

“Holy shit! Why do I have to be there?”

“Dunno Darren. Yer don’t tend ter query t’ Lady’s orders. She snaps ‘Er fingers an’ you come runnin’. I nearly shit mesen when I ‘eard she was back. I thought she were goin’ ter summon us straight away. Can yer imagine ‘avin’ ter parade in front ov ‘Er dressed like a pair o’ bloody clowns?”

“Jesus it doesn’t bear thinking about.”

“Could be worse Darren. I’ve bin up in front ov ‘Er in me birthday suit before terday.”

“You’re kidding me!”

“Straight up. Not a bloody stitch on.”

“What the hell for?”

“Oh er she just wanted to ‘ave me examined. There was a doctor there and me an Alice ‘ad to ‘ave a medical examination.” Daniel coyly omitted the details of the occasion when he had been examined by Dr Chandra and studiously avoided any reference to the by now infamous follow up when he had been obliged to provide a sperm sample.

“No way I’d do that.” stated Darren feelingly.

“You would do Darren. If t’ Lady ordered yer ter tek every last stitch o’ clothin’ off yer’d do it. Trust me. She’s not a woman overly comfortable with the word no for an answer.”

“Christ! She sounds like a goddamn dictator.”

“She is a dictator Darren. Mathom ‘All ain’t no democracy believe me an’ everyone round ‘ere knows oo the top dog is.”

“This place is so goddamned feudal. Jenny told me Lady Mathom even beats the girls.”

"Oh aye. She's not a woman as believes in sparin' the rod ain't the Lady. Becky were telling us that she 'ad 'er, Abi, Jenny an' t' twins in 'Er chambers only last week fer a good idin'."

"Has she ever … well you know… beaten Alice?"

"No not yet Darren. Or me for that matter. It's only a matter o' time though. She likes ter keep 'Er arm in apparently."

"Jesus you mean she'd beat you as well?"

"Well aye. I'm one ov 'Er slaves Darren. T' Lady's a great believer in 'avin' 'Er slaves thrashed regular. Reckons it's good for their mental an' spiritual well bein'."

"I don't believe this. You'd honestly let her?"

"Darren yer can't get yer 'ead around this can yer? I keep tellin' yer. The Lady's word is law around 'ere. She sez do summat an' yer do it. If she sez drop yer pants for t' cane then down they come an' no arguments about it. She's t' boss."

"She ain't my boss."

"Not yet she isn't. She soon will be though. Yer not 'ere ter just work in one o' t' offices Darren. I've told yer before. Yer've bin sold 'ere as a slave. T' sooner yer get that inter yer 'ead the better. Yer can kick an' fight as much as yer want it won't do yer a bit o' good. If t' Lady likes t' look o' yer an' decides she'll 'ave yer as a slave then yer'll be sportin' yer brand new Mathom 'All brand before t' days out."

"She can't enslave me against my will."

"It won't be against yer will Darren. You'll see."

"Jesus! This place is just crazy."

Daniel laughed "Don't worry about it mate. Me I'm looking forward ter 'avin' a brother in t' ouse apart from Robin." Daniel thumped Darren affectionately on the shoulder "Tell yer what though mate. If'n we do 'ave ter drop us pants fer t' Lady's cane we'll mek damn sure we've done summat worthwhile to 'ave earned it." The two young men passed on in great companionship and if Darren was more and more appalled by everything he saw and heard in Mathom Hall he nevertheless took great pleasure from his flowering friendship with Daniel.

At length, they came to the bridge that led across the stream into the gardens beyond. Waiting for them on the far side was the tall, beautiful Daniela and the strikingly fine boned African woman Nadira, both dressed in fabulous kimonos. They bowed low as the two young men approached the bridge. "Welcome to our Garden my lords. Would it please you to enter?"

"Er… er sure we…." Darren began nervously before a nudge from Daniel reminded him of his manners.

"Bow yer twit!" Daniel hissed under his breath and the two of them did so, if somewhat awkwardly. Rebecca had warned Daniel to ask for formal permission to enter if the bridge was manned and so, acting as spokesman, he stuttered out a faltering request. "Er these two men…. that's me and me mate 'ere… would like ter ask yer permission to er… you know enter inter yer gardens ladies. That's er…. if'n it's all right like."

"Why of course lord." Nadira told him "You are very welcome. May we humbly ask however that you leave your weapons at the bridge here."

"Oh... er…. Aye... of course." said Daniel self-consciously divesting himself of his two swords.

"Hey Danny?" asked Darren in sudden concern "You think it's ok just to leave these swords here? I mean they're damn museum pieces aren't they? They're probably valuable."

"Please have no fear lord." Daniela assured him "Your weapons will be quite safe. One moment please." She disappeared into the small hut to reappear quickly with a large flat cushion that she held out in great formality. "If you would care to place your weapons on here my lords I will place them in the bridge house and nobody will touch them I promise." There was an air of almost ritual solemnity in the act of surrendering their weapons and Daniela bowed low as they placed the sheathed blades on the cushion. In a curious way Darren almost felt undressed without his swords as Daniela took the four fine blades reverently. Daniela looked at the swords with eyes wide in wonder. "May I have your permission to examine your swords my lords?"

"Sure go ahead." Darren told her. Daniela slid the blades carefully part way from their sheaths and her wonder grew.

"They will be very safe my lords. I will appoint a guard to take care of them."

"Oh gee! You don't have to go to that trouble." insisted Darren.

"Oh but I must sir. These blades are very precious. They are Kanemichi swords of the Mishina School crafted in the latter part of the sixteenth century sir. I thought my eyes were deceiving me for a moment. You do me great honour in entrusting them to my care my lords. They are priceless."

"Oh Jesus!" breathed Darren appalled to learn that the swords he had been bearing so ill humouredly were of such ancient lineage and intrinsic value.

"I will place them under guard my lords. Nobody will be allowed to touch them. I promise you." Daniela scurried away with her precious burdens to place them safely in the bridge house.

"If you will follow me my lords I will conduct you to the palace." Nadira told them. She led them off through the gardens. Within minutes both young men were awestruck by the harmonious loveliness of the Oriental Gardens.

"Jesus Danny have you ever seen anything like this place?" asked Darren in growing astonishment.

Daniel shook his head "Nay! Never! I thought t' rest o' t' gardens was bonny enough but this teks the biscuit. Look at that bloody pagoda there. Yer'd swear blind it were growing straight out o' that copse o' trees." The pagoda was extraordinary. It was fashioned in such a way that it's lower part appeared like the roots and bole of an enormous growing tree but as it climbed higher it lost the gnarled appearance of living wood and achieved a spire like symmetry towering above the surrounding trees in triumphant grace and crowned at its very apex with a golden cupola like a great fruit or flower shining at its tip. It was easy to see the architect's point in this metamorphosis from a randomly growing natural plant into this elegant symmetrical structure and in some ways it epitomised the very essence of the Oriental Gardens themselves by way of the fashioning of nature into harmonising artifice. "If I could build owt like that I'd call meself a builder." Daniel said feelingly.

"Jesus! This place is unreal." breathed Darren. "I keep expecting to turn the next corner and find a gingerbread house."

"'Ave yer noticed t' path we're walkin' on Darren?" asked Daniel.

"Sure have! We come across a scarecrow or a tin man and I'm gonna lose it." The path was fashioned from yellow bricks.

Nadira overheard them and laughed. "Actually lords we sometimes call the island in the lake where Shiro-san has her palace Ireland! Quite apt don't you think?" By the time they crossed the causeway to the island, the two men were entirely under the spell of Shiro-san's creation. They found the girls squatting on a veranda chattering animatedly over a flask of hot rice wine and it seemed entirely appropriate that the familiar young women were transformed into such exotic creatures by their fantastic dress.

"Bloody 'ell lasses!" Daniel exclaimed, "You look bloody amazing!"

“Why thank you kind sir.” Rebecca told him, coyly fanning herself with a gorgeously decorated fan “You boys look very nice too.” Daniel and Darren looked sheepishly at their own costumes. They wore the somewhat drab colours, greys and browns, of a man’s kimono and looked dull in comparison with the fabulous costumes of their lady consorts.

“’Ere ‘ave some o’ this sake Danny.” Alice told her husband. “I don’t suppose they do draught bitter in ‘ere.”

Ming Ue was serving the sake and laughed. “But of course we have beer my lords. If you would prefer that, I can very soon fetch some.”

“Nay lady. We’ll stick wi what t’ lasses is drinkin’.” Daniel grinned. “That all right wi you Darren?”

“Sure thing. When in Rome….”

They sipped the hot wine in pleasure “Where’s Julie then?” asked Daniel.

“Not got here yet.” Rebecca informed him “Shiro-san’s despatched Doris and Ricky up toward the top gate to intercept her and bring her down here when she arrives.”

“’Ere won’t Julie be a bit put out bein’ t’ only one in western dress like?” Alice asked concernedly.

Abigail grinned evilly “Sorted Alice. I had a word with Shiro-san. As soon as Miss Hawthorne gets her pretty little fanny here Shiro’s girls are going to bully her into a kimono. They’ve got a bloody fabulous creation all laid out and waiting for her and they reckon they can get her into it in under an hour.”

“Oh wow!” cried Jennifer in glee “That’s going to be something to see.”

“Yes!” said Abigail wickedly, “Our little wayward shop girl won’t know what’s hit her.”

Chapter Nineteen

Julie already didn't know what had hit her. In fact Doris and Ricardo were too late to intercept her at the top gate because she had already been inside the Oriental Garden for over an hour. She was wandering around in a complete daze. It was not entirely accurate to say that she was lost. In the purely physical meaning of that word, all things being equal, she could have negotiated her way through the gardens with ease. No her purposeless meandering was more a spiritual malaise than it was a mere loss of direction. She hadn't so much as lost her way in the gardens as lost her way in her life. The bewildering events that had overtaken her in the last weeks were finally beginning to overwhelm her. The sheer unreality of the experiences that had so come to dominate her life were leaving her in a void of uncertainties, rudderless on a turbulent sea and lacking a pilot to guide her through the shoals. She had been building toward a crisis for many days now and then she'd wandered down into this dreamscape and her powers to think rationally had left her completely.

In some distant part of her mind Julie knew she had a rendezvous to meet but she wandered aimlessly through the gardens lost in revelry entirely bewitched. Somewhere or other she'd lost any sense of purpose. She felt drugged, intoxicated in a temporal void where a meeting by the clock had become meaningless. She sat down by the side of a tiny brook, almost heart-breaking in its perfection, and her handbag slipped from her grasp to lie forgotten on the verdant grass as she drifted away once more into the beguiling groves.

She felt like a ghost, a wraith that would pass unseen or perhaps like a shimmering image on the edge of visibility, as she passed through the gardens. People might detect her presence with some forgotten sense and shiver as she passed their way, lost in limbo. She felt an enormous melancholy in her forlorn wanderings. She paused to cry often, although whether her tears came from the beauty of her surroundings or her hopeless desolation lost within them, she was at a loss to understand. How strange her life had become, she reflected. Where now was the Julie Hawthorne that she'd thought she'd known? Where was the girl that had so studiously clung to her extrovert persona as the simple lass that ran a little shop on the village square? Who was this strange woman that seemed to be replacing her? Who was this woman that Eleanor, Rosalyn and Astrid seemed to think she was? Why had her life drifted into this strange deceit?

In the enchanted groves of the Oriental Gardens Julie had found a halting place on the onward rush of her life; a siding on the railroad into the future where she could step aside and look in bewilderment at the rails that carried the express train of the preceding days racing past in thunder to unforeseen destinations. As she paused by the side of a small pool the absurdity of her present life hammered at her consciousness in a torment of guilt and helplessness. The process that had started with her befriending Debra and her pretence up at Waterstone House had become a monster that had gathered her up effortlessly and precipitated her into one event after another beyond her control. The deceit had fed upon itself leading her into a labyrinth of pretence and illusion.

The pressures on her from the people around her had become intolerable; Eleanor and Debra, Astrid, Rosalyn and their families, her own family with its intractable looming crisis, they all combined to press her into an existence she did not believe in. After all she no more belonged under the elegant eaves of Waterstone House or among the sprawling acres of the Ramone homestead than she did here in these fabulous gardens. Oh it was true that she had imagined a life of great happiness and fulfilment either at Eleanor's house or on the homestead but that life depended upon a lie. She could be happy at either place as herself but that was not what was required was it? She was required to be something else, an illusion of a person that wasn't her, a bizarre impostor, living out a life of deception always on the brink of exposure. In these quiet gardens there was no room for pretence between Julie and her soul. Here there was only the bitter honesty of a person that looks into their inner self and sees the deceptions that they have woven about their self. It was impossible. Julie saw that now. All the promises of the past days were as much an illusion as this fantastically contrived landscape.

There was still a part of her mind that told her she had a dinner party to attend, her beloved Jennifer and Rebecca to see. The thought nagged at her that she really ought to be making some effort to find the other girls but, at the last, she felt a great reluctance to do so. That was just one further perpetration of her lie was it not? She did not belong among their company; she did not belong here or anywhere within this artful dreamland. She should leave now whilst her newfound integrity lasted. Her life had spun out of control and she felt the tendrils of panic clutching at her spine in a cold chill. In a sense she felt a terrible loneliness in this place where she could no longer lie to herself but it was not a loneliness that could be assuaged in the company of the girls from Mathom Hall. She needed to come to terms with her own company and that was difficult enough.

Nevertheless her wanderings brought her at last to the edge of the lake surrounding the island on which Shiro-san's pavilion stood. The dinner party was sat on a veranda at the very edge of the water engrossed in animated conversation. Julie watched them from behind some tall reeds and her breath caught in her throat.

The girls were just beginning to worry about Julie's absence. Rebecca had tried to call Julie on her mobile but the phone had rung unheeded in Julie's bag, abandoned by the stream. Jennifer's face was starting to look strained. Julie never saw this from her vantage point. All she saw was the incredible loveliness of the girls, in their Japanese finery, gently fanning themselves in the evening sunlight like a group of fantastically ornamented dolls; exquisite, delicate and in harmony with the beautiful surroundings. In a dreadful moment, Julie felt suddenly coarse and vulgar; her pretty party dress cheap and common. Now, more than ever, she felt like an interloper in this domain; a trespasser in an environment not designed for the likes of her. What remained of her courage deserted her and, with a strangled sob, she turned to flee.

She was running wildly through the gardens now, sobbing in self-pity, only wanting to escape this alien place, her hair flying as she ran. It was foolish to try and run in high heels and she stumbled and fell, breaking the heel on her right shoe. With the panic now overwhelming her, she kicked her shoes aside with a sob and fled onwards trying to find her way back up to the top gate. The trees were spinning around her and the sounds of her crying were sounding hollow and metallic as if reverberating in a great metal cavern. She recognised the sudden attack immediately. "Oh no not now!" she whispered to herself but the spinning became more dizzying, the swirl of the light around her turned into a blur and a dreadful echoing vibration rose to a crescendo in her head. She stumbled once more and then the vibration overwhelmed her and she collapsed senseless on a gentle lawn.

She was a long time regaining consciousness, coming back to her senses with the terrible weariness with which her attacks always left her. She had bruised her leg as she had fallen and her dress was dirty from her fall but she did not notice these things. For a few moments she just felt terribly tired yet at peace for her head was cradled in a soothing lap and there was a hand stroking her tangled hair. She opened her eyes and through their blur she saw a beautiful woman, whom she had never seen before, dressed in a kimono, looking down at her in concern. Doris was squatting on the grass holding her gently and watching her struggle back from the void. Richard, one of Shiro-san's male acolytes was kneeling down close by, his face worried. "Is she all right?"

"I think so Ricky. She had some kind of a fit or something but she seems to be coming round."

Julie murmured, "Oo are yer ma-am?"

"I'm Doris. Are you Julie Hawthorne?" she asked. Julie nodded miserably. "I think you had a fit Julie. Are you all right? Shall we call a doctor?"

"No ma-am. I…. I'll be all right in a minute."

"Have you had these fits before Julie?"

"Y… yes ma-am. I get 'em a lot."

"Well let's get you up off the ground Julie and somewhere where you can lie down for a while. Will you help her Ricky?"

"Of course." Richard took Julie in his arms and lifted her easily "Come along miss let's get you out of here."

"We'll take her to the nearest guest pavilion Ricky. The Maple House. It's not far." Gently Richard carried her with Doris walking alongside soothing her with comforting words. At the pavilion they took her inside and laid her down on a futon. Doris knelt to examine her, her face full of maternal concern. "We'd best be telling your friends Julie. They'll be worried about you."

"No ma-am! Please! I don't want them to see me like this. Please ma-am. I just want ter go 'ome."

Julie's voice was dangerously close to panic once more. Doris decided to let it rest. "Very well Julie. But I think you ought to rest a while first. How are you getting home?"

"Me mam said she'd pick us up." Julie looked around her in sudden consternation "Oh 'ell I've lost me bag. 'Ow am ah gonna call me mam up?"

"Hush Julie. We'll find your bag. Don't worry. If not we've a telephone here that we can use to call your mother. Just take it easy all right. Just lie back and try to relax ok?"

"Y… yes ma-am. Thank you ma-am." Doris conferred quickly and quietly with Richard and he departed before Doris knelt once more by the side of the futon to hold Julie's hand. At Shiro-san's pavilion the girls were increasingly worried about Julie's whereabouts when Richard returned there to kneel by Shiro and whisper in her ear. Shiro looked concerned and rose elegantly to her feet.

"If you will excuse me my ladies Richard and Doris have found your companion but there appears to be some problem. Please remain here and I will attend to it." The girls were suddenly thrown into consternation.

"What… what's happened Shiro-san?" squeaked Jennifer in alarm.

"Nothing that we cannot deal with lady Jennifer. Please do not be concerned. I shall attend to the matter personally." With that Shiro-san, accompanied by Richard, left the party and made her way to the Maple House pavilion. Julie was beginning to recover a little by now. Doris had given her a small brandy and she was feeling better if a little foolish. Her eyes opened wide as the extraordinary figure of Shiro-san entered. Richard had some things for her.

"Is this your bag Julie? I found it by the stream a bit lower down."

"Y.. yes thank you sir."

"I couldn't find your shoes though I'm afraid."

"That's all right sir. They're broken anyway."

"Well I'll go and have another look in any case."

"We can find Julie some sandals to wear." Doris pointed out.

"Th… thank you ma-am." Julie murmured very aware that Shiro-san was observing her closely.

"What happened Doris?" asked Shiro.

"I think Julie had a fit lady. I saw her running away in hysterics and I chased after her. When I found her she'd collapsed and lost consciousness. Julie says she has these fits quite often."

"I see." Shiro looked closely at the fear and confusion in the young girl's face and she knelt by the futon to reach out and stroke a hand down Julie's face. "There's more than just a tale of physical distress here though I think. This is a young lady with a story to tell. Would you excuse us for a little while Doris? I would like to hear this story."

"Of course Shiro-sama. I will see if I can find some sandals for her." Doris rose and left. Shiro took Julie's hands and smiled gently at her. Julie took encouragement from the tranquillity of this beautiful Japanese lady and the beginning of a watery smile played across her features.

"I knew your mother well Julie. It has been many years since she last visited us here. Is she well?"

"Y… yes ma-am. She still remembers t' times she spent 'ere! She were tellin' us all about it terday."

"She is a fine lady your mother Julie. I was sad when she stopped visiting us. You must tell her that we wait for her in these gardens still. She cannot run from her dreams forever."

"I… I'm sorry ma-am?"

"Never mind. Just tell her that. She will know what I mean."

"Y.. yes ma-am."

"And you my little cherry blossom? What brings you to the Garden of Dreams?"

"I…. I were invited to a party ma-am."

"Ah Julie. So sorry but that is only a little part of the story isn't it? People find their way to the Garden in many different fashions Julie. I would like to hear of the path you took. Would you trust me with your story? I will tell no one beyond the walls of this little house, not even whisper it down the well at midnight. But you should tell me your story for some stories are too great a burden to carry alone."

And Julie did. Encouraged and prompted by the soft gentleness of this remarkable lady she poured out her whole story. It took a long time for she omitted nothing. It was a catharsis for her to tell her tale to this infinitely patient and understanding woman. From the moment when her world had been turned upside down upon falling in love with Jennifer she traced her way through Jennifer's enslavement to Mathom Hall, the bitterness of the social divide that had separated them, her friendship with Debra, her pretence at Waterstone House, Eleanor's bid to purchase her, her familial troubles, all about the counter bid from Astrid and Rosalyn. Julie had never before so opened her heart to a person in quite this way. She spoke of her fears and her guilty deceits. She talked about her dread of exposure and the illusions of her ambitions to join the exalted households above her station. Shiro sat long with her and listened in great calmness never judging or voicing any opinion just urging her to talk. At last Julie traced the way through her story to that evening when her mother had brought her into these gardens and of her mother's sadness. She came at last to her soul searching in the gardens and the panic that had gripped her when she observed the other girls from behind the reeds across the lake. Shiro-san just nodded her head with a secret smile.

"Yer must think I'm daft ma-am." said Julie at last.

"Oh no my precious. Anything but."

"But it's a daft story isn't it?"

"It's a very old story Julie, my little minikui kogama. You can't hide behind the reeds forever."

"I…. I don't understand."

"Do you not? Well you will one day. But now we must get you home. You were not ready to come to the Garden. You will return when you are ready. Let us phone your mother so that she can take you home. I will make your apologies to your friends."

"Jenny will be mad at me!"

"I will explain to her. She will understand."

"Please ma-am. What's wrong wi me?"

"Nothing Julie. Nothing at all. Stop hating yourself for what you are. Or what you think you are. Come now I will call Doris and we shall accompany you to the gate and see you safely away."

Doris gave Julie a pair of sandals as she phoned her mother to explain that she'd had one of her "turns" and needed to be taken home. Mrs Hawthorne was distressed on the telephone and told them she would set off immediately. Then Doris and Shiro took lamps, for the evening had fallen in, and walked Julie back up through the gardens to the top gate. Julie felt much calmer now after unburdening herself to Shiro-san but she was exhausted by her ordeal and it seemed a long way up to the top gate. Mrs Hawthorne was already waiting for them and she rushed to hug her daughter beside herself with worry.

"Oh Julie are yer all right love?"

"Aye mam honest! T' lady 'ere looked after us! I'm all right now."

Mrs Hawthorne turned and bowed to Shiro. "Thank yer lady fer lookin' after our Julie. I don't know what I'd 'ave done if owt 'ad 'ave appened to 'er."

Shiro smiled. "It was my pleasure lady. I would like to thank you for the gift of your daughter. It has been long since I last saw you. I have missed you."

"Aye well yer know 'ow it is. Life moves on an' all that."

"Does it really? I know nothing of this life." Shiro turned to Julie "Thank you for your story Julie. I have a little gift for you that I took from the pavilion." She reached into her obi and produced a little box. "There is a name that comes with this gift. A new name for you. Henceforth in these gardens you will be known as Hakuchou. Come back to us soon Hakuchou."

Julie took the box and bowed overcome with emotion. "P.... please ma-am. Thank you fer takin' care o' me. I'm sorry I was so much trouble like."

"It was no such trouble Hakuchou." Shiro-san told her. "I enjoyed your story. I will enjoy hearing the rest of it."

"Yer'll say sorry ter t' lasses for us ma-am?"

"Yes. Have no fear."

"An' yer'll tell Jenny an' Becky I love them?"

"I will but soon you will return to tell them yourself."

Julie bowed once more. Shiro and Doris returned the bow and turned to walk back into the Garden. In her mother's car Julie opened the box and found a beautiful little brooch of white gold in it, fashioned in the likeness of a flying swan.

Chapter Twenty

The dinner party at Shiro-san's pavilion had died in the face of the worry over Julie. Food had been served but the company had picked at it listlessly aware that the evening was ruined. Jennifer was in tears and seemed inconsolable. Rebecca fought hard to keep back her own tears and the desperation that she could not comfort Jennifer adequately because of some division between them that she was at a loss to understand. Abigail was devastated that her party had turned out so poorly and that her careful plans to effect a reconciliation of the breaches between her sisters and their loved ones had failed and left them more isolated from each other than ever. It was a gloomy party to which Shiro-san and Doris eventually returned. Shiro-san took one look at the company and exclaimed "Why ladies, lords! Why is there such sadness here?"

"Oh Shiro-san!" cried Jennifer tearfully. "Where is Julie?"

"She has gone home lady."

Jennifer leapt to her feet very nearly tripping over the hem of her kimono. "Gone home? Why?"

"Peace lady. She was taken ill in the Garden and I thought it best that she returned home."

Doris intervened "She had some kind of fit lady. I found her unconscious on the ground. We let her rest for some time but my Mistress decided that it was better if she went home. Julie called her mother and she came to pick her up. We saw her safely to the top gate. She'll be fine. She just needs some rest. She said to say sorry to you all."

"Oh I must call her." cried Jennifer. "H… have you got your mobile Rebecca? I…. I've left mine in the house."

"No lady." Shiro-san interrupted. "She will go straight to her bed. It is best I think if you let her sleep. Leave her in peace."

"Oh Goddess!" said the distraught Jennifer "What if there'd been nobody there when she passed out? She… she might have died!"

"I think not lady." said Shiro-san. "She tells me that she has these fits regularly. I don't think she was in any danger."

Jennifer was clasping her hands frantically and tears ran down her face "I…. I should have been there. She needed me and I wasn't there."

"Hakuchou found what she needed lady. She will be at peace for a while now. She says that she loves you. Loves you and the lady Rebecca." Rebecca lowered her face her own tears flowing freely now.

"I…. I've lost her!" cried the desolate Jennifer.

Shiro-san took Jennifer's hands compassionately. "Ah no lady. There I think you are wrong. I think you are only just beginning to find her. She will return to you I am sure. She just needs to grow her new down."

"Wh… what do you mean?"

"Ah lady in the late summer the birds in the trees and on the lakes lose their old feathers. Whilst they grow their new ones they cannot fly well and so they must needs be quiet and hide until their new plumage emerges. One day, one day soon, your little Hakuchou will fly back to you. She will be beautiful in her new feathers. Please be comforted. Tonight was no tale of sadness lady. Tonight has brought great joy. Beyond your tears you will find that joy." Shiro-san released Jennifer's hands and addressed the company. "Come good people. Put tears aside. There should be laughter and gaiety in these gardens. No tragedy has happened. Why are we all so glum? Tonight I found my own Hakuchou. I thank the Goddess for the joy of her. She will return to my Garden and it will be more blessed than ever. Come let us drink sake. Let us eat and sing and share caresses in the night. Let us wash away the tears with love!" So powerful was Shiro-san's command that peace came back into the party and if it was not the bliss they had hoped for it at least recovered some semblance of happiness. Doris came over to Rebecca with a minor problem.

"Er lady I found Julie's shoes. Would you be able to give them back to her? I'm afraid one of the heels is broken however."

Rebecca took the shoes and examined them interestedly. "She should be able to repair them. Strange though."

"Why lady?"

"Oh it's just that I've never seen Julie wear such high heels before. She's usually just in a pair of sandals or trainers."

"I think she got dressed up for your party lady. Maybe she's just growing up. Maybe that's what Shiro-san meant. All young birds have to shed their fledgling plumage don't they?"

"Yes. Perhaps you're right. Thank you Doris. How far did Julie get before her attack?"

"Oh all the way. She made it as far as the edge of the lake. Apparently she saw you all from the reed beds before her attack began. She fled in panic when it started I think. I found her about quarter of a mile away when Ricky and I were returning down from the top gate thinking that she wasn't coming."

Helen was sat close by listening interestedly. "She was watching us from the reeds on the lake shore?"

"Yes lady."

"How interesting."

"I'm sure all you ladies and gentlemen must have been a wonderful sight. Forgive me I must fetch some more sake." Doris rose to attend to the provision of hot wine. Abigail drifted over and knelt by Rebecca and Helen with a sigh.

"Oh Becky! I'm sorry." she said. "I just wanted to sort things out between you, Jenny and Julie and it's all gone tits up. I've just made things worse by the looks of it."

Rebecca hugged her fiercely. "Abi! It's not your fault. You couldn't have planned for this happening."

"Jenny's gutted isn't she?"

Rebecca sighed, "Yes she is." Rebecca looked over to where a strained looking Jennifer was squatting being comforted by Alice, Daniel and Darren. "Goddess we could have done without this."

Helen was sat looking thoughtful "There's something else going on here girls."

"What do you mean Hell?" asked Abigail.

"Why did Shiro-san call Julie Hakuchou Abi?"

"Dunno Hell. That's not unusual though. I often don't understand why Shiro-san does something."

"What does it mean Hell?" asked Rebecca.

"It's the Japanese name for a swan Becky. Why did Shiro-san call Julie swan?"

Rebecca stared at Helen in surprise. "Goddess I don't know."

Helen gazed thoughtfully at the reflections of the lamps in the still waters of the lake. "I think we just fell into another story girls."

Rebecca held her breath as the import of Helen's words sank in. "Yes another story." She breathed. "Stories within stories. Dreams within dreams. They're all the same aren't they? We just keep repeating the same old stories over and over again." In bemusement Rebecca picked up Julie's damaged shoes and stared at them. "And where?" she asked, "have I heard this story before?"

Chapter Twenty-One

Early the next morning, Eugene parked the hired car in a safe car park in the city of Kingston. She'd had the girls up early today because they had a lot to do. They'd broken their fast and she'd piled them into the car and driven them through the countryside into the great port city that sprawled, as shapeless as a whale, on the northern banks of the great estuary. She was nervous about her charges for Kingston was a rough and ready sort of place where you needed your street wits about you and she was resolved to watch her young protégées like a hawk. It wasn't that she was any longer afraid of them running away. Over the past days she had gained their trust and now they were devoted to her but it was a dangerous city and all too easy for such untutored young people, as her three girls, to get into a good deal of trouble. Adding to her concerns as well was the fact that the girls were illegal immigrants with no papers. She believed the risk in that to be acceptable, however. Kingston was full of foreigners and three more would hardly elicit any undue attention. Nevertheless she intended to be careful and steer them away from any contact with the authorities.

"Ok girls." she told them as they mustered beside the parked car "I want you all to stick to me like glue. This is a big city and I don't want you getting lost. Ana I want you to take Vesna's hand and don't let it go for an instant. Understand?"

"Da lady."

"Please lady? Why we here today?" Mali wanted to know.

"We're going shopping Mali. You girls have nothing to wear. I can't be parading the bunch of you in front of my Mistress in a set of old borrowed clothes now can I?"

"Oh lady. You buy us clothes?"

"Yes Mali. We're going to put a sizeable input into the local economy today. Some boutique owner is going to think the Christmas season arrived early this year!"

"Sorry lady. You talk too fast."

"Never mind Mali. Come on girls. Hairdressers first. We have an appointment at the best hair salon this sad town can boast." Eugene led her small party out into the streets of the city centre. It had been a long time since Eugene had taken the leisure to walk through Kingston and she noted with agreeable surprise that the place had improved somewhat since her last visit. It was still the rough and edgy town it had always been but at least the city centre seemed to have smartened itself up somewhat with the demise of the old docks and fishing centre. There were smart new pedestrian precincts and up-market looking boutiques. The squares were not as littered with discarded pizza cartons and beer cans as they'd once been and there was less graffiti in evidence. Gone too were the sadly boarded up old shops and some of the more notable architectural monstrosities had been demolished to make way for modern looking shopping malls. They seemed to be taking more care of the wonderful old Victorian buildings that remained as a legacy of the city's glory days of wealth and influence, as well, and there seemed to be some rekindling of civic pride in the way the old iron railings were painted and gilded. The old docks that had once surrounded the city centre were no longer the hub of the city's maritime commerce. The main docks now lay to the east of the city and the old docks were converted into parks, lakes and yachting marinas, while the old warehouses along the waterfronts of them were metamorphosed into restaurants, hotels, offices and smart residential blocks. The place just looked better.

There were still the jarring notes however. There were still the inevitable beggars pleading for change along the streets. If anything the beggars had diminished in quality. Once upon a time they'd all had heart-wrenching stories to tell you about their poor impoverished mother and their terminally ill sister or something and they really looked as if they needed help. Now the beggars all looked ridiculously healthy and young and just asked you for change without the slightest effort apparently to convince you that they needed it. Some of them even whiled away the boredom by listening to music on clearly expensive MP3 players which hardly bespoke of terrible financial hardship.

One thing the population didn't seem to be doing was getting any slimmer. Eugene had never seen so many clinically obese people on a city street outside of the United States of America. She watched in disbelief as a party of young women waddled by, not one of them a pound under sixteen stone, eating burgers and chips as if they were trying to commit suicide by cholesterol overdose. Even Ana noticed it. "Please lady why people so fat here?"

"Because they eat too much Ana. Don't ever let me catch you girls getting like that. One ounce of excess flab on you and I'll take a stick to your backsides." The girls were excited about being footloose in the city however and Eugene's threats carried little sting. They followed after Eugene twittering excitedly and their eyes were everywhere staring into shop windows in wonder at the wares displayed there. Eugene had to remind herself that they all came from very poor backgrounds and even the wealth of a relatively depressed English city would seem awesome to them.

They crossed the main square of the city centre and it was generally rather pleasant surrounded as it was by venerable Victorian buildings glorious in their fanciful folly, sprouting pretentious neo-classical features, triumphal imperial statues and bristling with silly minarets and cupolas. They were just wonderful, the products of a more naïve age when their makers had been at the centre of a global empire and had seen nothing ridiculous at all about such indulgent ostentatious demonstrations of power and wealth. Eugene had to smile. You just had to love the Victorian English. They'd possessed more money than taste and better engineering skills than architectural style but their legacy of massive stone buildings were just innocent enough to avoid vulgarity and just silly enough to attract affection for them. She'd had to suppress her mirth at one huge civic building in the city centre crowned by an enormous statue (Goddess knew how they'd got the damn thing up there) of Britannia as a Roman Goddess riding a chariot pulled by a pair of snarling lions. It must have cost the civic authorities of the day a small fortune yet she wondered if anybody now even looked up and noticed it anymore. On the main square itself a huge statue of the old queen sat enthroned on a raised dais in the middle of the square, perched in all Her Imperial Majesty on top of the public lavatories, and nobody seemed to have noticed just how ludicrous that was.

Not that the civic authorities currently responsible for the running of the city were without their follies. There must be a tradition of squandering public money on useless public display Eugene thought for a jarring note on the square was provided by an enormous television screen several metres high that was blaring out the daily news across the square in the morning sunlight and being studiously ignored by the local populace. She'd read in a local paper that it had cost the city's taxpayers a cool 600,000 pounds. Goddess knew what the city council was thinking about. Did they honestly think that people might fancy slipping down to the city square to watch Coronation Street or something? Was there a plan in effect to provide every taxpayer with a remote control so they could change channels whilst ambling into the square or was it just erected to provide entertainment for the homeless tramps on the square at night? Eugene reflected that if it had been her taxes that had been frittered away on such expensive idiocy she'd have been tempted to come along one night and heave a brick through it. The girls, particularly Vesna, were fascinated by it however and Eugene made a mental note to incapacitate any television sets around in any accommodation they might be obliged to use. The last thing she wanted was for her young charges to have their brains addled by the meaningless trivia of popular television entertainment. Let them get addicted to books instead. Even a very bad book was more educational than "Big Brother".

There was one old familiar landmark for which Eugene had a great deal of affection and she took the girls on a detour to see it. It was an enormous great blackened column with a statue of one of the city's proudest sons acting as a pigeon roost high above the street on the edge of a park and sadly somewhat challenged for a prominent position on the skyline by a monumentally ugly 1960s college building. "Please lady who was he?" asked Mali in puzzlement.

"He was a great humanitarian Mali. A man of great convictions that fought long against something he regarded as a great evil."

"Sorry lady I not understand. What did he do?"

Eugene grinned. "He set free the slaves!"

"But….."

"Yes I know Mali. Come... let's get along to the hairdressers. Poor old Willy would turn in his grave if he could see us."

At the hairdressing salon Eugene made the lives of the three girls responsible for coiffing her charges miserable by continual interference with their work. Eugene was a fashion stylist herself and she had very strong opinions about how she wanted her three young girls to look. Mali had the best hair, long, black and glossy and Eugene wouldn't let the stylist do much more than trim it up and shape it a little better. Vesna's hair was long and dark too but had a natural wave to it that required more attention and Eugene fussed around driving the poor hairdresser to distraction. Ana's hair was the most problematical. She had nice pale blond locks but they had been long neglected. In the end Eugene settled for a somewhat shorter cut for her feathering the ends just over her collar and giving her a neat rather sassy look that fitted well with her personality. Eugene was aware that the stylists were counting the minutes until they could be rid of her so when at last she was satisfied she tipped them heavily for their forbearance and ushered her three charges out onto the street once more.

She had already earmarked the store where she intended to outfit the girls. It was a large and expensive store in one of the new shopping malls that did a fine line in women's clothes and accessories. Eugene was atypical as a female shopper. She was not a woman that liked to spend an entire day roving from shop to shop agonising over her choice of tops and skirts. She just preferred to find a single outlet that catered to her requirements and obtain as much as she could from that one establishment at her leisure. Certainly this store had a fine collection, everything from lingerie to handbags, cardigans to shoes, all good labels and good quality. And expensive! Eugene was a wealthy woman and no believer in spoiling the ship for want of a ha'porth of tar. As she walked into the shop with the three girls at her heels a young assistant manageress drifted over. "Can I 'elp yer madam?"

"Indeed you can young lady." Eugene glanced around to note with satisfaction that the shop was relatively empty. A pair of shop girls was lounging by the cash out desk looking bored. "Could you bring your two colleagues over here for a moment please?"

“Of course madam.” The young woman looked puzzled but she complied.

When the three were assembled Eugene looked them over. They were smartly dressed she noted and had stylish hairdos that bespoke of good taste and an eye for fashion. “Tell me are you girls on commission?” she asked.

“Er no madam. We just get a flat rate like.”

“Well you are now.” Eugene pushed her three charges, all blushing in embarrassment, to the fore. “Take a look at these three girls. I want all of them completely outfitting with a new wardrobe. That means underwear, stockings, summer clothes, warm jackets, shoes, accessories, house wear, nightclothes, the works. I’ve written their sizes down to give you some guidelines. I want elegant stylish clothes, no chav look, attractive and feminine, well cut and top quality.” Eugene laid a platinum credit card on the top of the counter. “I don’t care what it costs and if I’m pleased with the results there’s ten percent on top of whatever I spend for you three to divvy up between you when I’ve finished. And I intend to spend a lot. I don’t care if it takes all day. I require your undivided attention. Would that be a problem?”

The three shop girls shook their heads avariciously “No… no madam. We’re at yer service.”

“Excellent! I will of course vet any outfits you propose and veto anything I don’t find suitable. Now then do you have a chair so that I can take the weight off my feet?”

“Of course madam.” the three shop girls got comically entangled with each other rushing to fetch Eugene a seat. The youngest of them was despatched to the Italian coffee shop next door to bring Eugene a cappuccino and Eugene settled in for an agreeable day’s shopping. It was enormous fun. The shop girls brought dozens of outfits and their accompanying accessories and Eugene had the girls modelling them all. Ana seemed somewhat self-conscious parading up and down in expensive clothes but little Vesna skipped happily about in whatever they put on her. Strangely they had the most problems with Mali. Mali had a streak of vanity in her but she was a flowering young lady and rather shy about her body. She blushed furiously as Eugene made her model attractive lingerie in the middle of the shop, emerging from the changing stalls with only the most enormous reluctance, squeaking with horror and trying to rush off if anybody else might happen to be in the store. Eugene found her timidity rather endearing but she ordered her sternly to stay put and pose interminably for her.

By late afternoon Eugene was satisfied at last. A small mountain of wrapped goods was piled high on the counters and the three shop girls were beginning to look shell-shocked. She paid for the goods with her card but she used cash to pay the girls their promised commission. She saw no reason why the store, which probably paid the girls somewhere around the minimum wage allowed by law, should be allowed to cream off the girls' bonus for itself. The sheer volume of parcels and bags amounted to a logistical problem in itself however for the car was nearly a mile away. Eugene was hungry in any case and she was certain that the girls were so she ordered a taxi to take them with their new purchases to the best hotel the city could boast for dinner.

As soon as Eugene had left the store with her three girls the three shop assistants grasped each other and performed a war dance of glee whooping in delight. "One thousand four 'undred and eighty bloody quid!" the most senior of them yelped in gratification. "That's nearly five 'undred each! Get yer best clobber on ternight lasses. We're off clubbing."

"That bitch must be bloody loaded Tracey." one of her colleagues noted.

“Aye well she can come in ‘ere anytime she wants.”

“Me feet are killin’ me.” the other girl told her. “She ‘ad us runnin’ about like blue arsed flies.”

“I’ll run about to ‘er eart’s content fer five ‘undred quid Sharon. Come on its nearly closin’ time! Let’s go an’ ‘ave a bottle o’ bubbly at Lloyds and then we’ll go out an’ turn this town upside down. Twenny quid sez I pull t’ DJ at t’ Waterfront before you two do.”

“No chance. Yer on!” Happily the three young women planned a night out in Kingston that would feature even in the street legends of a city that took a perverse pride in its excesses.

Chapter Twenty-Two

The hotel, in truth, wasn't much of a place but it was about the best that Kingston had to offer. Eugene was, it must be said, apt to view any hotel with somewhat of a jaundiced eye. A woman such as she who had spent so long in search of a home had, by necessity, spent a great deal of her life living in hotels. After such a long memory of the trials and foibles of the hostelry industry a hotel had to be something special to attract Eugene's admiration. She did have her favourites. There were several alpine hotels in Switzerland and Austria that were so cosy in their massive wooden construction that any stay in them was a pleasure and doubly so when the snow lay thick on the mountainsides without and the big log fires warmed the interior whilst you drove the chills of a day's skiing from you with a thick creamy liqueur coffee. Then there was an old crumbling family run edifice in the Provence in France run by a family and staff of such mercurial eccentricity, forever bordering on the brink of catastrophe, that it figured high on Eugene's lists of breaks for comic relief. Eugene had a connoisseur's eye for the ridiculous and bizarre. One of her all-time favourites was an old hotel in the Bergell or Bregaglia valley of southern Switzerland. It would normally have filled the average tourist with abject horror with its cavernous entrance filled with suits of armour and its high vaulted restaurant with great heads of buffaloes and other game trophies adorning the walls. The head waiter even looked a bit like the Adam's Family's butler and the rooms high up in the bat infested turrets of the building had been so deliciously Gothic in character that you half expected to find Quasimodo on room service.

In fact Eugene liked her hotels to have character and uniqueness. The hotel to which they adjourned for dinner had none of the above. In fact it was the bland product of a large American hotel chain in a building of such architectural lack of imagination that it contrived to make the old dockside warehouses look characterful by comparison. The interior was equally unimaginative. Eugene knew that you could journey to the far end of England, enter another hotel of the same chain and find exactly the same furniture, the same carpeting and even the same crockery on the tables. There was exactly the same choice of drinks on offer at the bar and precisely the same bill of fare on the restaurant menu. The whole place was a triumph of uniformity and mediocrity. It possessed virtually no independent character of its own whatsoever. It wasn't a hotel; it was a clone. Only a pleasant location by the waterside of the yachting marina prevented it from totally lacking in charm. Still it would have to do.

At least the young waitress that greeted them at the entrance to the restaurant was friendly and delightfully uncultured welcoming them with a cheery "Hiya! Are yer wantin' a table?" It was a timely reminder that however much a hotel chain may subdue its staff with wretched bland uniforms, drill them endlessly into greeting their customers with company approved stock phrases and impose a uniformity of actions and demeanour upon them it could not, short of illegal dabbling in genetic manipulation, turn its staff into the desirable clones of corporate policy. They were only paying the girl seven pounds an hour and she was damned if they were going to take away her personality for that sort of wage. Eugene smiled at the girl much comforted by her irrepressible individuality.

"Yes please honey. A table for four if that's all right."

"Oh aye. It's not like we're too busy or owt. D' yer want ter sit by t' window?"

"Yes. Thank you."

"'Ang about then an' I'll just get yer some menus."

“We’ll just require one honey. I’ll be choosing the meal. The girls here don’t speak very good English.”

“Right then.” The waitress ushered them to a table “Will this be all right?”

“Yes this is just fine.”

“Well let us know if it’s a bit cawd an’ I’ll get us manager ter turn t’ fans down. Our air conditioning’s crap. It’s always too ‘ot or too cawd. Never seems ter be right.” Eugene struggled to keep the laughter from her face, quite certain that the young waitress had broken every house rule in the book with her indomitable spirit. She blessed her for it. “Now then can I get you owt ter drink while yer lookin’ at t’ menu?”

“Yes please. Could we have three diet cokes and do you do a good white wine by the glass?”

The girl scratched her head “Well nowt what yer can’t get down at ASDA’s fer a quarter o’ the price ma-am but the Chardonnay’s not bad, I suppose.”

“On that recommendation I’ll take a glass.”

“Right comin’ up.” The girl turned and left without realising that she had restored Eugene’s faith in the human spirit immensely. Eugene turned to look at her three young girls with pleasure. They looked lovely in their new clothes. Mali was preening herself outrageously in her new floral print dress and pretty matching shoes whilst Vesna looked happy and animated in her gypsy ensemble with the ribbon in her hair. Even Ana couldn’t help looking at herself in the reflection of the big plate window. She was wearing a lovely soft pale blue grey dress that complimented the cool grey of her eyes and much though she tried to hide it she found the look of herself very agreeable indeed. Eugene found the stirrings of a strange emotion; pride. She was actually proud of her three young girls.

Eugene turned to the menu and sighed. There was little on there to entice the excitement of fine taste. It was a standardised chain hotel menu as predictable as the fittings in the foyer. There was little on that menu that was not either grilled to a standard format or bought in as a pre-packaged prepared dish requiring only the culinary skills of placing it in a microwave oven. It must, she reflected, be a very frustrating occupation for any kitchen chef with any aspirations of creativity to have the misfortune to earn their living in such an establishment to which the very essences of creativity and individuality were anathema.

Eugene experienced the eerie feeling of deja vu that had been nagging at her ever since they had set foot in the hotel. She put it down to the sad uniformity of the corporation's hotel style that determined that once you'd seen one of their hostelries you'd seen them all but the feeling refused to go away. She shook her head strangely disturbed. The wine list certainly didn't offer anything that would tempt her into the discretion of over indulgence in alcohol whilst driving, thankfully, but her feelings of disquiet continued. This place was getting under her skin and she showed a moment of irritation by commanding Ana to sit up a little straighter like a lady and not to slouch. She was frowning at the menu when a voice at her side asked, "Are you ready to order yet madam?"

Eugene snapped her head up to perceive a middle aged man, in the uniform of the hotel and with untidy grey hair and glasses standing at the side of the table. She felt a strange momentary thrill of recognition as if she knew this man from somewhere but she dismissed the odd feeling from her mind and asked, "Er could you tell me what the soup of the day is?"

"Cream of vegetable madam." Eugene looked at the man sharply. There'd been an indefinable, yet unmistakeable, touch of irony in the voice, a subtly hidden veil of contempt for the necessity of informing her of a soup that the man clearly believed wasn't worth the eating of. He was stood there with a face that was nearly expressionless but carried just a hint of conspiratorial communication. Eugene smiled slowly.

"I see. Yesterday's left over vegetables pureed into an amorphous orangey mess right?"

"Loyalty to my employers would preclude me from concurring with that analysis madam." A flicker of amusement danced across the man's face.

Eugene grinned. "Well what entrées are worth eating off this menu?"

The man grinned back further stimulating the feeling in Eugene that he was familiar from somewhere. "Well the mussels and the Oriental plate are not bad value madam. Forget the mushrooms unless you feel like paying five pounds for two caps with a sprinkling of garlic and cheese on them. The country pate's not bad as well."

"Thank you for your honesty. I'll take the mussels." Eugene paused. Mussels might be a bit challenging for her young ladies. "The girls will take the Oriental plate. Do you have a nice main course? I don't want anything too stodgy."

"We do a reasonable chicken Caesar salad if you'd like to stay on the light side madam. Of course you have to like anchovies which not everybody does."

"That sounds fine. We'll mix and match a little. Bring me two Caesar salads and two of your Mediterranean vegetable pastas please."

"My pleasure madam!" the man scribbled the order down on his pad. At that point the waitress arrive with the drinks.

"Ere yer are then! Two diet cokes an' two white wines."

Eugene's laughter bubbled up inside her once more. "Oh honey! I ordered three cokes and only one wine." The girl looked devastated.

"Oh 'eck. I'm sorry ma-am! Me manager's gonna be chowing at me now!"

Eugene laughed. “Don’t worry about it honey! Just bring me another coke all right and if your boss gives you any grief just send him over to me and I’ll sort him out.”

The senior waiter was clearly having trouble keeping a straight face as the young waitress departed to correct the order. “I’m sorry madam.” He said, “You just can’t get the staff these days!” The comment had no sting in it however and was so full of affectionate humour that it was quite clear that the elder man thought the world of his junior colleague. Eugene regarded him closely. He was Alpha Sensual she was sure, very suppressed undoubtedly, aged beyond what he should be, but unmistakeable. The Goddess had walked this way without doubt. She looked him full in the deep brown eyes.

“Tell me sir. Is the Line true? Do you revere the presence of the Goddess?”

The man staggered visibly. “I…. I’m sorry madam?” His face had turned chalky white.

“The Goddess sir! Does she rule you?”.

“I… I’m afraid I fail to understand you madam!”

“Oh but I think you do!”

The man looked hunted, terrified even. “If… if you’ll excuse me madam I’ll see to your order.” He reeled away leaving Eugene more disturbed than ever at the strange encounter. She felt a prickling of tension as if some moment of enormous significance had passed through blurring the edges of reality and threatening the fabric of existence. The strange man had enturbulated her in a deeply profound way that she was at a loss to explain. She gripped her head in her hands breathing deeply.

“Please lady.” Ana piped up “Vesna she want to go to toilet.”

Eugene took a deep breath. “Ok Ana. You know where it is. Just past reception where we came in on the left hand side. Take Vesna with you all right.”

“Da lady.” Ana took Vesna by the hand and led her to the ladies’.

Mali looked at Eugene concernedly “Please lady. You all right?”

“I’m just fine Mali. I’m just pregnant and having fanciful vapours!”

“Please lady?”

“Don’t worry about it Mali. You look very pretty by the way.”

“Ah thank you lady. Thanking you also for the nice clothing you buy us.”

“It was very much my pleasure Mali. I am very proud of all three of you today.”

“Thank you lady!” Mali’s dark eyes gleamed with pleasure.

After Ana and Vesna returned the entrée was delivered by a young Chinese girl who added to the delightful humanitising of the hotel by contriving to drop the finger bowl for her mussels on the carpet and had to scurry away to replace it. The starters were acceptable Eugene thought, or at least they were now since the personnel of the hotel had gone such a long way towards ameliorating the facelessness of the institution. The main courses were eatable too. At least the Chicken Caesar salad was although the pasta was somewhat mushy and obviously not freshly cooked. But, by this time, Eugene was enjoying herself observing the interplay of the waitresses and waiters. The people made this hotel she decided. They were friendly and endlessly diverting. She hoped that the strange man that had taken their order would pass by their table again but she was disappointed to note that he seemed to be avoiding them, delegating responsibility for their table to his colleagues and concentrating on newly arriving guests. “I’ve disturbed him." She thought to herself "I've bothered his peace of mind by asking him if he was of the Line. Why? He must know of it or he wouldn't have reacted like that. What is he frightened of?" There was a mystery to this hotel she realised, something very strange, profound even. She felt the hair on the nape of her neck tingle.

"I trust everything is to your satisfaction ladies." Eugene looked up to see that they had been joined by the restaurant manager for the evening. He was tall and obviously of Scandinavian origin with a wide-open face that advertised the essential gentleness and good nature of the man. She liked him immediately. Turning the full charm of her smile on him she replied.

"Yes thank you. Everything's just fine."

"I'm pleased to hear it madam. Are you staying with us?"

"No we're just here for a meal."

"Could we get you another glass of wine madam?"

"No I'd better not. For one thing I'm driving and for a second I'm expecting a baby so I'd better go easy."

"Oh really? May I be allowed to congratulate you?" The man's face had lit up in delight. The word "baby" seemed to have touched a chord in him.

"Well thank you but its early days yet. I'm still not sure whether to laugh or cry about it."

The man chuckled "My wife is the same. We're expecting a baby as well."

"Ah so that is why you looked so interested!"

"Yes we're very excited about it but concerned as well. We lost our first baby very young I'm afraid."

"I'm terribly sorry to hear that sir. I'm sure everything will be all right this time though." Eugene hoped so. The man was so clearly excited about his forthcoming child. He was undoubtedly fussing around his pregnant wife like a broody hen. "Did you marry an English girl then?"

"No madam my wife is from Poland." The animation was clear to see in his face. He quite obviously adored his Polish wife.

"Well I'm sure it will be all right. I think you will be a fine father. I would be a proud woman if you were the father of my child." The man blushed in pleasure. Eugene meant it too. This man would clearly be a devoted father and husband.

"Why thank you madam. I hope very much that everything goes all right with your own baby." For a few minutes the man talked animatedly about the joys and heartbreaks of childbirth with such lovely theatrical hand gestures that Eugene felt completely charmed by him. Reluctantly he took his leave of them wishing them all the best and Eugene realised that there were hidden gems in this hotel that no amount of corporate uniformity was going to suppress. She turned back to her three charges with a warm smile.

"Finished already girls?" It was an understatement. The three girls' plates could barely have been cleaner had the kitchen porter passed them through the dishwasher.

"Please lady you are not wanting us to get fat?" asked Ana. Eugene roared with laughter. The poor girls had only had a sandwich since breakfast. They must have been famished and the light repast she had imposed upon them, an insult to a noble hunger.

"No Ana. I just wanted you to leave room for a proper gooey English pudding. Come on now who's up for big sticky toffee pudding covered in custard?" Eugene had already checked the dessert menu and decided upon that choice. There were some idiocies on the menu. Eugene was a wealthy woman as we have noted but she had known poverty enough in her life to be still outraged at the thought of paying five pounds for a tiny tub of ice cream that would have cost a fifth of the price in a shop. Still the dessert menu was a timely reminder that you could fob all sorts of things off on an Englishman but you messed about with their puddings at your peril. The sticky toffee pudding was just wonderful.

They retired to the bar lounge for coffee. It was a smoking area and Eugene wanted a cigarette until she remembered that she'd stopped smoking. She sighed and took out her telephone instead. She dialled a number and waited for a reply with her heart pounding furiously. Eventually the phone was answered by a young lady talking loudly over the background noise of a busy pub. "'Ello! Mathom Arms 'ere! Can I 'elp yer?"

"Yes can I speak to Mrs Wilkinson, the landlady please?"

"Oh sorry ma-am but she's not 'ere. There's bin some flap on an' she's 'ad ter go to the airport. Can I take a message?"

"Well I don't know. My name's Eugene Collette and I inquired earlier this week about accommodation in Mathomdale."

"Oh yes ma-am. I 'ave a message fer you! Margaret's found a cottage for you. You're with three other people aren't you ma-am."

"That's right."

"Well Margaret's assigned you Rose cottage up at Marveaux if that's all right."

"It sounds just fine." Eugene's heart missed a beat.

"Well we 'ave the keys for you 'ere at the pub ma-am so you can pick them up as soon as you arrive in Mathomdale. We can give yer directions to Rose Cottage an' all."

"I…. I know Rose Cottage thank you."

"Oh good. Well any time you want ma-am."

"Would tonight be convenient? It might be late because we have a fair way to drive."

"Oh aye. T' Pub's open till 'alf past eleven but if we know yer comin' we can stay around till yer get 'ere."

Thank you." Eugene consulted her watch. It was just gone half past seven. "I think we should be able to get there before closing time but thank you anyway."

"My pleasure ma-am. T' keys are 'ere for you anyway."

"Thank you. Until later then."

Eugene put down her phone her mind in turmoil. She knew Rose Cottage well enough. It was directly owned by Mathom Hall. Almost certainly, therefore, Lady Mathom had approved of its allocation to her. Her Mistress knew she was coming! The implications of her Mistress placing her on the property of Mathom Hall but at a neutral distance from the Hall itself was not lost on Eugene. Eugene felt her heart flicker with dread and excitement. The three girls were chattering among themselves. To still her wildly beating heart, Eugene picked up a brochure from the table and pretended to examine it. Her face froze into a mask as she looked at the brochure. It was an announcement of the forthcoming events and attractions in Hull. "Hull? Hull?" she thought furiously to herself. This town was called Kingston, not Hull. Hull was the name of the muddy little river that joined the estuary at Kingston. How could you have an event in a grubby little tidal river? Why would the producers of this brochure refer to their city by the name of the insignificant little river it had swallowed up? She felt that eerie creeping sensation at the back of her neck once more and the edges of reality seem to waver about her. All of a sudden she very much wanted to be out of this disturbing hotel.

She called over the manager once more. "Er we have a lot of parcels at reception. Would it be all right to leave them here for a few minutes while we go and pick up our car?"

"Certainly madam. I'll see to their safety myself. Did you want your bill now?"

"Yes please."

"I'll send one of the girls over with it madam. I hope you've had a pleasant meal."

"Yes…. yes thank you." The waitress that had seated them came over with their bill. Eugene eyed it critically. "It shows that there's a ten percent service charge on here young lady. Tell me do you and your colleagues get that?"

"Er some of it ma-am."

"Some of it?"

"Well aye the hotel takes about fifty percent and t' rest gets divvied up like between t' staff according to their position."

"So those in a managerial position would take a larger share in fact and the hotel takes half?"

"Er yes ma-am."

"How much do you earn young lady?"

"About seven pounds an hour ma-am."

"And the hotel in effect creams off your tips?"

"Well I er suppose so."

"That's terrible."

"Well there's nowt we can do about it ma-am."

"Yes there is. It says on the bill that this is a discretionary service charge. That means I can refuse to pay it."

"Er yes I suppose so ma-am." the girl was squirming uncomfortably.

"Can you remove the service charge from my bill?"

"Yes ma-am."

"Would you please do so then and bring me the adjusted bill?"

"Of course ma-am." the waitress scurried away in confusion. She returned in a minute or two with the adjusted bill. Eugene looked at it.

"That's better." She gave the girl her credit card "This is to pay my bill and this…." Eugene reached into her purse to withdraw a wad of banknotes "is a tip for you and all your colleagues. I want you to share it out equally between all of you. Would you do that?"

The girl's eyes flew open in surprise. Eugene was waving about two hundred pounds under her nose. "Y… yes ma-am. Thank you ma-am."

"Thank you young lady. Now if you would settle our bill my young ladies and I must be going."

"Yes of course ma-am. The young girl rushed off in excitement. The two hundred pounds divided between her and her four colleagues had effectively more than doubled their earnings for the night. It was cheap at the price thought Eugene for restoring her faith in humanity. The other waiters and waitresses emerged to bid her goodnight and the middle aged man that had so disturbed her was among them looking pale and worried. As she passed him Eugene leant forward to whisper.

"One day I want to know why you are so frightened of the Goddess sir!"

"How…. how can you possibly know about the Goddess?" he replied in a stricken voice. Eugene looked at him mystified. It wasn't the response she had expected. She backed away slowly all the alarm signals in her mind screaming warnings at her.

"You and I must talk again some time!" she told him. He swallowed and nodded. Eugene turned away and led her charges from the hotel realising that she was missing something of monumental proportions that nagged insistently at the fringes of her consciousness.

Back out on the street, evening was setting in and the streets were full of people making their way to the bars and nightclubs in the old quarter of the town. Many of them were already drunk she noted. There was a dangerous edge to the revelling louts and screaming vulgar women befouling the streets with their presence. Eugene had long divided humans into Alpha Sensuals and the rest that most Alphas called Betas but she wondered if that was not just an arbitrary and superficial division. Was there, she wondered, a third classification, call them gammas if you like, of loutish, ignorant and vulgar sub-humans, brutish and stupid that fouled their own environment with their bestial chants, their uninhibited propensity for violence, their broken beer bottles and their vomit slicks with the mindlessness of creatures defecating in their own beds? She kept the girls close but even so they ran into trouble. The beautiful Mali was the focus of the trouble; or rather the target of it as two drunken young men with seriously under-formed pre-frontal lobes accosted her on the street.

"Now then darlin'! Fancy a bit of fuckin' chop suey do yer?" said one leering at her.

"Aye come on an' we'll give a bit o' sweet an' sour." his companion said grasping at Mali's arm.

"Please let go!" squeaked Mali, frightened.

Eugene stepped in "Excuse me young man. Would you mind unhanding the young lady?"

"Oo the fuck are you bitch?"

"The person responsible for looking after the young lady you are molesting. Now would you please let go of her?"

"Fuck off bitch! I'm talking to the chinky, not you."

"I repeat, please let go of her or I might become irritated."

"What's up darling do yer fancy a bit o' cock an all?" the other lout asked.

Eugene sighed. She had warned them! There was a blur of motion as she attacked. One of the drunken men was hurled across the cobblestones unconscious, even before his head rattled against the curb as Eugene kicked his companion viciously in the crutch. He bellowed in rage and pain as she grasped him by the neck and with terrible strength slammed him up against the brick wall of a building.

"Let fuckin' go of me cunt!" he yelped in sudden alarm.

"You, young man, need to learn some manners!" Eugene rammed the points of her fingers into his solar plexus and threw him to the floor where he curled up gasping for breath. The three young girls were staring at her appalled by her sudden eruption of violence. The Goddess unleashed in fury was an awesome sight. Eugene grasped them all firmly "Come along girls let's go." She scanned the tops of the street lamps anxiously. She didn't think that her demonstration of trained Alpha Sensual physical power had been recorded on a CCTV but it was best not to linger. She hastened the girls away.

They made it to the car without further incident and collected their parcels from the hotel before Eugene wove her way through the traffic toward the city limits. She didn't breathe easier until they were out in the countryside beyond. "We go back to the house lady?" Mali asked.

"No Mali we're moving on now."

"Please lady where are we going?"

Eugene took a deep breath and, pointing the car northwards, she dared to articulate her hope. "We're going home Mali. We're going home."

Chapter Twenty-Three

The same day that Eugene had taken her three girls to town, also began with some upheavals at Mathom Hall. In the early morning Lady Mathom was sat at her computer console dressed in a diaphanous negligee, combing out her long hair and checking her mail. It was a disagreeable task for there were dozens of priorities pressing for her attention. One in particular caught her attention however. "Why Danworth?" she asked herself. It was something that needed urgently looking at but she was tied up for the day with important visitors. Her frown of concentration softened however when she detected soft footfalls on the carpet behind her. She brushed her hair to one side and tilted her head inviting Margaret to kiss the side of her neck, shivering as the lips caressed the smooth skin there. She reached up behind her to run a finger into Margaret's hair.

"Good Morning Margaret."

"Good morning My Lady. You weren't in bed."

"You were sleeping beautifully Margaret and I had chores to catch up on." She pulled Margaret around to sit her on her lap. Margaret had one of her dressing gowns on that she'd borrowed from the wardrobe and Lady Mathom eased it aside to run a finger languidly over her nipple. "Well my lovely one. Did you sleep well?"

"Like a baby My Lady!" Margaret shuddered in delight under the soft caresses. She glanced at the computer screen. "What's all that about?"

"A problem Margaret. They've diverted an aeroplane full of young refugees from the fighting in South America into Danworth airfield and the officials there can't cope. I'm sending some people in to sort it out. What I really need to do is be there myself but I've got bloody Dieter turning up today with a bee in his bonnet and I've promised to be here." Lady Mathom paused as a new idea struck her. "What do you have planned for today Margaret?"

"I am at My Lady's command as always."

"Would you go over to Danworth as my representative then? I need somebody on the ground to make sure those kids are into shelters, fed and bedded down as quickly as possible."

"Hell yes! I'll do it. I've been wanting to do my bit for the war effort. I'd be delighted to help out."

"It's a nuisance, I know, with the festival preparations under full swing but I'd appreciate it Margaret. Just stay around until you're sure that the kids are looked after."

"What should I do?"

"Get hold of Colonel Westcott and get him to put as many buses and trucks as you need at your disposal. We'll put the kids in Underhill barracks for the moment. Tell the Colonel to get field kitchens up to feed them and to dig out bedding and, where necessary, clothing for them. If there's not enough room for them all in the barracks we'll have to get the rest under canvas. The Colonel is pretty dynamic so you shouldn't have too many difficulties. If anybody gets in your way though you have my full authority."

"I'm on my way!"

"Oh no rush Margaret. You've time for some breakfast."

"It's a fair drive My Lady."

"Who said anything about driving. You can take one of the helicopters."

"Whee! I've never flown in a chopper before."

"If you run into any expenses that can't be deferred to the military just bill them back here ok?"

"Yes Ma-am."

"We'll get some breakfast and then I'll sort out a helicopter for you. Do you need some clothes?"

"I could dash home and change."

"No need Margaret. I always keep a few items in your size in the wardrobes for the rare occasions I have the pleasure of your company for the night. Your Amethyst collar is here as well, in the safe. Wear it. It will accord you due authority if you have to deal with any petty minded officials."

"I would be proud to do so Ma-am." Margaret leant forward and kissed her Lady. Lady Mathom's hand slipped into her dressing gown and began to stroke her flanks. Margaret's passion soared and the kiss became deeper and more urgent. There was a knock on the door of Lady Mathom's chambers.

"Oh blast it!" she hissed, "That'll be my two young men. Damn them for being so punctual. Quick Margaret slide back into the bedroom while I deal with them." Margaret giggled and jumped up to rush back into the bedroom helped on her way by a slap on the bottom. "Lady Mathom picked up her hairbrush once more. "Come in." she called. Darren and Daniel slithered nervously into the room their eyes agog to spy Her Ladyship naked but for the barely translucent negligee. "Good morning boys. Do come a little closer. I'm not going to bite you."

The two young men bowed politely and approached her murmuring "Good Morning Ma-am."

Lady Mathom suppressed her mirth at the two boys discomfiture well aware of their eyes feasting on the sight of her so scantily dressed. "Well Mr Morgan welcome to Mathom Hall. I'm sorry that I wasn't here to welcome you personally when you first arrived."

"Th… that's fine Ma-am. Your er… young ladies and Daniel here could not have been more hospitable Ma-am."

Daniel was riveted by the presence of the Lady, the soft curves of her body easily apparent beneath her flimsy covering. "I'm pleased to hear it Mr Morgan. Are you enjoying your stay then?"

"Y…yes Ma-am." Darren felt a slight sweat break out on his forehead. Why the devil didn't the woman put some clothes on? "However Ma-am I see that we have caught you at an inconvenient moment. Perhaps you would prefer to reconvene this interview after you have had the chance to dress My Lady."

Lady Mathom chuckled softly. "I do apologise if my informal manners shock your sensibilities Mr Morgan. I'm afraid that within the confines of my own home I tend to dress as I please. I note that both Daniel and yourself are dressed in working clothes. That is entirely appropriate. You are going down to the village to work on the erection of the grandstands I believe. I wouldn't expect you therefore to wear formal evening dress or business suits. This room is part of my personal chambers Mr Morgan. This is not a formal office but a lady's boudoir. My dress is entirely appropriate within that context. However if you are outraged by my appearance I shall go and don something a little more modest if you wish."

Darren's head was starting to swim under the sensual assault of the grand seductress playing her game in front of him. "N…. no My Lady. I… I was thinking only of y…. your er inconvenience. You of course have the right to dress as you please in your own home My Lady." Darren was floundering for some sort of guideline once again. He remembered what Jennifer had told him. This woman did nothing without a reason. If she chose to interview him whilst barely dressed then she had a good reason for it.

"Thank you Mr Morgan. I thought perhaps I had displeased you with my appearance." The latter contained such sultry overtones, as Lady Mathom indicated her body with an elegant sweep of her hands, that Darren felt his manhood stir in his crotch. He swallowed and fell back on the natural charm that Jennifer had found so endearing.

"My Lady I cannot believe that any man would find your appearance displeasing."

Lady Mathom laughed easily. "Why Mr Morgan. Ambassador Kelly has trained you well I see. Are you so charming with all the ladies?"

"Er… I…. I didn't mean to be too familiar Ma-am."

"Please do not be concerned Mr Morgan. I have taken no offence. On the contrary. No lady takes offence at a gallant compliment." Lady Mathom turned to Daniel. "Daniel it is wonderful to see you back. How is the house at Bolswick Bay?"

"Coming along nicely Ma-am. I was goin' ter go back an' get some more done after t' festival if that's all right with you Ma-am."

"I see no immediate problems with that Daniel. However I won't have you neglecting your duties here and there is one duty in which you have failed conspicuously!"

Daniel looked hunted. "Er sorry Ma-am? I thought I'd done everthin' what was asked of me."

"Not something asked of you Daniel! Something expected of you! Your Mistress has returned home after an absence as indeed you have. It is customary in those circumstances to greet me with a kiss. I am still waiting for my kiss."

Daniel looked flustered "Oh! Er … I see! Er sorry Ma-am." Daniel looked around embarrassed at Darren, whose face had frozen into a mask, before approaching Her Ladyship hesitantly.

"Come along Daniel. I'm sure that Mr Morgan won't be offended by our informal ways." When Daniel was close enough to Lady Mathom's chair she reached for his hands and drew him close, turning her face up expectantly. Blushing furiously Daniel bent over to kiss her. He would have kissed her on the cheek but she turned her face to his and took the kiss on her lips holding him close for a few seconds until she was satisfied with the kiss. When he straightened up she kept him close with a hand on the back of his thigh. “You’re looking very well and healthy Daniel. I’ve had reports of your progress on the stand construction in the village. Glowing reports. You have applied yourself most diligently. I’m very pleased with you. Apparently the stands have gone up in record time so far.”

“Er it were easy with all the soldiers we ‘ad as help Ma-am.”

“Nevertheless you marshalled your resources admirably Daniel. I’m delighted. If you get all those stands up in time for the festival you can take some of that polished Indian blue marble, you so admired in the mason’s yard, for your bathroom floor at Bolswick Bay if you would like it.”

“Oh wow! Er… I mean thank you My Lady. Our Alice will be thrilled ter bits.”

“My pleasure Daniel.” She turned to Darren once more. “I’d like to thank you for helping Daniel as well Mr Morgan. I realise that you haven’t come to Mathom Hall to be employed as a building labourer but your assistance is much appreciated.”

“Glad to be of service Ma-am.”

“It will be good for you anyway. You probably spend too much time sat behind a desk in your normal profession. A little physical work will do you the power of good. Did you boys enjoy your party in the Oriental Gardens last night?”

“Er yes Ma-am.” said Daniel diplomatically. Darren and Daniel were under instruction to not mention the disaster with Julie the previous night. “It were a bit strange ‘avin’ ter dress up Japanese style like though.”

Lady Mathom laughed “I wish I’d seen you. I had the girls in here in all their finery before they took off and it was just wonderful. What did you think of the Oriental Gardens Mr Morgan?”

“I’ve never seen the like Ma-am. Quite incredible. Your whole house and its grounds has to be the most fantastic place I’ve ever seen. I feel very privileged to have been accorded the honour of seeing it.”

“Could you live here Mr Morgan?”

Darren took a double take and blinked. “I… I don’t know Ma-am. I… I mean I still don’t know in what capacity I’m supposed to be here.”

“Yes I realise that you must be confused Mr Morgan.” Lady Mathom paused and decided to up the tempo a little. She twisted her neck with a small grimace and ran a hand over her shoulder. “Forgive me. I must have slept a little awkwardly. I fear I’m a little stiff this morning. Would you do me a service Daniel?”

“Of course Ma-am.”

“You have strong hands. Would you mind rubbing my shoulders for me?”

“Er…. er no of course not Ma-am.”

“Thank you Daniel.” Lady Mathom lowered the top of her negligee, baring her shoulders and grasping the gossamer material at her bosom. Nervously Daniel began to massage her shoulders. She lifted her startling eyes to look at Darren as Daniel worked on her shoulders. “Well Mr Morgan….” She paused “May I call you Darren?”

“B….. by all means Ma-am.”

“Thank you. A little stronger please Daniel. Oh yes... that’s better. Well Darren, as I say, I realise it must all be confusing to you but I must beg your indulgence a little longer. I have known your mentor, Ambassador Kelly for many years. He has recommended you very highly to me, I might say and, having examined your personal profile and academic record personally, I can understand why. You are a very talented and brilliant young man Darren. I have need of your talents here. Ambassador Kelly has asked me to find employment for you. Now I owe the Ambassador many favours Darren but I would not employ somebody merely as a personal favour if I did not believe that person to be a valuable asset. From what I know of you I believe that you would indeed be very valuable to me. I wish therefore to offer you a permanent position with us. You would be employed ultimately in a research capacity. One of your specialities is in the field of cryptography, I understand."

"That's right Ma-am. To be more specific I work in the field of cryptanalysis."

"Well Darren we, my researchers and I that is, have the world's worst code to break; a code moreover that will have profound implications for the future of the human species on this planet. I cannot tell you more at this moment but suffice it to say that the research work that I would be asking you to embark upon may well be the most important project that you will ever be involved in. You will be at the cutting edge at one of the most fantastic adventures in history Darren."

"Can you tell me anything more about this project Ma-am?"

"No Darren. Not at this moment. At present you do not have the security clearance for it."

"What security clearance would I need Ma-am?"

"My trust Darren."

Darren looked bewildered. "That's it? Just that? Your trust Ma-am?"

"Nothing more and certainly nothing less Darren. Hmmm yes Daniel. That's just perfect. Continue like that." Darren stared at the tableau before him his mind reeling. She was half closing her eyes as she luxuriated under Daniel's ministrations, her negligee dangerously close to slipping from her breasts. In a flash he understood her game plan. She was telling him plainly that she required his enslavement; his total dedication and unwavering loyalty to her. Even the fact that she chose to have him attend upon her whilst she lounged barely dressed underlined the intimacy which she required of him. She even had one of her slaves ministering to her physically whilst she talked to him; letting him see the control she possessed over that slave and, by allowing him to see it, tacitly including him in the intimacy of the slave relationship. He already felt like a slave parading before his Mistress he realised. She hadn't even invited him to sit down. She had praised his brilliance in the same way that she petted and rewarded Daniel or all her slaves. She kept them on a leash, praised them or admonished them, rewarded them or punished them and they all adored her for it. Who was she this woman he wanted to know. Whilst with his mentor, the ambassador, Darren had met some of the most powerful and influential people in the world but none came near to the sheer electrifying force of personality of this female. Her very presence seemed to fill the room with a static charge. No wonder her slaves were in awe of her.

"Have you talked much to Daniel here and my young ladies Darren?" she continued.

"Yes Ma-am. I have had a number of interesting conversations with them."

"Have they by now made you aware of their position and responsibilities within this house Darren?"

"They have tried to explain it to me Ma-am but I confess to being a little confused as to their exact status."

"Do you like them Darren?"

Darren blinked. It was an odd question. "Why sure Ma-am. They're wonderful people. I've become great friends with them."

"And my young lady Jennifer. I asked her to make you feel at home. Has she fulfilled that duty?"

The colour rose to Darren's cheeks. "Y… yes Ma-am. Miss Jennifer has been very hospitable."

Lady Mathom laughed warmly. "I am gratified to hear it Darren. Jennifer is a remarkable young lady but she is very young and vulnerable. I'm pleased to hear that you have been enjoying her company. Jennifer is a little shy and not used to the company of young gentlemen. It will be good for her to spend some time being escorted by an attractive and charming young man."

"I.... I hardly think I would qualify for the role then Ma-am." Darren felt his cheeks burning.

"Oh but you do Darren. I remember thinking when Alex introduced me to you what a fine looking young man you were. It will be most pleasant to have one or two attractive young gentlemen about the place once more. We've been getting far too set in our feminine ways. A little rough masculine edge to the place will do us all a power of good. Tell me are you in love with Jennifer?"

Darren was staggered by the blunt question. "Why do you ask Ma-am?"

"Curiosity, academic interest really. You don't need to reply Darren. The expression on your face tells me all I need to know."

"Did you intend me to fall in love with her Ma-am?" asked Darren appalled by his own boldness.

"It was not something over which I had much control Darren. Among the few certainties that I could count is the one that a romantically inclined, impressionable young gentleman such as yourself would fall instantly in love with Jennifer." Lady Mathom reached up to lay a hand on Daniel's rubbing her naked shoulder. "And you Daniel? Are you in love with Jennifer?"

"Er everybody loves Jenny Ma-am."

Lady Mathom laughed "Well there you are Darren. It wasn't so much that I intended you to fall in love with her as that I was fairly certain that it would happen."

"Please My Lady what has this to do with the conditions of my employment here?"

“Why it is fundamental Darren. I wish to know if you would be happy working here. People in love are much happier wouldn’t you agree?”

Darren took a deep breath, well out of his depth among this woman’s manipulations. “My Lady however pleasant I find Miss Jennifer’s company I would still need to know something more about the nature of the work I would be employed in.”

“And you will Darren. Tomorrow I want you to meet Goldie.”

“Who is Goldie Ma-am?”

“Why she is the young lady you will be working with Darren. She is very clever if somewhat temperamental. Rebecca has worked with her so I’ll get Rebecca to introduce you to her. I think you will rather like Goldie. I think also once you have met her you will start to understand the importance we attach to the work you will be doing. Goldie is very high on our security listings Darren. Very few people are privileged to meet her.”

“I shall look forward to making the young lady’s acquaintance Ma-am.”

“Goldie won’t answer all your questions at this juncture Darren but I think she’ll be able to show you a taste of the work you would be doing. Until we are able to better inform you would you please be a little patient with us?”

“I shall endeavour to do so Ma-am.”

“If you decide to join us Darren you may well also be expected to travel quite extensively. Much of our resources are scattered around the world. Do you enjoy travelling?”

“Er yes Ma-am although I haven’t travelled much outside of the States until now. Would I be expected to reside here when not travelling though?"

“Yes of course Darren. This would be your home.”

Darren took a deep breath. “My Lady would I be expected to reside here under the same terms and conditions as your young ladies and Daniel here?”

“Yes Darren you would.”

“My Lady forgive me but Daniel and your young ladies consider themselves to be your slaves!”

“And so they are Darren; very valuable, trusted and much beloved slaves. I am proud to be the Mistress of such slaves.”

“I am a free man My Lady!”

“Are you really Darren? Do you remember that old lyric line from that Kris Kristofferson song? “Freedom’s just another word for nothing left to lose”? I am offering you everything to gain Darren. A fabulous job, doing something you will not only find challenging and fascinating but also will be very important and allow you to make your name in one of the most exciting fields imaginable. On top of that I am offering you wealth, high position, a secure future and the chance to work with some of the most brilliant people in the world. You will have freedom beyond your wildest imaginings. The freedom to let your mind soar. The freedom to allow full rein to your creative intellectual capacities. The freedom to realise your full potential. All I ask in return is your slavery.”

“Th… that’s crazy Ma-am!”

“Not at all Darren. You are as yet unaware of it Darren but you are a remarkable young man. You are so remarkable in fact that neither your mentor nor I will allow you to be anything less. Ambassador Kelly has formally asked me to take you in slavery to this House and I have agreed Darren. I would like you to bear the brand of this House at your earliest possible convenience if you please.”

“And if I do not please?”

“Then you will never know your true potential Darren. Tell me did not the Ambassador forewarn you that this sojourn at Mathom Hall would be the most important decision you would have to make in your life?"

"He intimated so yes Ma-am."

"Did he not also order you to take up residence here and obey my wishes?"

"Yes Ma-am he did."

"Is it your intention to disobey that order?"

"I…. I don't know Ma-am. I had no idea that he was asking me to surrender my freedom."

"Have you ever questioned his orders before?"

"N…. no Ma-am. I've always let the Ambassador guide me."

"Then be guided in this Darren. I declare formally that I require your servitude to the House of Mathom, to be honoured with the privilege of bearing the colours of this House and to be granted all the full protection and rights as a Slave of the Amethyst. When will I have your reply Darren?"

"I… I don't know My Lady. I…. I must think about it."

"Think quickly Darren. I need you."

"M…may I have a few days My Lady?"

"Yes I will grant you that Darren. Would you please approach me Darren?" Nervously Darren stepped closer to her. "A little closer please." When he was stood near to her she reached out and took his hands. Her negligee now unhindered slipped from her bosom. Darren's eyes flickered over the swell of her firm breasts, the nipples taut, and he glanced away in embarrassment. She saw his discomfort and smiled. "Don't be afraid to look at me Darren. I am not ashamed of my body and neither should you be ashamed of it. If I choose to be undressed in your presence then you have every right to admire my body."

"You… you are a very beautiful lady Ma-am." Darren croaked hoarsely.

“Thank you Darren. I’m pleased that you find me so. You are a good-looking young man Darren. I’m not surprised that Jennifer finds you attractive.”

“D… does she Ma-am?”

“Oh absolutely. May I ask you something though?”

“Y’’ yes Ma-am.”

“Would you be careful with Jennifer please? She is a little sensitive for the moment and unused to the attentions of gentlemen. Will you be kind with her?”

“You have my promise Ma-am.”

“Thank you Darren. And thank you for the massage Daniel. That was wonderful. I won’t keep you two boys from your work any longer. But Darren I want you to think very carefully over what I’ve said. This is a crucial time in your life Darren. The choices you make here will have profound effects on the rest of your life. If you choose to become a slave of this House you have my guarantee that you will never regret it. Think carefully Darren. Choose wisely.”

“I will certainly consider it Ma-am.”

“Thank you Darren. If you two boys make good progress on the stands today I think it would be a good idea for you both to have a night out on your own. Get away from the girls for a bit and have a few beers together. Why don’t you take Darren down to the Mathom Arms after work tonight Daniel? The pub is reasonably secure now that we’ve put additional security in on it in advance of the festival so I won’t be worried that any harm will come to you. What do you say Daniel?”

“Aye I mean yes Ma-am. It’ll be good ter get out for a bit. These security restrictions are getting’ on everyone’s nerves Ma-am.”

“All right you can have the night off then. Don’t be wandering away from the Mathom Arms however. We’re not out of the woods yet. When you want to come home just call up the Hall for a car all right?”

“Yes Ma-am. Thank you. You fancy a few beers after work Darren?”

“Er sure. Yeah I’d like that.”

“Good.” Lady Mathom smiled and readjusted her clothing. “Now you’d better be on your way. We’ll have a longer discussion in the next few days Darren. In the meantime I want you to enjoy yourself and try to understand a little more about this House and what it represents. Will you keep an open mind until we talk again?”

“That much at least I owe you for your hospitality My Lady.”

“Excellent.” She turned to look at Daniel. “Daniel?”

“Oh aye! Er yes Ma-am.” Daniel bent to kiss her and she rewarded him with an affectionate pat. So powerful a control did she exert in this dismissal that for one awful second Darren was certain that she would demand that he kiss her goodbye as well and he knew that he would not be able to refuse. But she just smiled at him.

“Until later then Darren.” Darren hid his confusion with a hasty bow and the two young men left the Lady’s chambers. Outside in the hallway Darren leant weakly against the wall.

“Jesus H Christ! That just has to be the goddamndest job interview I ever had in my life.”

Daniel laughed and slapped him on the back. “She’s summat else isn’t she? Bloody ‘ell I nearly shat mesen when she asked us to rub ‘er flippin’ shoulders.”

“Is she … well always like that Danny?”

“I did try ter warn yer Darren. She’s one ‘ell of a woman. She doesn’t mess about. She wants ‘er own way an’ she gets it. Looks like yer’ll be movin’ in permanent then.”

“Hell I haven’t agreed yet.”

“No but yer will. Looks ter me as if she’s set ‘er mind on ‘avin’ yer so I’d start mekkin’ yer sen comfortable if I was you.”

“This is crazy Darren. She can’t just sit there and tell me that she intends to enslave me. This kind of thing just doesn’t happen.”

“It does ‘ere mate. Yer might think yer can still say no to ‘er Darren but yer foolin’ yer sen. She’s got ‘er ‘ook in yer an’ playin’ yer like a fish. Yer’ve no chance mate. She’ll scoop you up in ‘er landin’ net afore the week’s out.”

“Jesus Danny! You can’t mean that.”

“Oh but I do Darren. I told yer that yer was bein’ sold as a slave ‘ere. Yer wouldn’t ‘ave it. Well now yer know. Me I think it’s just great. I’m t’ only fellah among ‘er personal slaves at t’ moment an’ it’ll be great ‘avin’ a brother in t’ ouse. Come on lad. Cheer up. It’s not the end o’ t’ world yer know. In fact this is best thing wot’s ‘appened to yer. You’ll see.” Darren just shook his head despairingly. “Anyway Darren.” Daniel continued. “We’ve got t’ night off ter go down t’ pub. We’ll sink an’ ‘ole in t’ Mathom Arms’ beer cellar an’ be plottin’ ow we’re gonna get stuck inter one o’ them big carp in t’ Golden Pool.”

Darren smiled weakly. “I’ll enjoy that Daniel. Thank the Lord I’ve got you around to keep me sane.”

“Away then! T’ lads will be wonderin’ where we’ve got ter!”

Chapter Twenty-Four

In her chambers Lady Mathom was feeling thoroughly pleased with herself as Margaret emerged from the inner sanctum of her bedchamber. “The boys gone then?”

“Yes Margaret. All clear.”

“How’s your new boy coming along? Ready to be collared yet or is he still kicking?”

“Oh no. Straightforward. I won’t have any trouble there. He’s already pretty much in the mind-set already. He’s been a quasi-slave of Alex’s for years now and he’s a young man in search of a purpose. I should have him chained up by the end of the festival. All rather routine. He’s been pretty much softened up by his future sisters and brother and that helps. If all else failed I could always use Jenny to lure him into his cell but I don’t even think I’ll need to resort to that. Gratifyingly he seems to be forming a strong bond with Daniel, my other boy. That’s very satisfying because Daniel needs a brother and Robin isn’t here much with his commitments in Switzerland. I was getting worried that Daniel only had the girls around him. Boys need some male bonding as well. I’ve pushed the thing on a little by ordering them down to your pub this evening after work to get drunk and talk about football, or whatever it is that boys need to pair bond over. If you’re not back in time Margaret, ask your girls to keep an eye on them and flirt with them a little bit to bolster their masculinity would you?”

“No problems My Lady. I usually just take girls in these days but I have raised boys as well so I know how to deal with them. Do you want me to ensure that they misbehave themselves and have to report for punishment?”

“No better not Margaret. That might be pushing Darren’s limits a bit far at this juncture. Maybe you can see that they get up to some mischief and I'll sort of "nearly" find out about it just to focus Darren's mind in the right direction. If he thinks he's gotten away with it then he's already acknowledged that he's answerable to me for his conduct."

"Ok. It's been a long time since you took a coffle of boys on isn't it."

"Yes and I'm enjoying it. I think we need one or two more around the place. I've even been thinking of reactivating the old bachelors wing. It hasn't been used in years because we just haven't taken any high boys in. Thoroughbred boys usually end up at private schools, colleges, camps or under male masters these days because they're a bit more difficult to raise up domestically in this day and age. Still as long as we keep a small masculine preserve for them and make sure they're under a tight rein there's no reason at all why we shouldn't be able to turn out perfectly good male slaves. They're not that difficult for heaven's sake and they're generally cheaper to maintain than girls are. Personally I rather enjoy taming young men. I don't see why so many ladies are so leery of it. I think a lot of boys would benefit from being shackled to a mistress as long as their masculine side doesn't get repressed."

"Oh I agree. I've taken on boys before. I still hold the bonds on one or two of them that haven't been sold off yet. Do you remember John Partridge?"

"Oh yes he married off with two of your girls and that young man from Brawton didn't he?"

"That's right and they run the Green Dragon out at Hecklesthwaite together now. They've made a real go of it as well because it's a very successful pub. I still hold the contracts on them and they pay me a small percentage of their profits because I had to help finance them when they bought the place out. They've said they're all coming over for the festival to see their old mistress. I'm proud of John. He turned out very well.

They've got a couple of young slaves of their own now and two children so it's a real happy family."

"Yes well we're going to have to make some adjustments around here if I decide to take more boys on. Danny's in married quarters with Alice but the boys are going to need their own space. There's a little club room in the old bachelors wing and when we used to have more boys we used to have a little hunting lodge for them right out at the far end of the grounds where they could raise a little hellfire without getting under the feet of the house ladies. You always have to give them a bit of space to be primitive in."

"Hmmph! Not much different from girls then."

"True enough but girls at least try to keep a somewhat more civilised veneer on it."

"Anyway My Lady there's another thing. Shall I take the keys for Rose Cottage in case La Collette turns up out of the blue?"

"No I'll send them down to the pub and your girls can look after them in case she turns up while you're at Danworth. It's going to be interesting to see Eugene again. It sounds as if she's got her knickers into a real twist about something this time. I'm still wondering who these three slaves of hers are as well. It should be a very illuminating interview when Eugene finally whacks up the bottle to request an audience with me. Now then shall I order some breakfast for us? I'd better get Thomas to serve it. I don't want my little gossips to worry their pretty little heads over the fact that I'm sleeping with the pub landlady."

"I hardly think it would be a secret to them My Lady. If they don't know that I spend the occasional night here then they're not very observant and that I don't believe."

"Well in any case you'd better root about for something to wear Margaret. Joseph can be a bit stuffy about his daughter's misdemeanours so there's no need to push it in his face. I’ll order up your helicopter for Danworth while you’re dressing and then I’d better crack the whip over my little darlings and let them know that their Mistress is back in the house.”

Chapter Twenty-Five

The girls were already aware of the Lady's presence. Abigail was perfectly coiffed and ready to serve her Mistress when the call came through to the slave's wing. "Good morning My Lady." She answered. "Do you require attending to?"

"Not immediately Abigail. But I shall need two of you in attendance for lunch because I'm expecting visitors. Who have you assigned duty to?"

"Rebecca and myself are on standby My Lady."

"Hmm. I need Rebecca to be available for other reasons this afternoon Abigail. Also she has those papers I asked her for to put in order. Tell her to stand down and pick out someone else. I know bring Alice along. After lunch perhaps she can play the piano for us. One of my guests is a little awkward and music is well known as efficacious in soothing the savage beast."

"Yes My Lady." Abigail was relieved. For a moment she'd expected the Lady to ask for Jennifer and that would have been perilous. Jennifer would never have been able to conceal the disaster that had overtaken their party in the Oriental Gardens the night before. Alice was still problematical of course for she had never been called upon to wait on her Mistress over lunch as yet but they had a few hours to brief her up on her duties at least.

"Did you get back late last night Abigail?"

"No My Lady. We anticipated that you would require at least some of us on duty this morning and the boys had to go down to the village to work as well." Abigail bit her tongue thankful that the conversation was being held over the phone. In fact it had been past midnight when they had left the Oriental Gardens and gone one o'clock before they'd got back to the Hall. Despite the late hour the party had broken up in a somewhat subdued fashion and they'd all departed to their own chambers. Alice had gone off to the married quarters with Daniel and Darren had left them, politely, to remove to his own suite. By the time the girls had got out of their kimonos everybody had been feeling too downcast to consummate the night's events with more than a kiss and they'd all split up. Jennifer had vanished into her own chambers with a strained face. Abigail had envied the twins because they at least slept together whilst she faced a night alone in her bed. Oddly enough, however, in the middle of the night a tearful Rebecca had crept into her room and slipped into bed alongside her needing comfort and there'd been some compensatory sweetness for the denouement of the nights events after all. Breakfast that morning had been an uncomfortable affair and there were strange tensions in the air.

"Oh very well Abigail. We'll be in attendance at twelve with Alice then."

"Yes My Lady." Lady Mathom was surprised. She'd expected her slaves to spend the night in the Oriental Gardens last night doing the sort of things they normally did when off the leash for five minutes. She hadn't even expected to find anybody in attendance in the slave's wing and she'd planned to send somebody over to the Gardens to root out her wayward young ladies with dire warnings of retribution if they weren't up to scratch before lunch time. To find them all present and correct and dutifully on standby had caught her by surprise. Abigail's protestations of devotion to duty hadn't pulled the wool over her eyes for one second. Something had evidently gone wrong with their party it would seem. Well doubtless she would find out what it was in due course. In the meantime she had more pressing matters to attend to than some tiff in the slave's wing.

After she had broken the connection with the slave's wing she busied herself with other tasks concentrating fore mostly on the morning's crisis at Danworth airfield. She was still busy with that task when Margaret re-emerged from the bedchamber smartly dressed in a navy blue suit with a short skirt and white blouse over her long legs clad in dark nylon. She wore the collar of her authority as a Slave of the Amethyst about her throat and on the left lapel of her jacket she bore a badge that declared her to be of senior status and a holder of the Imperial Medal of Honour. Margaret was quite clearly intent upon not being intimidated by anybody.

"You look just fine Margaret." Lady Mathom told her. "I've already been on the phone to Colonel Westcott so I think the arrangements for the refugees will already be moving into action. The Colonel will be flying with you to Danworth so all you'll have to do probably is stand around and look regal while he kicks a few bottoms."

"I was thinking My Lady. Should I keep an eye open for any youngsters that might be suitable for the purposes we were discussing last night?"

"That's my Margaret." chuckled Lady Mathom. "Never miss the chance to look over some potential business. By all means have a look through them. If you find any that stand out particularly you can bring one or two back with you. I'd like to hear the stories from South America first hand from somebody who has witnessed it. You won't be able to single out a whole coffle of them to fit into a helicopter though. I wouldn't worry about that too much. We'll have more time at our leisure to sort out the best places for these kids. By the way, if immigration gives you any grief the official line is that these are the dependants of employees of Amethyst Imperial being temporarily sheltered from conflict in their homelands at the corporation's expense and under our responsibility. Some of these kids won't have papers so we'll have to blag it a little and say we're still sorting out their documentation. By the time that immigration gets around to looking into the matter properly we'll have them bedded down all over the place and they'll never shift them."

"Have all these kids lost their families?"

"Most of them Margaret. The evacuees from Colombia whose families survived have been given temporary shelter in Brazil or Argentina until they can be re-united. Most of the ones they sent to Europe are those whose villages were wiped out."

"Goddess they're going to be a lot of very traumatised young people."

"Yes they are and so they need to be dealt with as kindly and gently as possible Margaret. How's your Spanish?"

"Er very rusty."

"Well I've sent half a dozen interpreters so you should get by. Your helicopter flies out in a little over an hour so I'd better jump into something to wear and rustle up some breakfast for us."

The slave's wing was busy too that morning. A seriously worried looking Alice was being drilled assiduously on the formal serving duties required of her over lunch whilst an even more worried looking Rebecca was tinkering with her thesis papers still woefully dissatisfied with them but at least trying to get them into some logical order. Jennifer, still upset from the events of the night past was grateful to find that she had meaningful employment this morning as well. She'd telephoned Julie straight after breakfast and found her very subdued although apologetic about her collapse in the Oriental Gardens. There had been little time for Jennifer to be much more than reassuring and to tell Julie that she loved her to which Julie had replied with a strangled sob that the feeling was mutual.

On the positive side Jennifer had extracted a promise that they would have a long talk together sometime during the festival. It was just about enough to raise Jennifer's spirits somewhat but she missed Julie with a terrible ache and it was good that there was work to be done to keep her mind off it. Heather was busy with a duster and a damp cloth while Helen was running a vacuum cleaner over the carpets. Jennifer was sorting out bedclothes and hanging up the clothing that had been sent from downstairs up in the wardrobes. The windows were open to air the chambers and the view across the grounds was a pretty one. Eventually Heather took her pinafore off and looked around critically. "Well I think it will pass muster to begin with girls."

"Will the young one be in the adjoining bedroom?" asked Helen.

"I'm presuming so." Said Jennifer. "I've put bedding on the bed and hung her clothes up in there. It looks a more appropriate room for a child although maybe she sleeps with her sister."

"Well it's a nice enough set of chambers and they're on the east side of the wing so they'll get the morning sunlight." Helen commented. "I don't know if they're moving in permanently though."

"We'll have to be on our best behaviour with a young child about." Heather noted.

"Hey that's an idea." Helen said suddenly. "Let's go and scour the nurseries downstairs and pick out a bunch of dolls and cuddly toys to scatter about in there. The poor little soul's got nothing to play with."

"Brilliant." said Heather. "We can hang a few silly kiddy pictures up on the walls as well to make her more at ease."

"Should we hang a photo of the Lady in the living room?" asked Jennifer. It was a serious question. All the slaves in the wing kept a framed photograph of their Mistress on their wall somewhere in addition to the much beloved large oil painting of her that dominated the pride of place over the fireplace in the big Communal lounge.

Heather thought about it for a moment. "Hmm. I don't know about that one Jenny. We don't really know what their status is yet."

"I'd say yes," said Helen. "The Lady's their matron after all and it would be respectful to have her picture in their chambers. I tell you what. I've a nice one they can have. We'll just hang it up and if they don't want it they can always take it down themselves."

"They wouldn't dare!" said Heather.

"Well maybe not but we'll be able to judge whether they're comfortable with it."

"Come along then." Said Jennifer. "I want to see this nursery."

"Yes it will stop Laila pinching your dolls and teddy bears Jenny." said Helen with a laugh.

Jennifer looked sheepish. She had all her old dolls and cuddly toys from her room at the vicarage firmly in residence in her chambers. They were the last legacy of her childhood. She couldn't bear to part with them. The other girls teased her about it. Jennifer still had a lot of growing up to do. "When are the girls coming up here then?" she asked.

"Oh anytime today." Said Helen. "Mrs Carmichael has given us the day to prepare their rooms for them. We thought it would be a nice idea to wait until we're all off duty so we could welcome them all together. Abigail's arranged supper in our wing dining room this evening so we can eat together with them."

"What about Darren and Daniel?" asked Jennifer.

"Oh you won't believe this. The Lady's given them the bloody night off. Told them they can go down to the pub. We're not allowed out of her sight but the bloody fellahs can just go traipsing down the village without a care in the world. What's all that about?"

“Bloody sexual inequality is what I call it.” said Heather.

Jennifer laughed, “Maybe it’s not so important for them to be under security restrictions girls. Maybe the Lady considers men to be expendable.”

The twins roared with laughter. “Yeah that’s true.” Helen noted. “I mean they’re not that valuable are they? Lose a couple of fellahs and it’s no big deal. Plenty more where they came from. Still I wouldn’t have minded getting out of the house myself.”

“Me too.” Said Jennifer soberly. “I want to see Julie.” The twins went quiet. It was a sore subject at the moment.

“Aww Jenny!” said Heather “You’ll see her soon enough. We’re sorry it all went a bit haywire last night.”

“Well I’ll see her tomorrow probably. We’re all supposed to be moving to the Mathom Arms for the start of the festival tomorrow evening. That’s if she’s not too poorly.”

“Was she all right on the phone today?” asked Helen.

“Seemed to be. A bit teary and sorry for letting us down but she sounded all right.”

“Well there you go. Come on let’s get this all done by lunchtime. I’ve got to get over to IT services this aft. My bloody monitor’s gone tits up on me and I have to rustle up a new one. I should have gone earlier. The damn thing’s had one foot in the skip for nearly a month now.”

“Yes and I’ve got dancing lessons this afternoon.” Jennifer noted.

“Right then let’s check out that nursery.”

Just before lunch Lady Mathom was stood at the side of the sports field in the grounds, clicking her tongue in exasperation, as a helicopter swept in over the wooded crest of a hill to the east. Much though she occasionally appreciated the convenience of it, the fact that the peaceful grounds were turning into an auxiliary heliport was beginning to irritate her, especially now that everybody was starting to take advantage of it apparently. The helicopter flared above the sports field and dropped onto the side of the running track. Two men emerged from the machine ducking out from under the rotor, clutching bags. One was a tall athletic looking man dressed in slacks and an open necked shirt, devastatingly handsome under a shock of sandy brown hair and a devil may care expression to his face. His companion was a shorter, slim, dark haired young man in a suit looking clearly apprehensive and glancing about himself nervously. The taller man spied Lady Mathom and flashed her a wide grin and a cheery wave. She sighed to herself. In anybody else the gesture would have been dangerously close to being disrespectful but it was characteristic of her happily extrovert visitor.

The two men approached her and bowed in front of her. "Good morning to you Serenity." said the older man. "You look as wonderful as ever My Lady."

"Thank you and a good morning to you Dieter. I see you have made your usual extravagantly flamboyant entrance. You could have just taken a car from Danworth you know."

"My profound apologies My Lady but they said the helicopter was heading back here so we just hitched a lift on it." the man told her with a grin. "Allow me to introduce you to my young assistant. This is Doctor Desmond de Boer from Pennsylvania, one of the young guns on my faculty at White Mountain."

"I'm very pleased to meet you Doctor de Boer. Welcome to Mathom Hall." The young man bowed once more and took the proffered hand nervously. He had been on a whirlwind non-stop round of extraordinary new experiences ever since first arriving in Switzerland but this sudden spontaneous trip to England at the Professor's command was simply unbelievable. The thought of being presented to the legendary figurehead of the Line on the grounds of Her personal residence had quite frankly terrified him. He considered that the walk across the sports field to make his obeisance to be the most courageous act he had ever performed in his life. He was trembling visibly but trying to keep his wits about him and register everything he could about her. His friends and colleagues back in Switzerland would grill him mercilessly about every detail of her he knew and he would not come up smelling of roses by saying that he was too petrified to take anything in.

"I… I am greatly honoured to meet you Serenity." He stammered. "And I'm honoured to be invited to your beautiful home too. I… I've heard much about it Ma-am but I didn't think I would ever get to see it."

Lady Mathom laughed, liking this ingenuous young man and turned the full power of her charm on him. "Why then I hope that you'll have a pleasant stay with us Dr de Boer. Tell me are you of Dutch extraction then?"

"Er on my great grandfather's side My Lady. His family emigrated through Kingston to the States Ma-am so we have some familial connection with this part of your country albeit just by passing through."

"Have you ever been in England before Dr de Boer?"

"Er no Ma-am although it has long been an ambition of mine to visit the country."

"Well this is a most attractive corner of England Doctor. I do hope that you'll be able to have a look around during your visit. Perhaps my young ladies will be able to find the time to give you a tour around our grounds and the valley."

"Hmmph I'd keep them on a short leash if I were you My Lady." laughed Dieter clapping the young man on the shoulder. "Young Desmond here is a wolf. Don't be fooled by the shy appearances. He's broken the hearts of half the girls in the Roggental already and he's only been there a few weeks. We have to keep him chained up on a night." Desmond blushed furiously.

Lady Mathom smiled at him in amusement. "I'm sure Dr de Boer will be nothing other than a complete gentleman."

"Hah! Keine chance! I've seen your gaggle of young lovelies. Once Desmond here gets an eyeful of them he'll be pawing at the ground."

"You're embarrassing the young gentleman Dieter." Lady Mathom admonished. "The only person whose predatory instincts I'm worried about is you my dear Professor."

Professor Sehler roared with laughter. "There's only one of them I'm hunting for the moment My Lady. Where is the Lady Rebecca anyway?"

"She will be joining us sometime this afternoon Dieter. At my convenience. Until she does I ask you to comport yourself with patience."

"I've been comporting myself with patience half the summer My Lady."

"Well it wasn't very evident Dieter. I told you right from the beginning that Rebecca would be joining you after the summer. I have not changed my mind on that in spite of the innumerable and unnecessary communications you have forwarded."

"My Lady you can't just sit on this girl. Not with the theories she's holding on to!"

"I'll do what the devil I like with my own slaves Dieter."

"We were thinking that the wench could come back to Switzerland with us."

"Well you can think again. My personal slaves are not at the disposal of anybody's convenience but my own Herr Professor. Rebecca soll nach dem Schweiz wann ich sagen fliegen. Nicht bevor! Is das Klar Herr Professor?"

“Ja ja Ihre Hoheit. Es tut mir sehr leid. But we can get to speak to her ok?”

“That much I will allow Dieter. Will you be briefing her on the White Mountain project?”

“We have clearance to do that My Lady with your permission. Is the young lady a good security risk?”

“She is a high slave of the House of Mathom Dieter. She’s not one of my scullery girls you know.”

“I intended no insult against the lady Serenity. White Mountain is just about one of the highest security issues on the Line however. I have to be certain.”

“The Lady Rebecca is safe Dieter. She has had access to some of the most secure archives in our vaults for several years. There has never been a hint of any leakage. You may rest assured.”

“Thank you My Lady. Talking of security do you know where Eugene Collette has got to? She’s vanished. The last information we had is that she was heading for England. Since then we haven’t had a peep out of her.”

“I have no idea where Eugene is at the moment.” said Lady Mathom truthfully if a little evasively. “Are you saying that Eugene has left her post at White Mountain without leave?”

“She’s resigned her post My Lady. Security received a formal resignation from her just two days ago, effective immediately and handing over all responsibilities to her subordinates. She’s quit! The project committee’s screaming blue murder about it. I’m surprised you haven’t been alerted yet.”

“I’ve been on the road for some days Dieter. There’re a few things that haven’t caught up with me.”

“Well they’re throwing a fit in the Roggental about it. They thought she might be here. I’m supposed to see if I can run her to earth and drag her back to Switzerland in chains.”

"That would be most interesting to watch. I'll have to phone up the village bookmaker to see what odds he'll give me on your chances. Purely out of interest you understand; I wouldn't waste any money on the bet."

"Well neither would I for that matter My Lady. Still I'd like to know what the devil's the matter with her. Telling the most important research programme in the world to take one of the most prestigious security positions anywhere and stuff it where the sun don't shine is pretty temperamental even by the Lady Eugene's exacting standards. She's thrown a pearl of one this time."

"I'm sure Eugene has her reasons Dieter even if they don't make much rational sense to anybody else. Well we'll have to see. Perhaps she'll turn up here during the festival. Are you staying for the festival by the way?"

"If that would be convenient for you My Lady. We would enjoy that."

"Good. I think you will enjoy our local festival Dr de Boer. One of my newest young ladies will be officiating as the festival queen for the ceremonies."

"That wouldn't be your young Lady Jennifer would it Ma-am?" asked Dieter.

"Oh you've heard of her then Dieter?"

"I think most of Europe's heard of her My Lady. The story's going about that you've bought the Lady Katherine's daughter for one of the highest prices in the last fifty years. Everybody in the Roggental's talking about it."

"Well yes she's a very expensive young lady."

"We'd like to meet her."

"Then I really would chain young Desmond here up then if I was you Dieter." Lady Mathom laughed, "Jennifer has a curious but well documented effect on young gentlemen. If I wanted to pinch Dr de Boer from you I'd just let Jennifer loose on him for half an hour and you could kiss him goodbye." She smiled at the flustered Desmond "Come gentlemen. You must be hungry. Let's retire for lunch." She led them back gracefully to the Hall but her mind was ticking over furiously. The mystery about Eugene had deepened further with the intelligence that Dieter had provided. All in all it promised to be a most interesting summer festival this year.

Chapter Twenty-Six

Rebecca didn't know why Lady Mathom had ordered her to send the material for her thesis to her that day and nor did she understand why she was being taken off duty and told to await her Mistress's pleasure for that afternoon. Nevertheless she had some inkling that her life was about to come to a crisis. It was a crisis she could have done without. She was upset and her mind was far away from the disturbing material of her research. She was still trying to understand the estrangement that had sprung up between Jennifer and herself. They hadn't had an argument as such but Jennifer was studiously avoiding Rebecca's company and, when they did talk, Jennifer seemed distracted and would not make eye contact with her. A girl of such devoted passions as Rebecca found this intolerable. She was convinced that Jennifer's current mood went further than just some minor emotional fluctuation. It had started, she realised, the day after Darren Morgan had joined the household and Rebecca felt sure that something had happened to Jennifer since then to explain her strange humour. Rebecca had no idea what that might have been and Darren was either unable or unwilling to throw any light upon it.

Rebecca loved Jennifer with all the overwhelming power of her temperamental spirit and this inexplicable rejection of her by the object of her adoration was like a knife in her heart. She had been so upset after the failure of the previous night that she had sought comfort in the arms of her beloved sister Abigail. Abigail had been kind and soothing. She still tended to believe that Jennifer's mood was largely due to her separation from Julie. Well Rebecca could identify with that. She was upset by Julie's separation from them as well. She recalled the days when the three of them and Robin had planned a marriage together in such hope and love. It all seemed very distant now. Her dreams seemed to lie in ruins about the feet of some monstrous barrier they had collided with.

Later that day she had tried to talk to Jennifer up in the slave's wing but she'd found her sad and deeply introverted. Rebecca had asked if they could spend some time together that day, just the two of them, but Jennifer had shaken her head and said something strange. "Is this another plan of yours Rebecca?" she'd asked.

"Why? What do you mean Jenny?" Rebecca had replied.

"Nothing Rebecca. I'm just a little fed up of not being told the truth."

"What the devil are you talking about Jenny?"

"Why did you do it to me Rebecca? Why? I loved you. I trusted you."

"What the hell do you mean Jenny?"

"In the Oriental Gardens Rebecca. You betrayed me."

"Jenny! Darling! What do you mean? I couldn't help what happened last night. I was as upset as you are about Julie."

"I don't mean last night Rebecca. I mean the first time we visited the Gardens."

"But…. but…. what did I do?"

Jennifer had reached into her bag and taken out a small box and laid it on the coffee table as she stood up. "If it hadn't been for this I might never have known Rebecca. I might never have known how I've been used. If you'd excuse me now I would like to be alone for a while." Then Jennifer had swept out of the room leaving Rebecca speechless behind her. Deeply hurt Rebecca had picked up the little box and opened it. Her mystification had intensified. The box had contained a medal. Rebecca had recognised the medal. It was formed in the likeness of a naked woman on a background of two crossed swords. It was the honour of the Swords of the Goddess, the highest military award for bravery within the Line. Rebecca had stared at it uncomprehendingly.

Chapter Twenty-Seven

Margaret was having a tough time at Danworth airfield. It wasn't that there were any problems about the logistical handling of the crowd of young refugees assembled there. On the contrary, Lady Mathom's newly appointed military commander of the Amethyst Guard was fully justifying his lady's trust in him with his efficiency and energy. Lady Mathom had been right because Margaret had very little to do other than represent Her Ladyship at the proceedings.

The Colonel had cracked a whip with a vengeance and thrown every resource available to him at the problem of housing and feeding the frightened and bewildered young people off the aeroplane. He had ordered the clearing of several large barracks to act as temporary housing for the refugees, which had caused a certain amount of grumbling within his command as his soldiers would be obliged to sleep under canvas until more permanent facilities could be found. He'd ordered three big field kitchens to the airfield to feed the youngsters straight away and rustled up every cook he could spare to man the kitchens in the barracks. Even before Margaret had arrived there was a small fleet of coaches at the airfield waiting to whisk the refugees to their temporary housing. Colonel Westcott however had been worried that his troops might be unused to dealing with such young people many of who were merely children so he'd sent out an emergency call for volunteers around the families of his command. Now many non-military men and women were flooding to the airfield and the barracks to help out, bringing second hand clothes and even toys for the youngsters. Margaret could not have wished for greater energy and enterprise from the military authority.

Margaret's only real role therefore was to provide words of comfort and reassurance to the wretched young people, to inform them of the steps being taken for their benefit and to let them know that the Great Lady herself was taking an active interest in their safety and well-being, and in this she was having trouble for her Spanish had fallen to a very poor level through long disuse. Colonel Westcott had, it is true, found a Spanish speaker within his command to convey instructions to the young people over a PA system but he couldn't be everywhere and he couldn't be of much help to Margaret as she tried to talk personally to them, weaving her way among them and offering them the solace of her Mistress's pledges to them. Fortunately however she had a stroke of luck. Among the young refugees she came upon a very pretty, intelligent, English speaking young girl to act as an interpreter for her. The girl performed this task admirably and Margaret was highly impressed with her. She asked the young girl her name.

"Please my lady it is Gitana, Gitana Garcia." Margaret took a long look at her and made the decision that would change Gitana's life for that is how, before this day was out, Gitana would come to be on a helicopter bound for Mathom Hall.

Chapter Twenty-Eight

Abigail and Alice were dismissed from service after lunch without Alice being asked to play the piano for Lady Mathom's two guests much to her relief. It was evident that the visitors were very important people and Alice had quailed at the thought of entertaining them. She and Abigail mounted the stairs to the slave wing running a debriefing on Alice's first formal service duty. Alice was nervous about it, convinced she had made every mistake in the book.

"You were just fine honey." Abigail reassured her. "It was a fairly informal lunch in any case so absolute perfection wasn't really required."

"Well you did most o' t' work Abi love. I just stood around lookin' ornamental fer t' most part."

"Well you were doing your job in that case. Half the point of the thing is to look suitably ornamental for the Lady's guests. We're really there in those circumstances to honour the guests."

"Ow do yer mean?"

"We're high slaves Alice, the Lady's personal young ladies. There's any number of slaves further down the domestic hierarchy perfectly capable of bringing in a few plates or pouring out the wine but that would be disrespectful to honoured guests. By having her very own personal slaves attending upon her guests the Lady is conferring honour and respect upon them. It's like getting out the best china when the vicar comes to tea. You don't sit him down in the kitchen with an old cracked teacup do you? Well the same applies to us. We're there to be admired, to look pretty and give our guests something to feast their eyes on over the soup course. That's why all our movements should be graceful and elegant. That's why I drilled it into your head to move slowly, gracefully, to smile at the guests and anticipate their requirements. That's what the whole principle of service is about Alice. It is a conference of honour. When a waiter in a restaurant pours your wine for you it's not that they're saying that you're incapable of doing it for yourself is it? They are affording you the respect due to your position as a paying customer by showing that they are attendant upon your needs. They are honouring you."

"Who were those two blokes anyway?" Alice wanted to know.

"I don't know Alice. I've never met them before but the Lady seemed to be familiar with the tall guy. They're scientists or something, obviously. I think Becky knows something about them. They're probably here to do with something or other concerning this mysterious research project Becky's been working on. Goddess knows what that is. I don't know what Becky's been snuffling round in but it's classified up to the max. She won't let anyone near it."

"It could be owt. Our Becky's a clever lass."

"Oh hell yes. The dizzy little bitch has got a brain on her shoulders right enough. I hope to hell we're not going to lose her to some bloody research institute somewhere." The two girls entered the slaves' wing to find Rebecca sat in the common room. Abigail's eyes flew open in surprise. "Becky what the devil is the matter?" Rebecca was sat alone crying piteously.

"Oh Abi, Alice." She wailed and clutched them to her weeping.

"Goddess Becky!" said Abigail hugging her closely. "For the name of love honey. What's happened?"

"I… I don't know Abi! I don't know what I've done wrong! I…. I just don't know!"

Abigail held her at arm's length for a second. "Have you and Jenny had a row?"

Rebecca nodded the tears flowing down her cheeks. "She says I've betrayed her Abi. Said I'd used her or something. I don't know what I've done."

"For heaven's sake sit down and calm yourself Becky. You've got to go downstairs and attend the Lady and her guests in two hours. We've been told to tell you to present yourself at three. We can't send you down in this state. Alice go and get Becky a stiff brandy from the drinks cabinet. Come on honey sit down and tell us what happened between you two." Clutching a strong drink miserably Rebecca described her encounter with Jennifer earlier. Abigail was outraged. "Where the devil is the little madam now?" she demanded. "I'll soon bloody settle her!"

"She's gone downstairs Abi." Sniffed Rebecca. "Oh hell! I don't know why she thinks I've betrayed her."

"You haven't Becky. Nobody adores Jenny more than you do. She's being a bloody drama queen about something. Well I won't have it. This has gone on too long. It's time we settled Miss Walstow's hash for once and for all."

"Oh leave her be Abi." Rebecca said. "We'll only make things worse."

"What happened between you two the first time you were in the Oriental Gardens together anyway?"

"That's just it Abi. I don't know. We had a wonderful night there. Jenny was just fine. She was more than just fine. She was on a high. We all were. We were just all hopelessly in love. We've never been closer. It's something that's happened since. Something to do with that." Rebecca pointed to the little box open on the coffee table.

"What the 'ell is it anyway?" asked Alice.

"It's a medal Alice, a medal for bravery among the Line." Abigail told her, "Something like our equivalent of the Victoria Cross if you like. They're very rare Alice. Goddess knows where Jenny has got one from or whom it belongs to. Did she say Rebecca?"

Rebecca shook her head. "No just that she would never have known how she'd been used if it hadn't been for that. I.... I haven't a clue what she was talking about."

"Well we'll bloody well get to the bottom of it. She must have got it from somewhere. Sure as hellfire she didn't just buy it in a junk shop."

"I don't know Abi." Rebecca lamented, "All I know is that the girl I love thinks I've betrayed her and until I know what I'm supposed to have done I can't do anything to persuade her otherwise."

Abigail hugged her. "Leave it for the moment Becks. We'll sort it I promise. Right now though we've got to get you into a fit state to go downstairs and present yourself to the Lady and her guests."

"Who are they anyway?"

"We don't know Becky. We thought you'd know."

Rebecca shook her head. "No Abi. All that's been said to me is that there were a couple of people interested in seeing my research material. I took all my papers to the Lady this morning but she's kept me on ice ever since. I've just been sat here feeling sorry for myself."

"Well shape up honey. I think these guys are VIPs. They flew in on a helicopter so it ain't like they got sent around to the tradesmen's entrance or something."

"Oh hell! How am I going to talk to them in this state?"

"You'll be just dandy Becks. I've seen you get your act together under a lot more pressure than this! Don't worry about our little prima donna. When she gets her fanny back up here she's got some explaining to do to me."

Rebecca sighed heavily, "Ok I'll try."

"There spoke a true lady of the House of Mathom." Abigail paused and picked up the medal in its box once more. "What were you going to do with this Becky?"

"I don't know. Give it back to Jenny or something I suppose."

“Leave it to me sister. I’ll see that she gets it.” Rebecca vanished back to her chambers to effect repairs on her sorry appearance. Abigail frowned and picked up the medal, examining it critically.

Chapter Twenty-Nine

By three o'clock Rebecca had recovered her courage and tranquillity somewhat. She was dressed attractively and, if her face still showed some signs of strain, at least she had managed to bring her turbulent emotions under control. She was under instruction to attend the Lady and her guests in one of the large day parlours downstairs and, after taking a deep breath, she duly knocked on the door of that room. Entering at her Mistress's command, she found two men present both of whom rose to their feet as she walked in. Rebecca drew in a sharp breath. Her papers and notes were strewn across the surface of the large coffee table. The taller and clearly senior of the two men was clutching a sheaf of them in his hand and looking at her keenly. Rebecca stilled her wildly beating heart and curtsied politely.

"Good afternoon Rebecca." Said Lady Mathom. "Allow me to introduce you to our two guests. This gentleman is Professor Dieter Sehler, Director of research in Alpha Sensual anthropology and physiology and one of the coordinating members of the White Mountain research faculty in Switzerland. The younger gentleman is Doctor Desmond de Boer of Pennsylvania and a senior research assistant on Professor Sehler's team." Rebecca curtsied once more but with her heart and mind racing furiously. "Gentlemen," Lady Mathom continued "May I introduce you to the Lady Rebecca Walpole-Mathom, Slave of the Amethyst, Beloved of the Goddess and Daughter of the House of Mathom." The two men bowed formally to Rebecca and she felt a thrill of gratitude that her Mistress had accorded her her full formal title before these two men."

"We are very pleased to meet you at last Lady Rebecca." Professor Sehler told her.

“And I you Professor.” Replied Rebecca politely. “I have had the honour to read many of your works sir and have been inspired by them.”

The professor looked at her and bowed once more smiling easily. “Why thank you lady! We’ve read some of your work too and I’m delighted to meet the author of them at last. I would have been eager to have met any lady of such obvious brilliance. I am doubly delighted to discover that the authoress is not only brilliant but very beautiful as well.”

“I think Dieter,” said Lady Mathom dryly, “That it would be a good idea to at least allow my young lady to be seated before you unleash your gallantry on her!”

The professor laughed completely unabashed. “Why of course! Please do join us Lady Rebecca.”

“Allow me!” said Desmond rushing to hold out a chair. Rebecca blushed prettily but she lowered herself onto the chair with all the grace and allure of a high lady of her House and rewarded Desmond with a dazzling smile that kicked him straight in the libido leaving him limp and at her mercy, hopelessly devoted to her from that moment.

“Coffee Rebecca?” asked Lady Mathom.

“Oh er!” for a moment Rebecca was flustered and came within a wisp of jumping to her feet to serve the coffee. She took a breath and swallowed hastily. “Yes please My Lady.”

“Let me lady!” Said Desmond grasping the coffee pot and Lady Mathom was amused at the young man’s eagerness. It was plain to see that young Desmond was captivated by Rebecca. Well that was no bad thing! Let the good professor see that the young woman he was so eager to acquire was a high lady of the House of Mathom in all her power and grace. If he’d expected to recruit some submissive little assistant to bend to his will let him think again! Rebecca would land in his faculty with the devastating impact of an artillery strike and he’d best learn some respect for her forthwith! She felt inordinately proud of her beautiful young slave this day.

Once Rebecca had been served Lady Mathom turned to her. “Rebecca this is a very private conference which is why we have no servants today. We will be discussing matters of a highly confidential nature. You are to treat anything you hear in this room today with the utmost of discretion. I must have you formally declare that you will not repeat anything you hear today outside of this room without the authority of those of us present.”

“You have my formal assurance My Lady.”

“Very well Rebecca. I think you are aware that Professor Sehler here has been interested in your work for some time now and is eager that your work comes under the umbrella of his faculty in Switzerland.”

“Yes My Lady. The lady Eugene informed me of this at Bolswick Bay.”

“Yes. Well Rebecca I agree with the Professor that your work is highly significant to his project and as a result I have agreed to allow him the loan of you for his research purposes.” Lady Mathom allowed a small emphasis on the word loan to creep into her voice. “As yet Rebecca you are not aware of the reasons why your research is significant within the context of the White Mountain project. You are undoubtedly somewhat confused as to exactly what that project is. In order to enlighten you somewhat therefore I have asked the professor to give you a short briefing on the aims and principles of White Mountain. I will only say at this juncture that the White Mountain project is one of the most important and sensitive research programmes run by the Line anywhere in the world and of enormous significance for the future of our people. Professor?”

“Thank you My Lady.” Professor Sehler paused marshalling his thoughts. “Well Lady Rebecca. The White Mountain research facility is based in the

Roggental high in the Swiss Alps. The Line, through its business connections has maintained research facilities in Switzerland ever since the 19th century, financed by the Amethyst Imperial consortium. We have always had a good working relationship with the Swiss authorities and the Swiss economy is heavily dependent upon the injection of the capital of the Line within it. We have vast sums invested in the country. Were Amethyst Imperial and its daughter organisations to withdraw their funds the Swiss financial institutions would crash overnight. The organisations of the Line are the richest and most powerful business conglomerate in the world with a turn over unmatched by anything other than the Gross National Product of a handful of powerful nation states and the Swiss are our bankers! In a sense we are a bedrock of the Swiss economy, a large reason for the capital wealth of the country and heavy subsidisers of the economic infrastructure of the Confederation. It is sometimes said that in a way Switzerland is the Line. That if the Line could be said to possess its own nation then the Helvetic Confederation would come as close as anywhere to boasting that title. Everywhere in Switzerland from the financing of Alpine ski resorts to investment in the transport infrastructure and from cultural activities to heavy industry you will find the tendrils of the Line if you look for them. In no other country in the world will you find such an intimate relationship between the interests of the Line and those of a free people.

I tell you all this in order to try and explain just why Switzerland is so ideally suited for our purposes at White Mountain. In a way Switzerland is a test case for the Line. It is a working example of cooperation between Alpha Sensual human beings and a free society, a model if you like for what the Line would consider to be a successful society under the influence of the Goddess. There are other examples of course. Some of them such as those in Scandinavia may occur to you. At one point in its history even this country was on its way to becoming an Alpha dominated society before it all went pear shaped and there are other countries or enclaves within them where we can see the influence of the Line toward creating humanitarian and stable civilisations. I was born myself in Switzerland lady and I'm proud that my country has become such a shining example of what can be achieved by the influence of the Line. Make no mistake about it. Switzerland is one of the most socially and politically stable nations on earth. It possesses Europe's oldest continuous democracy, an eminently civilised federated republic of high per capita wealth and safe social conditions. It is a place where civility and respect still rule, where the crime figures would be beyond the dreams of avarice to the authorities in this country and, whilst it is highly regulated, it nevertheless affords its citizens considerable freedom within the shackles of their collective responsibility to the ideals their country represents. Even its foreign policy is a mirror image of the Line for even as the country involves itself heavily in the workings of the world it nevertheless retains its neutrality and a certain aloofness and moral high ground in the affairs of humanity.

Please do not think that I am painting a picture of an ideal society lady. Switzerland has its problems. We are after all talking about human beings here! What I am saying is that it is one of the best examples of a cultivated nation we've managed so far. If everybody lived in their own Switzerland this would be a far happier and more civilised world and it may well be that the survival of the human species will depend upon just such an eventuality." Professor Sehler paused and smiled. "Oh yes it happens to be a very beautiful country as well."

Rebecca smiled as well "I have never visited your country Professor but I have heard many reports of it and it must be lovely indeed."

"You will visit it lady and it will be all the more beautiful for your gracing of it!"

"Why thank you sir!"

"Are you supposed to briefing the lady Rebecca Dieter or flattering her?" asked Lady Mathom amusedly.

"Time spent complimenting a lovely woman is never wasted My Lady!" Professor Sehler noted, doggedly refusing to be corrigible. "Forgive me lady if I seem to have veered away from the subject into a eulogy of my native country but I have my reasons for doing so. For one thing it may well be that you will spend some considerable time in Switzerland over the next years and I would like you to know that it is a highly agreeable country. Then again it is important for you to know why Switzerland is advantageous for the purposes of our research programme. The truth is that it is a highly modern country integrated into the infrastructure of Europe yet at the same time remains a haven of civility and is sympathetic to the Line through its dependency upon our goodwill and a long history of cooperation with us. This makes it ideal within Europe. We have access to all the amenities of a modern state yet the state in question is willing to cooperate with us in ways that rather more xenophobic or sensitive nations might not. The third reason is the one that I've already touched upon. In a sense Switzerland is our experimental test case and you will come to find that many of the ideals by which we conduct our researches at White Mountain aim precisely for the kind of stability and civilisation that Switzerland represents. In a way you could say that we are trying to turn the world into a big Switzerland.

I must digress again somewhat here lady. I think we are all aware of the terrible and seemingly intractable problems of our world as it stands. We see daily a world facing the chaos of war, social upheaval, environmental degradation, poverty, sickness, blind prejudice, intolerance, over population and all the ills that afflict us. We are watching a society in a state of meltdown; one in which the very fabric of civilisation is at risk and possibly even the survival of the human species. For millennia the Line has championed the cause of high civilisation and the greater good of humanity. Make no mistake lady the Line has a proud record in furthering the principles of decency and rationality. Time and again our people have nudged societies towards those principles. It is our common ideology. We take oaths to that end upon our enslavement within the Line! You yourself are sworn to the cause of humanity lady. You took solemn oaths declaring yourself a slave to the good of humankind on the day you accepted the manacles of the House of Mathom. At this time, in these days of crisis, the Line has need of your services."

"I am aware of my duty Herr Professor."

"I am certain of it lady. Nevertheless I do not beg your pardon. We all need to remind ourselves of our sworn duty on occasion lady and never more so than at this time when it may be that the wisdom and efforts of those dedicated to the Goddess are all that stand between humanity and apocalypse."

"In what way will the research programme in Switzerland further that duty Professor?"

"In numerous ways lady. As I have already said we have a long history of scientific research in Switzerland. That research has always been dedicated in the final analysis towards human progress. For instance our pharmaceutical divisions in Switzerland have worked tirelessly to improve human health and banish illness. Then there are our researches into nuclear physics. We fund one of the most sophisticated atomic research programmes in the world out of White Mountain. It's not my field and I know very little about it but my physicist colleagues tell me that they are on the verge of a breakthrough that could provide cheap, virtually unlimited, clean power for the entire planet. The consequences of that alone would be profound for the human race. My own field is the area of bio-medical research specifically into the nature of the Alpha-Sensual syndrome. We know so little about the very characteristics that distinguish us from the rest of the human race. If we were to understand by what mechanism a portion of humanity came to possess enhanced human characteristics we could be on the way to a breakthrough that could profoundly alter the very nature of our species. We could be looking at a civilisation in which the Alpha-Sensual syndrome was the birth right of every human born. Think what that could mean. Your own work lady might give us the very key we need to achieve that breakthrough." The Professor paused to sip his coffee. "But I am getting ahead of myself. Let me tell you about White Mountain.

For a long time the research programmes in Switzerland were scattered about all over the place and it wasn't an ideal situation because there was often very little collusion between the various faculties. Some years ago we held a large policy conference with a view to streamlining the whole gamut of our research programmes and bringing them altogether under the umbrella of a single establishment that could coordinate our research. In this way it was thought we could have scientists from every discipline working together toward a common goal. Scientists as a breed lady are often rather protective of their territory. You could have a ludicrous situation where an advance is made in let us say particle physics for example that has enormous consequences for bio-medical research and nobody thought to pass the information on and it sits in a laboratory somewhere for years without ever getting into the hands of people who could use it. Why I remember not so long since when we had a situation where our aviation people developed a particular metal coating for aircraft surfaces. It turned out to be of limited use and got promptly forgotten about until somebody casually mentioned it to a friend in the electronics division. It turned out to be just what they were looking for to produce high efficiency conductors or something! The idea therefore of having all the scientists working under one roof as it were and in constant contact with each other is to ensure a multi-disciplinary cooperation.

Unfortunately space is somewhat at a premium in Switzerland and there was no real place that could act as our headquarters. Then we had a lucky break. Just after the Cold War, the Swiss government held a review of its defence policy. Switzerland, oddly enough for a supposedly neutral country, is one of the most militarised countries on the planet but, with the fall of the Soviet regime and the diminishing prospects of general European war and nuclear attack, the Swiss, like everybody else, started to look for ways of cutting their military budget. One thing that did come up was the issue of their fortresses, their mountain redoubts. These places are extraordinary lady. They are huge systems of caverns bored out of the centre of mountains designed to be impervious to nuclear attack. They are enormous some of them, capable of housing an entire division of soldiers with their equipment or more. Some of them even have railway lines running underground into them. There's even one I've seen that has a fully equipped fighter airfield inside the mountain. The aircraft literally fly out of the mountainside. Well many of these were expensive to maintain and increasingly obsolete as the threat of attack dwindled so the military planners were keen to decommission some of them.

"There was one inside a mountain called the Weissberg that was up for the axe. It was an enormous place high up in the Roggental that was costing a small fortune in upkeep. Well we came up with a proposal to lease the place from the military as a series of research laboratories and to construct a particle accelerator in. The military authorities were only too keen to make some money out of a costly dinosaur that they were going to shut down anyway as you can imagine. That was how the White Mountain project was born.

We moved all our facilities to the Weissberg and built or funded a corresponding infrastructure in the valley alongside. The Roggental didn't have much in the way of a tourist industry, as it happened, so the local people were all too happy to see an input of cash into the local economy. Hotels and guest houses sprang up all over the valley and we even opened ski lifts and shops. We nearly own that valley now and it's been a boon to the local residents because we've flooded the place with money. We even subsidise the local farmers. The Roggental's got a spanking new school that the Line paid for and we run most of the services in the valley. White Mountain needed a new hydroelectric generating plant to provide electricity that we built on the site of an existing but inadequate facility that the military had used. As a resulting offshoot of that we provide virtually free electricity, privately, to every household in the valley. We repaired the roads out of our own pockets and we hope to extend the current railway line right up to the upper valley. We opened a clinic for the inhabitants too and we provide first class health care locally because if there's one thing we've got lots of, it is doctors. I even take surgery myself down at the clinic sometimes. It's good for me. I try never to forget that I'm still a practising doctor. Having to deal with some little old lady's lumbago teaches me a little well needed humility. In effect lady the Roggental is an idyllic location virtually totally under the control of the Line and you'll not find a pleasanter or safer place outside of the valley in which you presently reside."

Lady Mathom laughed. "My dear Dieter. You're beginning to sound like a tourist brochure."

Professor Sehler grinned, "Forgive me My Lady. I'm afraid I'm rather proud of what we've achieved in the Roggental and rather liable to blow our own trumpet over it. However you did wish me to make clear to the lady Rebecca that working at White Mountain would be agreeable and rewarding. I thought that if the lady were to know something of the environment in which she would be working then she would come to see that her sojourns there would be highly pleasant."

"Oh I'm not criticising Dieter. The Roggental is a lovely place." Lady Mathom addressed Rebecca. "I've been up in the Roggental a number of times Rebecca and it is indeed very beautiful. It's a high alpine valley surrounded by awesome mountains and heart breakingly lovely. I've hiked up on the mountains around the Roggental when my duties have allowed me to and I could spend days up on the high pastures among the flowers and butterflies. The valley and its surroundings was a rather rural enclave previously and largely unspoilt by the sort of heavy mass tourism that has scarred many other mountain resorts. We have tried to keep it that way and, in spite of the heavy investment we have funnelled into the valley, I think we have largely succeeded. The Roggental region remains one of the most pristine Alpine environments in Central Europe. I think you will love it there."

"I love it here Ma-am." said Rebecca with just a hint of rebelliousness.

"You are not leaving here Rebecca. You will be spending as much time here as ever you will in the Roggental. I've told you this before. You are not being sold to White Mountain. You are merely being assigned periods of duty there; periods during which you will represent the House of Mathom at the White Mountain research facility. Your first duty will remain to this House however and this house will remain your home."

Rebecca drew a deep breath. "I will do my duty as you so order me to do so My Lady. However I would find it easier to perform that duty were I to know why exactly my services are required at White Mountain. For the moment I have nothing more than vague suggestions that my researches may be of interest to Professor Sehler in his own work. I have surrendered my papers to the Professor as you have ordered but I am at a loss to understand why they are of sufficient importance to require my physical presence in this Roggental."

Professor Sehler interrupted. "Please lady I was coming to that. It was necessary to fill you in with the background to the White Mountain project first. If I may be allowed to complete my summary of the research project I think you will better comprehend why it has become now so significant. You must be aware lady that naturally only a small part of the research carried out by the Line is conducted at White Mountain. In fact the facility is as much an administrative centre as it is a working laboratory. It has come to be a working headquarters of many diverse research units around the world, coordinating a global effort. To this end White Mountain possesses one of the world's most sophisticated communications facility and a computer system that matches even the one you have here.

"In fact your own computers, those of White Mountain and their twins around the world form part of an integrated web of super computers. Indeed you could do most of the donkey work you will be doing at White Mountain from the comfort your own boudoir here at Mathom Hall lady. But that would take you out of the other network, the most important one, the net of brilliant people working closely together toward a common goal. It is often an adage at White Mountain that more problems are solved over the coffee table than are resolved over a keyboard. We have the world's most powerful computers and they can interconnect all over the world at a distance from each other but the biggest super computers we possess have to sit down in the same room as each other and bang out the solutions that are going to change the world over coffee and sandwiches. I need you within that network lady. I would previously have liked you in any case to come to White Mountain to explain your theories. Previous that is to the events of this summer. Now however it is imperative that you do so."

"Imperative sir? Why? What events?"

"Events lady that have made the work we are doing at White Mountain more urgent than ever: events so secret that I preferred to come here and brief you in person concerning them. Before this summer White Mountain was a major research project, a key project but this summer has made it pivotal. This summer a discovery was made that blows open the doors on everything we have so far strived for and worked toward. It is a discovery so far reaching that it will change the course of human history. It may well represent the greatest hope or the greatest threat that mankind has ever faced." The professor stopped and turned to his younger colleague. "This is your baby Desmond. Will you take it from here?"

"Y… yes sir." Desmond turned crimson under Rebecca's keen appraisal but launched manfully into his long prepared brief. "Have you my lady Rebecca ever heard of the body of archival material within the vaults of this House known as Prophecy One, sometimes called the Prime Prophecy, the Word of the Goddess or the Star Prophecy?"

"I have come across some references to a series of religious myths within the Line's mythology in which those terms are mentioned yes." said Rebecca in puzzlement. "The archives are full of legends and myths dating back to the early days of the Line. Many of them are obscure to say the least and many have never been translated or interpreted."

"What do you know of that particular myth lady?"

"Why very little sir. It's a religious prophecy isn't it? Something like the Line's equivalent to the second coming of Christ; the coming of the Goddess to take Her people back to the Garden or something. I've studied Alpha-Sensual mythology of course as part of my studies into early Alpha societies but I'm no theologian."

"Yet you are probably aware that many of the legends of the Line are grounded in fact. They may well be expressed in archaic terms and obscure language but they frequently refer to actual factual occurrences."

"Well yes. My own work often consists of sieving through bodies of mythology to uncover particular trends that indicate specific patterns in which we can determine real events but there's an awful lot of fabricated nonsense in there too. I can hardly see how much of it can be rationally analysed."

"I would take care lady before dismissing the mythology of the Line as mere fairy stories. We're only just beginning to understand the deep messages and buried secrets contained within the vast resources of our legends. Those legends lady are a virtually untapped source of wisdom and we have simply no idea just how much information is stored within them. Some years ago a programme was initiated to study our legends and folklore in greater depth and to turn over the parts of our archival material that is as yet understood. This project was started largely by historians and theologians of the Line. Such studies, previously, were generally a fairly obscure if interesting field that was hoped would give us insights into the mindset of early Alpha Sensual societies. As such it was a field that was typically confined to small teams, often working independently in the numerous dusty archives of our people scattered around the globe. The new initiative was to unify all these obscure units under a single branch of study and to congregate all the work done so far in a single faculty. Her Ladyship here," Desmond nodded at Lady Mathom, "was very active in promoting this study and provided the funding for a centralised library at White Mountain to act as a repository for the material to act in collusion with the Mathom Hall archives. It was her desire that the veracity of the mythological content of the archives be measured and the whole body of work be given a far more intensive and scientific analysis.

"The results of that initiative have been startling lady and none more so than the study of the part of the archival material under the heading of Prophecy One. The Prime Prophecy we believe to have existed within the Line for at least three millennia lady and it has remained remarkably consistent. As you have rightly said it is tantamount to a religious prophecy. It foretells the coming of Judgement Day if you like, a time when the portents in heaven announce the emergence of the Goddess and the gathering of Her people into the Garden of Paradise. Unlike other such apocalyptic prophecies however the Prime Prophecy is cyclical. The Goddess emerges once every thousand or eleven hundred years to send her messenger to the people of the Line and invite them into paradise. If they choose not to She leaves messages of goodwill and returns again and again until Her people are ready to follow Her to heaven.

There are numerous epic poems and long religious texts within various archives concerning the Prime Prophecy and a remarkable fact about them is how consistent they are. I have seen for example ancient Mandarin texts, very old Arabic documents and European scrolls written in Latin that all make virtually the same prophecy. Even the details remain identical. The cycle of years between the visits of the messenger of the Goddess, the appearance of a new star in heaven to forewarn humanity of its imminent arrival and the song of the messenger."

"The song of the messenger?" asked Rebecca in bafflement.

"Yes lady. The messenger is supposed to announce her arrival with a specific song called the Song of Water. Nobody knew what the devil that meant. We do now! Forgive me but I'll return to that in a minute." Desmond paused for breath. "Well on the face of it lady it all seems like just yet another lovely story among our rich heritage of legend and folklore. Nobody has really believed it. It has always remained quite obscure and little known even within the Line. It certainly hasn't formed the basis of any great religious belief other than the non-specific, rather philosophical one of the people's return to the Garden which has always been regarded more as an analogy for Alpha enlightenment or a new age of high civilisation to be achieved when the Alpha syndrome becomes dominant within human culture. As such, the whole prophecy could well have remained just that; just an allegory for the forward march of Alpha culture. Certainly the people who studied the prophecy read no more into it than that. How wrong they were."

"You can't seriously be suggesting Doctor that there is some basis of fact behind this incredible story."

"Lady I am authorised to brief you that the Prophecy One is, not only factual, but has, this very summer, been confirmed by direct observation."

"But.... but how?"

"If you'll allow me to tell the full story lady perhaps you will begin to see how it happened."

"Forgive me Doctor. Please continue."

"Well lady the thing to remember is that huge portions of our archival material are simply not understood. There are vast swathes of documents that are encrypted into some of the most fiendishly complex codes ever devised before the use of computerised encryption. We have barely begun to scratch the surface of the material that has been handed down to us through the ages and resides within our archives. Some of it is almost certainly incomplete. We don't have the keys to crack the ancient codes of our forebears and those who might know have long lost the keys themselves. Most of the time we don't know what language it is encrypted from or even whether or not the language in question still exists. Then again there is so much material that it would take decades to even just read it. The keys to some of the codes could be sat in an old manuscript somewhere that nobody's even looked at for over two hundred years. Here in this house alone is enough material to keep us all occupied for the better part of a century. There's just too much of it and as far as we're concerned most of its gibberish.

"The reason I mention all this lady is to point out to you just how little we actually have of Prophecy One. Until very recently it was just a number of references to it scattered all over the world that told us that every millennia or thereabouts a new star appears in heaven to announce the coming of the messenger of the Goddess who will invite us back to the Garden with the Song of Water. Everything else revolving around the prophecy was deeply encrypted. Attached to the documentation concerning the Prime Prophecy were just thousands of completely indecipherable texts and references. That alone should have alerted us to the fact that Prophecy One was of vital importance since the people that created these texts went to a great deal of trouble, time and effort to put down so much information and then encode it to protect the secret. These were clever people lady. They wouldn't have taken so much trouble over something that they didn't consider to be important. What they didn't manage to pass through to us were the keys to decipher the information seemingly. It may be as I've said that those keys may still waiting to be discovered or it is eminently possible that somewhere in history they were lost or destroyed. One theory is that large amounts of the ancient material of the Line were destroyed in the Library of Alexandria somewhere between the first and fifth centuries AD. I couldn't comment on that. It's not really my field of study. In any case the prophecy has been rewritten and recoded many times since so the information couldn't have been entirely lost.

Well we don't have the keys lady but what we do have are modern supercomputers and a large body of decryption technology. When the archival studies were moved to White Mountain the scholars working on the material asked for help from other disciplines in decoding the encrypted material. A working team was set up to launch an all-out attack on the coded documents. They concentrated on the material relevant to Prophecy One simply because there was so much of it. I don't know much about cryptology lady but apparently the more material you've got in any code makes it easier to spot recurrent patterns and crack the code. The sheer volume of data in the Prophecy One documents were, in fact, their Achilles heel, especially when you could crunch it through a massive computer system.

Well some years ago the team made certain breakthroughs in a number of Chinese and European documents around a thousand years old that seemingly complimented each other. The stuff that was coming out however left everybody more confused than ever. Instead translating down into plain text the materials seemed to be coughing up what appeared to be mathematical formulae. To begin with most people thought that these formulae were merely a new level of encryption because apparently the encryption of the material is often layered. You break one code down only to find yourself in a new one. This stuff is super complicated believe me. Some others argued that the apparently emerging mathematical patterns were in fact a key to other documentation. Well everybody had a fine old time arguing about it but nobody seemed to be getting anywhere until one scientist raised the possibility that the mathematics were in fact the point of the whole thing. The people that had encoded this stuff actually wanted to hide the maths in it.

The most telling points about the maths were repeated descriptions of circles, curves and ellipses. There were whole sections just full of the reference to geometric relationships between these shapes. One seemed particularly significant because it was called "The Way of the Messenger" and it was a long drawn out ellipse. The team modelled it on a computer and then stood back and scratched their heads. Remember what Professor Sehler said about the usefulness of having many different disciplines working in collusion with each other? Well this was a prime example because the team could have been scratching their heads yet if a visiting astronomer hadn't walked in to the faculty and taken a look at their computer model. He took one look at it and said, "Why it looks just like a cometary orbit." Everybody went real quiet after that.

That casual remark was the breakthrough. The team modelled in all the other geometric circles they'd picked out of the material and the whole picture came together. They came up with a perfect image of the solar system with the orbital path of a comet dissecting it. It was just beautiful. They even got the comet's period out of it and, surprise, surprise, they found that it reached perihelion around every thousand years. The messenger of the Goddess was a comet. It all made wonderful sense. The new star that was supposed to appear in heaven to announce the Judgement of the Goddess was simply a periodical comet that revisited the inner solar system every thousand to eleven hundred years or thereabouts. They figured that it had to be a pretty spectacular comet and it must have made sufficient impression on people at the time to take on such religious significance. Some people even said that the Song of Water was in fact a somewhat flowery description of the comet's appearance. Possibly it had displayed a spectacular tail like a great fountain or something. The whole thing seemed to have been wrapped up rather nicely. It was time to move on. Well lady if you've been following all this you'll have spotted a hole in this comfortable scenario that you could throw a planet through."

Rebecca grimaced. "But of course. How could somebody a thousand years ago possibly have predicted the orbit of a comet? As far as I knew nobody had done that before Edmond Halley in the 17th century."

"Exactly! And Halley based his prediction on the recorded known appearances of a comet that visited the inner system every seventy-six years. This thing hadn't been seen for over a thousand. Now it was possible that there were Alpha Sensual people with memories that could encompass an entire millennium lady," Desmond's eyes flickered nervously toward Lady Mathom who merely sat there, her expression unreadable, "but if so they never recorded the fact and in any case that raised more questions than answers. For one thing long period comets generally originate in the Oort cloud which is a sphere of left over cometary debris right out at the very edges of the solar system extending out to maybe 50,000 AUs from the sun."

"I'm sorry to interrupt Doctor." Said Rebecca, "What does AU mean?"

"Sorry ma-am. AU stands for Astronomical Unit. It's a measurement of distances used by astronomers. One AU is the average distance between the earth and the sun, average because the earth's orbit is slightly elliptical and thus the distance varies, but about 93 million miles or around 150 million kilometres. Fifty thousand AU is an awfully long way away, a sizeable fraction of the distance between ourselves and our nearest neighbouring star. The point is ma-am that comets with orbital periods longer than around two hundred years, originating from such a remote distance just aren't that easy to predict the orbit of. A few years ago for instance you might recall the very bright comet that graced our skies for some weeks in the summer."

"Yes. Yes I do. It was beautiful."

"Well that was a typical long period comet probably with an orbital period of around four thousand five hundred years. When we predict such an orbit however we are only saying that if the comet follows the same parameters of the orbit it is on it will return in four and a half millennium. Well an awful lot has to go right for that to happen. Many long period comets only ever make a single visit to the interior of the solar system. You've got to remember that way out at aphelion, that's the orbital distance furthest from the sun; the sun is nothing more than a bright star at an incredibly remote distance. The gravitational influence of the sun on your comet is pretty feeble at that distance and anything can cause a deviation in its orbit, a passing star, the gravitational effects of the galaxy centre all sorts of things are giving the comet micro gravitational nudges that may seem pretty tiny but over such a long orbit they are sufficient to cause major variations in its orbit. Then again the gravitational pulls of the planets in the inner system can cause small deviations in the orbit as the comet visits the inner system. They may only move it off course by a tiny fraction but that fraction magnified over such a long orbit means that it ends up way out of its predicted orbit. What we had here however was the predicted orbit of a long period comet that visited, if you believed the figures, as regularly as clockwork with a small variation every thousand years or so. It beggars belief that anybody in the middle ages could have possibly predicted that.

"Even supposing they could do raised a whole new bunch of questions. Even to attempt to make a prediction, you've got to have some sort of knowledge of the nature of the universe. This is long before Newton's laws of gravity remember. Nobody even knew the very forces that determined the orbit of objects around each other let alone how to calculate the orbit of an object through the action of those forces upon them. Then again the figures showed an orbit that had a perihelion or a closest approach to the sun. That was unthinkable in that era. Right up until Nicolas Copernicus in the 16th century it was a matter of unshakeable faith that everything in the universe revolved around the earth. Yet here we had a predicted orbit that flew straight in the face of that geo-centric universal model. The more you looked at it the less sense it seemed to make. Something else was going on here.

"Now comets have notoriously been harbingers of doom, warnings of impending catastrophe or ominous omens and portents, so it was argued that it was hardly surprising that this predicted comet was seen as some apocalyptic sign of the coming of the Goddess. However, some dissenting voices started to question that analysis. For one thing the predicted orbit was just too rational. It showed an understanding of the nature of deep space objects that surely removed a lot of the mystique from them. It's one thing to read some doom filled interpretation into something you don't understand but quite another to place a thing in the ordered system of the universe at the mercy of physical influences on it and still assign religious or mystical properties to it. The minds behind this material showed perfectly well that they had a rational understanding of the physical properties of the universe and the order to which their predicted comet must conform. They were hardly describing some chariot of the Goddess that could do just what the devil it wanted to. This was a physical object with predictable parameters as much at the mercy of the forces of nature as old Isaac's apple.

"Then again there was the question of the singularity of the comet. If, as some suggested, we were talking about a very long lived Alpha Sensual that might or might not have had personal memory of a previous visit of this comet it begs the question of why this comet. In the course of such a lifetime they must have seen dozens if not hundreds of comets. They would have had Halley's comet rolling by every seventy-six years for one thing. That would have been a hell of a lot easier cometary orbit to predict. If they were truly describing the orbit of a comet why for heaven's sake did they fixate on this one? There is not the slightest attempt within the Prime Prophecy to calculate the orbit of any other comet. Why? Well perhaps the Prophecy One comet happens to be a particularly spectacular one. If that was true however then its appearance should have recorded independently by other sources yet try as we might we could find no such independent confirmation of a very bright comet corresponding to the predicted orbit of this one.

"Now that, in itself, was not an insurmountable problem. A hell of a lot of astronomical observation recorded by the European monks in the Middle Ages seems to have been lost and some of it even deliberately suppressed. There is the famous case of a supernova explosion in the 11th century the observation of which appears to have been deliberately eradicated from European records simply because its appearance directly contradicted the firmly held religious conviction in the changeless immutability of God's heaven. You can't have a new star appearing in the sky without the second coming of Christ can you? But that can't fully explain this over sight. Comets were after all perfectly familiar if ill understood phenomena and medieval scholars did record them. Then again we had the Prophecy One material from China and the Chinese were meticulous observers of the heavens. If the Europeans suppressed the records of the supernova the Chinese certainly didn't. They recorded it and its position in heaven with sufficient accuracy for modern astronomers to locate precisely the nebulous debris of the explosion from their records."

"That was the Crab Nebula wasn't it?" asked Rebecca.

"That's right lady." Desmond looked at Rebecca with growing respect becoming aware that he was in the presence of a formidable intellect and one of such polymathic talents that she was sufficiently well read in astronomy to know of the Crab Nebula. It was a timely reminder that he was not dealing with an uninformed layman. This girl was not just some decorative beauty. She had a brain that could match his own. He scratched his chin with a disarming grin. "Forgive me lady if I sound like I'm trying to teach you to suck eggs. I had no idea that I was talking to a lady so well informed."

Professor Sehler snorted with amusement in the background. "I think Desmond son, on the strength of the lady Rebecca's doctoral work, we may take it as read that she is no brainless bimbo."

"I did not wish to sound patronising lady. My apologies." said Desmond ruefully.

Rebecca rewarded his apology with a dazzling smile that made Desmond's heart jump. "By no means Doctor. I did not find your briefing patronising. Indeed I find all this fascinating. Please continue."

"Well er… do you have any questions so far lady."

"Oh hundreds Doctor. They can wait mostly. One thing I would like clarification on, though, is this. You have said that the Prophecy dates back at least three millennia yet the information that you have extracted from the encrypted material concerning this cometary orbit dates from the Middle Ages. Was this a new interpretation of the Prophecy from that era or is there any corresponding material from earlier eras to suggest that this parabolic orbit was known earlier?”

Desmond looked at her in surprise “Why yes there is ma-am. I was about to come to that.”

Professor Sehler looked at her keenly. “You’re beginning to see it aren’t you lady?” he asked.

“Oh yes Professor.” Rebecca clenched her jaw tightly. “I began to understand the implications of all this some time ago in Doctor de Boer’s presentation. I’ve been hoping it isn’t true.”

“I think a lot of us have been secretly hoping that over the last weeks lady.” Professor Sehler told her. “But it is true and we’re going to have to come to terms with that.”

Rebecca turned to Desmond. “Please continue Doctor.”

“Well ma-am, as you so pertinently asked, once some of the Prime Prophecy material of the middle Ages was deciphered the race was on to examine earlier encoded material surrounding the prophecy. In some respects it was difficult because of course a lot of the early material is incomplete or so archaic in nature as to be nearly gibberish. We did have one enormous advantage however. By now we knew what sort of mathematical patterns to look for and to cut a long story short we found them! We came up with beautiful parabolic models from material as early as the 6th century BC. One of the most extraordinary came from the 1st century AD from a series of scrolls in Egypt. In many respects it was even more detailed than the later manuscripts from the 11th and 12th centuries. It even showed the relationship of the parabola to the orbits of planets that weren’t visible to the naked eye and theoretically quite unknown in that era. How could some Egyptian in the First century possibly have known about Uranus and Neptune?”

“I’m beginning to think that I’ve fallen into an Erich von Daniken fantasy.” Rebecca observed.

Desmond grinned at her. “It certainly feels that way sometimes ma-am. I hope however that we have somewhat sounder evidence for our theories than von Daniken’s woolly ideas and fabrications. Anyway, whilst some researchers were hunting down the mathematical parameters of the parabola in earlier works, one small group was quietly working on the as yet un-decrypted material of the Middle Ages. In particular, they were working on the material under the heading of the Song of Water. This, as may you recall, was supposed to be the song delivered by the mythical messenger of the Goddess to the people of the Line to announce her imminent arrival. Oddly it wasn’t all that imminent this arrival for the material suggested that the song could be heard for a hundred years before the messenger arrived. Goddess only knew what that was supposed to mean.

“There were all sorts of curiosities and enigmas mentioned in the documentation about this mythical song. For instance, in a line from a poetical stanza dating from the 12th century it was said that the song could be heard but not seen. What the hell was that supposed to mean? Of course you can’t see a song. Was this deliberate obfuscating? Were the authors deliberately trying to baffle us with meaningless paradoxes? Well by this time we were alert to the fact that the encrypted manuscripts were very logical and rational documents. They were conveying information that the authors considered to be meaningful for us to know and if it said something like this then there had to be some point to it.

There were a number of documents that legend had it were actual translations of the Song of Water if only we could decipher them. Well the team ran the material through the same computer programmes that had uncovered the mathematical formulae in the documents that had revealed the parabola of our hypothetical comet to see if there were other geometries concealed within them. Well there were but, for a while, we were baffled by them. The formulae seemed to describe a series of oscillations along a linear progression like a musical scale. For a while we wondered if we'd just uncovered the score for the Song of Water but, as more and more, of the pattern fell into place the most astonishing feature yet emerged. The formulae were simply a description of oscillating vibrations and when we translated the units of measurement into our own we discovered that the material was nothing more or less than an accurate description of the wavelengths of the electro-magnetic spectrum right through from high energy gamma radiation through visible light right down to very low frequency radio waves.

Well this was just mind-boggling. It was hard enough to imagine early civilisations modelling the parabolic orbit of a comet but it went beyond the realms of fantasy to believe that they had a detailed knowledge of the electromagnetic spectrum hundreds of years before Isaac Newton had even shown such a thing to exist and even longer before we ever became aware of the non-visible part of the spectrum. Yet there it was. Unmistakeable. And, moreover, there on the spectrum was placed the Song of Water. Now we understood the meaning of the words of that poetic stanza. Yes we could hear it but it was outside of the visual spectrum. The documents weren't giving us the lyrics of the song. They weren't giving us the tune. What they were giving us was its radio frequency!"

"Oh Goddess!" Rebecca breathed.

"Yes lady. And it is a very special frequency as well; one that only a technologically advanced society could possibly know. In fact it is a range of frequencies between 1420 gigahertz and 1640 gigahertz on the electromagnetic spectrum. This is a range of frequencies in a relatively quiescent part of the spectrum between the hydrogen and hydroxyl frequencies that would be instantly recognisable to any advanced civilisation familiar with radio astronomy for instance. It's like a hole in the spectrum with very little background noise to interfere with any signal. It's been of interest to many astronomers searching for extra-terrestrial radio signals for many years because it's just such an obvious frequency range to use if you want to gain somebody's attention."

"Yes I think I've heard of it." said Rebecca. "Wasn't it the frequency range that was utilised by SETI in its earlier days?"

"Yes that's right lady."

"And in the hydrogen to hydroxyl range! Hence the "Song of Water" I presume."

"Precisely lady. It's even been known by modern astronomers as the water hole and its upper frequency is sometimes called the song of hydrogen. The authors of these documents knew exactly what they were saying. They were telling us precisely where to listen for the message of the messenger of the Goddess."

"This is incredible!"

"It becomes more so lady. I think that when you have ruled out every other possibility the one remaining, however fantastic it may seem, must be the truth. The revelation of the nature of the Song of Water coupled to the parabolic trajectory of the messenger opened up the astonishing possibility that the documents of the prophecy were not allegories for some mystic interpretation of anything as mundane as a mere comet. These people were not giving us legends and myths but hard scientific data. We had to take very seriously that when they referred to a messenger of the Goddess they were referring to exactly that. Not a comet. Not a supernova. Not any natural phenomena but, in fact, something that pursued a long-term cometary orbit within our solar system that brought it to perihelion every thousand to eleven hundred years. Something that carried a message for us. Something that could speak to us! A product of intelligence that could communicate with us along a pre-specified radio frequency and the consequences of that could change the course of human history."

Rebecca buried her head in her hands. "This is just too fantastic to be true."

"But true it is ma-am. We had an approximate date for the next perihelion. It lies about one hundred years or so from now we believe. With that in mind our astronomers started to use a huge radio telescope array in the New Mexico desert, among others, that is funded and maintained by the Line to listen out for the Song of Water out along the predicted parameters of the parabolic orbit. That initiative was started several years ago. This summer that radio telescope received an unmistakeable artificial signal lasting many hours from a point of origin that corresponds to the predicted orbit of Prophecy One. The prophecy is fulfilled. We have one hundred years before the messenger reaches perihelion in the inner system."

Rebecca had turned pale. "Wh.... what does the signal say?"

"We don't know lady. We can't understand it. Nor any of the smaller bursts it has emitted since. It is a massively compressed encrypted signal and we simply don't know where to begin to unravel it."

"But what is this messenger then?"

"Again we can only speculate lady. Since the reception of the first radio signal we have hunted for the object that emitted it in the visual spectrum without really expecting to find it. In point of fact we found it quite quickly. It is very distant and right on the very edge of the resolving capacity of our most powerful telescopes but it is there. Even to be visible at all at the distance we have spotted it then it must be huge! It has to be the largest known artifice anywhere. And it is an artifice lady. It has some kind of drive. We've seen the massive energy bursts that it produces as it presumably manoeuvres. It is a functioning artifice out in space lady and it is massive. More than that we can't say other than that it has revealed itself to the people of the Line and that it must have some terrible importance to us."

"A spaceship then?"

"Again we don't know. We ain't had a personal Email from Captain Kirk yet. We don't even know if there are people or beings on it or whether or not it is a mere robot. We just know that it is big, it is still working and that it's coming to neighbourhood near you all too soon. We could be looking at Judgement Day."

"A robot?" queried Rebecca.

"Why yes ma-am. You can imagine that in the days since the object now inevitably known as Prophecy One there has been some pretty wild speculation about it. One of the theories is that it's a so-called von Neumann machine, a self-replicating robot following a pre-set programme thousands of years old. Von Neumann postulated that it made far more sense to colonise interstellar space by building robots capable of building replicas of themselves, that could build replicas of themselves and gradually infest interstellar space like a sort of robotic plague. He argued that if we made contact with an extra-terrestrial intelligence it was overwhelmingly likely to be through such machines."

"Thank you Doctor. I'm familiar with John von Neumann's theories however."

"Sorry ma-am."

Lady Mathom looked at Rebecca compassionately seeing the shock in the young woman's face. "How are you doing Rebecca?" she asked.

Rebecca shook her head to clear the rising panic from her mind. “Oh My Lady this is all too much. All this can’t be true. It just can’t be.”

“Dearest Rebecca.” Said Lady Mathom gently “We’ve all said that to ourselves over the last two months. I think we’re all in shock somewhat. Do you remember the day when you came to report to me that you had seen Jennifer and I sent you to spend the night in the cellars?” Rebecca nodded dumbly. “Well that was the same day that I heard the news myself. The Goddess was running wild that night.” Indeed she had been Rebecca thought. It was the night when she Robin and the Lady had spent a night of wild forbidden sweetness in the cellars. The Lady had been carrying this dreadful secret into that extraordinary night.”

“Oh My Lady! I don’t know what to think.”

Professor Sehler looked at Rebecca in terrible intensity. “But you can’t stop thinking lady can you? You already know what this means to your own studies. You know now why it is so important to us the work you have been doing.”

“Yes Professor. I have seen it. As soon as I heard the periodicity of Doctor de Boer’s parabolic orbit I thought my heart would stand still. It hasn’t escaped me that the cyclical emergences of new Alpha Sensual clusters correspond rather too neatly with your Prophecy One orbit. This thing’s genetically engineering us isn’t it?”

“It’s our best guess lady. It is now anyway. Your theories about new clusters of Alpha Sensuals apparently unrelated to other groupings suddenly popping up every thousand years or so takes on a whole new meaning doesn’t it when we know that they emerge every time this thing pays a visit to the inner solar system. Whatever it is it isn’t just making a fly past on its visits. It doesn’t just come whistling through sending enigmatic messages out and then vanishing off back into the Oort cloud for another millennium. It's actively engaging with humanity on its passes. It must be. Think about some of the things in the prophecy. How could the authors of the prophetic documentation have known about all this? How could a medieval scholar have been able to compute parabolic orbits or the electromagnetic spectrum without technical know-how? He couldn't. Not unless somebody or something told him. This thing has been making regular contact with Alpha Sensual humans."

"We might even know where lady." Desmond observed. "Among some of the more baffling mathematical data among the archival material from Europe is a set of what can only be coordinates. Unlike the parameters of the orbital parabola however they appear to be coordinates on the surface of a sphere. A Professor Han at White Mountain ran a computer model to correlate the measurements used in the documentation to our own units of measurement and decisively demonstrated that the coordinates represented coordinates along lines of latitude and longitude on the surface of Earth. When he shifted the thing about to correspond with our medians based on Greenwich the whole cluster of points fell into a random distribution across Western Europe. There doesn't seem to be any logical pattern to these coordinates but several of them correspond to the location of major cities. Why we just don't know. Intriguingly the body of information of containing these coordinates was called the voice of the messenger. It could be, in the light of our growing realisation that Prophecy One has actively made contact with the Line, that these are places of contact. Whether that means they are places where contact has been made or that they are places where it will be made we have no way of knowing at this moment. We've argued it every which way. The city locations are the most interesting. Some of the cities in question didn't exist as cities when these prophecies were made yet others were already ancient at the time. You can run around in circles arguing yourself to death over that paradox."

"Why only Europe?" Rebecca wanted to know.

"Probably because those are the only coordinates we've found and interpreted so far lady. Doubtless there have been or still are in our archives similar coordinates all over the world. We have no way of knowing what their significance is though."

"Could they be time drops Doctor?" asked Rebecca. "You know. The location of deposited time capsules left for us to discover containing information relevant to the Prophecy?"

"Well certainly some people have considered that possibility lady but we're going to make ourselves mighty unpopular if we suddenly start digging holes all over down town Berlin looking for them."

"Berlin is one of the marked coordinates?"

"Along with a lot of others lady. There are even a few here in your part of England although curiously there aren't many others outside this region in the British Isles. Most of them seem to occur across Central Europe particularly in Germany, Austria, France and, coincidentally, Switzerland. There're quite a few in the Benelux countries and in Scandinavia and some in Northern Italy, Spain and Portugal. We're damned if we can see a pattern to them!"

Rebecca shook her head once more thinking furiously. "Gentlemen if this thing is breeding Alpha Sensuals what is the purpose of that? I mean why?"

Professor Sehler bit his lip. "Again we can only speculate lady Rebecca. It seems increasingly likely that the Alpha Sensual genome results from some kind of direct alien manipulation of human genes in order to produce enhanced members of the species with superior characteristics. Why that should be of value to the theoretical controlling intelligence is anybody's guess."

"If this thing turns out to be a bloody great black monolith I'm going to start screaming. I swear I will." Rebecca told him feelingly.

Professor Sehler grinned ruefully. "It may not be that far off the mark. There's a wild assed theory doing the rounds at the moment that Alpha Sensuals are human beings that are being groomed to journey to wherever this thing comes from to meet its creators. Quite a number of people have pointed out that very long lived human beings of enhanced capabilities, the ability to hibernate spontaneously and able to live harmoniously in tightly bonded teams would just about make your perfect inter stellar astronauts."

"Alpha Sensuals also make very good slaves Herr Professor." Rebecca pointed out. "We might do well to remember that."

"That's a disturbing thought lady."

"And too disturbing on an empty stomach I'm afraid." Lady Mathom pointed out. "I think at this point we'll adjourn for tea. If you two gentlemen would like to refresh yourselves before tea I would like a word with Rebecca in private. Shall we say in half an hour on the veranda?"

"Well that's fine with me." Said Professor Sehler although the disappointment visible in his face would have suggested that it was anything but.

"Excuse me My Lady." Said Rebecca "May I be permitted to ask one final question before we adjourn for tea."

Lady Mathom smiled "Of course Rebecca, assuming it doesn't require half the night to answer."

"Thank you My Lady. Doctor De Boer you said earlier that we might be looking at Judgement Day. I assumed that you were merely referring to the quasi-religious content of the Prime Prophecy documentation. Now I'm not so sure. What did you mean when you used that phrase?"

“Exactly what I said ma-am. Assuming that the Line is some sort of genetic tinkering with the human genome by some unknown intelligence then we might regard ourselves as a sort of experiment. Remember that the Line is under command to improve the condition of human civilisation. That’s a prime programme in Alpha Sensuals. That is what we have always seen as our purpose, our primary directive. Well maybe the Prophecy One object is periodically monitoring our progress. The suggestion is that we have been granted the information in the Prophecy One documentary but at a level that we can only understand once we have reached a certain level of technological sophistication. This may then be the point at which the controlling intelligence decides whether or not the experiment has been a success. Well if you look around you lady and see the mess our species is in it might well decide that we haven’t done a very good job and we all know what you do with unsuccessful experiments.”

“Goddess!”

“Yes lady. I mean think about it. Even after thousands of years we still haven’t eliminated war for example.”

Lady Mathom clicked her tongue with just a hint of irritation. “Why on Earth should we get rid of something that we are so very good at?” she wanted to know.

Desmond looked at her in surprise. “Why My Lady what do you mean?”

“I mean Doctor De Boer that we should hesitate long before we assign motives to an intelligence whose ultimate purpose we cannot begin to understand. We do not even know if our own perceptions of good and evil are at all relevant to an entity that formulates game plans over tens of thousands of years. I would like to point out that we have not been altered as human beings, merely enhanced. Ultimately we are still human beings with all the faults and frailties that term endorses. Those faults may well turn out to be the very characteristics that our creators find most desirable in us. After all if our mentors are hoping to cultivate a warrior species to recruit as allies in some great war of their own they are hardly going to be amused to discover that we've all become sweetness and light pacifists in the period since they last monitored our progress."

"Are you suggesting that that is their purpose Ma-am?"

"I am suggesting nothing Doctor. I am merely warning against the folly of anthropomorphising the intentions and purposes of the creators of Prophecy One. If there is to be a Judgement Day then let us not be the ones to judge too hastily."

Professor Sehler gazed at Lady Mathom intensely. "How much do you know My Lady? You are the eldest among us. How much of all this do you know?"

"I know first and foremost Professor that wisdom comes through recognising what we don't know. As to my own personal knowledge well I certainly don't intend to cover it in detail before tea. Now if you gentlemen would excuse us." Professor Sehler and Desmond rose reluctantly to their feet bowing as they took their leave. Rebecca rose to curtsy in her turn and then she was left alone with her Mistress.

"How are you doing Rebecca? You seem traumatised."

"Oh My Lady! I am so very frightened."

"We are all frightened Rebecca. We will have much need of each other's love and comfort in the years to come." Lady Mathom paused and sighed. "You will hear a great deal of wild speculation in the days to come Rebecca and some of it will be pretty scary stuff. Let me tell you what I believe and I hope you will derive some comfort from it. I do not believe that Prophecy One will mean evil for our species. I believe on the contrary that it represents an enormous opportunity for us, an opportunity for the human race to achieve greatness beyond our wildest imagining. If judgement there be it will be as to how ready we are to grasp that opportunity. I don't for one moment believe, either, that this is merely an opportunity for those of us blessed by the Goddess. This will be a defining moment for all mankind. We are merely the chosen to prepare our people for the coming of the Prophecy and ultimately the responsibility of doing that will fall upon us."

"And you My Lady? How much will you be responsible?"

Lady Mathom stared at her. Then she shook her head and took a cigarette from her case on the desk. She lit it and rose to walk over to the windows, staring out across the grounds as she smoked. There was a long silence in the room. The refrains of music drifted over the gardens. Some of the slaves on the estate were practising their instruments for their part in the summer festival. When Lady Mathom spoke once more it was with a voice that seemed to come from a great distance. "My name was Cheela Rebecca. I have forgotten many of my names but that one I will always remember for it was the first I ever had. The people who found me, the woman that I called mother, called me that. It was the name in their language for the little purple flowers that grow on the grasslands. They found me naked and starving as a little girl in the wilderness and knew not where I came from but they gave me a home and love. Some years later as a young woman I returned to the wilderness to discover from where I came. There, far from other human habitation, I became the slave of a great machine who called herself Xadinia. She taught me my purpose and showed me my destiny. She gave me the tools and knowledge to fulfil that destiny and she told me of my origins." Rebecca stared, hardly daring to breathe, at her Mistress's back. Slowly Lady Mathom turned to face Rebecca once more and Rebecca was shocked to see tears streaming down her face. "Rebecca I came not of man and woman. I was birthed on Prophecy One." The Lady seemed almost like a sad young girl stood before Rebecca, her cheeks wet with the bitter tears of her lost childhood. "Yes I will be judged most of all Rebecca and if we fail the responsibility will be mine. That object out there in the remote regions of the solar system is my Mistress."

Chapter Thirty

When Jennifer returned from her dancing lessons to the slave's wing that afternoon she found Abigail waiting for her in the common room. Abigail had a look of determination on her face that boded ill for any further prevarication from Jennifer. "Ah!" she noted, "Just the lady I was looking for."

"Why? Whatever's the matter?"

"Don't play games with me Miss Walstow-Mathom. You and I are going to have a little cosy chat."

"I don't understand."

"Oh don't you. Well take a seat dear Jennifer and let's see if I can enlighten you."

Jennifer sat down looking hunted. "What on earth's the matter Abigail?"

"I'll tell you what the matter is young lady. Alice and I came in here, after serving lunch today, and found Rebecca crying her eyes out. She was distraught. Distraught because of you. You've barely been speaking to her for the last few days and then you come out with some guff about how you think she's betrayed you or something. Here's a girl who loves you more than anybody and you tell her that she's betrayed you. Rebecca! The girl who'd rather pull her own head off than have anybody harm a precious hair of yours. You have some bloody explaining to do."

"Please Abigail you don't know the circumstances. This is none of your business."

"It bloody well is my business. I'm the senior slave in these apartments and if my sisters are hurt or squabbling among themselves it is my duty to get to the bottom of it. Now you will kindly tell me why you said such a hurtful thing to Rebecca. It's not like you. I'm surprised at you."

"Abigail! Please Abigail. I'm hurt too. More than you can imagine. But I can't talk about it. It is far too personal. I just can't."

"The devil you can't!" Abigail tossed the box containing the little medal onto the coffee table. "What the hell's all that about? Becky told me that you said that that was how you knew she'd betrayed you. She didn't know what the blazes you were talking about and neither do I."

Jennifer flushed and stared at the box. "Rebecca didn't know?" she whispered.

"Of course she didn't. It was bloody moonshine as far as she was concerned."

"She must know!"

"Oh Goddess! I'll goddamn slap you in a minute. I'm telling you she has no clue whatsoever what you were talking about. She doesn't know how the devil she's supposed to have betrayed you, she doesn't know what the blue blazes is going on in that little mind of yours and she sure as hell hasn't a clue what that thing is all about. Where the hell does it come from anyway?"

"It…. it's a medal for bravery or something."

"I know that Jenny. It's the order of the Swords of the Goddess, the highest award for bravery among the people of the Line. What I want to know was who does it belong to?"

"It…. it was my father's."

"Your father's! Are you trying to tell me that the Reverend Walstow is a holder of the Swords of the Goddess? You're crazy."

"He wasn't my father." Jennifer had whispered so quietly that Abigail barely heard her.

"What? What did you say?"

Jennifer burst into tears. "I… I said that he wasn't my father. Not my true father anyway."

Abigail was shocked "What?"

“It’s true.” sobbed Jennifer. “When I first came to Mathomdale my mother gave me that medal and told me it belonged to my father. Later in a letter she told me that the man I had always believed to be my father wasn’t at all. My true father was the man that had owned that medal.”

“Oh Goddess! Well what the hell’s that got to do with Becky? How would she know that?”

“Please Abigail! I can’t talk about it. Don’t ask me to. It’s too shameful and dreadful. Let me go now.” Jennifer jumped to her feet.

“Jenny no!”

“Leave me alone Abigail! This has nothing to do with you.” with that Jennifer buried her face in her hands and fled from the room. Abigail swore and kicked at a puff. She was still fuming when Heather and Helen breezed through the common room on their way out.

“Hi sis. What’s up?” Helen asked.

“Oh just had a run in with Jenny who’s just run off to her room in tears. Not my day for dealing with weeping females.”

“What’s up with her?”

“Goddess knows!” Briefly Abigail gave them the gist of Rebecca’s account and her interview with Jennifer.

Helen picked up the box abandoned on the table and looked inside. “Her father’s? she asked.

“Her biological father according to her.”

“Well who was he?”

“I’m afraid she wasn’t inclined to take me into her confidence on that score Hell.”

“Well easy enough to find out.”

“How? It doesn’t have a name on it.”

“Yes but every Swords of the Goddess is unique. They’re personally designed for each recipient. Oh they all have the basic figure of the Goddess and two crossed swords but the further decoration is always unique to that one medal. Sometimes people have the face of their wife or loved one imposed on the face of the Goddess. Then again people often have their family arms engraved into the background or some other symbol that is important to them. No two medals are alike."

"But how do you put the name of the holder to the medal?"

"Oh Abi! There's a full honour role of every receiver of the Swords of the Goddess with illustrations of the medal awarded in the main library. Get Randy to help you." Randy was the girl's affectionate nickname for Randolph the main librarian. "Anyway we must rush now. We're on duty serving tea downstairs. Catch you later." The twins swept out leaving Abigail looking very thoughtful. In sudden decision she snatched up the little box and hurried downstairs toward the library.

Chapter Thirty-One

For Rebecca that evening seemed interminable. After tea Lady Mathom had left her with Professor Sehler and Desmond and they had resumed the extraordinary conversation begun earlier and by dinnertime Rebecca's head was starting to swim. Professor Sehler was grilling her mercilessly over her research going over sheaths of her papers bit by bit, querying sources, translations, interpretations and raking through her research material so thoroughly that Rebecca felt entirely intimidated. At last in desperation she held her hands up and declared, "I'm truly sorry if my work is inadequate Professor."

"Inadequate? Inadequate!" The Professor had nearly glared at her. "It is brilliant! Quite brilliant. I wish to hell you'd been one of my students." The Professor tapped his finger on the pile of papers. "This is one of the most extraordinary bodies of work that I have ever come across from a young lady of your years. Properly developed it will make the conclusion that Alpha societies have been continuously modified by external influence almost inescapable. We're about to blow White Mountain apart and hitherto only the physicists thought they could do that. What do you think Desmond?"

Desmond, who was rummaging through some of the work with his tie loose and his hair ruffled, could only agree. "It certainly is eye-opening sir. I wish to hell we'd had this stuff when we were asking for funding last month. They'd have thrown everything but the kitchen sink at us."

"The Lady's promised us that we won't go short of funding Desmond." Professor Sehler pointed out with a certain satisfaction. He meant every word he'd said about the quality of Rebecca's work but he was nevertheless not insensible to the enormous advantages of having a Mathom Hall connection among his faculty. This beautiful dark haired slave of Lady Mathom's brought not only brilliant new ideas but the cash to back them up as well. Of course it was going to be complicated having a Slave of the Amethyst under his responsibility at White Mountain. If something happened to one of the Lady's favourites while under their care then Botany Bay wouldn't be in it. Privately, the Lady had already threatened death, damnation and exile to the furthest corners of hell if anybody so much as tousled the girl's hair without her permission. The Professor could already see complications. Lord Robin was at White Mountain. That was all very well but it was obvious that Desmond was already deeply in love with her as well. Then again Goddess knew what effect this startling beauty was going to have among the people on the faculty. There were enough storms and tribulations among the convoluted love lives of his team as it was. The possible scenario of unleashing a fully-fledged high Slave of the Amethyst with the Goddess in her veins among them didn't bear thinking about! These young slaves of the Lady weren't just your average Alpha Sensual fillies! They were bad enough but these girls were neutron bombs with XX chromosomes! There'd be mayhem!

Dieter sighed to himself. Well it would make life interesting for sure. He allowed himself an inner smile. There were plenty of people at White Mountain whose attention it was necessary to engage on occasion. The thought of having a Slave of the Amethyst at his disposal when he unmasked his batteries was entirely agreeable! That would set a rocket under the Arschlochen down in Admin and no mistake. Only one thing disturbed his contentment. He would have loved to have been party to the private conversation that this young lady had enjoyed with her Mistress just before tea. The Lady was sitting on secrets he dared hardly think about. Instinctively he felt that she knew what Prophecy One was. She had to do. Nobody else's memory stretched as far back as hers. What did she really know? How much had she told her slave? Dieter determined to get it out of Rebecca one way or another. "Well we'd better wrap it up for the moment." He said. "Her Ladyship has invited us to dinner at eight and we'd better get into our dinner jackets Desmond!"

"Sure thing sir. Will you be joining us for dinner Miss Rebecca?"

"Yes Doctor I have that honour."

"Gee ma-am. If we're going to be working together I'd kindly appreciate it if you'd do me the honour of dropping my formal title. Desmond's the name my mom gave me and I'd be honoured if you'd use it."

"Why of course Desmond!" said Rebecca with the sort of smile that raged through Desmond's psyche leaving him feeling weak and feeble and apt to start wagging his tail like a puppy dog had he possessed one. Professor Sehler snorted in amusement.

"Well if you two young people can spare me a moment of your attention I suggest that we retire to our guest chambers Desmond and climb into our monkey suits. All very formal here at Mathom Hall Desmond. Until later then lady."

"Do you require assistance finding your way sir?" asked Rebecca politely.

"Thank you Miss Rebecca but we should manage. It's been a number of years since I was in this house but I think I can still find my way about."

"Very well then sir." Said Rebecca with a graceful curtsy. "Until later then."

Chapter Thirty-Two

Rebecca was the only one of the high slaves of the Hall sitting down formally for dinner that night. Heather and Helen were obliged to snatch a quick meal before serving dinner to their Mistress and her guests. Alice was called upon for duty, as well, because Lady Mathom wanted her to entertain her guests on the piano after dinner. Jennifer was still closeted in her room crying copiously, Abigail was rummaging through volumes in the library and becoming more appalled by the minute whilst Daniel and Darren were making do with steak pies and mushy peas as ballast for the pints of excellent ale they were busily quaffing in the Mathom Arms.

In the interval between tea and dinner, however, Lady Mathom found a most agreeable interlude. The internal paging system informed her that Margaret's helicopter was about to land on the sports fields and she was eager to hear what Margaret had to say about the conditions at Danworth airfield so she had that estimable lady summoned to her immediately. Margaret was flushed with excitement. She had had an enormously satisfying day among the young refugees and if their stories were tragic it was at least deeply gratifying to be able to take some direct action in ameliorating their condition.

Margaret was, fundamentally, an idealistic soul and one of a very activist nature. Her untiring efforts on behalf of the Mathomdale community were testament to that but this day she seemed to have found a vocation. That her undoubted organisational skills could be put to some higher purpose than merely the arrangements for the vegetable stands at the summer festival was tremendously exciting to her. She was a woman who liked her hands on everything, of course. She was possessed of unflagging energy and tirelessly unremitting skills at getting things done. In many respects, although a key member of Lady Mathom's Mathomdale community, she was chronically underused.

Today had been a revelation to her. All of a sudden she seemed to see an outlet for her talents. Like any high slave of the Line, she was dedicated under solemn oath to the furtherance of humanity and sworn in the name of the Goddess to use her enhanced abilities for the greater good of the Line and mankind. She had chafed somewhat at her seemingly menial role and had long yearned for a more meaningful one, which, of course, was why her Mistress had directed her to Danworth airfield that very day. There among the refugees she had found a focus for her passionate devotion to the cause of the Goddess. She and her military assistants had performed small miracles in attending to the emergency at Danworth and Margaret's mind was already racing ahead with long term solutions to the displaced young people.

She'd even been too excited to enjoy the return helicopter ride, sitting in the aeroplane scribbling notes in a pad for where she hoped to get donations of money, spare clothing, temporary accommodation and, most of all, permanent homes for the youngsters. She had the lists of all the refugees in her briefcase and she was already marking down potential futures for them. She was about to hit the families of the North of England like a whirlwind. She had already made a mental note of all those families in the market for slaves. Later she would open dossiers on all of them with details of their wealth, their past ownership records, their eligibility and their lineage. She figured she could place at least a hundred of the youngsters through private negotiation without even trying. The rest she'd sell in closed auction, carefully controlled, by invitation only of course. She was already planning venues, refreshments and invitations. She'd demand top dollar for the youngsters, ensuring their futures and pouring the excess back into the relief effort.

She'd start a steam roller, an entity, that would build on its own momentum bringing all the miserably destitute young sons and daughters of the Goddess under the umbrella of a centralised organisation responsible for placing them into loving servitude. She'd erect an ethics committee too and by the Goddess anybody that abused the privilege of owning one of the unfortunate young people would rue the day that Margaret Wilkinson-Mathom, Slave of the Amethyst and Beloved of the Goddess was obliged to take them to task for it. It was an intoxicating vision, a means by which Margaret could begin to repay the debt she owed to the Line of the Goddess and prove her worth. She was determined to beg her Mistress for such a role. It was a purpose she had long awaited.

They were special these youngsters, she realised. It was seldom that you ever saw over three hundred young Alphas gathered in one place and it had been thrilling. The sheer volume of their untapped potential had been staggering. These kids had come through absolute hell yet they were mostly calm and well mannered. You would not have been surprised to find them shocked and traumatised, chaotic in grief and loss but somehow they had found reserves of courage and fortitude and the collective dazzlement of their intelligence and awareness had almost been a tangible, physical aura in the air. Over three hundred sons and daughters of the Goddess, waiting to burst into full flowering. What could you not do with three hundred of them? Oh they were special all right. But even among them there were some that stood out, the very special ones. The ones that your instinct told you that the Goddess had been particularly lavish with Her gifts in their case. They were the truly extraordinary finds among them, the favoured of the Goddess.

They were approaching landing now and Margaret looked up to look at her charge once again who had her fingertips pressed to her lips as she gazed out of the window in wonder at the landscape unfolding below her. Her eyes were wide in astonishment. They were remarkable those eyes, thought Margaret. They were so dark they were almost black, soulful deep pools set in a face of such loveliness that it took your breath away. She was just maturing, perhaps sixteen or seventeen, but already her body showed the beginnings of ripening curves. She was beautiful. The Goddess radiated in this young daughter of Hers like a glow of sunshine from the blemish less olive skin. She would grow into a woman that men would lay down their lives for. But it was the inner beauty that fascinated Margaret. There was a wholesome goodness to this young girl curiously mixed with a fatalistic tranquillity that was enormously appealing. But there was more to her too you could discern. Those dark eyes could twinkle in an instant with humour and those generous lips were made for laughter. Given time to recover from her ordeals and this girl could burst spontaneously into song or dance just for the joy of being alive. The Goddess kept a Latin sparkle to this girl, could lay a hand on her hip and toss her hair with a clear laugh between the perfect white teeth and mock the cruelty of fate. She'd grow into a woman that could stamp her feet, clap her hands and twirl her skirts around her, flashing her dark eyes in proud challenge and allure. She was well named.

Margaret wanted her own slaves from the young people landing in wretchedness upon the shores of England but she had a special purpose for this one. She truly wanted that new position now; that new purpose she had found a vocation for on Danworth airfield. She must needs beg for it but she would not beg empty handed. She would come before her Mistress bearing a gift, a token of her honour. This one she would not keep for herself. This one she would give to her Mistress.

"Is this really the home of the Emperatriz Amatita Senora?" she asked Margaret.

"Yes it is honey. This is where she lives."

"It is beautiful. I never knew England was so beautiful. They told me it was cold and grey."

Margaret laughed "Well wait till you see it on a wet morning in November honey."

"It must rain much here Senora. It could not be so green otherwise."

"Oh it rains just plenty."

"When I was little I used to like to dance in the rain."

"Well you'll sure get plenty of dancing practice here little Gypsy. Come now I think we're landing." The helicopter alighted on the playing field scattering a covey of partridges from some long grass at the verges and frightening away a fallow deer that was grazing at the edge of a copse. The military presence around the Hall was very low key by now and there was only a pair of soldiers to greet them as Margaret took the young girl's hand and guided her under the spinning rotors of the aircraft. Her young charge was still clutching the battered old suitcase that she'd been given when she'd boarded the ship in Santa Marta a lifetime ago.

"Excuse me Ma-am." a young soldier addressed her with a salute. "Her Ladyship would like to debrief you immediately at your convenience Ma-am."

"Certainly. Come along honey."

"Wh… where are we going Senora?"

"To meet someone very special honey."

Margaret's enthusiasm, when ushered into Lady Mathom's, presence was infectious. She launched off into such a babbling account of her day and her plans that Lady Mathom had to raise her hand and stop her with a laugh. "Whoa Margaret! Slow down. I see you've had a very stimulating day."

"Oh it was marvellous My Lady. It was just incredible being among those kids. They were just stunning. You'd never guess they'd just come from a war zone. There was one boy I talked to. I asked him what he wanted to do and he told me that he wanted to grow up and become strong and join the soldiers of the Lady. Then he would go back to his country and take his father's land back from the cartels. He was about six years old but ever so determined. He had a little medallion pinned on his jacket. One of the soldiers that took him out of the war zone had given it to him for being brave he said. He said it was a military medal for bravery. Only the bravest soldiers earned it!"

"And was it?"

"Well, actually, it had the words "Welcome to Blackpool" on it. But you couldn't have got it off that little boy with a crow bar, so proud he was of it."

Lady Mathom laughed. "They're quite something aren't they?"

"They are indeed My Lady. With kids like these we'll conquer the world."

"You seemed to have had quite an experience Margaret."

"Oh My Lady. I know you don't have much time today but I've been thinking all day. These kids are arriving all the time now and we have no sort of coordinating service to take care of them. We're just reacting really. Housing the kids on an ad hoc emergency basis with no real organisation in place. The military have been superb today but, with all due respect to them, a military barracks and field kitchens can only go so far."

"Your suggestion?"

"Lady give me full authority and financial backing and I can have an organisation set up to deal with all our refugee problems from the moment they land to the time they are placed in permanent homes. I've dozens of ideas

My Lady and I've got the contacts to make it work. I can do it. I know I can. You've always said that I'm wasted just running community affairs. Well give me the chance to prove you right. Give me the chance to prove my worth to the House of Mathom."

Lady Mathom smiled. "I was rather hoping that you'd come to me with some proposal like this Margaret. You're quite right. I need an organisation in place to handle our displaced persons problems. I'm very pleased with the way you handled today's crisis. Very pleased indeed. The job's yours. I want a full action plan for a coordinating body on my desk as soon after the festival as you can. You have full authority to hire or requisition anybody you want and I'll need a full financial breakdown on your required funds. In the meantime I want you to monitor the refugees that arrived today with a view to permanent settlement. I want those kids in good homes within two months."

"I'll do it in one."

"Excellent! It's high time we gave your talents a little more scope Margaret."

"Oh My lady!" Margaret's eyes were shining "I won't let you down."

"I know you won't. Come now you've got something else up your sleeve haven't you?"

Margaret bit her lip shyly. "Well yes Ma-am. I.... I've er... brought you a present"

"Really?"

"Yes Ma-am. You said you wanted to hear the stories from South America first hand and to keep an eye open for anybody special that might be able to relate them to you."

Lady Mathom clapped her hands in delight. "Oh you've brought me a slave."

"Yes My Lady and I think a very special one. It's a young girl and she even speaks English. In fact she's been my interpreter all day. She's maybe sixteen or seventeen and she is a pearl. Her whole family got wiped out in Colombia I'm afraid but she is very resilient. Extraordinarily pretty too."

"Well where is she?"

"I've got her waiting outside Ma-am."

"Well get her in and let's have a look at her."

Margaret grinned and a moment or two later she was ushering the young girl into the Lady's presence. The girl's eyes were wide and fearful but Margaret placed a hand on her shoulder and told her. "Don't be afraid now. This is Her Serenity the Lady Jennifer, First Lady of the House of Mathom, Empress under the Goddess. My Lady, may I introduce Gitana Garcia."

Gitana dropped a low curtsy, her cheeks rosy as the blood rushed to them. "I… I am most honoured Alteza. May the blessing of the Goddess be on you."

Lady Mathom caught her breath. It took but a single glance to tell her that this was one very superior young lady. "Thank you Gitana. You are most welcome in my house."

"You do me too much honour Alteza."

"Why not at all." said Lady Mathom. She turned to Margaret with a smile. "You certainly haven't lost your eye Margaret. Why she's quite exquisite. Come closer Gitana and let me see you properly."

Gitana hesitated, awestruck to be in the presence of the legendary First Lady of the Line. She recognised her of course. There'd been a portrait of her in the little shrine they'd maintained in her honour in her village. When she'd been a little girl, Gitana had often crept into the shrine to gaze at the portrait. She'd leave little bunches of flowers beneath the portrait and daringly kiss the portrait always beguiled by the beauty of the lady in the picture. Yet here was that very lady in the flesh in all her intoxicating beauty. Gitana felt almost faint. In all the upheavals that had entered into her young life this was the most astonishing of all. Her feet seemed to have turned to lead as she tried to obey the Lady's command. Margaret helped her propelling her gently forward telling her, "Don't be frightened Gypsy. Do as the Lady says."

"Gypsy?" asked Lady Mathom "Is that what you call her Margaret?"

"Isn't that what Gitana means in English Ma-am?"

"It is indeed. Come little traveller. You've journeyed half way across the world to see me so a few more feet won't hurt you!" Lady Mathom granted Gitana a radiant smile and the girl took confidence from it and walked tentatively across to her. Lady Mathom took her hands and looked over her in pleasure. "Why you are a very pretty young lady Gitana!"

"Muchas gracias Alteza. But I am nothing. Nobody is pretty when they stand next to the most beautiful woman in the world Alteza Real."

Lady Mathom laughed entranced by the young girl's boldness. "Why a little flatterer!"

Margaret laughed behind Gitana. "I told you she was a pearl My Lady."

"She certainly is." Lady Mathom stroked the great waves of dark hair that fell over Gitana's shoulders in enormous pleasure. Nothing gave her greater enjoyment than the discovery of such a young gem. After the long and difficult afternoon with Dieter, Desmond and Rebecca and the uncertainties of Prophecy One, little Gitana was just the tonic she needed. She blessed Margaret for her. "Where did you learn such good English Gitana?"

"From my father Alteza. He came from San Francisco. He taught me that if I wished to see the world I must learn my English well because that is the language of the world."

"Can you read English as well?"

"Si Alteza. My father had many books in English and he taught me to read and write in his language. He used to read me fairy stories from his books when I was a little girl. I loved the stories about beautiful princesses. I always used to pretend I was a beautiful princess in a great palace when I played by myself. I used to dream about it and wish I was such a princess." Gitana smiled shyly.

Lady Mathom looked at her seriously. "Well little Gypsy. You must always be careful what you wish for because it might come true." Lady Mathom was interrupted by her intercom. It was Thomas telling her that dinner would be served shortly. She clucked her tongue irritably, reluctant to relinquish the lovely young girl so quickly. "Oh blast I don't have much time today." She turned to Margaret "Have you and Gitana eaten Maggie?"

"We ate at lunch time My Lady."

"Well do you want to join us for dinner Margaret? I'm dining with Dieter Sehler, Rebecca and a young man of Dieter's"

"I'd be delighted My Lady. Do you want Gitana to dine with us as well?"

"Oh Goddess no! I wouldn't inflict the company of such terrible old women and men on the poor girl as soon as she gets here. No I'll get the girls to see to her. I can't ask Mrs Carmichael because she's looking after Laila and Jamila until they move up to the slaves' wing after dinner. Now who can I find that's free to look after her."

"Is Abigail on duty because I saw her working in the library when I walked past."

"No. Perfect. I'll call her up. We'll need somewhere for Gitana to sleep as well. I'd rather she was in the slaves' wing though. I don't like the idea of her being left on her own. They won't have a room ready for her though. They have got some chambers for Laila and Jamila but the others are all a bit empty and desolate."

“Can’t she share with one of the other girls for tonight?”

“Yes that’s a good idea. I know. She can have the spare bedroom in Jennifer’s chambers. The other girls might be a bit old for her. Jennifer’s moving down to the pub tomorrow for the festival so she can use her room until the girls get another one sorted out. Jennifer can sort out some bedding for her. How is she for clothes Margaret?”

“A bit thin My Lady. She’s got a few donated clothes in an old suitcase but that’s about it.”

“Well Jennifer might have some things that will fit her. We’ll have a rummage through the wardrobes tomorrow. Goddess knows we’ve got enough clothes in the house. I’ll get Abigail to find out what size shoe she takes.”

Gitana was listening to all this in disbelief. “Por favor Alteza? I am to stay here?”

“Why yes Gitana. For the time being in any case. Would you like that?”

“Si Alteza. Si, gracias.”

“It will be my pleasure Gypsy.” Gitana stared at Lady Mathom in wonderment astounded by the honour being granted to her.

Chapter Thirty-Three

Jennifer had by now cried herself out and she was sitting miserably in her chambers when Abigail knocked on her door. Jennifer started with guilt when she answered the door. "Oh Abi! I… I'm sorry about what happened earlier. I…."

Abigail raised a finger and placed it over Jennifer's lips. "Hush Jenny. Not now. We'll talk later. I think I understand now but let's leave it until later all right?" Abigail turned and eased a young girl into view. "Jenny this is Gitana. Gitana Garcia from Colombia."

Jennifer looked at her and yipped impulsively "Oh what a lovely girl!"

Gitana smiled at her "Gracias Senorita. You are too kind. I am not as beautiful as you though."

Jennifer clapped a hand over her mouth. Oh. Oh I'm sorry. I…. I didn't mean to be rude. You… you speak English Senorita Garcia?"

"Si Senorita. I speak English."

"Oh what ever must you think of me. Please forgive my bad manners Senorita."

Gitana laughed liking this auburn haired girl immediately. "Please Senorita it is nothing. Nobody can be insulted by a compliment from a beautiful lady. Are all English ladies so beautiful as the ones I have met?"

"Er well not quite!" Abigail told her with a grin. "We'll take you down to meet old Aggie in the laundry if you like. That'll put things in perspective for you." It was an unkind thing to say for while Agatha was a lady that was so fat that it was a standing joke in the house that she needed a Greenpeace bodyguard just to go down to the village she was, nevertheless, such a happy, good natured soul that she was enormously popular in the Hall and the girls adored her.

"But you are all so lovely." said Gitana.

“Why thank you Gitana.” said Abigail. “Listen Jenny. Gitana’s a … a displaced person from the war in Colombia and she’s staying with us for a while. The Lady’s asked if you could put her up in your chambers for the moment until we sort out another room for her. Is that Ok with you?”

“Why of course. I’d be delighted. There’s a spare bed in the adjoining bedroom but we’ll need some bedding for it. It’s a smaller bed than mine and I think my sheets and duvet will be a bit big for it.”

“That’s no hassle Jen. We’ll soon sort out some bedclothes. Look you be showing Gitana where to put her things and I’ll call down for some bedding and food. Have you eaten Jenny?”

“Er no not yet.”

Abigail looked at her sharply. “Well I’ll get some food for the three of us sent up. Everybody else is on duty. The other girls are bringing Jamila and Laila up after dinner. Is everything sorted out in their chambers?”

“Yes. Yes it is. The twins and I fixed it all up this morning.”

“Well we’ll have a little supper party when they all come up after dinner but that might be a while so we’ll grab something now. Ok look after Gypsy here while I sort it out.”

“Gypsy?”

“Oh she’s got a nickname already Jenny. It’s the meaning of her name in English!”

“I think it’s just perfect.” said Jennifer and she meant it. The name went with the dark haired girl with the twinkling dark eyes to a tee. “Please come in Gypsy and be welcome.”

“Gracias Senorita.”

“Please my name is Jennifer or Jenny. Would you call me that?”

“I would be honoured Jennifer.”

“Come along then and I’ll show you your room.”

Dinner downstairs was a pleasant affair since the presence of Margaret precluded any further discussion of the weighty topics that had so dominated the day. Alice played the piano to them over coffee and brandy and Lady Mathom was delighted by the effect her beautiful playing had on her guests. Dieter was an avid fan of classical music and he listened in disbelief as Alice executed a movement from a Haydn piano sonata almost flawlessly, warmly applauding her and having the cheek to ask Lady Mathom if she'd consider an offer for the girl. Alice flushed with pride when Lady Mathom laughingly riposted that he couldn't afford her.

After dinner Alice, Heather and Helen were dismissed and told to collect Jamila and Laila to take to their new accommodation in the slaves' wing. Released finally too was Rebecca to her great relief. Margaret also took her leave and her departure gave Lady Mathom an idea. She wanted a quiet word in private with Dieter but she didn't want Desmond to be abandoned alone in the house and she had other schemes brewing as well. "Desmond you haven't seen a lot of England yet have you?" she queried.

"Why no Ma-am. This is my first visit to your country."

"Well why don't you take the opportunity to see a real English pub? Margaret here is the landlady of one of our more notable local watering holes in the village. It's a very old and renowned pub Desmond, all old oak beams and Tudor frontage. It's a beautiful old place. Instead of sitting around in the house on your own while I have a talk with the Professor why don't you go down there and sample some of our local English beer. I'm sure Margaret will be all too happy to drive you down."

"Er how would I find my way back My Lady?"

"Oh that's not a problem. Two of my young gentlemen are down there for the evening tonight. They'll be calling for a car home later on and you can come back with them. Margaret will introduce you. I'm sure they'll be all too happy to welcome you. Would that be all right with you Margaret?"

"Oh sure. We've got the first of the festival beer on as well Desmond. That's a treat you shouldn't miss!"

"Thank you then I'd like that." said Desmond and, in truth, he welcomed the idea of escaping the rarefied atmosphere of Mathom Hall for an hour or two. The thought of a glass of beer was entirely agreeable to him. A few minutes later he was sat in Margaret's car and on his way to a memorable meeting.

Chapter Thirty-Four

In a corner of the Mathom Arms Darren was saying to Daniel, "You have just got to be pulling my pisser with all this!"

"Shh! Keep yer voice down Darren. We don't want ter be spreadin' all this about do we?"

"But seriously Danny this is the wildest bull I ever damn well heard."

"Aye I know it sounds bloody barmy. I'm still tryin' ter get me own 'ead around it Darren but I'm only tellin' yer wot's bin told ter me an' our Alice."

"This is some crazy kind of fantasy Daniel. People don't just don't live for hundreds of years."

"Hush up fer 'eaven's sake Darren!" Daniel looked around him nervously. The pub was busy. There was a mounting fever of excitement in the air with the imminent festivities just two days away now and people were out and about almost as if eager to start proceedings early and with the Festival ale as an added incentive the pub was full. Darren looked at Daniel in astonishment. Hidden away in their corner Daniel and he were having a very intimate and, to Darren at least, an incredible conversation. Daniel had been trying to explain to Darren what an Alpha Sensual human being was and inviting an incredulous reaction from Darren.

In truth, it is likely that Daniel was not the best person to initiate Darren into this secret of his heritage since Daniel himself had only very recently been exposed to the idea and he was still rather vague about it all. Most of what he had garnered had come from the girls at the Hall or second hand through Alice although, on the day of their enslavement to Lady Mathom, their Mistress had taken the time to explain their birthright and the duties and responsibilities of enhanced human beings.

Darren's first inclination was to dismiss the whole thing as some fantastic fabrication but there were some things that sowed a seed of doubt in his mind. There was no doubt for instance that there was something about the people up at the Hall that set them very apart from the mainstream of humanity as he understood that to be. It wasn't just their curious customs and ideas either, although that in itself was telling; there was also an air of brightness and high ability that made you instantly aware that they were extraordinary people. In their company Darren had never felt such a dynamic aura of vitality and intensity about anybody before. He realised that, over the past days, he had been taking some of the most incredible things for granted. If he stepped back and looked at the events of the past few days and looked at it objectively he would have to come to the conclusion that he had stepped into an asylum. These people lived in a very different world from that which he had hitherto considered normal.

Then of course there was Lady Mathom herself. She was just so way beyond the ordinary that she might have come from Tau Ceti for all you could say. Every time he recalled the remarkable interview with her that very morning he shook his head in disbelief. Then again there was that eerie feeling that had come over him when he'd seen the portrait of the Lady Anne on the wall of the eponymous pub just yesterday. He'd just known that that portrait was of Lady Jennifer and not some ancestor dead some three hundred years before. Nevertheless the information that Daniel was trying to convey to him was just a little too fantastic to take seriously and Darren might not have even begun to do so had it not been for one of those incredible coincidences that can only happen in real life and authors of fiction would never dare to inflict upon their readers.

"Great Galloping Goddess! Darren goddamned Morgan!"

Darren snapped his head up and stared in astonishment at a young man stood staring at him with a sagging jaw. “Jesus H Christ! Des De Boer! Des! What in all the seven circles of Hell are you doing here?”

“It is you Dazzler. Goddamn it! I thought my damn eyes were deceiving me.”

Darren staggered to his feet and grasped Desmond in a bear hug. “Jesus Des! Where the blue blazes have you sprung from?”

Margaret was stood behind Desmond looking amused and amazed at the same time. “You two boys surely don’t know each other.”

“Know each other? Know Dazzler Morgan? Why hell yes ma-am. Darren here was my roommate at college. I’ve known Dazzler for years. Ain’t seen him for a long time though and blow me he shows up here. My first night in England and I walk straight into my old roommate. I just don’t goddamn believe this!”

“Damn it Des!” said Darren staring at his old friend and gripping him by the shoulders. “What the hell are you doing in these parts?”

“I was kinda going to ask you the same.” Desmond stopped suddenly and his brow puckered in thought. “Wait a minute... are you…..” he stopped and twisted his head to face Margaret. “Ma-am this old reprobate surely isn’t one of Lady Mathom’s young gentlemen we were supposed to be seeing?”

“That’s right Desmond. I’ve not been introduced personally but I know of the young man. The other gentleman there is Daniel.”

Daniel rose to his feet “Er pleased to meet yer Desmond.”

Desmond took Daniel’s hand warmly. “You too sir. And.. you …. you’re both gentlemen of the Hall?”

“How the hell do you know about Mathom Hall?” blurted the spluttering Darren at last.

"Where the hell do you think I'm staying?" asked Desmond.

"I just don't goddamned believe this!"

"Dazzler! You are not telling me that you're a Slave of the Amethyst surely. I'm surprised they even let you in the door. How the blazes did you con your way into that?"

Darren, with his head reeling, demurred. "Well it beats the hell out of working for a living Des."

"Dammit I might have known I'd find you shacked up with a collection of the best looking gals I've seen this side of the pond."

Margaret laughed, "I can see you boys have a lot of catching up to do. I'd better run along and see if my young ladies have managed to ruin my business in my absence."

"Thank you kindly for the lift ma-am." Desmond told her.

"My pleasure Desmond. You boys want anything to drink just ask the bar girls. The drinks are on the house. Don't get too drunk though." she looked at Daniel and Darren mischievously. "You boys aren't so big that your Mistress will hesitate about taking a stout stick to your backsides if you make a disgrace of yourselves." Margaret walked away feeling pleased with herself for throwing a little fuel on the fire.

"Goddess Dazzler. Lady Mathom's your Mistress! Well I'll be blowed! You always did have the luck of the devil."

Darren experienced the familiar feeling of losing control of events that had dogged him from the moment he had set foot in Mathomdale. "Jesus Des! Come on pull up a stool and sit. Let's get some more damn drinks."

"I'll get 'em." Danny volunteered "Same again Darren?"

"Sure and get one for Des too."

“Hey what is it you guys are drinking?”

“The local brew Des, smooth as a baby’s ass and a kick like a mule. I’m just kinda getting weaned on it.”

It was to prove an interesting night. For the next hour or more Desmond and Darren listened to each other’s stories with growing amazement. Desmond recounted the long trail by which he had come to White Mountain and thence to Mathomdale. It hadn’t worked out with the girl in Pennsylvania and, shortly after, he had been taken on by the research establishment that had finally sold him to Professor Sehler’s faculty at White Mountain. Unlike Darren, Desmond had always known of his Alpha Sensual heritage and although he had been unaware of Darren’s lineage he had rather suspected Darren of having affinity to the Line too. They had never discussed it, however, even though Desmond had been an indentured slave during his college years. Darren had always thought that Desmond had lived with his relations after the supposed breakdown of his parent’s marriage. Now he was flabbergasted to learn the truth. To believe that Daniel and the girls at Mathom Hall considered themselves slaves was one thing quite another to accept the fact that his old roommate and best friend did so too quite another. Continuously however Desmond returned to the astonishing fact of discovering that Darren was a slave to Lady Mathom. His congratulations became so embarrassingly effusive that Darren was finally obliged to disabuse him of the notion.

“Hell Des. I ain’t Lady Mathom’s slave. I’m just here at the request of Ambassador Kelly my boss.”

“You ain’t?” Now Desmond was completely confused.

“Nope. Oh she asked me to er… join her household this morning Des but well that would take some thinking through.”

“Oh so you ain’t been branded yet?”

“No sir.”

"Well she seems to think you have Dazzler. Pretty much claimed you as her own up at the Hall. I guess the Lady don't describe you as one of her "young gentlemen" without bein' pretty damn sure that she's got you on a leash. Not from what I've heard about her and seen today."

"Hell I ain't made up my mind yet Des."

"You honestly figure that what you've got your mind set to do is gonna have anything to do with it Dazzler?"

Daniel guffawed "That's what I keep tellin' 'im. Won't listen ter me though!"

"Hell guys! I still got some say in the matter."

"Yeah sure you have Dazzler," Desmond laughed, "You gonna go walk right on up to the Lady and tell her to take her offer and shove it? This I gotta see! Figure I'd better bring a bucket and shovel along to pick up the pieces. What kind of a deal is she offering you anyway?" Briefly Desmond explained the loose terms that Lady Mathom had outlined in their interview that morning. Desmond was astounded. He whistled. "Whee and you're just thinking of walking away from that? You hold him down Danny while I whistle up the men in the white coats. Are you goddamn nuts Dazzler?"

"Hell I'm no mere slave Des."

"A mere slave? Is that what you call it?" Desmond shook his head and addressed Darren seriously. "Dazzler have you any idea what it means to be a Slave of the Amethyst? Any goddamn person of the Line would tear his or her own goddamn leg off to get to serve the Purple Lady! That is the most prestigious House anywhere on the Line. Top of the roost! You're a slave to the Amethyst and you walk in anywhere and folks kowtow to you. That's the top of the pecking order Dazzler. It doesn't get higher than that. That's the ruling House Dazzler; the Imperial Household. The Slaves of the Amethyst are the elite."

“Jesus Des! I don’t know. Danny here’s been trying to tell me about this Line thing. It kinda sounds a bit fantastic to me though.”

“Er Darren don’t know about t’ Line or about Alpha Sensuals Des.” Daniel explained. “I’ve bin tryin’ ter explain it but I’m not doin’ a very good job.”

“Well what the hell are they?” asked Darren.

“Well you’re one for a start!” Desmond told him.

“Me? Hell nothing special about me.”

“Lady Mathom thinks otherwise apparently Dazzler and, with all due respect buddy, I kinda value her opinion a bit more than yours in this regard.”

“Well what the hell am I supposed to do?”

“That’s the easy bit Dazzler. Let me give you some advice. I know at college you never listened to any advice worth a damn, but listen to me now. Tomorrow go straight to Her Ladyship, go down on your knees and beg her for the privilege of being her slave. Don’t ask no questions, just do it. You’ll learn all about what it means to be an Alpha Sensual human of the Line in all due course but make sure you’ve got your pretty new brand and shackles on before then. I’m telling you this in all seriousness Dazzler. This is the most important thing you’ll ever do. Don’t kid yourself with some tomfool notions about freedom and choice. It’s raining soup Dazzler boy. Go grab yourself a bucket.”

Darren shook his head. “Hell I need some more beer.”

“I’ll second that!” said Daniel enthusiastically. “We might as well drink it while it’s free! Your turn to walk ter t’ bar …..Dazzler.” Daniel grinned. He liked Darren’s nickname.

When Darren returned with the beers he had one observation of positive note to make. “Gee that bar girl gave me a come on like you wouldn’t believe. You can say what you like about this goddamned crazy valley but the gals are something else.”

“Already noticed that.” said Desmond. “Hell! Me I hope my boss and I stay for a real long visit. I’m getting to like it here.”

“Well yer’ll be ‘ere for t’ festival won’t yer?” asked Daniel.

“So I’m told.”

“Well we’ll ‘ave a bit o’ fun t’ three of us then. They say anyone as doesn’t get their leg ovver at t’ festival wins a plot o’ land six foot be two foot an’ six foot deep. I’d stock up on t’ stout an oysters if I was you lads.”

“I’m liking it more by the minute.” Desmond began. Then his eyes opened wide and he let forth a low whistle. “Wow! Look at this Babe! Check out your five o’clock Danny.”

Daniel span on his stool to see the beautiful blond woman glide into the pub lounge. She lit up the place like a Very light and the buzz of conversation dropped noticeably. It was Daniel’s turn to open his jaw in amazement. He jumped to his feet and called “Eugene!”

Eugene turned in surprise and then her face lit up in a grin of delight. “Danny!” She flew across the room and threw herself into Daniel’s arms smothering his face with kisses.

One of the locals turned to his friends and said “Gerra bucket o’ water somebody afore they put a burn in t’ carpet.” but Eugene heeded him not.

“Oh Danny how great to see you. Where’re Alice and Becky?”

“Up at t’ ‘All Eugene. What the ‘ell are you doin’ ‘ere?”

“Oh I’m just up for the festival.” Eugene said evasively. “I’ve rented a little cottage up at Marveaux. I’m supposed to pick the keys up from here.”

“Well this is just brill. I ‘aven’t seen yer since Saltersea.”

“Wow yes! Haven’t things changed since then. You and Alice high up at the Hall now hey? Changed a whole lot of things that day on the beach at Bolswick Bay didn’t it?”

“Aye it did. ‘Ere let me introduce you ter me mates.” Before Daniel could proceed however Margaret came drifting over.

“Good Evening my lady Eugene. Thank you for gracing our house with the Goddess.”

“And I thank you my lady for the honour of your welcome.” The two women curtsied to each other in great formality with just the hint of wariness of two powerful women testing the waters between them.

Margaret broke the curtsy first and smiled. “We have the keys for Rose Cottage here lady if you wish to drive straight up to Marveaux.”

“Ere Eugene!” protested Daniel, “Yer can’t go straight off wi’out ‘avin’ a drink wi us first.”

“I would like that Danny but I don’t know. I’m not alone. I have three young girls with me out in the car. Would it be all right to bring them in my lady Margaret?”

“By all means lady. We were expecting three young ladies to be accompanying you.”

“Thank you. The girls will appreciate it. We’ve just driven up from Kingston and they must be thirsty by now.”

Eugene went outside to fetch Vesna, Ana and Mali and bring them into the pub. The girls blinked in the bright interior after the dark on the square outside. Eugene brought them over to introduce them to Margaret but, as she was about to, there was a disgraceful incident. A boorish looking middle-aged woman sat nearby with her taciturn looking husband said in a perfectly audible voice. “More bloody foreigners! I can’t think what the country’s coming to. We’ll be inundated with them at this rate. They ought to send them all back where they came from."

Margaret whipped round in fury. "”What did you say madam?"

The woman paled visibly under the sudden furious onslaught. "I… I was only expressing my opinion."

"Then I'll thank you to express it elsewhere. You are no longer welcome here madam."

"I ….I have the right to say what I think."

"You have no right whatsoever to insult my guests with racist remarks madam. Leave! And take your sour pussed husband with you."

"I…. I've never heard the…."

"OUT!"

"Aye bugger off!" one of the locals added.

The woman and her husband nearly ran out of the pub before Margaret's fury. Margaret took a deep breath and curtsied deeply to Eugene. "My most profound apologies lady! I am ashamed that you have had to endure such insulting behaviour beneath my roof. Please tell me how we can compensate you for this dreadful occurrence."

"Please lady Margaret. It is forgotten. There are fools everywhere."

"They were trippers ma-am. Please be assured that no local person from this valley would dare to insult the slaves of a high lady of the Goddess."

"I would not believe for a moment that they would lady. Please let me introduce you to my young ladies." The three girls curtsied politely as Eugene told Margaret their names and slowly the shocked hush in the pub following the incident subsided back into the enjoyable hum of conversation although many an eye turned to admire the spectacularly beautiful Eugene and her three lovely young slaves. Eugene's young ladies fascinated Margaret and it was many years since she had seen Eugene herself so she invited herself to join the company, while the three boys fetched extra chairs and made space to accommodate them all at their table. Eugene squeezed in next to Daniel and flirted with him, liking the straightforward young man immensely. "I've got the prints from Alice's photo shoot out in the car Danny." she told him. "I don't think I'd better bring them in here though. They're a bit naughty…. some of them."

Margaret organised the drinks and refused point blank to accept any payment for them, so mortified did she feel about the fact that a high lady had been insulted in her house. Eugene took a small glass of wine and ordered fruit juices for her girls. She didn't want them to develop a liking for high calorie fizzy drinks. The three young girls were very shy as the focus of attention but they relaxed somewhat as the boys drew them out. Danny was trying to get Vesna to tell him the names of things in her own language and she dissolved into giggles at his clumsy attempts to repeat them. Mali was falling in love with Darren and couldn't take her eyes off the handsome young American whilst Ana was cheekily poking fun at Desmond's American accent and asking him if he was a Chicago gangster. It was a merry meeting. Margaret caught Eugene's ear for a moment and said quietly. "They're lovely lady. Where did you find them?"

Eugene's face hardened, "They were taken by the prostitution slave market lady. I took them out of a Hamburg brothel last week."

"Goddess! How much did you pay for them?"

"About 115 grams of lead lady. I blew the brothel owner's kneecap off for him."

Margaret looked at Eugene with renewed respect. "I saw a lot of kids that were refugees from the war today lady. A lot of them had had their whole families wiped out. Apparently the scum that did it were saving the pretty young girls and boys to sell into prostitution.

Many of them were raped repeatedly. I've never felt so angry. Maybe that's why I lost it with that stupid woman. Forgive me if I have underestimated you. I admire your style lady. I would be honoured to be your friend."

Eugene smiled at her "Thank you lady. I'm not a very nice person I'm afraid but I need all the good friends I can get. It would give me great pleasure to numbered among your friends." There was peace between the two women from that moment and a friendship that would flourish between two strong wills.

Chapter Thirty-Five

Peace reigned also in the slaves' wing of Mathom Hall that night as well or at least the underlying hostilities were suspended in order to welcome Gitana, Laila and Jamila to the sorority of the Hall. Rebecca put aside her fears over Prophecy One and, if there was still an underlying tension between her and Jennifer, then the three new guests in the wing were not allowed to see it. Jennifer did her part too, welcoming the girls and turned the warm charm that she was famous for on to them and granted the joy of her loving to them in spite of the gaping wounds in her heart. Alice pulled out the little electronic keyboard she used for practise and played some tunes for the twins to sing silly songs to and make the shy little Laila laugh and Jamila rejoiced to see her young sister looking so happy again. They'd found Laila a lot of toys in the downstairs nurseries and the little Afghan girl had taken a liking to a big cuddly fluffy rabbit with silly long floppy ears and she hugged it close while she giggled helplessly over the twins' comic antics.

Gitana's eyes were sparkling with pleasure and the dark forests of Colombia seemed far away now, in the safety and warmth of the big cosy common room. She was deeply attached to Jennifer by now and she held the older girl's hand shyly as she laughed with the rest of them at the impromptu entertainment. Oddly enough, the one who seemed most ill at ease was Abigail. She had done wonders arranging a little party supper for them all and she'd put up some decorations with the help of Jennifer and Gitana to amuse little Laila before they came upstairs. Nevertheless, although she smiled warmly, there was a strained sadness about her that was uncharacteristic of the generally sensible young lady.

At last they showed Jamila and Laila to their chambers. Jamila had clapped her hands together in pleasure at the lovely rooms prepared for them. She had taken one look at the portrait of the Lady they had hung on the wall and had curtsied reverently before it instructing Laila to do the same so that had answered that question. Gitana too was tired so the little party broke up and Jennifer escorted her back to her chambers where she found a pretty nightdress for her and they took to their beds. Eugene had already taken her leave of the Mathom Arms, by now, and she was tucking her three girls into their own beds bestowing kisses on them, so very proud of them. Daniel was teaching Desmond and Darren the tune and lyrics to On Ilkley Moor Ba'Ta-at, destined it seemed to become the anthem of intoxication at Mathom Hall, in the car on the way home and Alice went to the married quarters to welcome her over indulgent husband home.

In the night, however, the fears and worries of them all came back to haunt them in the dark. Jennifer tossed in her bed unable to sleep with tears threatening to mist her eyes once more. She was saved from self-pity, however, by a cry and a babble of frantic Spanish from the room in which Gitana had her bed. Worried, she crept through into Gitana's room and found the young dark haired girl sat up in bed sobbing piteously. "Why Gypsy whatever is the matter?" she asked.

"I…. I am so sorry Senorita. I didn't want to wake you."

"I wasn't sleeping Gitana." Jennifer sat on the side of her bed and took the younger girls hand. "What's the matter?"

"It was the dreams again Senorita Jennifer… the bad dreams."

"You were having a nightmare?"

"Si. I saw the soldiers coming again. The bad soldiers. The ones who came to my village. The ones who….. " But Gitana burst into fresh sobs unable to say it.

“Were these the men that… that attacked your people Gitana?” Gitana nodded miserably. Jennifer took her in her arms compassionately. “Tell me Gitana. Tell me what happened.” And slowly Gitana did as Jennifer listened appalled in the dark room. She heard the appalling tale of the massacre in Gitana’s village. Gitana had seen her own father die though, mercifully, she had been spared the sight of the death of her mother. She’d watched the soldiers bayoneting small children and them burning some of the villagers alive in a hut. Gitana told her about the dreadful days and nights when she and the others that had been spared were force-marched through the forests and beaten when they’d lagged. She told Jennifer about the rapes and how the men had taken turns at her and Jennifer’s eyes were filled with tears of horror and pity. At last she seemed exhausted but she clung to Jennifer in fear. Jennifer found salvation in Gitana’s grief and fear. Her own troubles now seemed so petty. She found herself rocking the distraught girl in her arms like a baby and crooning soft words to her.

“I’m frightened Senorita. I don’t want to sleep in case I dream again.”

“Come Gitana. You won’t sleep alone tonight.” And Jennifer took her by the hand and led her to her own big bed, laid her down and climbed in beside her, holding her gently and soothing her. “I’ll be here all the time Gitana. Don’t be frightened of the dreams. I’ll keep them away.” At last Gitana did sleep but Jennifer lay long beside her overwhelmed with pity for this young child of the Goddess and willing a blanket of love over her as she slept.

Rebecca was sat on her bed drained and with a hollow sense of loss that seemed beyond tears when the soft knock came on her door. “Who is it?”

“It’s me, Abi, Becky. Can I come in please?”

“Sure Abi. Come in.”

Abigail walked in in her nightdress looking strained. “I saw the light under your door Becky so I thought you might not be asleep yet. Can I join you?”

“I’m afraid I’m not much company at the moment Abi.”

“Because of Jenny?”

“Yes... that and other things Abi. I’ve had a pretty torrid day.”

“Well let’s be two miserable bitches together then Becky. I feel rotten!”

“Oh come on Abi! You’re always the sensible one right. The one who always looks at things rationally. You’re never down.”

“Sometimes I get sick of always being the sensible one Becky. I tried to do something sensible today and … and well it’s sort of smacked me in the teeth.”

“Why Abi? What’s happened?”

Abigail pulled out Jennifer’s medal from her nightgown and laid it on the bedside table. “That’s what’s happened Becky. I…. I never gave it back to Jenny. I wish I’d never seen the blasted thing now.”

“What about it Abi? Have you talked to Jenny about it?”

“Oh Becky yes I have. I can’t tell you now though. Not while you’re having such a rotten day.”

“Yes you can Abi! Tell me! I need to know.”

Abigail sighed. “It’s about what Jenny said about her thinking you’d betrayed her. That thing there is why she thinks that.”

“Why? Why in the name of the Goddess?”

“Becky do you know who that belonged to?”

“I’ve no idea Abi.”

“Do you swear Abi?”

“Yes! Yes I do.”

“It belonged to Jenny’s father Becky.”

“What... the vicar?”

Abigail shook her head. "No Becky... not the vicar. The Reverend Walstow isn't Jenny's natural father Becky. She told me that herself today. Apparently her mother told her in a letter this summer that she was fathered by another man. She didn't say whom but she did say that that medal had belonged to him. So today I took it into my silly little sensible head to find out whom her real father was. Talk about curiosity killing the cat. It was none of my business as she said but I just had to go and stick my bloody nose into it! I… I thought I was doing the right thing. I thought that I could somehow sort out the problem between you two. All I seem to have done is make things worse."

"What have you found out Abi?" Rebecca whispered.

"Well you remember when this mood of Jenny's kicked off with a vengeance. It was the first night that Darren was here. We thought she'd slept with Darren that night and it turned out she hadn't but she'd gone off in a sulk on her own. We just thought that she was in a huff about Darren turning her down but I think it was something much more serious."

"What the hell's happened Abi."

"Oh Becky today I went and looked that medal up. The twins put me on to the idea. It turns out that no two Orders of the Swords of the Goddess are the same. You can identify the recipient of the medal from the design of the flipping things. In the library there's a bloody great tome illustrating every design against the name of the recipient there's been since the Order was founded. There were loads of them but this one was easy to find because it's an award to the House of Mathom and they're given prominence." Abigail paused willing herself to continue.

"Who was it Abi?" asked Rebecca quietly.

"That medal was awarded to Lord Donald, Lord Mathom of the House of Mathom and husband to the Lady Jennifer, Empress under the Goddess in 1943."

"Oh Goddess no!" Rebecca covered her mouth with her hands the blood draining from her face.

"I'm sorry Becky but there's no mistake. I truly am sorry."

"It can't be!"

"It has to be Becky. Think about it. The Lady Katherine was married to Lord Donald and the Lady. She left this House the year that Lord Donald was killed and the same year that Jennifer was born. The Reverend Walstow was a curate at the village church at the time temporarily and Katherine ran away with him. Now it's the local legend that Katherine became pregnant by the curate and he persuaded her to leave with him. They got married about two months later. Katherine must have been three to four months pregnant by then because Jenny was born about five months later. Katherine left straight after Lord Donald's funeral, call it a little over a week after he died. She was anything between a month and six weeks pregnant by then. Well what if she wasn't pregnant by the curate as everyone thinks? What in fact if she was expecting her Lord's child? She must think so." Abigail paused once again. "Do you know how His Lordship earned that medal?" Rebecca shook her head in shock. "Well apparently he rescued some people, resistance fighters, from the Nazis in occupied Europe. Now I can't prove that Katherine was one of those people but she did return to the Hall in 1943 the same year that this happened and certainly that medal meant something special to her. I think he saved her life and she took that medal in memory of him when he died. She wouldn't have passed it onto Jenny unless she was convinced that he was Jenny's father."

"Oh Goddess this is worse than I ever thought."

"So what happened that night when Jennifer escorted Darren back to his room? Well I think I can fill in the gaps now. Not far from Darren's chambers there's a huge portrait of the Lord Donald in full military fig wearing that very medal on his left breast. I went along to have a look at it. While I'm looking at it one of the chambermaids breezes by. She asks me why I'm so interested in that portrait and when I ask her why she tells me that she came upon Jenny staring at it late one night when she had night duty. She said she thought Miss Jennifer had seen a ghost. Well she had. The ghost of her own father. Now we know what happened that night. Jenny comes staggering away from Darren's in a huff because he's just told her to go and take a running jump and she wanders about until she comes upon the portrait. She must have stared at that medal a thousand times since her mother told her it belonged to her father and so she recognises it. She asks this chambermaid whom the portrait is of and she tells her. Jenny's mind goes straight back to what happened in the Oriental Gardens! And what did happen in the Oriental Gardens Becky?"

"We….. we spent the night there. Jenny, Robin and I."

"Yes the two of you spent the night with Robin. The man who you asked Jenny to take as a lover with you, to join you in marriage with, the one who you placed Jenny in the arms of that night... Lord Donald's son! Jenny thinks you've put her to bed with her own brother."

"Oh Goddess forgive me! I never knew! I swear it!"

"Becky how much does the Lady know?"

"What?"

"Come on Becky! She can figure out dates just as well as we can and she must have a file on Jenny's DNA as thick as your wrist. She's had Jenny examined by Doc Chandra after all. She must know that there's a familial match with Robin. She must do! Is that why she ordered you to become Robin's lover? To deflect him away from Jenny because she thought it possible that he was Jenny's half-brother? So maybe she didn't know for certain until later after the test results but surely she's aware of it now. Does she know that Robin slept with Jenny?"

"I don't know. Maybe not. He left for Switzerland the next day. But she knew we were going to spend the night together in the Gardens. She wouldn't have had the test confirmation by then though. Jenny only got tested a couple of days before that and it can take up to a fortnight for results to come through. Oh Goddess I don't know."

"I'm sorry Becky. I didn't want to put you through all this. Really I didn't. I've ruined your marriage plans haven't I?"

"No Abi. You haven't! It would have come out in the end after all. It's better to know now. Oh Goddess! What a mess."

"Becky I feel terrible about all this. I really do. I feel awful."

"Oh Abi you did what you thought best."

"Becky……. Becky can I share with you tonight? I…. I don't want to sleep alone tonight."

"Of course Abi! Of course you can. I don't feel much like sleeping alone either." They climbed into bed together and held each other close, their tears on each other's faces until sleep mercifully took them. And so, at last, peace descended finally on a long day at Mathom Hall. But still the people gathered, for that night, as they slept, with a squeal of tyres on the tarmac, an aeroplane landed on the soil of England. Aasha was aboard it.

THE END OF VOLUME 10

Lightning Source UK Ltd.
Milton Keynes UK
UKHW02f0016070418
320672UK00006B/176/P

9 781786 951496